Twilight Of The Mountain Man

Two young men run from their homes in Arkansas to the 19th century frontier, seeking freedom and safety as mountain men.

James Oliver Virmala

Edition 1

Cover Photo James Oliver Virmala

"Teton Mountain With Lake"

Copyright © 2019 James Oliver Virmala

ISBN: 978-1-7340021-1-9

ACKNOWLEDGMENTS

In the face of the devastation caused by hurricane Harvey and Irma, I would like to acknowledge the many volunteers that came together to help rescue those trapped by the storm or rising waters, many of them using personal watercraft, vehicles and tools, while asking nothing in return.

CONTENTS

BOOKS BY THE AUTHOR

Oli's Gold Book One
Search For Oli's Gold Book Two
Return To Oli's Gold Book Three
To Be A Mountain Man
Trouble On The Kansas Plains
Frontier Justice
Return Of The Mountain Man
The Tall Man
The Prospector
The Green Valley
Twilight Of The Mountain Man
The Mother Lode
Quest Of The Mountain Man
Journey's End
Rufus Pike
Rufus And The Pup
The Winding Trail Home
Rufus The Lost Years
The Kankakee Kid
Bogus Island
Tyler Tomas The Brothers' War
War of 1812 The Choice
Kyle Oliver The Next Horizon

CHAPTER ONE

Sweat soaked the curly locks of the brown-haired man as he worked in the sweltering heat clearing land on the Arkansas Delta. Crowley's Ridge rose to the east of the plantation he was working on. Beauford Levesque was 22 years-old and was working off an indentured contract originally made between the landowner and his father.

Beauford, better known as Beau, was stripped to the waist. Sweat glistened off his work-hardened body. His calf-length canvas trousers were held up by a broad leather belt that supported a nine-inch Green River hunting knife. He wore low-heeled boots that had seen better days.

Beau was tasked with clearing rich delta land of trees for logs, and to make more tillable acreage. Six slaves and four freemen worked on the project, harvesting the logs and removing the stumps. Felling the trees was the most dangerous part, so Beau and the slaves were assigned this job. The large oak and hickory trees could jackknife, hang up, or have dead

1

branches that could fall, striking the man below during the felling process.

He had several scars on his back and arms from close calls. At the end of the day's work the freemen would go to their homes and families. The slaves had hastily assembled quarters near the work site. Beau walked the three miles to his small cabin on Crowley's Ridge.

The only day he had off was Sunday, and Beau believed that he couldn't be any closer to God than in the hills near the cabin. The nearest church was a three-hour walk. Beau had a .54 caliber Model 1803. The bore and rifling were somewhat worn from use, but he could still bring down game. He would spend the day hunting deer and bear. Between the fat and the skin, a black bear was worth $12 to $15, and there was still meat for meals.

Setting his axe against the next tree to be felled, Beau took a drink from the deerskin bag. Water dripped down his chin and he wiped it with the back of his hand. Drying his hands on the sides of his trousers, he gripped the axe handle and began the task of cutting the tree.

A freeman named Ralph came by, driving a team that was skidding out a hickory log. "Hey, Beau," he called over. "Did you hear the old man has been ill?"

"What's new?" Beau laughed. "He is always down with something."

"You're right there," the freeman replied.

Beau paused as he watched Ralph drive the horses toward the collection yard. The old man was the owner, Horst Weber. He had emigrated from Germany and had carved out an impressive plantation in Arkansas.

"This ain't no ladies' social!" a man snapped as he rode up on a gray gelding. "Keep your axe biting wood!"

The man had bushy eyebrows and a permanent scowl on his face. The blacks called him master, Beau called him sir, and the freemen called him Angus. For the past four years, he had run the plantation for Horst. Up in years and plagued with arthritis, the owner kept mostly to the big house. Angus was tough on the workers and enforced his dominance with a whip carried on his belt.

"Yes, sir," Beau replied and continued working on the tree.

An hour before sunset, the ringing of the axes stopped with the day's work completed. Beau picked up his shirt and a poke he carried over his shoulder. The large oak lay on the ground. Cutting the limbs would be his first job tomorrow morning. Beau always took his axe to the cabin and put a fresh edge on it for the next day's cutting.

As he walked, Beau watched flocks of egrets fly over him heading for the safety of the water for the night. Buzzards circled in the evening breezes, looking for a meal. It was April 7th, 1838. One more day of work and then he would be hunting in the hills he loved. He had another two years and his contract would be up. Thinking about the time, it seemed like forever.

The cabin was situated 300 feet above the delta. It had a single room with a fireplace on the back wall. A single stool and table sat in the left corner near the door, with a bunk along the wall to the right. There was no window and the floor was packed dirt. To Beau it was home, and when at the cabin he was happy.

His mother had died when Beau was two. He and his father had been on the move, scraping by on odd jobs. Three years ago, his father had borrowed a horse from Horst Weber to do a job and the animal had been injured and died. Unable to pay for the horse, Beau's father had agreed to a five-year contract with the owner to settle the debt. Fever had taken his father a year ago and Beau had become liable for the debt.

The door of the cabin hung open as Beau approached. He knew that it had been closed when he'd left shortly after sunrise. He recognized the smell of a bear before he reached the door, and could see the claw marks the animal had made along the logs as it clawed to rip it open.

Tracks in the dirt showed that it had been a mother and her cub. While he heard no sound coming from the inside, the smell was strong and it was possible that they hadn't left yet. Anger surged through Beau. He had little enough to get by with and could not afford to have it taken by scavenging animals.

Dropping the poke bag and his shirt onto the ground, he picked up a good-sized rock and threw it through the open door. He stood holding the axe, ready for anything that came out. The bears were gone. Still carrying the axe, Beau entered his home. Reaching on a small shelf, just inside next to the door, he grasped his flint and steel along with a short candle.

While he put together a small pile of tinder in his fire pit near the cabin, Beau continued to watch the hills. The animals that had been in his cabin could not be far away. Once he had the fire going, he lit the candle and entered his cabin.

"My good God!" he gasped.

His home was a shamble. Bags of cornmeal, flour, coffee, and rice had been ripped open and scattered in the dirt of the cabin floor. His bunk lay in a broken heap and the clay containers of wild honey he had stored under it were broken, the contents smeared around as the hungry bears had consumed it. While the bags had contained little product after the winter months, the honey meant cash for Beau and was needed to purchase future supplies. The feeble light from the candle told the story only too well. He was in trouble.

Shaking inside, he shouted, "Listen to me, you son-of-a-bear! Your hide and fat *will* replace the honey you took from me."

The cook fire he had started went unnoticed as Beau was numbed by what he had found. He slowly began to put his home back together, salvaging what he could. There were scat, urine, and vomit as a result of the animals gorging themselves. The air in the cabin was foul as a result.

It was dark as ink on the moonless night as Beau finished making the cabin livable. Even the stars were obscured by clouds that had moved in. Filling his coffee pot from a spring next to the cabin, he set it onto the coals of the fire pit. After poking a few fresh sticks into the dying coals, he sat with his back to the fire, waiting for the water to heat.

Below, on the delta, he could see lights from distant windows. He listened to the night, trying to catch a sound from the bears that had visited his cabin. The air coming up from the delta felt heavy and he hoped any rain would hold off. In the morning, he would have to go after the bears and accept any wrath he would receive from Angus for missing a day's work. Without the skin, oil, and meat that could be sold to replace the honey, his very survival would be in question.

Once the water started boiling, he put a measure of coffee mixed with dirt into the pot. Feeling drained of energy, he got a second pot and his poke. In the poke bag he had some cattail root and wild greens he had picked on the way to the delta that morning. He added these and some salt to the pot of water. He had planned to add some side meat, but that had also been under his bunk and had been eaten.

It was almost midnight when he sat in front of the cabin and ate his roots and greens, washing them down with muddy tasting coffee. The upside to his coffee was that most was still in beans and the dirt could be cleaned off them. Tonight's coffee had been ground earlier and had been scraped up with the dirt.

The night air had cooled somewhat and Beau went back into the cabin. He relit the candle. Cleaning up the cabin had used almost a week's worth of candle. Again, something he couldn't afford. His Model 1803 rested on pegs above the fireplace. His possible bag and powder horn hung on pegs next to the door. He took them down and readied them for the morning.

He smiled. "At least the damn bears didn't eat powder." Snorting, he added, "With luck, tomorrow they will eat lead."

Snuffing out the candle, he lay on his straw tick mattress. Some of the leather straps had been broken on the bunk frame and parts of his body hung through. While he would've liked to have left the door open for the cool night air, the thoughts of his uninvited company returning during the night forced him to close it.

CHAPTER TWO

Beau dreamt of his father that night. He was burying his father and when he tossed the first shovel full of dirt into the grave, the body began to move. He woke up in a cold sweat. It was a dream he had had more than once since the loss of his father. It always left him shaken.

The cabin was dark and the cracks in the door showed no sign of light. Beau went to the door and pushed it open. The fresh air that hit his face was a relief. He stepped outside, getting away from the stuffiness of the cabin. The frogs and water fowl on the ponds below filled the night with sound. The clouds had broken in the sky and the stars told him it was an hour or so from daybreak. This side of Crowley's Ridge would stay in the shadows well after sunrise.

Last night's fire had a few coals left in the ash, so he added a little tinder to them and blew on the embers until it caught fire. Adding a few sticks, he placed what was left of the prior night's coffee to heat.

Dipping his fingers into the cook pot, he pulled out a cold cattail tuber and chewed on it.

Having hunted bear over the years, Beau knew that they would have gone down toward the delta to spend the night. There were stands of evergreens and they liked to make a bed of the needles. As soon as it got light enough he should be able to find some tracks to confirm this.

Having made a meal of cold roots and dirty coffee, Beau got his .54 caliber and possible bag. He was wearing his faded wool shirt and had his knife on his belt. At first light, he began to sort out the bear tracks. They had come to the cabin from higher up on the ridge. Most likely they had been drawn by the scent of the honey. The tracks leaving led directly along the ridge for a way and they started down. While the older bear had kept to a direct path, the cub had played and explored while following its mother.

Walking with the rifle loaded, Beau moved quietly along the trail. As he went he used his senses of sight and hearing to detect the presence of the animals. A mother bear will attack without warning when defending its cub. The air was rising off the delta, preventing the bears from scenting him. That would give him little advantage if he stumbled upon them before they saw him.

For two hours he followed the trail, making little distance and losing the trail at times, only to find tracks again after working his way up and down the ridge. The trail had started back up the hill. Beau sat pondering the change in direction. Looking around, he saw that the bear could have seen him coming across the delta at this point. This may have caused it to change direction, wanting to avoid danger to her cub.

He was less than two miles from his cabin and slightly below it along the ridge. The wind had taken many of the trees down on this knob some years back. It left him exposed in all directions. If the bear was nearby, it couldn't miss seeing him. One of the rotting windfalls had been ripped apart by his quarry to find grubs or other edible things.

Making a decision, Beau decided to work his way up to the top of the ridge and try spotting the bear and cub from the higher vantage point. If he continued to try and track it, progress would be too slow, and if the animal was above him his scent would be carried to the bear before he would see it. About 100 yards up the ridge he would be back in the trees.

After taking a drink from his water skin, Beau picked up the .54 caliber rifle and continued up the ridge. Just after entering the trees, he stopped and sniffed the air. He felt a chill go through his body. The smell of bear was strong. Not far from his location was a bear, or one that had relieved itself recently. To his right came a loud tearing sound of wood being splintered.

With his rifle at the ready, Beau moved toward the sound, stalking the bear. He had just drunk, but his throat felt dry. If he had been after a lone bear, it would most likely run away at the sight or smell of a man. A mother bear would not. In front of him was an evergreen thicket and beyond was another area covered with windfalls. The bear was probably searching for grubs in the rotting trees.

Suddenly, he saw movement as the evergreens around him thinned. The female bear was just entering the trees beyond. The cub still played in the windfalls.

Beau remained still with his rifle raised, hoping that the mother bear would come back looking for the youngster. The crash of brush higher on the ridge startled Beau. Coming down the ridge at a full run was a large male bear, intent on catching and killing the cub.

The sound of brittle tree branches cracking and the sudden cries of the cub as it tried to run for its mother filled Beau's ears as he swung the rifle, sighting on the black raging hulk. The rifle recoiled, sending the ball into the shoulder of the male bear. It stumbled for a second before turning and running straight at Beau.

The male bear was within 30 paces before the curly-haired man had a chance to react. Dropping the rifle, Beau ran into the trees, looking for one that was high enough to get him out of reach of the wounded animal. Daring not to look back, he grabbed the limb of a live oak and climbed, his heart pounding in his chest. The growling sounds of the bear were ringing in his ears and he was sure it was right upon him.

Clinging to the tree, Beau looked down. What he saw shocked him. There was a battle between the mother bear and the large male. Responding to the cries of the cub, the female must have come back and took after the wounded bear. The confrontation was over quickly and the male ran north up the ridge. The female took a few steps in that direction before turning back to find her cub.

Giving both bears some time to move away from him, Beau climbed down from the oak and went to retrieve his rifle. The was no sign of any of the bears. As he poured powder and rammed a ball down the barrel, he looked in the direction where the male had gone.

"Well, boy," he mumbled. "You got a wounded bear to go after."

The prospect of tracking the male bear was nothing he looked forward to. He had heard stories of wounded animals circling and waiting for the unsuspecting hunter. The blood trail was plain to see. Often an injured animal would run until it became weak, then laid down and bled out. Beau hoped that this would be the case.

It was mid-afternoon and he was still tracking the animal. The bear had laid down once and left a large, bloody patch before continuing. Beau found saliva mixed with blood on some branches, confirming that it had been a lung shot. Given time, it should drown in its own blood. The trail led over the crest of the ridge.

Beau became concerned. It was headed down the east side, toward an area with several cabins. If it should be spotted by anyone living in the area, they would finish the kill and claim it for themselves. He knew that he should stop and let the bear lay down. Beau was sure he was pushing it and that was what was keeping it going. The fear of losing it wouldn't allow him to wait.

It was late afternoon when relief flooded over him. Just below him he spotted the black bear lying sprawled out on the hillside. Taking his time, Beau slowly went up to the animal. Using the barrel of his rifle he poked it, checking for life. When the bear had finally gone down it had slid ahead and come to stop against a large pine tree.

"You damn brute, you could have stayed on the west side of the ridge," Beau complained. "Now I got to get your carcass back up over the top."

The bear was a big male. Beau estimated that it would be over 400 pounds. It would take several trips back to the cabin to pack the animal home. Grunting, he pulled and pushed the animal away from the pine, preparing to gut it. He would save the liver, kidneys, and heart, leaving the rest of the guts to the wild animals.

After making the first cut, Beau froze. A twig snapped behind him and a low voice asked, "What you doin' huntin' in my woods?"

Turning slowly, he saw a bearded man dressed in well-worn clothing, holding a long rifle cradled in his arm and pointing it in the general direction of Beau.

Leaving the knife on the carcass, Beau stood up and faced his accuser. "I wasn't hunting on your side of the ridge. If you follow the blood trail, it will take you well beyond the other side where I shot the bear."

"It be on my side now," the man stated flatly.

"I need this bear, mister," Beau said, wishing he hadn't left the knife on the animal. "My winter harvest of honey was eaten when a bear broke into my cabin. I depended on the honey to get through the next year. I need this animal to survive."

"That's your hard luck, sonny," the man said as he shifted the rifle in line with Beau. "I got hungry young'uns back home that need feeding. You keep the innards, and I'll take the rest of the bear."

Panic surged through Beau. He was about to lose the oil and skin, not to mention the meat. As quickly as the panic came, it was replaced with cool calculation. His life was worth more than the $15 that the skin and oil would bring and he could live on greens and tubers until he shot another bear, or a deer.

He decided on one more try to reason with the man before giving up the animal. "You got hungry kids and I need money the bear would give me to get supplies for the coming year. Now, I don't need all the meat this big brute will provide. In fact, I ain't got enough salt to put it all up. Why don't I take what I need, and you take what you need, and we will both go on living?"

For a long minute the two men stood staring at each other, neither speaking. Finally, the man lowered the rifle. "I got me a mule back in the trees. We can drag the animal to your cabin and butcher this bugger. I'll haul home the meat and you can have what's left."

Nodding, Beau went to retrieve the .54 caliber leaning against the pine. "You can leave the rifle here and come with me to get the mule," the man instructed. "And, when we get back, we can cook up the liver before draggin' the bear back. By the way, my name is Homer Franks."

Suddenly, Beau realized that he was starving. Following Homer, he replied, "Beau, my name's Beau Levesque."

There was smoke rising from the chimney of the two-room cabin Homer Franks called home. Along with a wife, there were five children. The age difference between the couple was almost 10 years. She had lost her first husband and, needing a provider for her and the young'uns, she had chosen to marry the older bachelor. Seeing the family he was supporting helped Beau understand why Homer had defended the rights to the bear. A pole corral and a barn were to the north of the cabin.

True to his word, Homer used his mule to drag the bear over the ridge to the cabin. It was almost dark when the men finished cutting up the bear and removing the fat from the animal. A kill in the fall would have provided much more fat from a bear, but Beau needed what he could get right now. With the meat packed on the mule, Homer waved and led the animal up the ridge. Homer had left enough meat to last Beau for a month if he used it sparingly.

Sunday was spent rendering the fat and using what salt he had to preserve the meat. Scraping the hide provided some additional fat. Next Sunday he would walk to the village and sell the skin and oil. As he worked, he went over the items he needed to purchase. Beau thought about sitting around the fire and eating the liver with Homer. He kind of liked the man and would take a trip over the ridge and visit sometime this summer. Maybe bring him a haunch of venison, too.

Beau went to sleep that night in a good mood. He was happy living up on the ridge. He considered it his own little mountain. The bear would provide for things he needed through the summer, and he had enough meat to get by for a while. Tomorrow he would have to put up with Angus, but he planned to be at the plantation before daylight and start work. If needed, he could always promise to put in a Sunday.

Not far from the cabin the mother bear and her cub sat sniffing the air. The meal of honey was still fresh in her mind. The other smells from the cabin were disturbing. Somewhere about was the smell of the male she had fought with. Snorting, she and the cub moved away along the ridge.

CHAPTER THREE

It was an hour before daylight when Beau arrived at the delta. The oak he had felled on Friday still lay where he had left it. Stripping his shirt off and placing it next to the poke bag, he went to work limbing the tree. By the time the sun came over the ridge, he had the tree ready to skid to the bucking station. Resting for a minute, Beau took a long drink from the water skin.

He was dragging the branches and piling them for burning when movement caught his eye. It was Angus on the gelding coming his way. He noticed that the others had not come to work yet. Feeling good about the work he had already done, he waved to Angus.

The gray gelding stopped next to Beau. Angus sat there mean as ever, glaring at the curly-haired man. "Come to work when you feel like it I see," he snarled.

"Where are the others?" Beau asked.

"Not that you would care, but they're burying Mr. Weber," Angus snapped.

Shock ran through Beau. He did care. Beau and his father had done odd jobs for the owner over the years and Horst Weber had always paid them well and treated them with respect. Now the man was dead. What would happen with the contract?

"I am very sorry to hear about Mr. Weber. He was a good and fair man," Beau said, defending his feelings.

"You sure as hell show it, taking off whenever you want to!" Angus scoffed.

Not wanting to argue, he asked, "What is to become of my contract?"

An evil smile came over the face of the big man. "He left it to me. I own you, boy."

"That's not possible. Mr. Weber would never do that!" Beau exclaimed.

With a swift motion, Angus uncoiled the whip and raised it to strike the curly-haired man. "Don't you talk back to me!"

As the whip-yielding arm came forward, Beau pulled his knife, intending to slash the weapon in half. The braided leather whip cut into his shoulder and back. Grasping it in his hand, he jerked it tight and brought up his knife. The unsuspecting rider was caught off guard and fell forward, landing on top of Beau, and the two of them landed in a pile on the ground.

The weight of the big man trapped Beau as he struggled to free himself. Pushing Angus aside, he rolled clear and leaped to his feet. He had lost the knife when the big man had fallen on him. Beau stepped back, expecting Angus to come after him with the whip. His eyes widened when he saw his knife protruding from the side of Angus.

He heard voices. It was the freemen and slaves coming to work. There was no way he could explain or defend what had happened here. Beau pulled the knife from Angus' side. He noticed that there was also a gash on the man's temple caused when he had hit the ground. Beau knew that he had to go, and go fast.

Grabbing his poke and shirt, Beau headed for the ridge, using the sparse trees for cover. He could hear shouting behind him as he ran. His mind was racing. What was done could not be undone. He would have to leave the area and find a place where nobody knew him. Beau had lived with his father in Virginia and the Carolinas. A man without means would not fare well there, and he was definitely a man without means.

To the west, he would be facing hostiles and would be forced to live off the land. If he did survive through the summer, the coming winter would probably he his end. Beau could see the cabin as he climbed the ridge. The morning sun filtered through the trees. It was peaceful and a place he had called home. Now men would come here to arrest him for murder and he must be gone when they came.

"You did nothing wrong," he mumbled. "It was an accident." As he talked to himself, he was busy packing things he would need. He had a blanket, ground cloth, extra powder, lead and patches for the .54 caliber rifle. He looked at the shaving kit next to the small mirror and basin. He wouldn't be needing them.

With the poke and possible bags filled, he tied some line to his blanket roll so he could sling it over his shoulder. Beau had an extra well-worn shirt and a pair of socks rolled up inside. He also had his father's coat. It was a little small and threadbare, but would be some help if it was cold. He had his father's felt hat, which had a round top and a turned-up brim. His father had always said that a hat makes a man.

Beau looked out the door to see if anyone was coming his way. It was quiet below. He decided on his first move. His gear, the bear skin, and the oil would weigh about 150 pounds. He would go over the ridge and bring the skin and oil to Homer. He would leave the meat he couldn't take with him and the man could come to the cabin and get it if he wanted. He could also have anything else of value, which wasn't much.

As Beau went over the ridge he heard shouting from the direction of the delta. They were coming after him! Pulling the straps higher onto his shoulders, he headed down the east side of the ridge. A sudden crash in the brush to the south startled him. Dropping his gear to the ground, he swung the rifle in the direction of the noise. He breathed a sigh of relief when he spotted the white flash of a deer's tail as it ran through the brush.

"You best get out of this territory, boy, or you'll be jumping every time you hear a noise," he muttered. Picking up his bags and bedroll, Beau ducked through the brush and trees as he headed for Homer's.

Rushing to the cabin, Beau scattered the chickens scratching in the front yard. Dropping his packs, he knocked on the plank door. Homer opened it and hesitated a moment before recognizing the curly-haired man.

"Been hunting on my side of the ridge again?" he asked sternly. Then, smiling, he invited Beau in.

"I got trouble, Mr. Franks," Beau said.

Homer motioned to a chair near the scarred table and went to get the coffee pot next to the coals in the fireplace. Mrs. Franks was busy giving the young'uns their weekly bath in a wooden washtub sitting on two chairs. The three youngest ones ran around naked, waiting for their turn in the tub.

With coffee poured for the two men, Homer sat across from Beau. "What kind of trouble would that be?"

Staring at the tin mug of coffee, he replied, "The worst kind, Mr. Franks. I killed a man. I've got to leave Arkansas. I brung you the bear skin and oil. Back at the cabin is a barrel with some salted meat. You are welcome to it and anything else you find useful."

"When you tell a man that kind of news, you best look him in the eye, son," Homer said, his voice flat. "Did the man need killing?"

"I can't say he did," Beau replied. "He were mad at me for missing work and took the whip to me. I grabbed it to cut it and he fell on the knife when he come off the horse."

"Were you a free man working for him?" the man asked.

"I was working off a contract that he came to have."

Beau noticed that the bath routine had stopped and the wife and children were staring at him. Homer went over to the coffee pot and refilled his cup. The curly-haired man hadn't touched his. Sitting back down, Homer heaved a sigh.

"He had the right to put the whip to you, son," Homer concluded. "While I don't agree with the practice, a judge would send you to the hanging tree."

Beau gulped down the cold coffee and started to leave. "I can give you something for the skin and oil," the man said, stopping the young man.

He went to a tin can near the washboard. Homer returned with $5. "It is all I got. Take the mule and ride north until dark. Let it go and it will find its way back home. If they come here looking for you, I will tell them you took it. You won't be in any more trouble than you are now and I won't have to do any explaining when I go to your cabin and tell them I was hunting it."

Before leaving, Homer also gave him a fly tarp to sleep under and an old set of stained buckskins that he had outgrown. Beau rode bareback on the mule, heading north along the base of the ridge. His gear hung down on each side of the animal. Guiding it with a halter rope, he rode, the rifle cradled in the crook of his arm.

As instructed, Beau stopped just after the sun went down behind the ridge. He removed the halter rope and sent the mule back towards Homer's cabin. Building a small fire, he roasted some of the salted bear meat and made a meal of it along with water. Kicking dirt over the coals to put it out, Beau walked another hour north before spreading his blankets under some pines.

He lay in the dark, listening to the night. He half expected to see men with torches coming after him through the trees at any moment. He had traveled about 15 miles from his cabin. Beau's mind had been racing as he and Homer had been getting the mule ready to go.

The man had asked Beau where he intended to

go. It was a question that he did not have an answer for. All he could think of was far from here. Homer had talked of his wish to go to the Rocky Mountains. He had said that Crowley's Ridge was nothing compared to the grand peaks out west. Meeting his wife and the responsibility of the children had ended his dreams of going west and becoming a mountain man.

As the coolness of the night came on, Beau pulled his blanket closer under his chin. He began to rethink going west. If he had a plan, it could be possible. There were places in Missouri that he could earn money to outfit himself. He had heard that pack trains went out of St. Louis and he might be able to join one of them.

Exhaustion from the long day began to overcome Beau and he started to drift off. The snap of a twig brought him wide awake. Holding his breath, he strained his ears, trying to determine the source. It could be an animal, or even just the cooling night breezes. Then the sound came again. Something, or someone, was moving toward him.

His rifle was lying just under the blankets and was loaded and ready. Then there was a muffled cough. It was not an animal. "Whoever is out there, I got a rifle ready and will put a hole clean through you," he warned.

"Don't shoot," a voice out of the dark said. "I mean you no harm, suh."

"Step out so I can see you," Beau ordered.

In the meager light of the night stars, he saw a shadowy form appear. "Who are you?" he demanded.

"Elijah, suh," the voice said.

"Mr. Weber's Elijah?" the surprised curly-haired man asked.

"Yes suh."

Beau had seen Elijah around the plantation. He was a servant in the owner's home. It was rumored that his father was Horst Weber. It was said that he had been schooled by the owner. Word was that he had been taught to read and write as well as handling firearms. When Mr. Weber had gone into town, Elijah had always driven the carriage.

Sitting up, Beau asked, "What are you doing here? Are you running?"

"I had to, Massa Beau," the slave replied. "Angus didn't like the way Massa Horst treated me and would look for any reason to lay the whip on me."

"Well, first off, don't be calling me master," Beau said. "I don't own you and don't intend to own any slaves."

"Second, there ain't nothing I can offer you," he added. "I am one step ahead of a hangman's noose and if you're caught with me, we will be hanging from the same tree."

"I can't go back," Elijah replied. "Massa Weber promised me freedom, but died before he done it. If I go back, Angus will peel the hide off my back with the whip."

"Angus is gone, Elijah. I killed him this morning," Beau told the young slave.

Determined not to be turned back, Elijah replied, "If it wasn't him with the whip, it would be others. I would like to spend the night here with you, and then I will go on my own."

"Help yourself to a piece of ground." With that, Beau laid back down and snugged the blanket around himself.

* * *

The sun was just coming up when Beau awoke. The cool air was heavy with moisture. A dew covered the ground and his belongings. It was a moment before he became aware of his surroundings and the memories of yesterday flooded back. Tossing the blanket back, he sat up. Less than 20 feet from him lay the runaway slave. He lay curled up next to two bags, shivering.

Taking his blanket, Beau laid it, dry side down, over Elijah. He then searched around for some dry twigs and branches to start a fire. He was in a pine grove on the east side of Crowley's Ridge. He would have to take care to avoid others who lived on the ridge. There was one community with a trading post and several dwellings that had a local lawman. He would have to head west before coming to it.

Once the fire was going, Beau put some water on to heat for coffee. He would use the last of the grounds mixed with dirt from his cabin floor. He pulled a blackened frying pan from the poke bag and placed it on the fire. Beau looked at the sleeping slave, then decided to share the last of his salted bear meat with Elijah.

The sound and smell of the frying meat woke the young sleeper. Looking over at Beau, he said, "Thank you for the blanket."

"You looked cold. Come on over to the fire and dig into the meat," Beau invited.

"Is the water for coffee?" Elijah asked.

"It is. As soon as the water boils, I'll add some grounds, and I do mean *grounds*," Beau said, smiling.

Reaching into one of the bags, Elijah pulled out a tin. "Let me share my coffee."

There was no argument from Beau. Soon, the two of them were enjoying a hot meal. Beau began to talk. "I had first thought of going to St. Louis and then west, but word travels fast and I might find trouble traveling along the Mississippi. I best cut west over the mountains in Missouri. My father took me that way once until we run short of supplies."

"I got supplies," Elijah replied. "When word come that they was going to lock us all up after the massa died so things could be figured out, I filled two bags with as much as I could carry and took to the woods. Of course, you noticed, I forgot to grab a blanket."

"What brought you to my camp?" Beau asked.

"Coming over the ridge, I saw you on the mule, suh," Elijah explained. "I had seen you around the plantation. I remember your father meeting with Massa Weber. I was some confused when I watched you let the animal go. I figured you were also running and maybe you knew the best way to go."

Beau wiped his bear grease-covered fingers on the sides of his trousers. With his eyes on the supplies, he said, "We need to get one thing straight if I take you. I am not a master or a sir. You just call me Beau or Levesque. As of now, we are both free men."

"You can call me Eli, suh . . . ah, Beau," the young black said, smiling.

With their meal out of the way and an understanding of each other, the two men angled over Crowley's Ridge in a northwesterly direction.

CHAPTER FOUR

The terrain the two men were traveling was rugged, with a series of cuts and gorges from ancient rivers. While it looked mountainous, it was really high ground that had been eroded by time. Several of the ravines still had rivers flowing through them.

After two weeks on the trail, they passed a trading post. Eli decided to stay out of sight while Beau used a dollar of Homer's money to buy a blanket and ground tarp for his traveling companion. For another $2 he bought salt, flour, and a few other supplies.

Beau was wearing the buckskins that Homer had given him and had a good start of a beard. The burly trading post owner asked if he was headed for the rendezvous on the Green River. Whether he was kidding or not, Beau couldn't be sure. He had read about the wild times at the mountain man gatherings.

Suddenly, he thought, *Why not?*

"As a matter of fact, I am," Beau said with a degree of authority.

"You going to catch the pack train at Fort

William?" the owner asked.

It was the end of April right now, the exact date Beau was not sure of. He had no idea how far the fort was from his present location. "I hope to," he said. "That is, if they don't leave before I get there."

"It shouldn't be a problem if the Lakota or Arapahoe don't get you." The merchant walked away chuckling, leaving Beau holding his bags of supplies.

Leaving the trading post, he met with Eli next to a creek a mile away. The young black man had the fire going and was roasting two ruffed grouse they had killed earlier in the day. "We're going to the rendezvous."

Elijah looked up from his cooking. "The rendezvous?"

"It's a gathering where the mountain men sell their furs," Beau explained.

Nodding, Eli turned the birds. "Where is this rendezvous?"

"West, it's west of here near the Rocky Mountains," he replied.

The young black man seemed satisfied with the explanation. Beau's father had been an avid reader and often explained things using maps printed in the books. He had traced the route along the Missouri and Platte Rivers that frontier men had used for their trips to the west. Right now, they were about three weeks away from Independence.

By now, Beau was safe from the long arm of the law. For Elijah, it was another story. Missouri had laws that controlled the movement of blacks in the state. Eli had nothing to show that he was a free man. If questioned, he could be put in jail, only to be sold for the expenses of his incarceration. If Beau was identified as helping a runaway slave, he could end up in prison for five years.

Slave patrols roamed the towns and countryside, watching for blacks who might have strayed too far from their place of work. The two men were constantly alert to populated areas that might be a source of questions. One time, the two of them were stopped by a businessman who challenged them. Beau was able to convince the man that he was escorting Elijah through the state for the owner, and planned to catch a steamboat on the Missouri River.

They arrived in Independence on May 16th. The two fugitives camped outside of town along the banks of the Missouri River. This was the end of the line for the steamboats. To the east, they could see the billowing smoke rising into the air from the boilers on the boats. The long, lonely blasts of the steam whistles could be heard night and day. Supplies would be off-loaded and transferred to wagons to be shipped in all directions, including west to Fort William.

For the past week, the two men had been traveling on rolling prairie. It was said that the grasslands would continue all the way to the fort. They had the fly tarp rigged for sleeping. Eli had caught some fish and was frying them over their fire. Beau had offered to help with the meals, but Eli was good at it and insisted on doing the cooking. The results left Beau with little to argue about.

During their trip up from Arkansas they had killed two wolves, three fox, and a fisher. Beau took the furs and headed into Independence to sell them and purchase a few needed supplies. He walked with the bundle on his back when he noticed a wagon that was tilted to one side. A stocky man was in the process of emptying the cargo.

As Beau got closer he noticed that the back wheel was broken. The man was struggling with some of the larger items. Dropping his bundle of furs, he walked toward the wagon. "Can I help you with that?" Beau offered.

The man stepped back, mopping his face with a rag. "Sure could use it. The wagon hit a wash back there and the spokes gave way."

The two men finished unloading the wagon. The wagon had a spare wheel riding under the belly. With Beau's help, the wagon was repaired and the cargo was reloaded. While helping the man, he learned that after making this local delivery, the man, whose name was Elroy, was joining several other wagons hauling freight to Fort William.

Before heading on his way, Beau asked, "Would anyone on the trip to the fort need any extra helpers? My black and I are headed that way and could use the work."

Elroy climbed up onto the seat and took the horses' reins. "I got three wagons myself. Be at the dock in the morning. You can help with the loading. Maybe someone will need help. At the very least, I will find you and your black a ride to the fort for the help."

Picking up his pack, Beau headed for the town, whistling, feeling pretty good about the latest development. He had found a way to go west. Beau would have to be careful traveling with Elijah until they were well away from Missouri. Blacks were thought of as property and nothing more.

The furs weren't in prime condition, but still sold for enough to purchase supplies and have a little left over. One of the items Beau bought were new boots. He wore them on the walk back to their camp. His feet were aching before he got there.

"I got us some work, Eli," he announced as he strode into camp carrying his new boots.

"Do we have the time?" Elijah asked. "We have to catch the pack trains west at Fort William."

Smiling, Beau replied, "That's the best part. The work will get us to the fort."

That night the two men laughed and talked about the upcoming adventure traveling to the Rocky Mountains. The next morning the two men were walking toward town before the sun came up. Both men carried packs with their worldly supplies and Beau cradled the Model 1803 rifle.

The dock area was piled high with all types of goods. Men carrying short clubs walked among the freight, making sure that nothing was stolen. One of the guards stopped, scowling at the two men before continuing on. Beau and Eli sat, just up from the landing, on some discarded boxes, waiting for the wagons to arrive. There was the smell of coffee and side meat being made for someone's breakfast.

They had started the day with leftover fish and water to wash it down. The 17-year-old Elijah was humming a hymn as he whittled with a bone-handled clasp knife on a piece of apple wood. The young black had a slim build. He wore dark woolen trousers and a light gray shirt. He had taken to wearing Beau's father's coat, which fit the slim figure much better. His hair was close cropped and he had a thin growth of chin whiskers.

The sound of harnesses jangling caught the attention of the two men. Several wagons were slowly moving toward the landing. Beau tried to spot Elroy.

The glare of the rising sun made it impossible to recognize anyone. As each of the wagons got closer, none were driven by the man he had met.

He began to doubt that Elroy was even going to show when he spotted three slowly moving wagons coming from the south. Each wagon was pulled by six mules. Leroy drove the lead wagon and the other two were driven by younger men. Beau and Eli walked over to meet them. Noticing them, Elroy pulled the team to a halt and gave Elijah a hard stare.

"Is this the black you spoke of yesterday?" he asked.

"Yes, it is, sir. He is a good worker and will do you a good job," Beau assured the man.

"He looks kinda soft," Elroy replied. "I suppose you got papers on him?"

"I've had him for a long time and the need for papers never crossed my mind," Beau lied.

The other two wagons pulled up abreast of Elroy. A horse was tied to the back on the last wagon. "Climb in back," the man said. "I don't like it. No, I don't. Law says you can't stay in Missouri less'n you got papers."

As he and Eli got into the wagon, Beau thought, *That should work. We won't be in Missouri much longer.*

The wagon that the two men loaded was filled with kegs of gunpowder. Beau and Eli took care not to bump and bang them. Elroy told them not to worry about the powder, because it would take a lot to set it off. The question that remained was: *What was a lot?*

Once the wagons were loaded, one of the young men took the horse and headed back home. "My son's wife is ready to give birth. Kept him up all night with labor," Elroy explained. "I had hoped you could drive one of the wagons to the fort."

"As long as my black is part of the deal, I'd be happy to," Beau replied. "You should know he is a good man with a team."

"I will only pay one man for driving," Elroy said.

Just a little steamed by the news, Beau was tempted to tell the man that Eli would be the driver, but instead he replied, "Understood."

Beau and Eli also had an understanding. When necessary, the young black would be Beau's. Once they got away from the slave states, the charade could end.

A small army contingent was traveling with the wagons. Sergeant Howell was the senior man leading the caravan of 12 wagons. He rode by, giving instructions for the position of each wagon. Munition wagons would be at the end and were required to stay back a distance from the rest.

"What happened to it taking a lot to set it off?" Eli asked, chuckling at his own joke.

"I look at it this way," Beau said, grinning. "If it goes off, we will be the first to hear it." He liked the fact that Elijah was acting less timid.

There was one other wagon with munitions and it took the position in front of Beau and Eli. Two soldiers rode alongside each of the wagons. While they offered protection in the case of an attack, Beau had found out that their job was to detonate the powder before letting hostiles get it.

It was mid-afternoon when the freight wagons pulled away from the landing. All of the wagons except one had a tarp tightly tied over the cargo, leaving the driver exposed to the weather. Only the first wagon was a Conestoga, or covered wagon. It offered protection for the driver and any passengers riding inside.

Mules had been chosen to reduce the length of time the round trip would take. The 650-mile trip to the fort would take several weeks longer with oxen. While the oxen would have been slower, they could survive on prairie grass, while mules needed grain to supplement their diet. With the mules, they should arrive in just under six weeks.

Beau sat on the wooden seat, holding half of the reins in each hand, waiting for his turn to fall in. All of the teamsters were rough-looking men. So far they had pretty much avoided him and Eli. The dust from the other wagons was drifting back as Beau started his mules.

The road was rutted from earlier trips in the spring, giving the riders a bone-jarring ride. As they rode Beau sat, his stomach growling from hunger. The rest of the men had brought something that was quick to eat during a short break. There wasn't time for them to dig into their packs and make something. Beau understood that the rest of the meals would be provided during the trip, except for Eli, who was just hitching a ride.

The rest of the teamsters had no intention of mingling with a black. Beau and Elijah had not expected more than that, knowing the conflict over slavery that Missouri had faced when it had become a state. They were perfectly happy to keep to their selves. The pay would be given out at the end of the trip and it was assumed that Beau would be paid something for Eli helping with the loading and unloading of cargo.

The first night they camped on the far side of a creek that flowed into the Missouri River. It was the first of many tributaries they would have to cross before reaching the fort. Two major rivers would be the South Platte and then the Laramie. Crossing them in late summer would have been easier because the water would be down, but not so in May and June.

The soldiers left the munition wagons and joined the rest of the army bivouacked near the Conestoga. Each driver took care of their mules. Having Eli with him was an advantage. After being given water and grain, the animals were hobbled so they could graze. Beau went to the main fire and got his plate of beans and side meat. He also grabbed a couple of sourdough biscuits.

Eli had a small fire going and was making coffee. The two men shared the meal provided by the caravan. They also had some frying pan biscuits that the young black had made. Some would be saved for the morning meal.

"Tomorrow I will walk, and if you got anymore of the bird shot, I'll get us some fresh meat," Eli suggested.

"That sounds good," Beau agreed. "You'll have to wade the streams and I figure there will be a lot between here and the Platte."

"I'd trade wet feet for a sore bottom bouncing along on the wagon," Eli replied.

Fires were banked early in the evening and the teamsters began to turn in, spreading their blankets under the wagons. Over the next six weeks the days would be long and the nights short. Sundays would be a day off the trail to rest the mules, fix harnesses, lubricate axles, and take care of personal items. The normally hard drinking and fighting men were all business on the trail.

If a man let his mind drift from what he was doing due to being tired, a wheel could end up crosswise in a rut and break an axle. Spare axles and wheels were carried along, but the time lost making repairs could never be made up. One other thing was the army. The soldiers could stay with the caravan as long as they made good time. If they had to stop for any extended period, the sergeant would have to take the majority of the soldiers ahead.

Beau was up early and checking his cargo. He wanted to make sure that none of the kegs had loosened up, allowing them to slam against the rest. The powder kegs had hemp bands to prevent any sparks from metal against metal. He heard Eli bringing the mules in to be harnessed. Beau got the fire going and put water onto heat for coffee. He then went to the main fire to get his breakfast.

There were pancakes and molasses to sweeten them. The second wagon had some cargo, but most of the space was used for supplies needed to feed the teamsters. A bearded fellow with most of his teeth missing rode with the driver and did the cooking for the caravan. Only two meals were served a day. Many of the drivers would grab an extra biscuit or two to chew while on the trail. The cook's name was Abel. Beau held his tin plate out for some cakes. The old cook put on a couple and then added an extra portion.

Noticing, Beau said, "Thanks, Abel." He then scooped molasses from the tin and poured it over the pancakes.

Returning to their fire, he noticed that Eli was still working on the mules. "Your cakes are getting cold," he called out. "You best get over here."

"Keep them near the fire," Eli replied. "I got a couple more minutes here."

Beau was almost done eating when his friend came to the fire. "Having some trouble putting on the harnesses?"

"Trouble, no," Eli replied. "They were set up poorly and some of the mules were in the wrong position. Watch the one on the back left. He likes to bite and kick. I got him fixed so he can't get at the other mules. Now if he wants to kick, he'll just hit the wagon."

Beau watched as his friend wolfed down the pancakes. *What kind of servant were you?* he wondered.

The caravan was on the move an hour after sun up. Some of the teamsters began to sing songs they had learned in saloons and taverns. For the first two hours Eli rode on the wagon, watching the mules. After a long pull up a grade, the caravan stopped to give the animals a breather. The young black jumped down and worked on the harnesses, making an adjustment here and there.

Once the wagons started again, Eli watched for a short while and then he took the possible bag and the rifle and jumped off the slowly moving wagon. He trotted diagonally away from the caravan, disappearing into a swale.

"Sure hope the Lakota don't get him," Beau muttered.

The sun was getting low in the west and Beau was getting worried. He was thinking that it had been a mistake to let Eli go. He could be hurt or lost on the prairie. And then there were Indians. There was a shout from the front of the caravan. The dust prevented him from seeing what the ruckus was. A few minutes later he saw his friend standing beside the road, waiting for him.

Tossing the rifle and possible bag onto the back of the wagon, Eli climbed up and sat next to Beau. "No luck hunting?"

"There were some ducks on the river, but I couldn't get close enough for a shot," Eli replied.

"Well, you may as well wait a day or two and try again," Beau suggested.

"They'll be serving venison steaks for supper tonight," the young black said matter-of-factly.

"Took you all day to track it, hey?" Beau kidded.

That night everyone enjoyed the fresh meat with beans. Eli and Beau got one of the tenderloins and roasted it over their fire. While they were eating slices of the tender venison, a couple of the teamsters wandered by and thanked them for the meat. While they didn't stay and visit, their comments were appreciated.

The next morning, they awoke to rain. The chilling precipitation was falling from the steel gray sky. Abel was handing out rain slickers. Beau managed to get two. The high spirits of the caravan when they'd gotten the fresh meat had been dampened by the weather. The ground quickly became soft and the wheels of the wagon churned it to mud.

They huddled on the seat under their rain gear, the drizzle chilling Beau's hands as he held the reins. The wagon tended to slip and slide as they wound along the banks of the Missouri River. Steam came off the mules when they stopped to give them a breather.

Eli climbed down and checked on the mules

while Beau dug some biscuits out of their gear stored under the tarp. A quick check of his rifle confirmed that the moisture wasn't reaching it. He walked around the wagon, getting the kinks out of his legs while chewing on a biscuit. Passing his friend, he handed one to Eli.

The rain would be good for the new growth on the prairie. Green grass was spouting through last year's stems on the brown hills. They were sitting at the point where the Platte River joined the Missouri. The Platte was wide and shallow, with many islands of grass and brush. It was not well-suited for navigation with a canoe, much less larger water craft.

Both men's hats drooped as the rain dripped off the brims. The wind began to pick up as the caravan headed west along the Platte. The rain was driven sideways, making it difficult to see as the drops pelleted their faces.

"Miserable weather we're having," Eli complained.

"Once we get to the mountains, we can climb right above the clouds," Beau assured him.

Each of the men took turns driving the mules. The person riding could pull down their hat to protect their face and warm their hands inside the slicker. For two days the caravan slogged through the rain-soaked grassland. They watched as the current in the Platte gained strength. That would be a problem when they had to cross the south branch of the river.

Beau awoke on the third day to the sound of water dripping off the wagon above them, but the rain had stopped. There were breaks in the clouds to the west. Crawling out from under the wagon, mud oozed through his fingers. It would be some time before the prairie would dry out.

Elroy came back to the munition wagon, carrying a can of liniment. "We'll be spending the day here while things dry out. I got some stuff here to put on any harness sores on the mules."

Eli came out from under the wagon. "Won't need it, suh. The mules are fine."

"How the hell can that be?" the man asked, looking at Beau.

"My man here keeps the harnesses properly adjusted," he replied. "Good to know we got the stuff though, just in case."

The scowl on his face disappeared and Elroy said, "Well, okay. That's good to hear." Without another word, he turned and headed back toward the other wagons.

The caravan looked like it was laundry day. Clothing and blankets hung everywhere. The May weather was still on the cool side, but sitting against the wagon wheel with the sun in their faces felt good. Beau heated some water to clean the black powder out of his rifle. He noticed that the frizzen spring had weakened and he hoped to find a gunsmith at Fort William.

He looked over at Eli, who was brushing the mules. Two had feed bags on and were enjoying some grain. The tender new grass was keeping the animals in great shape. Of course, it did make them a little looser and one had to watch where they were standing when the animals coughed.

Beau felt good. They were out of Missouri and it was less likely that any authority would question Eli's status. He did realize that they had traded that concern for the new danger of Lakota or Arapahoes looking for scalps. He looked over at the other teamsters sitting around their fires and drinking coffee. Beau would have liked to be with them, listening to their stories, but he wouldn't abandon Eli.

The ground was still soft when the caravan pulled out the next morning, but the sun was warm. Smiling, Beau realized that it wouldn't be too long until they were again riding in the dust of the other wagons. He had been surprised when Elroy had asked Eli to ride on his wagon. That night the young black man spent time adjusting harnesses on the owner's team.

Figuring that Elroy had accepted Eli, Beau decided to let the black drive the wagon so he could do some hunting. During the rain, he had spotted some buffalo in the distance. At first he had thought they were patches of brush against the prairie grass until he saw one rolling onto its back to coat its hide against parasites.

Before the caravan started out, Beau was standing on a rise to the south. He could see the endless ruts of wagons that had made prior treks to the fort. Assured of the directions to intersect the route of the wagons, he headed west to find a buffalo or any other game that presented itself.

His new boots were broken in and he had sealed them against water. The heavy dew on the grass beaded off the leather. Soon the caravan was out of sight and Beau was alone on the vast expanse of grassland. He had grown up in the foothills and valleys along the Mississippi River and had never had such a feeling of openness.

By mid-day he had seen only one small bunch of woolly beasts. They were well south of the trail and too far away to make a kill and pack back to the wagons. If he'd had a horse or mule, the task would have been simple. He had seen several groups of pronghorns, but they stayed well out of range for him to shoot.

Beau worked his way back toward the trail and stopped near a sandstone mound to eat. He chewed on some jerky that Abel had given him. He was drinking from his water skin when something that sounded like rusty hinges startled him. A flock of gray birds flew over him, their long dark legs trailing in the back and long necks stretched out in front. They had enormous wing spans. He knew that they were cranes and probably good eating.

After several circles, they landed out of sight near the Platte River. Beau estimated that there were about 20 birds. Collecting up his gear, he worked his way toward the flock. He stopped below the ridge above the river. He could hear the birds beyond. Reaching into his possible bag, Beau withdrew a flat leather sheath. Inside he carried paper from a wasp nest.

Removing a piece, he then selected a half-dozen buck shot from a small leather bag and wrapped them with the piece of wasp nest. Pushing it into the end of his rifle, he used the ramrod and drove them down to the ball he had loaded the .54 caliber with. It was a buck and ball load that was used as far back as the Revolutionary War. He then primed the pan with fresh powder.

His heart was pounding with excitement as he slowly worked his way up the hill. The sounds of the cranes filled his ears with the promise of game for supper. He left his possible and water bag lying in the grass on the hillside to give himself freedom of movement. Removing his hat at the last minute, he wormed his way through the grass until he could see the birds.

Most were busy eating tender vegetation or insects along the riverbank. Four were keeping watch, their black bills with a red tuff of feathers pointing in the direction they watched. One crane was looking in Beau's direction. He lay still, the rifle stretched out in front of him. Beau watched the birds moving around, going about the business of feeding. He tried not to look directly at the watching cranes, fearing that they would feel his eyes on them.

He saw that several of the birds had lined up in a group, giving him the opportunity to hit several with one shot. Beau whispered a prayer that the lookouts wouldn't catch the slight movements he had to make. Lining up the rifle on the cranes, he squeezed the trigger. A split-second later, fire erupted from the .54 caliber.

Smoke from the black powder clouded the view of his target. Clinging to the rifle, Beau leaped to his feet, running toward the scattering birds. Several of the cranes lay flapping on the grass while the flock took to flight. He saw one running with a broken wing dragging. Not wanting to lose a bird nor leave one wounded, he sprinted toward it. Suddenly, the crane turned on him.

With the good wing outspread and the broken one dangling, it began to hiss a warning at Beau. Unable to stop quickly enough, he swung the muzzle loader like a club, striking the neck of the crane as he went by. Wheeling around, he came face-to-face with the undaunted bird. Realizing that it could drive the bill into him or take his eye out, Beau ducked as he pulled his knife. Managing to grab its neck, he swiped at it with the Green River blade, severing the arteries.

Quickly, he put distance between the bird and himself, waiting for it to bleed out. Gasping for breath, Beau stood with his hands on his knees, keeping an eye on the crane. He then noticed another wounded bird moving toward the river. It was harder hit and was crouching as it went. As he approached it the crane stopped moving. It was finished.

He had killed a total of five cranes. Beau collected up the 10-pound carcasses and carried them to the riverbank. He then went to collect up his scattered gear. He felt some stinging on his cheek bone. Touching it with his fingers, it came back bloody. The crane he had faced had gotten one thrust in. Before heading down to clean the cranes he rinsed the cut on his cheek with water from his bag.

Once the cranes were cleaned, Beau hung them over his shoulders with leather string from his possible bag and started walking back toward the caravan. The wagons had just stopped for the day when he reached them. Abel came running to meet him.

"You brung something for the cookpot?" he called out.

"I got you some birds to roast," Beau replied.

"Hot damn! It will be like a holiday," the cook exclaimed.

That night the teamsters were lively, enjoying the roasted crane. The meat was dark and stringy, but it was a nice break from beans and side meat. Abel saved the legs to make a soup the following day. Roasted, they would be too tough to eat. He let Beau know that he had a few root vegetables hidden away for the soup.

Several of the teamsters came by to chat briefly

with Beau and Eli. Two of the men even stayed awhile and shared some of the coffee. While most of the men weren't about to become pals with Beau and Eli, they were accepting them.

Once the men went back to their fire, Eli pointed at Beau's cheek. "I got something to put on your cut."

He climbed up onto the wagon and dug into his packs. Beau sat, thinking of all the things Eli was capable of doing and couldn't help but wonder where he had learned it all.

CHAPTER FIVE

When the caravan reached the confluence of the North Platte and South Platte Rivers they had to find a safe location to ford the South Platte. The soldiers rode their horses along the bank and eventually found an acceptable crossing. It was three miles from where the two rivers joined.

Beau sat on his munition wagon watching the wagons and mules struggle through the river current and silt-covered bottoms as they made their way across. His stomach felt tight knowing that his turn would come soon. As each wagon reached the other side, the exhausted mules stood with their heads hanging down, water dripping off them.

Eli poked Beau with his elbow. "Pull the wagon around. It's our turn to cross."

As he got the mules moving, Beau muttered, "I sure hope I keep this powder dry"

After all his worry and concern, the crossing went without a hitch. Eli had the harnesses adjusted to keep all the animals pulling evenly. Beau was successful keeping them moving and soon they also stood on the far side, water dripping onto the grassy bank.

The caravan went another mile before they set up camp. They would have the next day off to rest the mules and go through their wagons, making sure everything had come through okay. One of the soldiers told Beau that they were just over a week from a towering structure called Chimney Rock. They would be able to see the 300 feet-high pinnacle days before they would reach it. Another week after that, they would be at the fort.

It was early June, and the plains were covered with yellow buckbean and goats-beard. The reds and purples came from the wild rose and peavine. A carpet of blue stem and switchgrass covered the plain. The teamsters were drinking their morning coffee and Abel had made them pancakes. Eli and Beau had finished their meals and were getting the mule team harnessed.

Without warning the placid scene was shattered as several dark shapes came over the rise to the south. The shrill cries of Indians cut through the air. The wagons were sitting in a half-circle near the river, with an opening on the east side. The munition wagons were alone, away from the opening. The camp was in confusion, with teamsters running for their rifles and tripping over gear left near the wagons. The soldiers on watch began to fire at the attackers. The others were in the process of packing their tents. They left them lying on the prairie grass and scrambled to take up positions.

The Arapahoe had closed within striking distance and were showering the wagons with arrows before the teamsters fired the first shot. Eli had just finished hitching the team at the first cry. Seeing the

Indians coming, Beau leaped onto the wagon and pulled out the rifle, possible bag and powder horn. The sudden movement of the wagon almost caused him to fall off.

Eli drove the wagon to block the open side of the caravan before cutting the mules loose. He then joined the teamsters and began reloading the spare rifles as the men fired. The munition wagon now offered some cover from the open side of the caravan. Beau loaded and fired the .54 caliber as fast as he could, using his wagon for protection.

As Eli handed a loaded rifle to one of the teamsters, an arrow took the man in the chest. Picking up the rifle from the downed teamster, Eli fired at the circling Arapahoe. The shot knocked a brave from his horse. Clouds of black powder smoke filled the air along with the cries of wounded men.

Suddenly the Arapahoe broke off their attack, driving off some of the soldiers' horses. A few of the teamsters and soldiers kept firing after the departing Indians, but most began to give aid to the wounded. Beau chased after the scattered animals while Elijah began helping the injured. The man who had taken the arrow was dead. He was also one of Elroy's drivers.

The soldiers set up a perimeter in the event that the Arapahoe tried another run. It was soon apparent that their intent had been to scatter the stock and make off with as many as possible. Most of the mules had harnesses and hadn't strayed far. The soldier's horses were another story. Over half of them had been driven off.

One teamster was dead, three were wounded. The soldiers had fared better with two wounded. After the mules and remaining horses, including two Indian ponies, had been rounded up, Beau went to find Elroy. The man's face was drawn and he had tears in his eyes.

"They killed my daughter's husband," he said.

Standing awkwardly near the grieving man, Beau struggled to find words of comfort. He finally said, "I am very sorry. We'll give him a proper grave with a Christian burial."

Turning to help others get their wagons ready, Beau left the crushed owner near the blanket-covered body. Eli finished helping with the wounded and joined him. Beau told him about Elroy's son-in-law.

"I know," the young black said. "I was loading for him when he was hit."

Looking out in the direction where the attack had come from, Beau was surprised to see that there were no Arapahoe bodies in sight. "Eli, I saw you hit one at least. What happened?"

"While we were shootin' at the ones driving the horses, others swooped in to pick up their dead," he replied. "I could have shot one, but killing more didn't make no sense."

The decision was to move the caravan upriver to a more defensible location after burying Elroy's son-in-law. Beau helped with the digging while Eli carved a marker. With hats in hand, the men listened to Elroy say words over the grave and then several hymns were sung.

The owner wasn't ready to leave when the rest of the caravan departed. Beau stayed behind with Elroy while the man remained near the grave, praying. Beau stood watch near the munition wagon with Elroy's rifle and his .54 caliber loaded with buck and ball. If they were attacked again, he wanted to do as much damage as possible with the first shot.

It was getting dark when he and Elroy got back to the caravan. Elijah was talking with several of the teamsters and broke away when he saw Beau. "I'll help with the mules," he offered.

It was no longer necessary to build their own fire after the attack. Once the other men saw Elijah under fire, it had left them with an appreciation for the young black. While Beau was sure that the men wouldn't be willing to invite him to their homes back east, here on the open plains he was a man they wanted on their side.

That night, lying in their blankets under the wagon, Beau asked, "Where did you learn all the stuff you did today?"

"I learned it from Massa Weber," Eli replied. "He had fought the British in 1812 and spent long hours talking and teaching me about battle and tending wounds. Whenever someone was hurt on the plantation, he had me do the doctoring."

"When you say, Massa Weber, you mean your father," Beau said quietly.

After a long pause, Eli said, "Yes . . . My father."

Lying there, thinking for a while, Beau concluded, "I'll be darned. By blood, you now own my contract."

"I guess I do," Eli agreed, chuckling. "Well, I want you to know. I consider it paid off for taking me with you."

The next morning Elroy came over to the two men's wagon. His eyes were still sad, but his voice was brisk. "I'll need you to drive my third wagon, Elijah. Your choice, the munition one or my son-in-law's."

He turned to leave, then hesitated. "You'll be

on full pay for the trip."

Beau watched the surprised look on Eli's face, and then said, "Don't look here. I ain't giving up the munition wagon."

The caravan arrived at the Laramie River on June 20th. The soldiers who had lost horses were riding on the Conestoga or the cargo wagons. The unshod ponies were tied to the back of the lead wagon. Beau volunteered to take his wagon across first. He suggested that if the water was too deep, the sealed powder kegs would keep the wagon afloat.

It was a weak argument, but the decision was to let him go. Across the river, the adobe and log fort could be seen. As the mules entered the river their hooves churned the water, splashing it back toward Beau. Shouting encouragement and slapping them with the reins, he got the animals across the Laramie River, leaving a broad wake behind the wagon.

This crossing was much easier than the South Platte had been. Beau drove the animals away from the river and pulled up near some cottonwoods. He watched the other wagons come across. Eli's face was very serious as he guided his team and wagon across the river. The Conestoga and soldiers were the last to ford.

The mounted soldiers fell alongside the munition wagons as the caravan moved toward Fort William. The fort was privately owned and used mostly as a fur trading post. The powder on Beau's wagon would be held at the fort for a period of time, then be moved south. The fight at the Alamo had been two years earlier. Tensions between Mexico and the United States remained. The army was stocking for future conflicts that it was sure were coming.

Sergeant Howell guided the munitions wagons to an adobe building in the fort. The soldiers quickly began to unload the wagons. Beau noticed cannon barrels tied up against the room walls. Once done, the heavy plank door was closed and locked. Two of the soldiers took up positions to guard the powder.

The sergeant walked up to Beau, leading two ponies. "We have no need for these horses. You and your black can have them. Feed them proper and they'll carry you or your packs just fine."

Having other things to do, the sergeant turned on his heel and went back to instruct his men. Beau called out, "Thank you," to the departing man.

Tying them to the back of the empty wagon, Beau climbed up and drove the team toward the rest of the caravan. Eli was helping unload the cargo from Elroy's other wagons. Jumping down, Beau went to assist. Once the cargo was all tallied and stowed in the trading post store room, a gray-haired man invited them in for a drink.

The dimly lit trading post was filled with items a trapper or frontier family would need. The stocky man stepped behind the plank bar and smiled. "My name's Aloysius, but call me Louie."

The teamsters crowded around the bar, having a mighty thirst after the long trip from Missouri. While Louie poured the drinks, Beau and Eli walked around the rooms looking at the items they might need. There was a smoky smell in the room mixed with the smells of leather, rope, and oil from the metal traps hanging on the wall.

Elijah ran his fingers through the fur of a beaver pelt nailed to the log wall. "It sure is soft," he said. "My massa ... ah, father had a hat made of beaver. It was made from the fur and called felt."

Beau looked at the shelves lined with canned goods, tin cups, pots pans, lanterns, and every kind of thing one could want. Another wall was lined with barrels and bags of corn, oats, flour, coffee beans, and white beans. He could smell the coffee through the woven bags.

They circled back toward the bar, passing boots, blankets, long johns, trousers and shirts. Bolts of calico and other cloths stood in a half-barrel. Louie looked up as they approached the bar. He was smiling and looking at Eli.

"You remind me of Jim Beckwourth when I first met him. The first drink is free, gents, then they cost you."

The two men took the shot that Louie had poured and toasted each other. The whiskey burned all the way down, taking Beau's breath away. Coughing, they set their glasses down.

"Another?" Louie asked.

"We're good for now," Beau said. "We'll be back after Elroy pays us."

They walked out of the trading post, squinting at the bright sunshine. Their bellies were warmed by the whiskey and their spirits were high. They retrieved their gear from the wagons including another rifle and possible bag Elroy had given to Eli. The young black noticed the ponies.

"When is the army coming to get them?" he asked Beau.

"They're ours, Eli. Sergeant Howell gave them to us."

"I never owned a horse before," Elijah said, eyes wide, looking at the animals.

"Neither have I. We got some now, though," Beau said proudly.

Abel and the teamsters would spend the evening drinking in Louie's trading post. Two of the wounded teamsters had gone to the fort doctor, Herbert Ward, before joining the rest. It became apparent to Beau and Eli that they wouldn't get their pay until morning, so they led their horses to the livery and discovered that Louie also owned that. They asked that the horses be given grain along with their hay.

The hostler asked, "Where you heading?"

"We are on our way to the mountains," Beau replied.

Looking at the buckskins on Beau and the cotton shirt and wool britches on Eli, the man inquired, "Would you be heading for the rendezvous?"

"We plan to go to the Green River before we head into the mountains," Beau replied.

"You boys sure don't look like mountain men," the hostler said. "You missed the supply train heading for the rendezvous earlier this month. I also hear that it's at the Popo Agie, where it meets the Wind River, instead of the Green River."

Everything the old hostler was saying meant nothing to Beau and Elijah. They had heard about the mountain man rendezvous before, but the locations the man was talking about were foreign to them.

The hostler's brow furled as he looked at the two of them. He then asked Beau, "Is your black here a runaway? You might be a mountain man, but he's wearing clothes that would be found on a servant or something."

"We worked in a fancy eating place in Ohio," Beau lied. "We was drinking one night after work and decided to head for the mountains. I traded my fancy britches for these dirty buckskins. I think I got took."

"You sure as hell did," the hostler said. "You best see Louie and get some warm clothes. Where you're going, it's going to be damn cold."

"Can you recommend a gunsmith around here?" Beau asked. "I got to have the frizzen spring fixed."

"There's a smithy across the way, he can fix most anything," the hostler replied. "He can work on the bore also. If you done any amount of shooting with the old Model 1803, it will need it."

Thanking him, the two men turned to leave. Smiling, the hostler said, "You'll pass the local law office on the way. He got some posters looking for runaways or folks that are wanted back east. You might want to see if your names are on any."

The old hostler led the horses toward a stall, chuckling at his joke. Learning of the posters from the east shook Beau and Eli. They had thought that after getting out of Missouri their pasts would be behind them. The only comfort was that word on them wouldn't have reached here yet. More than likely it never would.

Carrying their rifles, Beau and Eli headed for the smithy, avoiding the law office. A burly German was working on some horse shoes. He looked up when the two men walked under the cover of his forge. He struck the shoe a few times, sending sparks flying. He then plunged it into some oily-looking water.

Beau waited until the steam from the red-hot shoe stopped. "I need some work done on my frizzen spring. Also need the bore looked at."

The big man spat into the hot coals. "Wasting

your money on the frizzen. I can change it to a cap. It is much better."

"I don't know much about caps, but if you could fix the spring," Beau said.

The man took the rifle with his leather-gloved hands and looked it over. "I got parts. Tomorrow at noon."

With that the man set the rifle against the wall and continued making shoes. Eli had a newer Hawken .50 caliber. It was patterned after the Harper's Ferry 1803 in length. It had a set and firing trigger, giving better control when shooting. It was also a flintlock.

As they walked by the trading post, the sounds of the merriment inside told them that they might as well set up their camp and make their supper. Toward the river there was a spreading oak. While Beau set up the fly tarp, Eli made a fire for their meal. After getting the coffee water on, he began mixing up some dough for biscuits. He would fry them in the grease of some side meat.

The two men sat against the oak, drinking coffee after their meal. "Frontier life is pretty good," Beau reflected.

"It sure is," Eli agreed. "That is, if you're not being shot at by Arapahoe."

As they finished their coffee, they wondered about the mountains and the life of a mountain man. They avoided the subject of being wanted back east. There was urgency to continue west.

The moon was still almost full and cast a pale light across the landscape. When the fire had burned down, they crawled into their blankets under the tarp. Once in a while they'd hear a whoop from the partiers at the trading post, who would be dealing with headaches come morning.

The next morning Beau and Eli walked toward the trading post. The caravan wagons were hitched and lined up next to the building. They found several of the teamsters sleeping in the beds of the wagons. One man lay on the front porch, just outside the door. As they walked up Louie came out, giving the sleeping teamster a shove with his boot, sending him rolling into the dirt.

Smiling, he said, "A good time tends to leave them littering up the place. I got hot coffee ready."

They followed the grizzled merchant into the building. Beau was pleased to find Elroy sitting at one of the tables, having morning coffee. They joined him with steaming mugs. The man's face was a bit puffy and he was sporting a blackened eye.

"It wasn't my best night," Elroy explained. "A couple of the men spoke poorly of Eli, and it kind of riled me."

Elijah tasted his coffee and then said, "I appreciate you sticking up for me, but I can't say it is worth getting beat up for."

"Heck," Elroy laughed. "They just got one good one in. Right now, they're out in the wagons nursing some painful lumps."

Louie appeared from the back room carrying a platter of pancakes and some tin plates. "I got some griddle cakes to settle the stomach."

Elroy shook his head. "You got to give me a minute. You guys dig in."

The merchant came back with a mug of coffee and some maple syrup. Beau and Eli got busy with the pancakes.

"You two are heading for the Popo Agie?"

Louie asked.

With a mouth full of food, Beau said, "We hope to leave tomorrow."

"Before you go, talk to Bauer, at the smithy," Louie replied. "His oldest son will be going to the rendezvous. He had to wait for percussion caps that came in with your caravan."

"I'll do that," Beau replied. "He is working on my .54 caliber right now."

The two men sat at the table with Elroy long after they had finished their meal. They were waiting for him to bring up the subject of their pay. Beau had hoped that saying that they were leaving tomorrow would prod the man to mention it.

Having drank too much coffee, Eli excused himself to use the little house. After fidgeting a bit, Beau decided to say, "Eli and I need to get a few things for our trip and hoped to get paid today."

"Soon as Louie pays me, I will pay you," Elroy said. "He is a clever cuss. He likes to have you drink up a portion of the money coming before he comes around."

Seeing the concern on Beau's face, he gave the curly-haired man a half-smile. "You don't have to worry. Louie is honest and ain't never cheated us. He will keep track of every drink you down, and every pancake you eat, and deduct it, but it will be fair. Now, I think I'll try some of those pancakes."

Thanking the wagon owner, Beau went out to find Eli. He found him looking at used saddles displayed on the front porch. "It might be a day or two before we get paid. And the pancakes weren't free."

"It was my first time," Eli said.

"First time?" Beau asked puzzled.

"Yes," the young black said, smiling. "The first time I set at a table and ate with white folks."

The two men headed for the smithy to check on the rifle. They could see smoke coming from the forge as Bauer pumped the bellows. The blacksmith looked up as they walked in and stopped what he was doing to retrieve the rifle.

"The bore didn't take much work," he said. "I replaced the spring. You owe six bits."

Beau carried his money in a leather bag under his shirt that hung from a string around his neck. Retrieving some coins, he settled up with the man.

Shaking his head, the blacksmith went back to his forge. "For another six bits, I could have changed it over to caps. Fixing a frizzen is a waste, just a waste."

The air outside was cool and the warmth of the smithy felt good. The two men watched the man finish the hinge he was shaping. After he plunged it into the water, Beau said, "Louie told us your son was going to the rendezvous on the Popo Agie. We were hoping he needed some help."

Bauer spat against his anvil block. "Can't say if he needs help or not, but a couple extra guns would be welcome."

"When does he plan to leave?" Beau asked.

"Peter will leave at first light tomorrow," the man said as he plunged another piece of iron into the forge.

Panic suddenly swept over Beau. What if they didn't get the pay in time?

"We will be back to talk to your son this afternoon," Beau said. Turning to go, he stopped. "Thank you, Mr. Bauer."

"It's okay," he replied, "but call me Pepper."

Eli led the way as they hurried to the trading post. They hoped to find Elroy. To their surprise, the teamsters and the wagons were gone. They had been at the smithy less than an hour. It was possible that the wagons had just been moved from the front of the trading post.

Running into the trading post, the two men collided with Louie, who was coming out. Grabbing at the big man, they prevented him from falling. "We didn't mean to run into you," Beau said, his breath coming in gasps.

"Where did the wagons go?" Eli asked.

Straightening his shirt and apron, Louie replied, "They went up river to pick up some buffalo hides to take back to Independence."

"Our pay . . ." Beau blurted out.

"Yes, Elroy left your pay with me," the merchant replied. Walking toward his counter, he continued. "You two will need clothing and other items that I can sell you much cheaper than you will find at the rendezvous."

Reaching under the counter, he placed two stacks of coins in front of the two men. Each had received $40. The amount of money, two horses, and the rifle for Eli had far exceeded their expectations. "And," Louie said, "this morning's meal was on me."

The next three hours were a blur. With Louie's help, they put together two impressive stacks of items needed. There were long johns, wool socks, boots, heavy wool trousers, shirts, rabbit skin hats, choppers with liners, flint, steel, candles, powder, lead for balls, patch material, spare knife, hatchets, buckskin jackets, side meat, jerky, salt, cold flour, canvas for packs, blankets, rope, sawbuck pack saddles, and beaver traps.

When Louie finished tallying each pile up, it left each man just over a dollar. Some of the items, like the sawbucks, were used, saving some money. The merchant cautioned them that not all of the mountain men were honest, and they would have to protect their winter clothes. He recommended they cache the stuff away from the gathering. Replacing their food would be impossible at rendezvous prices.

They already had pots, tin plates, mugs and utensils for preparing their meals. They also had possible bags with ball molds, melting ladles, line, fish hooks, needles, and other odds and ends useful on the trail.

Beau asked Louie about new buckskin outfits. Laughing, the merchant said, "They might keep the weather off, but you need wool to keep you warm."

He suggested that they get themselves some Flathead or Crow women at the rendezvous to set up housekeeping and they could make them a fine outfit. The thought of taking on a woman made Beau blush. While he hoped to take up with a wife someday, he had the problems back east to keep in mind.

With their gear purchased, the two men headed back toward the smithy to talk with Pepper's son, Peter. The son was older than they had expected. His blond hair stuck out from a leather hat and he was clean shaven except for the bushy moustache. Old scars on his bare forearms were evidence of years of working hot iron with his father.

Reaching his hand out, he said, "I'm Beau Levesque, and this here is Elijah Weber."

A look of skepticism flashed across the man's face as Eli was introduced. Then, with a broad smile, he said, "Peter is my name." Motioning toward his father, he continued. "Pa told me you are looking to work your way to the rendezvous. Just so happens some of the men that were promising to travel with me left with the earlier pack train. I'll pay $10 and one meal a day for the trip and another $10 if you would be willing to work with me at the rendezvous."

"Would that be for Eli and myself?" Beau asked.

"As long as someone don't come along and claim him for a runaway," Pete said. "It's the only reason I can figure he'd be looking for faraway places."

Beau liked Peter's honesty. The man was straight forward and said what was on his mind. "We both have reasons for going west, but I can promise you we will carry our weight on the trail and work hard for you at the rendezvous."

"I can't ask for more," Pete replied. "Be here with your gear at first light. You will both be leading pack animals."

"We can string them out behind our ponies," Beau said. All of a sudden, a thought came to the young man. "The ponies are unshod. Can we get shoes put on before we leave?"

"You done any smithing?" Pepper asked him.

"I haven't," Beau admitted.

"I've done a little," Eli replied.

"Well. Where you're going there are few places to have horses shoed, and you won't be packing the equipment to do it," Pepper pointed out. "Every six to eight weeks you'll be looking to have them done. You best keep them unshod and let the good earth wear the hoof naturally."

The young men left, having had their first lesson of being horse owners.

CHAPTER SIX

It was still dark when Beau and Eli led their horses, packed and ready. The fort had an eerie quietness to it. Toward the river there were a couple of fires burning. In another hour, the place would be bustling with activity. There was the creak of a door toward the back of the smithy.

Peter stuck his head out and called to the men, "We got coffee in here if you be wanting some."

The area in the back was sparsely furnished. It was what Pepper Bauer called home. It had two rooms, with the front having a cook stove, a table with four stools, and a side board for keeping supplies. Beau assumed behind the curtain covered doorway was their sleeping quarters.

Sitting at the table with steaming cups of coffee, Pete explained his plans at the rendezvous. "I sell and repair firearms. We will be carrying tools to work bores and rifling, also parts to convert flintlocks to percussion. I have a few smoothbore muskets and rifles. We are also packing knives, axes, molds, and lead. Basically, I am a gunsmith by trade."

"What would you have me and Eli do once we get there?" Beau asked.

"If the two of you are willing to learn, you will be fair gunsmiths by the time we leave the Popo Agie," Peter told them.

The sound of a cart was heard outside. "Time to go," Peter said.

Stepping outside, Beau saw a wheel cart hitched to two mules. It had a canvas stretched over wooden bows to provide protection for its cargo and some cover for the driver. There was also a string of mules with packs. "Everything's ready, Peter," a lean, stoop-shouldered man with tobacco-stained chin whiskers said.

"Meet Joshua," Peter said. "He will be riding in the cart with me."

There were twelve pack mules, which meant Eli and he would each be leading six, along with their horses. The trip to Popo Agie would take just under three weeks. Starting from the fort, they would be climbing in elevation to the rendezvous and crossing several tributaries flowing into the North Platte River. They would be crossing the Sweetwater River six times as it meandered back and forth.

Beau and Eli checked over the halters and lead ropes on the mules. They would use the horses as lead animals with the mules strung out behind. Pete and Joshua climbed onto the cart and led the way from the fort. Just upriver they were joined by a group of Cheyenne, consisting of six men and four women. They had four horses pulling their gear on travois.

Beau and Elijah were happy to leave the fort behind. Peter set a mile-eating pace that would challenge their stamina. Both men had worn one of their new woolen shirts. After an hour of walking, they both had stripped to the long john tops and stuffed the shirts into the packs of their horses. By mid-day the cart was a mile ahead of the pack animals and the Cheyenne trailed the mules by another mile. Walking steadily, Beau and Eli chewed on jerky and drank water as they attempted to catch up to the cart.

The sun was setting when they finally caught up to the cart. Joshua had a fire going and was working on their meal. Peter stood waiting, smiling as they tied the horses to some low bushes. "We done good today," he said. "I figure it was close to 30 miles, maybe more. From here on we will be faced with more cuts and valleys to travel through. Some days we might only make 20 miles. By the time you get the mules stripped and watered, Joshua should have the meal ready."

With that, Peter went back to the fire. "I think the boss found a way to get out of paying his help," Beau said. "He'll work us to death before the end of the trip."

"The meal that was offered was supper," Eli said. "We best plan for getting up early and fix our own breakfast."

It took an hour to strip the packs from the mules and their horses. Then they watered and hobbled the animals. The grass was good in the area and the mules would do well. They did worry about the ponies. They should have brought some grain for them. With the animals taken care of, they joined the boss at the fire.

The meal was hardy. Joshua had made fried side meat, beans, and johnnycake in the Dutch oven. A pot of coffee was steaming next to the coals. Beau and Eli ate their fill and then sat against the cart wheel drinking coffee.

"You make the brew nice and strong," Beau complimented the man. "Many a day I had to make due with yesterday's grounds."

Joshua came over while gnawing off a chew of some twisted tobacco. "Have a chew," he offered. Both men declined.

Taking a seat next to them, he spat and then said, "Boss likes to get a good start on the first day. Says it sets expectations. He was testing the two of you today and couldn't be happier with what he saw."

"So, we can expect an easier day tomorrow?" Eli asked.

"I can't say that," Joshua replied. "But today you done good."

As Eli and Beau removed their boots from their aching feet that night, they weren't sure that doing good was such a *good* thing. They had rigged their fly tarp and curled up in their blankets shortly after eating. Peter and Joshua continued to talk near the fire. The Cheyenne had set up a camp about a quarter-mile downriver. The sound of frogs, crickets, and an owl lulled them off to sleep.

The clang of a spoon on a fry pan brought them wide awake. "Time to get the packs on the mules," Peter called. It was still fully dark.

Stumbling out of their blankets, Beau and Eli headed for the brush to relieve themselves. They wrapped their bedding in the fly tarp and put it near the packs for their horses. It was just getting light when they had all the sawbuck pack saddles on the mules. Then Joshua said something that was music to their ears.

"Got coffee over here, boys. Bring your cups and plates."

There were beans and johnnycake left over from the night before. "No sense in wasting food, eat up," the old man said.

Gulping down the coffee and food, they thanked him and headed to put the packs onto the animals. Beau saw as they finished readying the mules that the Cheyenne had struck camp and were waiting for the cart to pull out.

Leading his horse and mules next to the cart, Beau asked Peter, "You let the Cheyenne come with us on this trip. We was hit by some Indians coming to the fort from Missouri. Ain't you worried about them?"

Rubbing his chin, the leader replied, "I can't say I asked them to come with us. We're both headed for the same rendezvous. I figure there is safety in numbers. The Cheyenne watch for marauders and I watch them."

The chill of the morning quickly turned to stifling heat as the group wound their way along the North Platte River. Time was lost filling in a washout caused by earlier rains that would have prevented the cart from passing. Beau and Eli had no problem keeping up on the rougher terrain.

The hot wind blowing across the Platte River valley was pushing in dark, threatening clouds. Heat lightning was flashing as the storm moved toward the pack train. Peter stopped at the lip of a rocky ridge that went to the south and west, creating a large, rock-strewn basin. "We best get the hell off this ridge before the storm hits," he shouted back at Beau and Eli.

All of a sudden, hail rained down on the men. "Leave the cart! Get the pack animals to the bottom!" Peter ordered.

At a reckless pace, the men led the startled animals down the winding ridge trail while the bruising mix of rain and hail pummeled them. The rocky path quickly became slick, causing the men and animals to slip and fight for footing. One of the mules fell, rolling several feet before coming up against a rock pinnacle.

With the wind tearing at his soaked clothes, Beau pulled his Green River knife and cut the pack and lead ropes free of the animal, then abandoned it to find its own way to safety. Grabbing the rope of the nearest mule, he continued down.

Hardly able to open his eyes against the vicious wind, Beau saw a wide funnel cloud swirling across the valley in front of them. He yelled, "Tornado!" The words were ripped from his lips and lost in the howling wind.

The valley was plunged into near darkness as the raging storm approached, with the only light coming from electrified particles swirling in the churning clouds. Unable to see the others, Beau reached the bottom and pulled the animals still with him behind a rock outcrop, which gave little relief from the storm.

Airborne debris flew by, striking Beau and the animals. Clutching the lead rope, he huddled, protecting his face. Unsure whether the others had made it down or had been caught on the trail, he prayed that they were out of danger.

The rain and hail stopped as the storm blew by. The deafening roar of the tornado was replaced by silence as it disappeared back into the clouds. Emerging from behind the outcrop, Beau was relieved to see the others safe.

Eli ran toward his friend, relief on his face. "Am I glad to see you! I thought you were caught on the trail when you went after the mule."

Still a little dazed by what they had just gone through, Beau said, "Thank God, we made it."

Joshua was the only one who had sustained any visible injuries. A piece of debris had struck his left cheek bone, leaving a two-inch gash and blackening his eye. Several mules were missing and packs were scattered along the trail coming down the ridge.

While Peter doctored Joshua's cheek, Beau and Eli caught up with the mules and their horses, picketing them on the boulder-strewn valley floor. They then climbed to the top of the ridge to find what was left of the cart. To their surprise, it had fared better than expected. It had been rolled by the storm and its contents scattered, but the cart was undamaged.

The Cheyenne traveling with them had been a mile behind the pack train when the storm had hit and had been spared the close encounter of the tornado. They approached carrying several items that had been in the cart.

Peter set up camp below the ridge and met briefly with the braves. Five animals were missing and one had broken a leg. Four of the younger Cheyenne men took their horses and rode away to look for the missing animals. Two of the elder Cheyenne stayed in their camp while the four women joined in gathering the scattered gear and moving it to the bottom of the ridge. Beau and Eli took two of the mules and brought the cart down after finding a place closer to the river where it could be driven down.

The bows on the cart had been broken and the canvas top was gone. Their food had been carried in the cart. Bags of flour and cornmeal had been soaked or strewn across the plain. They salvaged the beans and side meat. Well-sealed kegs of powder and wooden boxes of supplies survived the storm.

Once the gear was collected in the camp, the process of sorting the items began. Three of the missing animals had packs, while two had lost them on the ridge. One had been cut loose by Beau.

While Beau and Eli had expected Peter to be more upset, he appeared to be in a good mood. Evidently the most important items needed at the rendezvous had not been damaged or lost. The food could be replaced by hunting.

Toward dark the Cheyenne braves returned, leading three mules. Two still had their packs and one was without. The women had set up a camp and were using some of the wet cornmeal to make a porridge. Joshua was making the rest of it into corn dodgers in a blackened cast-iron pot. Beau and Eli had pitched their fly tarp a short distance from the rest.

"I don't think I have ever been so tired," Beau complained.

"Tired is a good feeling," Eli said. "I was terrified when that storm come over us. While fighting the mules, I was making peace with the man upstairs because I didn't figure I'd see another day. I made him some promises that will be hard to keep. Worse yet, I lost my hat."

Laughing, Beau replied, "Lost, heck. I figure our hats blew all the way back to Missouri."

The young black's face became serious. "What are we going to do after the rendezvous? We say we're going to be mountain men, but we don't know the first thing about trapping beaver or surviving in the mountains over a winter."

Beau ran his fingers through his hair, removing some of the dirt from the storm, trying to think of something that would assure his friend. "I figure we can listen and learn from the men at the rendezvous. We both know how to hunt, and I done some trapping back on Crowley's Ridge."

"There is more to surviving a winter that setting traps or killing game," Eli said. "We got to find the places to set the traps. In one of my father's books I read of men getting snowed in and starving in the mountains."

"We don't have a lot of options, Eli. We can't go back to Missouri. I would end up being hung and your future would probably be worse." After a moment, Beau continued. "We got supplies, and I figure we are smart enough to avoid most of the dangers in the mountains."

Joshua called them to supper. Beau was glad to see that Eli's spirits had rebounded as they went to test the corn dodgers. After the meal was done, Beau took his rifle and began cleaning it. Peter walked over and asked, "Is that the one my father fixed?"

"Yes, it is," Beau replied. "He said I wasted my money having the frizzen spring fixed. He said I should have had it converted to cap."

"That's my pa," Peter laughed. "He figures the cap requires less fussing and fires faster and surer, preventing the shooter from developing a flinch."

"I heard it is faster," Beau said.

"Most often it will be if the flintlock isn't tuned proper," Peter agreed. "If a man is careful and keeps the flint in good condition and the pan clean, it can be about the same. Most men like to ram the load in hard. If you leave the powder a bit looser, it ignites faster and both the cap and flintlock fire quicker when the hammer drops. Heck, if the spark hits the pan right, the flintlock fires before the hammer is all the way down."

Much of what Peter was saying was from a gunsmith's perspective and went over Beau's head. All he worried about was a misfire and having whatever he was shooting at get away. He also figured a flintlock would fire long after a man runs out of caps. Beau carried several 3/4 by 7/8-inch flints for the 1803. Plus, every trading post and frontier mercantile carried flint. The young man was curious about what Peter meant by properly tuned and hoped to learn more about that once they got to the rendezvous.

The caravan spent one additional day below the ridge, repairing broken gear and redistributing items on the remaining pack animals. Once back on the trail they crossed back and forth across the river, seeking the best route for the cart. The pack animals could have kept on a more direct path and many obstacles could have been improved to allow access for the cart, but they could not afford the time it would take for road building.

Once they reached the Sweetwater River, Peter said that they were just over a week from the rendezvous. They followed the trail that had been blazed by the earlier mountain men and trappers dating back to the early 1800s. Joshua told stories in the evening about the landmarks they had passed along the trail. He talked of an earlier trapper named Jedediah Smith who had cached his furs near a large, dome-shaped rock, Independence Rock, back in the '20s after being unable to haul them east by river. They had come back with horses to retrieve them.

A couple of days later they passed a spot where the Sweetwater River cut through a gap in a solid granite wall, Devil's Gate. Joshua had heard a story of how it had come to be while wintering with some Shoshone. In the early days, the area had offered plentiful game but was protected by a beast with large tusks. Some of the braves had decided to try and kill the huge animal. From the cover of the many ravines, they'd shot arrows into the beast, only angering the gigantic thing and it had torn the gap in the rock with its tusks and escaped.

Beau and Elijah looked forward to the many stories that the old man shared with them. At night, they would lie in their blankets and try to envision the trappers or monsters that wound through his tales.

Two days from the rendezvous they spotted several buckskin-clad men sitting around a fire on the river bank.

"Hello, the camp," Peter called out.

One heavyset man stood up and looked over the pack train. "Come on in," he replied. "Got a young deer on the spit."

Peter spoke in low tones to his men. "Keep your rifles ready. We don't want to lose our supplies so close to our destination. Joshua, you take the Dutch oven and make up a mess of biscuits to go with the venison."

The six men at the fire were all smiles as the pack train approached them. A short, barrel-chested fellow started the introductions. "They call me Reiner, the big fellow is Hoss, then there is Kinney, Walt, Uno, and Wes." Without hardly taking a breath, Reiner asked, "You ain't got some coffee, do ya?"

Peter introduced his crew, then said, "Joshua, make up a pot for these gents."

Listening to the cheers of the trappers, Beau and Eli led the mules a short distance upstream and began to strip the packs from the animals. After watering the mules, they were picketed in a grassy area. All the while, they kept their rifles within easy reach.

Walking back toward the fire, they watched the jubilant trappers. They had just come out of the mountains and were headed to the rendezvous with their furs. It had been months since they had run out of such luxuries as coffee and tobacco.

These were the first mountain men that Beau had seen. All of them wore stained buckskins and calf-high moccasins. Some had wool caps, and others had head gear made from skins they had caught. Three of the men had dug into the possible bag, pulled out clay pipes and filled them from the tobacco twist that Peter had given them. The others had bitten off a piece and were enjoying a chew.

Beau noticed their packs of furs under a live oak tree. The three large packs would hold up to 50 beaver pelts each. He listened during the meal while the men complained about the lack of good trapping where they'd been. They had traveled far to the north in the search of beaver. Next year would be better.

The trappers had heard about streams to the northwest that were so full of beaver you could walk across on their backs.

Eli and Beau enjoyed listening to the stories of the trappers. After the doubts they'd experienced following the storm, as they approached the rendezvous their excitement rose. Both men asked the trappers questions until late in the evening. The buckskin-clad men were more than happy to answer their questions with stories that were as much fiction as truth.

CHAPTER SEVEN

The west wind brought the smell of the rendezvous before the travelers could see it. The six trappers led the way, followed by Peter's pack train. The Cheyenne split toward the north to join up with others from their tribe. Sounds of the revelry came next. Then the rendezvous came into view located at the confluence of the Popo Agie and the Wind River. Tents, teepees, and every kind of shelter had been erected along the river. Many of the men chose to sleep under the stars next to their campfires. Someone had even built a low log cabin.

Larger tents had been set up by the American Fur Company and Hudson Bay Company. The trappers they had met said a quick goodbye and headed toward the company tents. Peter shook his head. "We're getting here a little late and the crowd don't look as big."

Beau looked at the number of people drinking, competing in races, wrestling, and shooting. He couldn't imagine there being more men. Both trappers and Indians mingled together, taking part in the fun.

Peter chose a location not far from the company tents to set up shop. He had brought two troop tents, one to do business from and the other for sleeping and extra supplies. After emptying the cart, he left for a couple of hours, returning with some items from a cache he had in the hills. The anvil and parts of the forge were too heavy to haul out each year.

He had warned Beau and Eli to keep a close eye on the items they had purchased at Fort William. Many of the down and out trappers would be looking to steal what they needed.

Eli was sent to get wood for their cook fire. Taking an axe and two mules, he headed for a tree-covered rise. The July sky was clear and blue. The wind coming off the mountains kept him cool as he swung the axe. A feeling came over Eli that he had never felt before. The vastness of the mountain range around them and the fact that he was being paid for swinging the axe made him realize that he was truly free.

When he wanted, he could take the horse that *he* owned, and leave without worrying about pursuit. With this freedom came the responsibility of providing for himself. As the chips flew from the windfalls he was cutting up, he thought *I'll take the responsibility*.

The sun was low in the western sky when the camp was set up, and Peter suggested that they go check out the doings. With the pay from making the trip in their pockets, Beau and Eli headed for the company tents.

The sound of a fiddle came from a crowded tent. "This looks like a good place to start," Beau suggested.

A plank bar was set up, and men pushed and shoved to get close enough to make a purchase. Two bartenders were busy handing out bottles and making change. Beau pushed his way in and purchased a bottle, then he and Eli moved away from the tent, sat under a willow tree, shared the liquor and watched the trappers.

Having no mugs, they passed the bottle back and forth. Having drunk little in their lives, it was hard to judge if the harsh-tasting brew would be considered good or not. Eli swallowed and coughed. "I wonder if this stuff would kill a man."

Laughing, Beau replied, "I don't see bodies lying about, so I got to figure it is safe."

Suddenly, two men came tumbling out of the tent opening. After a couple of swings, one tackled the other and they rolled in the dust, punching, kicking, and biting. The scene was quickly blocked as cheering trappers poured out and surrounded the fight, egging the two men on.

As quickly as it had begun the exhausted participants lay on the ground, gasping to catch their breath. The crowd headed back into the tent, laughing about the spectacle the two men had made of themselves. Slowly, one of the fighters got to his feet. Blood ran down the side of his neck from a torn ear. Staggering as he walked, he disappeared toward the river.

The other man sat up, coughing and spitting out blood. Feeling the glow of the rye, Beau called over, "Which one of you won?"

Groaning as he got up, the man headed toward the willow. "Damned if I know, but I think I swallowed a chunk of his ear."

Holding out their bottle, Eli said, "Wash it down with a slug of this."

Sitting heavily next to them, he accepted the bottle and took a long drink. His grin revealed a bloody gum that a dislodged tooth had come from. "I appreciate the drink. My name is Calvin Harp."

"I'm Beau and my friend here is Eli. We come in with Peter Bauer."

Calvin's eyes lit up. "Bauer's here? I was hoping he'd make it. I got some work I need done on my rifle."

"You do okay on your beaver?" Eli asked.

"With the two companies here, we can dicker on the price for our furs," Calvin told them, "but the goods they are selling are terrible high. Many men went to Fort Hall or even William to trade this year."

"What was the fight about, Calvin?" Beau asked.

Accepting another drink from the bottle, the man said, "It weren't no real fight. Frenchy thought I stole his woman last night. I told him she liked me better and that set him off."

Sitting in the dark, the bottle was finished thanks to the help of their new friend. Fires dotted the valley and lanterns or candles lit up the tents. Feeling a little tipsy, Beau and Eli bid Calvin goodnight and headed back toward their camp. Somewhat confused, they wandered to two other camps before finding theirs.

Joshua and Peter were sitting next to the fire, drinking coffee. "I see you two stayed out of trouble. Have a seat and some coffee."

"We met a man named Calvin Harp that needs work done," Beau volunteered.

Shaking his head, Peter said, "I don't doubt it. The man doesn't clean his Hawken. Probably has a ball stuck in it again."

After finishing their coffee, the two young men rolled out their bedrolls in the tent and went to sleep listening to the sounds of merriment beyond the canvas walls.

* * *

The next several days were busy, with little time to take part in the night life. Several of the mountain men had been waiting for Peter to arrive to have work done on their rifles. Used muskets and several types of rifled muzzle loaders were on display in front of the supply tent. There were also blankets spread out with knives, hatchets, powder horns, lead and molds, and some percussion and flintlock pistols.

True to his word, Peter put both Eli and Beau to work repairing firearms. Joshua loved to dicker and spent all his time selling items from the blankets or taking items of higher value in on trade. Both trappers and men from the tribes came by to do business. Often a musket or rifle would come in on trade. Beau would clean out the black powder with boiling water and then do minor repairs and the weapon would go to the display rack for sale. Eli worked with Peter off the back of the cart. He would work the forge or turn the reamer for truing bores. Peter also had him converting flintlocks to percussions. The used parts would go to Beau for repairs.

A Colt Paterson .28 caliber cap and ball revolver came in as a trade. The owner had bought it in St. Louis before coming west. He had wounded himself once after loading all the chambers in anticipation of a confrontation, and he had lost the loading lever during the trip west.

Beau cleaned the revolver before putting it out for display. The close-fitting parts of the folding trigger and the other components made it susceptible to fouling from the black powder. The bell-shaped grip felt good in his hand. The barrel had to be disassembled before removing the cylinder for loading. Peter told him that the arbor that the barrel and cylinder rode on could be used for seating the lead balls.

With regret, Beau placed the revolver and an extra cylinder on the sale blanket. He admired the revolver. It might not be practical for a trapper or mountain man in the field, but in his eyes, it was the finest weapon on the blanket.

That night the three of them worked on straightening some musket barrels. Beau worked the forge while Eli held one end of the glowing metal. Peter held the other end and struck it on the anvil. It was surprising how many men viewed their muskets as a lever bar. Once the barrels were straightened, the bore would be honed.

As they worked late into the evenings, the revelry continued around them. Beau and Eli did not mind. Peter had explained that the time they had to make money would be short. Soon, the attendees would start wandering away to summer camps.

Word went out through the rendezvous that the Hudson Bay Company would be pulling up in a week and head back for Fort Hall. With the repairs caught up, Peter gave Beau and Eli the day off. Eli wanted to go visit the Flathead camp. One of the braves had promised to show him how to use the bow.

The next day was sunny and warm. The breeze coming down the Wind River Range was refreshing. Beau headed for a group of men who were shooting. He carried his nine-pound Harper's Ferry Model 1803. He had worked on the sights and hoped to win a little money. Calvin was one of the men shooting and he gave Beau a hardy wave.

"We can use your money," he called, laughing.

Two men using Kentucky long rifles were shooting at a clay pot about 100 paces out. They had both missed their first shots and were loading for their second attempt. They offered to let Beau join, but competing with the 33" barrel of the Model 1803 against the long rifles was a sucker bet.

"I think I'll wait for the target to come in a little," he replied. The group appeared to think that it was a wise choice.

Once the target was placed at 50 paces, Beau joined in. For two hours the men competed, money changing hands back and forth. At the end, Beau was still ahead and offered to buy the first bottle. The conversation of the trappers had turned to where they were going to head to after the rendezvous was over.

A sour-smelling fellow joined the men to share the rye. He tended to complain about lack of beaver in the streams. "I barely got enough plew to outfit myself this year."

Feeling a little careless after enjoying the rye, Beau replied, "Take you a good bath and you wouldn't chase the beaver out of the territory."

The rest of the men probably agreed because they had positioned themselves upwind of the fellow, but Beau's comment stopped the conversation. For a moment it was quiet, and then the comment seemed to sink into the brain of the smelly fellow. With a roar, he came off the ground and headed for Beau.

The two men raised a cloud of dust as they rolled around on the ground, each trying to get punches and kicks in as they fought. The shouts of encouragement from the men around brought a crowd out of the company tents. Soon Beau and the sour-smelling man were surrounded by cheering mountain men.

Every time Beau tried to regain his feet, he was tripped by his scrappy opponent. He managed to get a headlock around his foe's filthy neck, but the man's foul-smelling breath was almost nauseating. The man tried clawing at Beau's face in an attempt to break free. After a couple minutes of struggling, Beau released the headlock and flopped onto his back, gasping for breath.

The anticipated attack from the sour-smelling man did not come. Instead he heard, "I'm too damn old to take on these young pilgrims. Hand me over a bottle."

Sitting up, Beau looked at his opponent. "Well, for an old coon you sure have a lot of scrap left in you. I'll join you in that drink."

With the fight over, the men headed back for the company tents. Beau accepted the bottle and sat next to an aspen near his rifle. His left eye was beginning to swell shut, and he felt aches and throbbing in several spots of his body. The smelly old trapper didn't seem to have been affected at all from the fight. To himself, Beau declared the old-timer the winner.

After a couple more drinks, Beau bid the men

a good afternoon and headed for the company tents to price some buckskins. The old stained and worn outfit he had wouldn't take him through the winter. The sun was low in the west when he headed back for camp. Everything he had looked at was too pricey for his budget. He hoped that before the companies pulled out they would drop prices rather than haul it back east.

Joshua was sitting next to the fire, stirring a pot of beans when Beau got back. Peter was out tending to the stock and Eli hadn't returned from visiting the Flathead camp. Waving to the old cook, Beau went to help with the animals before having his supper.

Returning with Peter, Beau filled his plate with beans and biscuits. Joshua looked up at him and grinned. "Did you bump into something this afternoon?"

Touching his swollen eye, Beau replied, "There is a smelly old trapper out there. If you should meet him, I wouldn't recommend you suggest he take a bath."

Wrinkling his nose, Joshua said, "I believe some of him rubbed off on you."

It was well after dark when Eli returned. Poking a couple of sticks into the dying fire, he sat down and poured some coffee into a tin mug. Hearing his friend, Beau got up from his blankets and joined him for coffee. Sitting on the ground next to his friend was a bow and several arrows.

"I see you done some trading."

Eli nodded. "I also found some buckskins for us." After a moment, he continued. "I had a great afternoon. All my life I have accepted my place. I was to do for those that owned me without question. The rest of the time, I was to stay out of sight. Today I felt a part of a family. I can't quite explain it, but it was different."

"One thing to keep in mind," Beau said. "The same group that is like family could come after your scalp tomorrow."

Beau woke up the next morning sporting a black eye that he received a lot of kidding about. His first job was converting a Hawken rifle from flintlock to percussion. After getting the parts and a few instructions from Peter, he went to the task. It was the first conversion that he had made.

Before starting, Peter always wanted the black powder residue removed with hot water and the bore checked. After the conversion was made, the rifle would be fired and then the stock metal would be rubbed down with oil. After finishing the installation, Beau moved away from the tent to test fire the Hawken.

He poured a measure of powder into the barrel. Then, taking an oiled patch and ball, he rammed it down the barrel. Placing a cap on the nipple, he chose an ant hill for a target. Taking careful aim, he set the rifle with the back trigger. He then touched off the front trigger. The instant recoil of the rifle caught him off guard. Up until firing the Hawken, he had only shot flintlocks. There was a slight delay between pulling the trigger and the shot while the powder is first ignited in the pan.

Walking back to his workbench, Beau could see the advantage in not having the delay, but in the mountains, all a man needed was powder to fire the rifle. Once out of caps, the percussion system was useless.

The days of the rendezvous went by quickly.

The American Fur Company didn't bring in as many furs as they had hoped. Some of the trappers had sold their furs at the forts. There was talk of cancelling the next year's rendezvous. The trappers complained of the high price for goods and low prices for beaver. Peter assured Beau and Eli that the same complaints were heard every year.

Business had slowed down for Peter. Each day the group would sit around the fire having breakfast and watch trappers pull up and leave. It wouldn't be long before Peter would do the same, then Beau and Eli would be on their own, looking for a place to trap beaver.

Peter had taken the anvil, forge, and some extra muskets to his cache for the coming year. Joshua continued to sell what he could from the supplies on the blankets. Beau and Eli kept busy with an occasional repair and getting the stock ready for the trip back to Fort William.

The two men began to take their ponies to explore areas beyond the rendezvous. Eli carried his bow to hunt with. Beau wanted to work their way up the Wind River when they headed out for trapping.

One evening, just after dark, they noticed that the fire had burned down. That meant that Peter and Joshua had made another trip to the cache. The two men were picketing the horses when Beau heard something spill over in the supply tent.

Grabbing his rifle, he headed over to investigate. As he approached the tent a man with his arms loaded with items burst from the tent, colliding with Beau. The ill-gotten items went flying as the man bowled him over. Beau swung the rifle in a futile attempt to strike the man.

There was a shout from the other tent and the sound of running footsteps. Beau leaped up, taking after the fleeing men as they disappeared into the darkness. The rifle was useless because he had discharged it prior to coming into camp, planning to clean it.

Unable to see where the men had gone, Beau stood swearing into the night. Eli came up beside him. "I got an arrow into one of them. I doubt it will kill him, but he will be hurting for a while."

The two men hurried back to the tents to check out the damage. The items from the supply tent were scattered on the ground in front. Eli lit a candle from the coals of the fire and the two of them went into the sleeping quarters. Beau gasped as he saw that their packs had been torn open and gone through. A large slit in the back of the tent indicated the exit of a third thief.

They would have to wait until morning to know the full extent of what had been taken. Eli got the fire going while Beau tried to collect the stuff on the ground in front of the supply tent. They closed up the slit in the tent the best they could. They had killed a couple of grouse and were roasting them over the fire when Peter and Joshua came back.

Beau met them coming into camp. "We had three men rob the tents."

Peter handed the reins to Joshua and asked him to take care of the cart and animals. Turning back to Beau, the cook fire reflected off his face, showing his anger. "Do you know what they got?"

"We interrupted them, boss," Beau explained. "I think the one in the supply tent dropped most of his stuff when he ran into me. Two others in the sleeping tent got away with their arms full. I think Eli got an arrow into one of them."

"I heard that they have been having trouble with thieves in the company tents," Peter said. "The companies aren't offering credit this year and trappers that wasted their last winter's catch have been blamed for the robberies."

Joshua came back with a long face. He had heard most of what had been discussed. "Every year there are a few hard cases that will steal from another man," he said. "Damn useless sons-of-bitches in my opinion."

The mood remained somber at the fire that night. Beau's and Eli's stomachs were tight, not knowing how much of their gear might have been taken. Without the needed supplies the winter would be very difficult. A quick check under candle light told them that their traps were still there, but much of the clothing and food staples might be gone.

They were all up at daylight. Peter went to see what was missing in the supply tent. Eli searched in the direction of the man he had gotten an arrow into. Beau went to take care of the animals while Joshua started their breakfast. By the time Beau got back he saw Eli returning, carrying a bag.

"Did you find some of our supplies?" Beau called to his friend.

He saw that Elijah's face was drawn. "I killed the man, Beau. The arrow hit him low in the back and he ran away before he fell. He was lying there, flies all on him. The bag was still in his hand."

Attempting to support his friend, Beau said, "He shouldn't have been stealing another man's gear. It weren't your fault. You had to try and stop him."

"I ain't never killed a man before, Beau. I'll be hung for sure. A black man can't kill a white and get away with it."

"We're not back in Arkansas or Missouri, Eli. Out here they look at right and wrong, not what a man's skin color is."

Peter came out of the supply tent and saw them talking. "Only a few small things missing in here. The fellow has a bag filled but left it when he heard you coming. I see you found a bag, Eli."

"Yes . . . Yes, I did," he replied.

While his friend put the bag back into the tent, Beau let Peter know about the man Eli had shot. "An arrow you say," Peter said, thinking. "It will be blamed on one of the tribes."

"It wouldn't be right to blame them," Beau replied. "It may cause trouble and get more folks killed."

"Elijah!" Peter called. "Get the bag and show me where the man is. Beau, you stay here."

Beau watched them walk away. The smell of side meat frying from Joshua's meal filled the air. Turning, he called out, "Is the coffee ready?"

It was two hours before Peter and Eli returned. A cold meal and stale coffee awaited them. Beau and Joshua sat waiting for the two of them to take what they wanted to eat. Once Peter sat down, he brought them up to date.

"Eli here won't be charged with the killing," he started. "The dead man is Brewster. He and two other trappers had a tough year and had spent what little they had on whiskey. Brewster's partners were gone when we went to look for them. Some figure they may have been involved with stealing from the company."

They all sat silently while Peter chewed on the side meat and took a drink of coffee. He then continued. "The men decided that you were right in killing him, Brewster's friends may not agree. We're almost done at this rendezvous and I would recommend the two of you start planning on leaving."

"We're gonna be short supplies," Beau said. "We'll have to try and get some from the company stores."

"I am afraid you won't get too far at the prices they're charging," Peter said. "We are low on supplies for the trip back, but I may be able to help you some."

"You could also join up with the trappers we come in with," Joshua suggested. "They work for the American Fur Company. You mostly work for groceries, but you won't go hungry this winter."

"It's settled then," Beau said. "We check with Reiner and his crew first."

CHAPTER EIGHT

It was late afternoon when Beau and Eli found Reiner. The barrel-chested trapper was nursing a gash on his forehead. "Damn skunk took after me yonder in the trees. I was off like a shot and missed seeing the low-hanging branch."

"By the lack of smell, you must have avoided the skunk," Beau said, trying to look at the bright side. "Me and Eli had a good part of our winter supplies stolen last night. We were wondering if you had any openings on your crew?"

"I heard about the man being killed last night," Reiner said, carefully setting his hat toward the back of his head. "It's not a big loss. Chug was a bad'un. He would lie to your face, cheat at cards, steal and think it was okay." Looking up, he asked, "Was it one of you that put the arrow in him?"

"I done it, Mr. Reiner," Eli admitted.

"Just Reiner, young man. I was just talking with Hoss. He and Wes plan to go free trapping this year. Figures they're going to hit it big in the Big

Horns." Reaching for his bottle, he took a slug and passed it on to Beau and Eli.

While the young men took a drink, he asked, "Have either of you trapped beaver before?"

Beau knew the man's experienced eye saw them as *beaver kittens* or new to the mountains, so trying a bluff wouldn't work. "This will be our first year trapping beaver. I have hunted and trapped on Crowley Ridge in Arkansas, with bear being the best prize. I think I can speak for Eli here, he has shown himself to be an expert with rifle or bow. He is a fair cook, and never backed down from a challenge."

"Well, any man can be taught to set a beaver trap," Reiner said. "If we was to take on anyone, they would have to have the sand to face anything the mountain throws at us."

Handing the bottle back to the barrel-chested man, the two men sat and watched him ponder while he took the last swallow. Appearing to make his decision, he looked at Eli. "So, you put the arrow in old Chug?"

"Yes, suh. He had our stuff," Eli replied.

"I can see we'll have to work on you calling me Reiner." Smiling, he said, "We can use a man that can use the bow. Now, let's see what you're going to need to replace. The company ain't extending any new credit, but working with us, you should be able to fill in the few things you need."

With the weight lifted about winter, both of the young men smiled. Beau headed for the company tent. "I'll get us another bottle while we figure what's needed."

"Grab a twist of tobacky also," Reiner called after him.

With the need for additional food satisfied, the list of remaining items was short. Eli had made arrangements with the Flathead for buckskins and calf-high moccasins for the two of them. Peter had helped out the trade with a couple of older muskets and knives.

Beau and Eli avoided extra trips to the company tents to prevent any confrontations with friends of Chug. After a couple of days, Uno came by and let them know that the trappers were pulling out the next morning. Eli and Beau began to put their packs onto the ponies. Peter called them over to the supply tent.

"I got your pay." He placed 10 silver dollars for each man onto a barrel being used for a table. "There is a blanket spread out beside the tent. As a bonus, you can each take an item from it."

Beau looked around the corner and broke into a wide smile. There lay the Colt Paterson revolver. Without hesitation, he scooped it up. Eli paced back and forth in front of the blanket, having a harder time deciding. Finally he picked up a bag of glass beads.

"Beads?" Beau asked in wonder.

"I met someone that will love these," Eli said, appearing a bit uncomfortable. Thanking Peter, he headed for the Flathead camp.

Peter reached inside the tent and brought out a leather bag. "I figured you would choose the revolver. There are caps, a mold, a spare cylinder, and a few other things you will need to maintain the Colt. As a rule, I wouldn't figure the revolver would be worth a darn in the mountains, but with what I taught you about taking care of gun, you should be able to keep it shooting just fine. Just remember, when you load the revolver, dab grease on the end of the cylinder to prevent setting off more than one charge when firing it."

"Eli and I can't thank you enough for what you did for us," Beau said, feeling regret at having to leave. "We will be looking forward to seeing you next year."

Joshua was sitting quietly next to the fire. Looking up, he said, "Take care, young'un. Don't go losing you top knot."

Beau felt excitement, realizing that he was about to embark on a new adventure. With a smile and with a quick wave, he went over to the ponies and led them out of camp on the way to Reiner's camp.

Arriving at the trapper's camp, he joined them at the fire. Hoss and Wes were still there and playing cards with Uno and Walt. Reiner met him and helped with pulling the packs from the horses.

"Where is Eli?" he asked.

"I think he met a woman in the Flathead camp and went to bring her a goodbye present," Beau replied.

The trapper chuckled. "Could be she'll give him something in return that will be a warm memory for cold winter nights."

It was sunset when Eli came walking toward the trapper's camp. Walking with a bounce in his step, he waved to the camp. Suddenly, a shadowy figure burst out of some evergreens, holding a knife. Beau and the trappers shouted a warning.

The attacker and Eli went down, disappearing from view. As one, the trappers and Beau raced toward the two men. They saw them struggling in the dirt. Then Eli's voice was heard. "Quit your damn moving or I will pull this knife across your scrawny neck!"

Walt and Uno reached the confrontation first. They pulled the two men apart. Eli stood ready with a knife while the attacker struggled to break free and continue fighting. Reiner pulled his knife and struck the man with the butt, knocking him unconscious.

The men stood around the attacker. "You were lucky. Good thing you had a knife," Reiner said.

"This is his knife," Eli said. "I took it from him and was about to bleed him like a hog."

"You best keep the knife," Wes said. "I seen this drunk around. He was a friend of Chug and likes to make trouble. Uno and I will drag him back to his camp."

The rest of the men went back to the fire. Beau looked at his friend. Eli was wearing his buckskin shirt and britches. Like Beau, he was sporting a short beard. His friend looked every bit a mountain man.

"We best get some sleep," Reiner said, tossing out the dregs from his mug. "I want to get an early start."

Sunrise found the group an hour from the rendezvous. It was mid-August. Reiner and Kinney led, riding horses while Beau, Eli, and the other two trappers led pack animals. They were headed for the Wind River Range. A day out from the rendezvous they would split into two groups and start working the tributaries flowing into the river.

Reiner had told Beau and Eli that they would be going with him. After working their way up river for two to three weeks, they would meet at a place that Kinney and Reiner were familiar with. The wide valley in front of them was covered with red and yellow wildflowers. The river wound back and forth, cutting through the mature summer grass. The sky was blue, with puffy clouds being pushed by the west wind.

Late that afternoon, Reiner stopped. "I'll be damned if we haven't found sign already." He was looking at a freshly gnawed stump. Marks of the chisel-sharp teeth of beaver were evident.

Swinging down from the horse, he said, "Looks like here is where we split up, Kinney. You and your men are welcome to spend the night here with us, unless you want to move further north."

Kinney chose to continue for another couple of hours. The plan was that Reiner's group would trap inlets coming from the south side of the river and Kinney the north.

Beau and Eli pulled the packs off Reiner's mule and their horses. They set camp up next to a large, rotting windfall. The leader rode upstream, looking for more sign or a dam. Twenty minutes later he returned.

"Supper will have to wait," he said. "We got some traps to set. Each of you grab a couple and some castor."

Both Beau and Eli wore broad belts on top of their buckskins that held their hatchets and knives. Under his shirt, Beau also carried the Colt in his waist band.

Each trap weight 5 pounds, including the 5-foot chain. The end had a metal ring that the securing stick would go through. With the traps over their shoulders, they followed along behind Reiner's horse as he wound through the aspen trees. They would soon learn that their leader seldom walked if he could ride.

Reaching the first location, Reiner stopped 30 feet away. "Just yonder is a spot they've been coming out of the stream. We don't want to mess it up with our scent. Go cut four sticks that will fit through the rings but won't allow it all the way through."

"How long?" Eli asked.

"Make 'em as tall as you are. Now get to it."

Returning with the six-foot sticks, they saw that Reiner had laid out two traps and lengths of leather cord. He also had two three-foot sticks. "Now I will make the first set. You both pay close attention," he said.

Removing his boots and socks, he entered the stream. Using his knife, he cut any brush or other debris out of the way. He then set the trap and placed it in the runway in six inches of water. He then waded out to the end of the chain and slipped the metal ring over the stick. Using the back of his hatchet, he drove the stick into the muddy bottom. After tying the cord to the stick, he waded back to the bank, and tied the other end to some low brush. He then positioned the shorter stick and drove it into the bank so the end of it was over the trap. Finally, he smeared the thick castor onto the end of the stick.

Reiner then stepped back and sloshed water around the area to rinse any of his scent away. He worked his way downstream before climbing out of the water.

"Well, that's the way it is done," he said. "The castor should attract it, then beaver will try and go deep once caught. The weight of the trap will keep it under water and it will be drowned. If by chance it pulls the stick out, the leather thong will hold it so you don't lose the beaver and your trap. If you are moving on, you can pull the stick and trap in with it without getting wet."

He then pointed at a spot about 15 paces upstream. "There's another good spot," Reiner said. "You set one there, Beau. Me and Eli will continue up to look for another path, or the dam."

Beau watched them move upstream. He hoped and prayed that he would remember everything that Reiner had shown him. Earlier, he and Eli had been told that setting the trap before or after entering the water was purely preference. They had double-long spring traps, and it took both feet on the springs to set them.

On Crowley Ridge, he had used smaller, single-long spring traps for mink, weasel, and the like. Those he could set by squeezing them with his hand. Setting the trap onto the ground, Beau compressed the springs with his feet. With care, he set the trigger and slowly released the pressure on the springs. Stepping away, he smiled with satisfaction at the set trap.

Pulling his boots and socks off, he collected the cord, securing stick, and the short stick for the castor. His hatchet was in his belt and he had a bottle of castor in his possible bag. Grasping the chain about two feet from the trap, he lifted it and turned toward the spot where he planned to enter the stream.

There was a snap, followed by a sharp pain on the back of his leg. Beau yelped, and jumped to get away. He did not have to look. Beau knew that he had let the trap swing and the trigger had bumped his leg, setting it off. Hanging onto his buckskin britches was the trap. Underneath there was a very painful bruise on his leg.

Beau slowly continued setting the trap, limping from the pain on the back of his leg. He had barely finished with the set and started upstream with the pack horse when he saw Reiner and Eli coming back.

The leader stopped near the trap and looked at Beau's work. "Looks about right. Come fall you'll want to be faster. You'll freeze standing that long in an icy stream."

It was dark when they reached their camp. Eli had noticed that Beau was favoring one leg. "Did ya misstep in the water?"

'Nah. I tested the trap on my own leg to make sure it worked," Beau muttered. Behind him he heard his friend chuckling.

The beaver was a nocturnal animal, and the group would set the traps each evening and check them in the morning. After trapping out a pond they would move on, looking for the next location. The thing about the beaver was that they left plain evidence that they were in the area.

They had set four traps. Reiner told them that they would probably move two of them tomorrow and look for canals that the beaver had made. Beau and Eli realized that tonight had been more for training than finding the most active entries.

Eli fried up some side meat and mixed a batch of frying pan biscuits. Beau took care of the horses and mule, giving them a rubdown before returning. The welcoming smell of coffee greeted him as he returned.

"You both done good today. Peter had told me I wouldn't regret taking the two of you along, and I tend to agree after watching you," Reiner said as he slid side meat and biscuits onto his plate.

Both Beau and Reiner cut a chew off a tobacco twist after the meal was done. Eli took out a clay pipe and chopped up enough tobacco to fill it, then lit the pipe with a firebrand from the fire. The men sat on the ground, leaning against the windfall, enjoying the cool evening breeze.

Beau sat cleaning his revolver. He was smiling, realizing that as of now he was a trapper and mountain man. Even the star-studded sky above had a new look to it. The freedom of the mountains suited him just fine. He looked at Eli, who sat peeling additional sticks to stake traps, his pipe glowing as he drew on it.

While they had a fly tarp to rig for camping, Reiner told them that most nights they would be sleeping under the stars. Simple camps and frequent moves would be the routine. They were trapping an area that had few beavers due to being trapped out. The pelts they would harvest until October would be lower quality than winter plew, or prime pelts.

Beau awoke well before daylight the next morning, anxious to find out what they had caught. He lay listening to the even breathing of his fellow campers. Not far away hung their buckskin britches, drying from the work in the stream. In the distance an owl hooted, calling to a mate. Mourning doves were cooing in the hills nearby.

Once the eastern sky got light, he couldn't lay still any longer. Under his blankets were his rifle and the Colt Paterson. Rising soundlessly from his blankets, he moved a distance away and relieved himself.

He crept back toward the camp when he heard Reiner. "Get the fire going and put on some coffee. Wake me when it's done."

With the water heating, Beau retrieved his britches. Before pulling them on he checked his leg. There was an ugly, bluish-green bruise. Sticking the

Colt into his waistband, he went to take care of the animals. By the time he got back, Reiner and Eli were at the fire drinking coffee.

They made their breakfast on corn dodgers that Reiner had in his pack. Once finished, the leader said, "Strike the camp. We'll pull the traps and continue upriver."

"We'll want to skin anything we caught first," Beau said.

"No beaver here for some time," Reiner said. "I wanted to make sure you both knew what to do once we do come on fresh sign." Smiling, he led the way up the stream.

"We must have passed the test," Eli whispered to Beau.

They climbed up a long canyon with limestone cliffs on both sides. The Wind River was left behind for the time being. The river that they were following up the valley was a fork of the Popo Agie. The valley and cliffs were covered with Douglas fir trees, snowberry, wild rose and an abundance of other shrubs. A goshawk circled in the blue sky, looking for a meal below.

Reiner told them that the canyon had navigable passes to go south over the mountains. His objective was to camp in the canyon and hunt for meat. What they couldn't eat fresh could be made into jerky for later.

Beau noticed that the Popo Agie suddenly became a boulder-strewn dry river bed, only to see the river flowing again, farther up the canyon. "Where did it go?" he asked.

"What go?" the leader questioned.

"The river. Does it run behind the canyon

wall?" Beau asked.

"Follow me," Reiner said.

He had them tie the animals to some low brush and led Beau and Eli over some rocks into a bowl cut into the canyon wall, Sinks Canyon. To their amazement, the river disappeared into the ground. "Come spring, the river floods this bowl and overflows down the bed we've been following and then meets up with the Popo Agie below. I wintered here a couple times." He pointed to an overhang in the bowl. "That makes a decent place to camp this time of year."

The men moved their gear under the overhang. The river flowed down over the boulders and then disappeared. The roar of the tumbling water would be their constant companion. The horses and mule were picketed a short distance away on some mature grass. A stand of lodge pole pines hid them from view from anyone traveling below.

Taking his rifle and revolver, Beau headed into the trees to hunt down some supper. Moving quietly through the forest, he heard the clucking of a grouse. There were clumps of chokecherry bushes loaded with the dark purple fruit. He pulled the Colt from his waistband. He had fired it very little and was looking forward to using it for small game.

Finally, the bird came into view. One was in plain sight, while a second one was just beyond the bush. Cocking the Colt Paterson brought the trigger out. The bell-shaped grip wasn't the best design for holding and aiming. Placing the front sight dead center on the grouse, he squeezed the trigger.

The sound of several birds being flushed filled the air, while the one he had shot flapped wildly on the ground. Hurrying to scoop up the bird, he stuffed it under his shirt and looked for any sign of the others. One of the fleeing birds had flown up into an aspen. Once again, he aimed the Colt. The bird under his shirt continued to struggle. Distracted, he fired and hit the branch the grouse was sitting on. It spread its wings and glided out of sight.

Pulling the struggling bird out from under his shirt, Beau broke its neck with a quick motion before moving on. Over the next three hours he managed to kill three more of the grouse. Several times he stopped to enjoy the ripe chokecherries.

Returning to camp, he found Eli cleaning a small mule deer. He had stalked the animal and shot it with his bow. He told Beau that Reiner was upstream fishing.

"We got these grouse for supper if the boss doesn't have any luck," Beau said. "In the meantime, I will start cutting poles to make a rack so we can dry the deer meat."

On the fourth day in the canyon, Beau was riding one of the ponies using Reiner's saddle. He caught sight of an animal with the largest rack he had ever seen. It was lying in the grass next to the river. It was the first bull elk he had come across. Sliding off the horse, Beau sank down close to the ground. He was no longer able to see the elk.

Trusting the horse to stay where it had stopped, the curly-haired man began to belly crawl in the direction he had seen the bull. With the rifle out in front of him, he worked his way forward, his heart pounding with anticipation at bagging such a large animal. A breeze was coming from his right, which should prevent the animal from scenting him.

He wished that he dared to poke his head up

to see if the animal was still there. Beau lay for a moment, trying to calm himself. He tried to listen for any sound from the elk, but his heart was pounding in his ears, which made catching any sound impossible. He did suddenly hear something coming behind him. Peeking out of the corner of his eye, he saw that it was his horse.

If you scare the damn elk away, we just might be eating you this winter, he thought, anger running through him.

Suddenly, the elk stood up. Looming in front of him, it snorted threateningly at the pony. Without hesitation Beau swung the rifle toward the elk, aiming down the side of the barrel at the shoulder of the bull, he squeezed the trigger. The quick movement of the elk as it attempted to flee caused his shot to be low and just behind the front leg.

Blood sprayed onto the grass and the bull ran for the trees, crossing the river and crashing blindly into the brush on the other side. Standing quickly, Beau turned to get the pony. It was running several hundred feet away, startled by the shot.

"Damn!" he shouted as he dug into his possible bag to reload the rifle. The low hit would be slow to kill the elk, and he would have to try and catch the pony before going after the elk.

He had another couple of hours of daylight, so if he could get the pony he should have time to track the elk. Beau also knew that he should wait a bit before tracking to allow it to lie down and bleed out, rather than keep the elk running ahead of him.

With the rifle loaded, he started after the pony. It had stopped down the canyon, standing with its head up looking at him. "You wanted to be my close buddy when I was stalking the elk. Now don't be running from me when I need you," he muttered.

After a short game of dodging him, the pony finally let Beau come up to it. He felt angry at the delay in tracking the elk, but Beau reminded himself that it was not the horse's fault. Forcing himself to be calm, he patted the animal on its shoulder and spoke softly to it while mounting the horse.

The blood trail of the elk was easy to follow. Beau's only fear was that he would run out of daylight. Once in the trees, he swung off the pony and led it. The deep tracks of the running elk were easy to see and the amount of blood loss gave him hope that it hadn't run too far.

Beau moved slowly in the long shadows of the trees. Straining his eyes, he looked ahead for any sight of the bull. Then he saw the animal. It was lying in some evergreens, looking at him. Beau's first thought was to tie the pony to one of the small saplings to prevent it from running again. He feared that the extra movement would startle the elk.

Wrapping the hackamore around his right hand, he brought the rifle up and took sight on the neck of the bull. After making sure that the hackamore didn't interfere with the hammer or frizzen, he slowly squeezed the trigger. Fire belched from the rifle, sending the .54 caliber ball at the elk, striking it. The pony pulled back, spinning Beau around. Fighting to keep a grip on the hackamore, he looked in time to see the elk lunge up and flounder, falling into the short brush.

Securing the pony to one of the saplings, Beau hurried over to the elk, poking it with the barrel of his rifle. The animal was dead. For a moment, he stood in awe of the huge animal he had just shot. The antlers alone were nearly as wide as the span of his arms. The sound of a wolf howling in the distance brought him back to the task at hand. Pulling his Green River knife, he began to cut up the animal.

Beau would have loved to drag the elk back to camp and show it to Eli, but bringing back the parts they wouldn't eat didn't make any sense. He gutted and quartered the elk, leaving the head, legs, and much of the rib cage. He did use his hatchet to remove the antlers which he carried on his back.

Leading the heavily loaded pony back toward camp, Beau was enjoying the moment. He was looking forward to the reaction of Reiner and Eli. It was an hour after dark when he arrived. A short distance away, he hailed the camp. The others came out from under the shelf.

While Reiner an Eli were pleased to see the amount of meat Beau brought back, they had been worried and were about to go out and look for him. The evening was cool and the elk would be fine until morning. Tossing ropes over the pine branches, they hauled the elk up to prevent wildlife from getting at it. Beau brought the large antlers to the campfire to show Eli.

What happened next had likely been happening for 10,000 years in this very canyon. By the light of their fire, Beau regaled the others with a story of the hunt.

It was full daylight when the sleeping trappers finally moved. Eli went out from the shelter to relieve himself. Shortly, he returned, concern on his face. "We got company," he said. "A whole tribe is outside."

Reiner got up quickly and pulled on his boots.

"Beau, give me the revolver." Accepting the Colt, he made a quick check of the loads and then put it into his waistband. "I'll go up first," he instructed. "Both of you follow a bit back with your rifles. Make sure you don't make any threatening moves."

"What if they're hostile?" Beau asked.

With a fixed stare, the leader said, "I'll empty the Colt at them and try and make it back to the bowl. It will make a good spot for you to make a defense." After a short pause, he added, "If I go down, leave me and get back to the shelter."

Slowly, the men emerged from under the ledge and climbed out of the bowl. There on the canyon floor were no less than 30 Lakota. Reiner felt some relief when he saw that the group consisted of elders, braves, women, and children. Their ponies carried their lodge poles as travois with items for an extended stay.

He motioned Beau and Eli to stay back as he walked out to see them. Using sign, he welcomed them. One of the braves rode up to Reiner and slid off his pony. For the next 15 minutes, the two of them conversed as best they could by using common sign and gestures known to both.

Eli whispered to Beau, "They are here to pick berries and hunt meat for the coming winter."

"How do you know?"

"It is the same sign used by the Flathead that I visited at the rendezvous," the young black replied.

Suddenly, Reiner spoke. Both of the young men missed what he said, not expecting him to speak to them. Again, the leader repeated, "Get down one of the elk hind quarters for our friends here."

"Stay here with the rifles," Beau whispered.

While walking to the pine tree, he noticed that the horses and mule were still there.

Lowering the meat, he turned and saw a woman leading a pony and travois toward him. With the help of the woman, the heavy hindquarter was loaded and the woman led the pony back toward the other Lakota.

Beau headed back to join Eli. He watched as Reiner turned and joined them. "I told the brave you have a special gift for him."

"A knife or hatchet?" Beau asked.

"Nope," the leader said. "Bring him the elk horns."

Beau hesitated a moment, confused at the request. Reiner added, "You'll have lots of horns in the future. The pair you got last night will buy us the friendship we need to be safe."

Realizing that the leader was right, Beau went into the shelter and picked up the large antlers. After taking just a second to admire them, he emerged and presented them to the brave. A broad smile broke out on the brave's face and he accepted the elk antlers. Holding them up for the rest of the Lakota to see, he headed back to join them.

The three men watched as the Lakota moved up the canyon to make camp. Reiner handed the revolver back to Beau. "While we have shown proper respect to our new neighbors," he said, "as soon as we get the rest of the elk dried we'll be on our way. It won't take too long before the feeling of goodwill will be overtaken by the desire to have our horses."

CHAPTER NINE

A week later the three men left the canyon, heading back north to the Wind River. They saw little of the Lakota, whose women and children were busy gathering baskets of chokecherries and other berries and herbs while the men hunted for meat. They would dry both and pound most of it into pemmican to be eaten during the winter.

The night before they'd left, the brave whom Reiner had spoken with and a couple others came to visit. They had sat on a blanket and smoked tobacco provided by the trappers. The gist of the conversation was that their hunt had been successful so far and their winter would have little starving time. Before they'd left, the brave had presented Beau with a pair of moccasins and a knife with the handle made from a deer antler.

As a parting gift, Reiner had given them the rest of the tobacco twist they had been smoking from. As they'd watched the neighbors leave, the leader had said, "It will be good to leave tomorrow. I noticed that one of the young braves spent all his time looking at our stock."

Beau figured that it had been two weeks since they'd left the rendezvous and they hadn't caught their first beaver. While in the canyon he had made several hoops to be used for drying the pelts. They caught up with Kinney and the others. They were camped below some red cliffs. It was now September and the nights were cool in the higher elevations. The hills were a blaze of yellow and red from the aspen and maple trees. The evergreens stood out as dark patches surrounded by bright fall colors.

Kinney complained at only catching four beavers so far. Beau sat on a log, warming his hands with a mug of coffee. *It sure beats what we caught, which is nothing,* he thought. Reiner brought out a bottle and the group sat around the fire, enjoying the rye and telling stories. Everyone liked the re-telling of Beau's bagging the elk.

Before breaking camp, Reiner gave some of the jerky to Kinney's group. Once again, plans were made for meeting in a couple of weeks. The cold nights and fair days would quickly improve the beaver pelts.

There was frost on the ground when they left the red cliff camp. Beau and Eli had put on their flat-brimmed leather hats. In their packs, they carried wool tuques gotten from the Hudson Fur Company for winter use. They rode through the golden-brown grass, with a scattering of sage and boulders, that covered the valley floor.

Reiner led the way, riding well up along the streams flowing into the Wind River. It was late afternoon when the sun glared off a pond through the trees. Excitement went through the group as they spotted recently chewed stumps, showing that it was an active beaver pond.

They set up camp downstream of the pond. The beavers had built a dam that was easily 200 feet long. Reiner began to pull the gear off his animals. He looked at the expectant young men. "Go ahead," he told them. "Grab a couple traps each and find some entry points or canals to set them."

The two men quickly stripped their packs off the ponies and dug out what they needed. With the horses picketed on a grassy area, they headed out to trap beaver. Beau crossed the stream using a windfall and searched for spots on the far side, while Eli remained on the nearside.

Beau found the first entry. Stripping to his long johns from the waist down, he took a trap, his stake and a stick for the castor. Wading in a bit downstream, he worked his way back to the entry path. Eli had disappeared farther toward the dam.

The entry was clear, so it took little time to set the trap into the shallow water. After driving the stake through the ring, Beau tied the leather cord to a low bush. He then positioned the short stick over the trap and applied the castor. Sloshing some water to eliminate some of his scent, he then went back downstream to exit the stream.

Returning to his britches and the second trap, he felt quite proud of how quickly he had set the trap. Slipping his feet into the low boots, he carried his socks and britches with the second trap as he looked for a another entry path. On the pond, he heard a beaver tail slapping the water, warning the others of danger.

He came across a canal that the beavers had dug out to drag branches to the stream. Feeling somewhat an expert by now, he quickly placed a trap in the canal. Beau headed back downstream, crossed on the windfall, and was pulling on his britches when Eli appeared. His friend was smiling.

"I saw three lodges in the pond," he said.

"Were you the one that scared them?" Beau asked.

"Could have been," he said. "I was near the spillway when they set to splashing."

It was dark when they returned to the camp. Reiner had a pot of beans going on the fire and the coffee was ready. The wet long johns chilled them, so they sat close to the fire and warmed their insides with the strong coffee.

Eli told Reiner about the three lodges. The leader looked up from stirring the bean pot. "That would make about six adult beaver in the pond, maybe a couple more with young'uns."

"That will make a good start for us," Beau said.

"We'll only take four out now," Reiner informed him. "Come spring we can swing by and maybe try for a couple more. Too many trappers forget that they'll need beaver to make more beaver."

Beau wanted to object and say that others would come and trap the rest, but he respected Reiner and kept quiet. The beans had side meat, molasses, and a little rye in them. Both of the young men complimented the leader on his cooking.

"When we get us some beaver I'll show you what good eating is," Reiner boasted.

They awoke to a threatening sky. Thick cloud cover could deliver a soaking rain or even snow due to the elevation. Beau and Eli rigged the fly tarp to protect their gear before eating or going to check the traps. They made their breakfast on warmed up beans. They just finished the meal when a mist began to fall. They both wore their flat-brimmed hats to keep the rain off their necks.

Reiner saddled his horse and rode out of camp to scout future trapping sites. Beau and Eli headed for the pond to check their traps. Eli continued toward his first trap while his friend crossed the stream on the windfall. The young black arrived at the first trap. Disappointed, he found it just as he had left it. After adding a little more castor to the stick over the trap, he continued to his second set.

It was at the end of a short canal. He stopped when he saw that the bait stick was gone. Slowly, he approached the canal. Sudden movement caught his eye. He had a beaver in his trap, but it was not drowned. The trap had been caught on some underwater roots, preventing the animal from getting back to the deeper water.

Eli stood in the cold rain, face to face with a very angry beaver. It snapped its teeth and uttered a cry which was unexpected by the young black. Removing his hatchet from his belt. Eli tried to get close enough to finish off the beaver with a strike to the head with the blunt end. For a short while it was a standoff as the beaver parried every move Eli made. Then, the trap came loose from the root and the large rodent disappeared into the stream.

Eli sat on the bank in the cold rain, a bit shaken as he watched where the beaver had gone. Killing an animal while hunting was not new to Eli, but the unexpected confrontation with the beaver was his first. After a few minutes, he waded into the water and pulled the trap with the 40-pound beaver out of the stream.

Before re-setting the trap, he cleared the roots from the canal. Pride in the catch quickly replaced the uncertainty that he had first felt. He hung the beaver on an aspen branch before going to check his next trap.

Beau was sitting on the end of the windfall with a beaver at his feet, when Eli came back proudly carrying his catch. "I see you got one," the curly-haired trapper said.

"For a moment, I wasn't sure it I was going to get it or if it was going to get me," Eli admitted. As they walked back to the camp with their catch, he told his friend about the angry rodent.

The rain was still falling when they got back. Along with the precipitation, the aspen leaves were cascading down. Reiner hadn't returned from scouting. After getting the fire going, Beau put a pot of water on to heat. Both men were familiar with the correct way to skin the beaver. Kneeling on the ground close enough to get a little warmth from the fire, they began by cutting a slit from the nose to the tail.

They had finished skinning their catch and were scraping the meat and fat off the pelt when Reiner returned. "I see we had some luck," the leader said.

"Yep, we each got one," Beau said proudly.

"Did you save the castor?" he asked.

"Yes, we did," Eli replied.

"And you didn't mess up the meat."

"All gutted and waiting for you under the tarp," Beau said as he worked on the fleshing of his pelt.

True to his word, Reiner made a fine supper for them. He cut the choice meat from both carcasses and, using grease from some side meat, some salt and wild onions, he cubed the beaver and fried it, making a gravy with a little cold flour.

Sitting under the golden branches of a willow tree to stay out of the rain, the three men feasted on the succulent meat. Reiner wiped his mouth with the back of his hand and told them, "Figure to eat beaver most of the winter when we're catching them. Once the pond and streams freeze it will be jerky and cold flour."

After their meal, Reiner showed them the best way to stretch the pelts on the hoops to dry. Beau ran his fingers through the thick fur, thinking that this very pelt could travel all the way to Europe to be made into a gentlemen's top hat.

While they sat drinking the last of the coffee with a shot of rye and enjoying some tobacco, Reiner suddenly said, "We been together almost a month and I don't know your last names. Mine is Wells. My first name come from my mother's family."

"My full name is Beauford Levesque. Beauford's too long. That's why I go by Beau," the curly-haired young man said.

Eli took a slow drag on his clay pipe and proudly said, "Elijah Weber is my name."

* * *

The trapping out of an area and moving on to find another pond became the men's routine. Beau enjoyed the challenge of outsmarting the cautious beaver, and the ever-changing terrain.

"Hey, Levesque," Reiner called. "After we get the traps set, see if you can bag some of the grouse we flushed up."

It was early October and most of the leaves had fallen in the high country. They were camped in a stand of pine with mountains looming above them in the distance. The Wind River wound through the basin in front of them. Kinney and his crew were to meet them in the next week or two. Their catch of beaver had been marginal at best. They had just over two dozen pelts. Reiner would tell them stories of getting that many over a two-week period in years past. His eyes would glow when he talked of years gone by.

The mountains were shrouded with snow. Patches remained in the basin from an earlier snowfall. The men wore wool shirts and trousers under their buckskins. Wading into the frigid streams would leave the men shivering by the time they got back to the fire.

Beau arrived back in camp, proudly carrying enough grouse for their supper. "I knocked two right out of the air with the Colt," he bragged.

"You're getting pretty damn good with that noisy shooter," Eli said as touched his bow lying next to him.

While the two young men cleaned the birds for roasting, Reiner built up the fire. He stood and looked at the sky. "Could get some more snow. As soon as Kinney gets here, we need to head through the pass and work the Green River area."

"I saw some big cat tracks north of here," Beau said.

"Probably after the same birds you were," Reiner replied. "We can get a good price for the cat skin, not to mention a couple good meals from the meat."

"You carry the big trap in your pack," Eli said. "We can set it in the pines."

"We can try," the leader told him, "but starting tonight, we bring the animals in close to camp."

As if on cue, the shrill cries of the cat were heard that night. The sound sent chills down Beau's spine. That night, he snuggled deeper under his blankets. At his side was the rifle and his Colt, offering a degree of comfort.

While Beau and Eli made breakfast, Reiner took a walk through the pines. He carried his Hawken, .50 caliber cradled in his arms. By the time he got back, Eli had crisp side meat and fried biscuits ready. He had just given the coffee pot a stir to settle the grounds.

"It's watching us," the leader told them. "The damn thing circled the camp several times and then lay on the rock ledge, eyeing our stock."

"I hope Kinney gets here soon so we can head for the Green River and leave the cat behind," Eli said.

"Wouldn't do any good if it's hungry and figures we'd be a good meal," Reiner replied. "I've had cats follow me most of the winter, feeding on beaver carcasses. Two years ago, Kinney lost a mule to a cat."

"If we have a beaver in the traps today, I'll bait the big trap with it," Beau suggested. "Maybe the hungry cat will like beaver meat."

The six traps they had set the night before had caught two prime beaver. The cold had thickened the fur, creating the plew they had hoped for. Beau and Eli arrived back at camp, their pants legs frozen stiff. The air temperature was below freezing, so they had to tend to the skinning, fleshing, and stretching quickly before the beaver froze.

They had a rack near the fire to dry their wet clothing. Beau donned his extra wool trousers and his low boots. Taking the trap and the carcass, he headed into the pines to find a place to set it for the cat. Out of the corner of his eye he saw a yellow flash as he startled the prey.

He had left the rifle back at camp and had the revolver in his waistband. The .28 caliber balls wouldn't be adequate to kill the big cat if he came face to face with it, but the sound might scare it off.

Beau set the trap about 150 paces from the camp. Clearing the ground below a large pine, he placed the trap. Hanging the beaver about five feet above, he then set the trap and sprinkled pine needles over it to make it less visible. He drove a two-foot stake into the ground to secure the chain. Once finished, he stepped back to look the set over.

The shadows were long as he hurried back to the camp. Beau had the uneasy feeling that the cat's eyes were on him. The security of the fire was welcome as he sat and poured another cup of coffee.

"I got a glimpse of the cat on the way out," Beau told the others.

"If the trap doesn't work," Reiner said, "we'll have to hunt the damn thing down. It means to make a meal out of one of our animals . . . or us."

Eli came back from watering the horses and the mule. He picketed them close to camp. "The stock could smell the cat. They were mighty skittish at the stream."

That night the cat could be heard screeching in the hills. Beau lay awake for the longest time, listening for any sign that the cat had stepped in the trap. The men were up at first light. Reiner said he would go up and check the big trap while Beau and Eli checked on the beaver.

Beau found that one of his traps was covered with a sheet of ice. Pulling it, he moved the set to another spot that was less likely to freeze. Eli joined him, carrying a muskrat that had been caught. They had split a cedar into boards to stretch and dry anything that was case skinned rather than open skinned like the beaver.

Returning to camp, they found Reiner putting on a pot of coffee. Looking up, he said, "The cat got the damn beaver. Looked like it leaped on it and snapped the limb and landed beyond the trap. It is one smart critter."

"The stream's starting to ice over," Beau said.

"I have a shanty in a valley off the Green River," Reiner said. "We'll hunker down there once all the streams freeze over. Come March, with the breakup, we can go after some plew."

"Does the valley have any marten or fisher?" Beau asked.

"Some of the men set up a trap line," he replied. "Most things you catch are yours to sell."

Beau and Eli were coming back from an evening check of the traps when they saw Kinney and the others coming slowly across the basin. That meant that they would be moving on soon and hopefully get away from the cat.

The group sat around the fire roasting venison steaks from the deer that Walt had shot earlier in the day. Between the two teams, they had caught 59 beaver and 6 muskrat. It was well below the number that had been trapped by this time last year. Reiner and Kinney were optimistic about the luck they would have in the Green River area.

A light snow was falling as the men sat drinking their evening coffee. The topic had switched to the big cat. Uno and Wes were in favor of heading across the pass and trying to put the animal behind them. Kinney was in favor of trying to hunt the cat.

He suggested that they put one of the mules out on the edge of the pines to lure the cat in, and then the six of them spread out for a shot when it came in. "If we can bag the cat we will get as much as six beaver pelts, maybe more," he said.

Beau and Eli sat listening to the discussion, keeping their thoughts to themselves. The decision would be made by Reiner and Kinney. In the morning, they would be pulling the traps in preparation for moving on. The two young men were proud to be a part of the group of trappers. The broad basins and looming mountains were breathtaking. The vastness of the untamed area gave them all the freedom that their inner spirits longed for.

The decision was made that they would hunt the cat. They awoke the next morning to three inches of new snow. Any tracks they found would be fresh. It was decided to use Reiner's mule as bait. Eli was stationed in a cluster of rocks about 200 paces from the mule. It would be his responsibility to kill the cat with his Hawken if it got by the rest of the watchers.

Beau found a place to watch near the ledge that the cat had used some days before. It was late afternoon when the men spread out to watch. The mule was not happy to be away from the other animals and began to bray. Reiner figured that it would help draw the cat in.

The men sat in the crisp, late afternoon air. The cold began to creep in, numbing their feet. Beau sat flexing his fingers, trying to warm his hands. After full dark, the men walked in. Walt had thought he'd caught a glimpse of the cat farther up in the pines. Eli was shivering and stomping his cold feet when Beau reached the cluster of rocks.

"I'm damn glad the cat didn't come after the mule," he said. "My hands were so cold that I doubt I could have fired the Hawken."

Beau smiled at his friend. "In the morning Kinney is going out to look for tracks. If the cat didn't come around, we should be heading out."

Eli built up the fire so everyone could warm up before crawling into their blankets. Walt continued to say that he had seen the cat. It had leaped across an opening in the pines above him. "I'll check in the morning," Kinney said. "My guess is you saw a deer."

After a little rye and a smoke or chew, the men went to their blankets. The cat had not been heard from the past few nights. Beau hoped that there were no tracks. He was ready to see the Green River area. He was looking forward to seeing over the next horizon.

It was pan-fried biscuits and venison for breakfast. Eli and Uno were doing the cooking. Kinney was gone at daylight, looking for tracks. Beau and Walt were tending to the animals. While the animals were being watered, the curly-haired young man walked around looking for a good spot to picket the horses and mules.

Suddenly, he called out, "Walt! Walt, come here."

The trapper came running over. In front of him were the tracks of the big cat. It had come down from the pines and had been circling the stock. "We were freezing up in the pines and it was down here looking over our animals."

"Will the mountain lion hunt during the day?" Beau wondered.

"Depends on how hungry they are," Walt said.

They put the animals on new grass and then headed in for breakfast. Kinney was coming from the pines. "I didn't find any tracks," he called out.

Once he got back, Beau took him to see the ones they'd found. "Damn," he muttered. "We sat up in the pines and it come almost into camp."

That morning it was decided that they'd try one more day for the cat. If they had no luck, then they'd pull up camp and head for the pass. They had another month, maybe a little more of trapping before things froze over.

The cat had been hunting during the day, so after breakfast the men spread out beyond the stock and found places to watch. Beau used a windfall that created a shelter from the wind with its root base. He sat with his back against the uplifted roots and settled down to wait.

Uno was just out of sight over a ridge. Beau had taken note of where each man was watching to make sure that he didn't fire in that direction should the cat come through. They had spread the horses and mules out a little to broaden the area that the cat would come to.

The upturned root base was a good windbreak. Beau was warm and comfortable, so comfortable that he had to fight the urge to fall asleep. Several times he shook his head and blinked his eyes trying to stay awake. Finally, he had to stand and take a short walk to wake up. He had just returned and was getting seated when there was a rifle shot.

It was from the direction where Uno had gone. The shot was followed by the snarling of the cat. Then there was a scream from Uno! Even before the scream, Beau was headed toward the ridge. His heart was in his throat as he heard the continuing snarling of the cat and the shouts of terror from the trapper.

Gaining the ridge, Beau saw the large cat dragging the struggling man. In desperation, Beau shouted, hoping to get the attention of the cat. Holding Uno down with its massive paws, it crouched behind the man and snarled threateningly toward Beau. Though he feared hitting the trapper, the young man felt he had no choice and he drew a bead on the cat's head and fired his rifle.

The cat spun and rolled on the ground, making sounds that chilled the young man. It came up and leaped back onto the trapper and hissed, refusing to give up its prey. Pulling the Colt Paterson from his waistband, he ran toward the stubborn beast, hollering at the top of his lungs.

Finally, unnerved, the cat leaped from the man and turned to run. Beau fired twice at the departing cat, seeing it flinch once. Sliding to his knees next to Uno, he rolled him over and grimaced at the sight of the mauled trapper. Uno was bloodied from his head to his waist. One of his bearded cheeks was ripped open to the jaw bone. He heard running footsteps behind him as the other trappers came to join him.

Seeing his friend, Walt gasped, "Oh my God! Is he dead?"

"Not yet, but he got it bad," Beau replied. "Do what you can to help him. I'm going after the damn cat!"

Kinney and Walt stayed with the injured man. After Beau reloaded the rifle, the rest of the trappers spread out to track the cat. Beau stayed on the trail, and saw that the animal had been wounded and was leaving a blood trail. The distance between the tracks was over 20 feet as it had sprinted through the woods.

The trail took them into the pines. Beau's eyes were fixed on the ground as he followed it. Then he heard a threatening hiss above him! Looking up, he saw the cat about 15 feet above in a gnarled pine. Skidding to a stop, Beau made a desperate effort to raise the rifle. There was a shot from behind him. The cat tried to leap but, unable to do so, it crashed to the ground next to the young trapper.

Jumping away, Beau watched the animal kick its last as its life slipped away. Eli came along side, smoke still coming from his rifle. "Thanks . . . Uh, thank you Eli," he said.

"I saw it above you and didn't want to let it get another man," Eli replied.

The rest of the trappers came up and stood around the large male cat. Gasping for breath, Reiner said, "That bugger must weigh 150 pounds, maybe more."

Cutting a pole, the cat's feet were tied around it and then, with Beau on one end and Eli on the other, they headed back to camp with the sober realization that the prize they carried had come at a high price.

Kinney had taken two of the fly tarps and made a shelter next to the fire. Uno was lying on the blankets and they were trying to stop the bleeding. The torn skin and punctures from the claws and teeth were numerous. The injured man was, mercifully, unconscious. A pot of water was steaming on the fire, the contents red from the bloody cloth being dipped into it.

Kinney and Walt continued working on the mauled man, attempting to sew up the cheek, while Beau and Eli hung the cat to start skinning. They skinned it from nose to tail and removed the paws to keep the claws.

Reiner sat next to the fire and appeared to be praying. Earlier, when the men had been talking of bagging the cat, they had been anticipating a celebration of the hunt. Instead of everyone sitting around the fire drinking to their success, the only rye used was for cleaning the wounds of the unfortunate trapper.

The leader came over to assist Eli in removing the best cuts of meat from the cat, while Beau cut four poles to stretch the skin for fleshing and drying. It appeared that Uno hadn't shot the animal. They guessed that it had jumped on him and instinctively he had fired the rifle. Beau's first shot with the rifle had creased the side of the cat's face, possibly stunning or confusing it, thus not scaring it off. One of the shots from the Colt had hit it just below the rib cage. Eli's shot had gone through the heart, finishing the cat.

Reiner told Eli that back east they had hunted the cats with dogs. The cats were good sprinters for a short distance and would tend to find safety to rest, which explained it being in the tree. Once they had the meat harvested, the leader took his mule and dragged the carcass deep into the pines. Wolves or coyotes would make short work of it.

It was dark when Uno began to moan as he slipped in and out of consciousness. Walt had made a broth out of some of the cat's meat and tried to get the man to swallow some. Reiner and Kinney had brought the animals to the stream for water. When they returned, Eli had a meal of roasted mountain lion ready.

Whether or not the meat tasted as good as Reiner had said it would earlier, Beau couldn't tell. He had little appetite and was worried about his fellow trapper. After the meal was finished, Reiner cleared his throat.

"Kinney and I discussed what would be best for Uno and our venture," he started. "It will be several days before Uno will be able to be moved. Even then it will be probably by travois. I will stay another two days. Then I'll take Beau and Eli and head for the Green River. We will work to the north until things ice over. We'll then head south for the shanty and meet up for the winter. We will be carrying all the pelts that have been caught so far. That will lessen the amount Kinney will have to take with him."

After a pause, when Uno cried out, Reiner continued. "When Kinney here gets through the pass, he, Walt and Uno will trap to the south on the Green until they get to the shanty."

Reiner didn't ask for any questions. What he and Kinney had decided was not up for debate. What was left unsaid was the plan if Uno didn't survive. They all knew that the human body could overcome some of the worst injuries. They all had heard the stories of Hugh Glass after he had been left after being mauled by a bear.

That evening, Reiner and Beau sat to the side while the rest of the party huddled near the fire. The two of them were chewing tobacco and drinking lukewarm coffee. "I went by the spot where the cat attacked Uno," the leader said. "From the tracks, it looked like the cat had come right up to him in plain sight before attacking."

Remembering how tired he had been, Beau asked, "You think he fell asleep?"

"Either that, or his attention had been in another direction," Reiner replied.

"I'd like to think he was looking in another direction," the young man said.

"I would also."

Reiner would never speak of what he found to anyone again. Beau figured that the attack was weighing heavily on the leader and he felt the need to talk to someone. The attack showed how quickly bad things could happen. They would never know what took Uno's attention away from seeing the cat come in.

Beau awoke the next morning. It had snowed again and the sun sparkled off the new, frozen precipitation. The basin was a white expanse, with the dark waters of the Wind River winding through. He heard muted voices coming from near Uno.

He pulled his boots on and shook the snow off his blankets. He then stopped and stared at the fly tarp protecting the injured trapper. The look on Kinney's and Walt's faces told the story. Uno had passed during the night.

The men sat near the fly tarp shelter, the cook fire remaining cold. Beau was numb inside, unsure of what he should do. He started to get the fire lit. He listened as he heard Walt say, "There was too much damage. The cat had bit his head. I didn't know what to do."

As he worked on the fire, Beau saw Kinney trying to comfort Walt. Once he had water heating, the young man knelt next to the two trappers. "I'm sorry," he whispered. They had pulled the blanket over their departed friend's face. Reiner and Eli were the last to learn of the bad news. They knelt with the others, each with their own thoughts and prayers.

Breakfast that morning was just coffee. Beau and Eli went to dig a grave. The ground was only frozen a couple inches deep and soon they had a proper hole dug. Both young men were glad to be busy and away from the sorrow. Walt and Uno had been partnered up for a score of years and Walt was taking the loss of his friend hard.

They laid Uno into the grave wrapped in his blanket. Once it was filled, Reiner said some words, remembering the quick wit and honesty of the man. Walt started to sing a hymn but his voice broke. The others pitched in and sang to their departed friend.

With the short service completed, Reiner ordered that the camp be struck. They were leaving the misery behind and heading for the Green River. Walt stayed near the grave until things were ready to travel. Beau heard him promise to bring a marker to his friend's grave next summer.

The group left the basin camp and headed for a pass that the leader had used in prior years. The rest of the cat meat remained, lying near the dying fire. None of the men had any appetite to eat it. Beau looked at the mountains they were heading for. He had been told that they would be crossing the continental divide. Kinney explained that it was the point where rivers on this side flowed east and those on the other flowed west. Looking at the snow-covered mountain tops, Beau couldn't understand how a river could even flow up there.

For the first two days, the group climbed steadily. The sky was clear, with sunshine, but the temperature remained below freezing. They had loaded firewood onto the pack animals. For a while they would be above the tree line. The views were spectacular, and if it had only been summer season Beau would have liked to spend several days camping.

Soon they were dealing with talus-covered hillsides. Care was taken choosing their trail. A man or animal could fall 1,000 feet on some of the slides. Sitting around their evening fire, Reiner and Kinney would tell the others the names of many of the mountains around them. While the names might be forgotten, the landmarks of the trail would be long remembered. "Tomorrow," Reiner said, "we will be crossing an area that remains frozen year-round. After that we start down and should be at the Green River in three or four days."

Part of the challenge of being so high in the mountains was the knowledge that a severe storm could blow in anytime and strand the trappers. The passes would be all but impassable, filled deep with snow. The wind-blown fire did little to warm the travelers. They huddled around it, wrapped in their blankets.

In the pass the thick crust on top of the snow was barely strong enough to support the men's weight. Their unfortunate animals continued to break through. They kept the pack animals strung out in single file, rotating the lead animal, which had the toughest going.

Frequent rests for the men were required to prevent sweating under their clothing. Should this happen, they would be sure to freeze at night.

It took two days to cross the snow-covered pass. Once through it, they began to work their way down. Within two days they were back in sparsely forested hillsides. They built a large fire to warm their chilled bones. Walt made a pot of beans while Eli mixed up a batch of frying pan biscuits. They were still too high for most game. They had caught sight of some bighorn sheep in the distance.

Reiner broke out a bottle of rye and poured drinks for everyone after the meal. "Let's drink to plentiful beaver on the Green," he toasted. After the men drank, he continued. "We will reach the river in two more days. Beau and I will work the river north. Kinney, Walt and Eli will work south. I figure most of October is gone and in another month or so, the snow and ice will make trapping near impossible. We'll meet at the shanty and winter. Last time I was in this area, I saw plenty of grizzly sign. They should be about ready to den up for the winter. If you get the opportunity, pick your shot carefully. The hide can replace a lot of beaver."

The leader couldn't help but look at Walt as he spoke of the bears. He had put Eli with Kinney because Walt worked best with a partner. After the second round of drinks, the men turned in. Eli lay awake in his blankets. While he got along with everyone in the group, it did come as a surprise that he and Beau had been split up.

"You be careful out there. I won't be there to shoot the cat out of the tree for you," he whispered to his friend.

Beau didn't respond, but he smiled. He had his own thoughts. He hadn't seen Reiner set a single trap except for the first time when he'd instructed him and Eli. Thinking about the frigid water, he hoped that it didn't continue.

The group killed a young bull elk the day they arrived at the Green River. Beau and Eli skinned and butchered the animal. The meat would last in the cold weather, so they didn't have to dry it. After the meat was divided, each team headed out. Beau felt the loss of the companionship of his young black friend. It had been many months now that they had depended on each other.

Reiner started to shift the packs around as the others headed south. "We'll both be walking soon enough. I figure by sharing our gear and supplies, we can both start out riding."

Coming down to the Green River, the leader had spotted a large pond about five miles away. He was anxious to get there and find out if it was made by beavers. The two men rode out with Beau holding the lead rope of the mule. He sat on his pony behind the sawbuck pack saddle, which held some of the supplies.

The pond had several lodges. While Beau set up camp in a grove of aspen, Reiner scouted the streams and pond for active runs. The golden leaves had fallen from the trees and created a thick blanket beneath them, their bare branches reaching for the sky. Some of the tender ends would make good feed for the stock.

The sun was setting when Reiner returned. "The pond was worked by trappers early in the season. I found their old camp a half-mile from here. I did see a fair amount of fresh sign, so come tomorrow we will put in traps."

Beau liked the word "we" in the sentence. They ate their fill of elk steaks that night. The rest of the meat was suspended high in an aspen tree. The mule and horses were picketed on some short grass in the trees. The men crawled into their blankets with the smell of snow in the air. While he hadn't expected it, Beau was anxious to start trapping again.

CHAPTER TEN

After a meal of weak coffee and roasted strips of elk whittled off a frozen haunch, the two men were ready to set their traps. Reiner said he was heading for the far side of the pond. Beau loaded his traps and sticks onto the pony. He'd be working the near side. Before leaving the camp, he put wood onto the fire, banking the ashes on the edges. When he got back from setting the traps in the icy water, he wanted to be able to build the fire up quickly.

Beau cut a chew of tobacco and stuffed it into his cheek. He led the pony toward the pond, his now experienced eye looking for the best places to set his traps. He came to a half-chewed aspen and found an entry path nearby. Tying the pony a short distance away, he spat. "May as well get my feet wet, horse."

Beau sported a full beard and his brown, curly hair was below his ears. Pulling the Colt out of his waistband, his stuck it into his possible bag. His rifle was slung on the pony alongside the pack. Shedding his buckskin britches and wool trousers, he put on his low moccasins. The cold air cut through the legs of his long johns.

Wading into the water, he went to work setting the trap. Emerging from the water, his teeth were chattering. He put the buckskin britches back on and pulled on the calf high moccasins. Shaking the water out of the wet moccasins, he took the pony's lead rope and went to look for his next spot. This act was repeated until four traps were set.

Beau then hurried back toward the camp. His feet and legs were numbed. He tied the pony to a sapling near the camp and quickly went to the fire. While the flames were gone, the remaining coals gave off welcomed heat. He added wood to the coals and spat the used tobacco chew into the ashes, spittle dribbling onto his beard.

As Beau's feet began to warm, he felt pins and needles from the circulation returning. Sitting on a log next to the fire, he curled and uncurled his toes against the pain. As soon as the long john legs dried a bit, he would pull the wool trousers back on.

Reiner returned, his buckskins frozen stiff. He had always kidded Beau about taking his pants off before entering the water. He said, "Levesque, a real trapper ain't never caught without his britches."

Continuing, he said, "More than one trapper come out of the water after setting traps to find his animal and all his gear had been taken by one of the local braves, or chased off by wolves, leaving him in a hard way."

Beau pulled the Colt from his possible bag. "Should that happen, I will send a parting shot after the culprits."

The pond yielded six plew quality pelts. They had to be careful skinning the beaver. As much water as possible had to be removed from the fur before starting. The surface had to be one that the fine outer hair of the pelt wouldn't freeze to. Pulling it loose from something it had frozen to could reduce the value of the plew.

Throughout the month of November, Reiner and Beau trapped the tributaries running into the Green River. They worked up one side of the river and then started down the other. The days were sunny and cold, while the nights were frigid. In many cases they had to remove ice to set their traps.

Beau was sitting in camp, skinning one of the two beavers he had in his traps. He glanced up at the clouds building over the mountains. "Could be some snow coming, horse," he said to the pony tied next to him. "It must be the end of November, maybe even December."

The animal snorted, causing the young man to smile at it. "Now, was that agreeing with me or not?"

"Hey, Levesque!" He looked up from his task and saw Reiner riding toward the camp, leading his mule. "We best keep our eye on the clouds. Could be a storm brewing!"

Finishing the skinning, Beau wiped his hands in the snow and then warmed them over their fire. "I noticed that they've been building up pretty good," he replied. "Any luck this morning?"

"Got one plew," the leader said.

"I'm all set up here," Beau said. "Toss it over and I'll skin it. After I finish, I will set up the fly tarp."

The wind was starting to gust, hitting the camp harder than usual. A few stray flakes were in the air.

By the time he finished the skinning, Beau noticed that the mountains were shrouded in snow.

"You best save the stretching and fleshing for later. We got to move to the trees," Reiner said. "With what's coming, the tarp would be gone in no time."

Sensing the urgency in the leader's voice, Beau began to break camp. They loaded the packs onto the mule and horses and headed away from the river, toward the growth of spruce trees. Choosing one with branches close to the ground, Reiner turned to the young man. "Collect us a good-size pile of wood. I'll start making a shelter."

With the wind tearing at his buckskins, Beau began piling branches and smaller windfalls near the new camp. The leader had made them a shelter under the spruce tree by pulling several of the upper branches together, then removing some of the lower branches and weaving them into the sides. The opening was downwind, with plans to build their fire near the opening. Several additional spruce nearby helped to cut the howling wind.

By the time that this was finished the wind was driving pellets of snow, which stung when it hit their faces. A short distance from the shelter, the two men stretched a picket line between two trees and tied the stock, allowing them to keep their backs to the storm.

Most of the packs were placed around the perimeter of the spruce to offer the men additional protection. By this time, the wind-blown snow made even the simplest task difficult. Reiner was able to build a small fire and put on some water for coffee. Beau arranged the packs they had brought into the shelter. They used some of the beaver meat for their meal.

By the time they had eaten, the full force of the blizzard had hit them. With the blinding snow, any movement away from the shelter would be taking one's life into one's hands. Despite the attempts to secure the shelter from the storm, some snow still blew through under the spruce. For three days, the blizzard tore at the crude shelter.

When they awoke the morning of the fourth day, there were just a few lazy flakes falling. Emerging to check out the effects of the storm, they found some places blown clear, while others had 10-foot high drifts. Much of the sheltered areas had snow to their waists.

While Reiner cleared away an area to start a fire, Beau went to check on the stock. The mule's and horses' winter hair was covered with snow. He cleared the frozen crust from around their eyes and noses. The animals had stood close together, their rumps to the storm. He led the animals through the deep snow, looking for some relief and some branches or brown grass to graze on.

The mountain-bred animals didn't hesitate to start pawing at the snow to expose the grass below. Unable to drive picket stakes into the frozen ground, Beau tied them to low brush or saplings. He headed back to the shelter. The leader had coffee ready and some chunks of beaver meat in the frying pan.

"I fear our trapping has been cut short by the storm," he said. "In the morning, we'll continue south and keep our eye open for any open water with beaver sign."

Smiling, Beau said, "I had read about the storms here in the west. The words on the pages came well short of just how weak one feels against such a blizzard."

While they chewed on the tough beaver meat, the sounds of wolves calling to each other reached them. Soon the remaining elk herds would become vulnerable to the hunting packs. Both men knew that their stock could also become the prey.

The swirling snow still obscured the mountains as they headed south. Their packs were now too heavy for both men to ride. Beau followed behind, leading his pony. Reiner's horse broke path when necessary. They camped on the lee side of a limestone butte. Beau was able to scrape and stretch the last of their beaver pelts.

"We are about a week north of the valley with the shanty," the leader said, "then another day's walk into the valley and we'll have all the comforts of home."

"I'm looking forward to seeing Eli," Beau said.

"While it ain't none of my business, talk at the rendezvous was he was a runaway," Reiner said.

"I met Elijah on the trail west," Beau said. After rolling his tobacco to the other cheek, he continued. "I reckon we both had reasons for coming to the mountains."

"He's a good man to travel with," the leader said. "You both are damn fine mountain men."

After a few days resting up at the butte, the two men continued toward the valley. That afternoon, Reiner pulled up and pointed to the southwest. "We got a pond yonder. It must have some springs, because I see open water."

The men stopped just shy of the pond and set up camp. Beau had mixed feelings. He had been looking forward to some months without wading in the icy water. Yet the catch to date hadn't been as good as they had hoped, and any additional pelts would be helpful.

Reiner rode away to scout the pond while Beau set up camp in some aspens. Movement caught his eye as he was picketing the pony. It was a good-sized snowshoe rabbit. Drawing the revolver from his waistband, he watched for it to come out from behind some brambles. The waiting game between prey and hunter went on for several minutes.

All of a sudden, the rabbit's head appeared from behind the snow-covered brush. Without hesitating, Beau lined up the sights and fired. A few minutes later Reiner came back leading his horse.

"Hey Levesque," he called. "I hope the hell that shot was supper. I was leaning over the dam and nearly fell in at the sound."

"We'll be eating roast rabbit tonight," he replied. "It's a big one. Should make a fine hat with the skin."

While they were enjoying the tender rabbit, Reiner let Beau know what he had found. "We got us several beavers in the pond. We also got wolves. They been circling the pond, trying to get at the beaver."

"We best keep our rifles loaded and with us at all times," Beau suggested.

"I wouldn't mind bagging a couple of them," the leader said. "Last rendezvous a wolf was worth two beavers."

The next morning, they headed out to set their traps. Beau headed beyond the pond to check out a rising mist. He found one of the reasons that the pond was still open. There was a pool of water from a heated spring. The excess spilled over the edge and flowed downhill into the pond. Sticking his hand into the water, he found it tolerably warm. It would be perfect for a bath before they left the area.

After finding areas to set their traps, the two men returned to the camp. "Did you see the tracks, Beau?" Reiner asked. "The wolves have checked out our camp. They were fearful to come in too close."

"I did see them," he answered. "I also found a warm spring that will be good for bathing. Maybe some laundry."

Snorting, the leader said, "Mountain men don't do laundry. When your clothes fall off, you get some more, or do without."

The men's kidding and laughter were heard by the dark forms lying in the snow beyond the firelight. The wolves tested the air. While they were tempted by the smell of the stock, the odor of man was a strong deterrent.

The morning was crisp as Beau crawled out of his blankets. Fog rose off the warmer pond water. The brightness of the sun made him squint as he looked over the river valley. He heard Reiner getting up. "It's a great day to be alive." the leader exclaimed.

"I'll check on the animals while you get the fire going," Beau said as he walked into the aspen. The horses and mule were dozing in the morning sunshine. "Time to wake up, you cayuses!"

The ground around the animals had been well-pawed to get at the grass below, and all of the reachable aspen branches were chewed. Walking toward the pond, Beau saw the tracks of their night visitors. So far, they remained well away from their camp.

Reiner had the coffee on when he returned. "Wolves have been checking us out," he told the leader.

"Any beaver we catch here, we'll skin down near the pond," Reiner said. "No sense in having the smell of a fresh kill drawing the critters into our camp."

The two men chewed on jerky and drank coffee made with last night's grounds. Some of their luxuries, such as coffee beans, were getting low. Their packs also carried a sack of tea leaves for later use.

Reiner headed out for his traps first. He was leading his horse and mule. Walking would help him stay warm in the frigid morning. Beau finished cleaning up after their simple breakfast and secured the camp before leaving.

He had two traps set in the pond. Both were empty. After a quick check of the set, he added a little more castor to the bait sticks. He then led the pony up a stream feeding into the pond. Even before he reached the first trap there, he could see that it had been triggered. The bait stick was knocked down and the securing stick was leaning a little toward the center of the stream.

Tying the pony downstream a bit, he pulled off the calf-high moccasins and stripped to his long johns from the waist down. He put the Colt into his possible bag and pulled on the stiff, low-cut moccasins. Shivering, he waded into the water, thinking, Too bad this isn't coming from the warm spring.

Feeling around the bottom in the knee-deep water, he found the beaver. Dragging the trap and his catch into the shallows, Beau removed the beaver and tossed it onto the bank. Then, giving the securing stick a few raps with his hatchet, he set and placed the trap.

While applying the castor, he heard the pony snorting. "Be patient, horse. I'm about done here."

Moving back downstream, Beau walked out of the water and grabbed his catch on the bank. His hands throbbed from the cold and the wet long johns offered no protection to his legs. Water squished in the soaked moccasins. As he approached the horse, he hesitated, dropping the beaver. The pony was looking intently toward the brush beside the stream.

Reaching into his possible bag, Beau withdrew the Colt Paterson. He was hardly able to hold on to the revolver with his stiff fingers. Straining his eyes, he tried to see what was bothering the horse. He saw a shadow move in the undergrowth and then it was gone.

The pony snorted and stomped in defiance to the unwelcome visitor. "You're a good horse. Whatever it was, you'd kick its butt if it got any closer," Beau said. He began to dress, his teeth chattering from the cold, then put the revolver back into his waistband. He had no doubt that it was a wolf following him.

Reaching the second trap, Beau found that it had not been sprung. After applying a bit more castor, he led the pony into the aspens a short distance and began to skin his catch. Several times he had to stick his hands inside his buckskins to warm his hands. He cut some of the meat from the carcass to have for the mid-day meal.

Beau was putting the meat into the pack on his pony when he heard a growl behind him. Wheeling around, his heel caught a chewed stump and he fell back, landing in a small, frozen pothole. Not ten feet away was a large wolf holding what was left of the beaver carcass. There were the shrill cries of the pony as it pulled on the lead rope to get away.

Without even thinking, Beau drew the Colt and fired after the fleeing wolf. A yelp from the wolf told him that he had hit the animal. The shot had caused the wolf to drop the beaver. From out of nowhere, a second wolf appeared, grabbing the skinned carcass and disappeared into the brush.

The cold forgotten, Beau scrambled to his feet and ran a few steps in the direction the wolves had gone. The fearful protests of the pony stopped him and he hurried back to the animal. The sapling that it was tied to had snapped but had not broken free.

Beau grabbed the halter rope and tried to calm the pony. "Getting to be mighty damn brave," he said as he rubbed the horse's neck.

"It's the smell of blood that makes them forget their fear," Reiner said when he heard about the confrontation. The two men sat near the fire, roasting the beaver meat using green aspen sticks. "If your shot at the first one was crippling, the other will kill it and make it the next meal."

"I should have followed it into the brush," Beau said. "For all I know, it only ran a short distance."

"You done the right thing," Reiner replied. "With a scared horse and fresh meat in your pack, the wisest thing was to get back to camp."

The leader had caught two beavers and had brought them back into camp. They were laid near the fire to prevent them from freezing. He intended to go toward the pond and skin them after he ate. Beau kept changing position as he roasted his meat.

"You sitting on an ant hill?" Reiner asked.

"When I fell, I banged up my tailbone," the young man replied.

"I got to thinking about what you said yesterday," the leader said. "I think we should go up to that warm spring and have a good soak. It will help take the bruise out of your butt."

After the beavers were skinned and the hides fleshed and stretched, Reiner hung them in an aspen near the pond. Then, taking their animals with them, the two men headed for the warm spring.

With the steam rising around them, the two men soaked in the soothing water. "I can't remember the last time I truly felt warm," Beau said.

Reiner scoffed when the young man took his dirty clothing and soaked it in the spring. "Your gonna give us mountain men a bad name."

The heat did help Beau's bruised tailbone. The two men sat in the spring for over two hours before climbing out and sitting on the edge to dry off. All of the young man's dirty clothes lay next to him, wrung dry the best he could. He would hang them on the aspen branches and let them freeze dry.

The two men arrived back at their camp in high spirits. When they saw that their beaver pelt packs had been torn open, anger soared through them. "Damn wolves are coming right into camp!" Reiner snapped.

A quick investigation told them that only a couple of pelts had been pulled out of the torn canvas packs. "It appears that the wolves are hungrier than they are scared," Beau concluded.

"I guess it could have been worse," Reiner said. "They went after the smell of beaver and left the food supplies alone."

Beau got out some waxed string and a large darning needle. He began to repair the torn canvas.

Reiner was still mad and sat looking out into the valley. "Got to make them pay. Them pelts had a value."

"What you got in mind?" Beau asked as he worked on the canvas.

"A couple of wolf skins would make us more than even," he replied.

Stopping his sewing, the young man replied, "I say we go after them."

"Can you hit a target at 100 paces?" the leader asked.

"I have been known to," Beau replied, stopping his sewing. "Of course, it depends on the size."

"Wolf size," Reiner said. "Big old wolf size."

While Beau finished repairing the pack, the leader rode out on his horse. Retrieving the two beaver carcasses he had hung near the pond, he rode out into the valley and tied the two bloody remains securely to two aspen that stood out by themselves. He then rode in a wide circle and returned to camp.

They had pulled a windfall near the camp to sit behind and support their rifles for the shot. It would be another three hours before dark. The moon had been almost full, so if necessary they might get a shot after dark.

Getting comfortable behind the windfall, the men watched. Looking around, Reiner grumbled, "With all your damn laundry hanging around here, the wolves will be scared away for miles."

"Who knows, they might take a fancy to a clean shirt," Beau kidded.

The men hoped that hunger had made the wolves more aggressive and less careful. After an hour of watching they caught a glimpse of movement within the aspen grove. Reiner kicked Beau with his toe. "You awake? Did you see that?"

"Sure did," the young man whispered.

The two men lay behind the log with their rifles at the ready, not daring to move. They had seen no less than three wolves trying to decide if they wanted to come out after the beaver. The men planned to wait until the wolves were at both beavers before taking a shot. Suddenly, a lighter colored animal dashed out of the trees and sunk its teeth into the closer carcass. Being unable to pull it lose, it ran back for cover.

Beau felt his heart pounding under his shirt. The thrill of the hunt had always excited him. If the wolves refused to come out and stay near the beavers, they might have to take a snap shot at a running wolf. The odds of a kill shot at this distance was slim.

All of a sudden, Beau's breath caught. Blinking his eyes, he realized that there were three wolves standing just outside the aspen. The lighter colored one and two dark ones. He heard Reiner whisper, "You take one on the right, I'll take one on the left. You fire first."

Reiner's Hawken was percussion and would fire instantly when the trigger was pulled. Beau's flintlock would have a slight hesitation. Now all their waiting depended on a steady eye. The young man fought to control his breathing as he took careful aim at one of the wolves. Slowly he squeezed the trigger.

Fire belched from both rifles almost simultaneously. The flash of the powder in Beau's pan obscured the target momentarily. Reiner jumped up and ran to his horse, which was saddled and ready near the camp. He galloped down the valley. In his hand he was carrying Beau's Colt.

Standing up, the young man could see one wolf down, kicking its last on the snow. The other they'd shot at could not be seen. He was sure that the one he could see was the one that Reiner had shot. Beau feared that he might have disappointed the leader. All it took was a slight flinch and the shot could go wide. He had also heard of men taking aim on longer shots and not realizing that the animal had moved just prior to firing.

He watched as Reiner checked the downed wolf. He then ran into the aspen, disappearing. There was the sound of a gunshot. Beau was hopeful. Maybe the one he had shot was severely wounded and had made it into the trees but couldn't get away. Either way, he felt better hearing the shot from Reiner.

Realizing that he was standing without a loaded gun, Beau measured powder into the rifle. Then he removed an oil patch from the brass patch box built into the stock. Wrapping it around the .54 caliber ball, he tamped it home with the rod. He was pouring some powder into the pan when he looked up and saw Reiner riding back.

With his rifle loaded, Beau waited. He was relieved when he noticed that there was more than one wolf at the end of the rope that Reiner was dragging behind the horse. As Reiner rode up, surprise showed on Beau's face.

"Three?" he questioned.

"That was a damn good shot you took, Levesque. One you shot clear through and then hit the wolf behind it, breaking its back. The one with the broken back and was trying to drag itself away, so I shot it again." Laughing as he dismounted, he pulled the wolves forward. "We got more than payback for the pelts they stole."

They skinned the wolves by the light of their fire and the moon. "Their young'uns. Maybe two-years old. More than likely poor hunters," Reiner pointed out. "I don't know what happened to their elders, but these pups were looking for ways to stop from starving."

He then pointed to a burn mark on the thigh of the light-colored wolf. "Looks like you were into this one twice. Here is where your Colt hit earlier."

Before dragging the wolf carcasses away from the camp, Reiner took several cuts of meat. Wolf wasn't a favorite of his, but any fresh meat available at the onset of winter was a good thing. Their side meat was almost gone and they had eaten more of their jerky than the leader had wanted. They had had beaver to eat most every day during prior winters.

While the leader was gone, Beau put frames together to stretch the skins. He ran his finger through the thick, soft fur. "I might have to make a coat out of a couple of these." The pony nickered as usual at the sound of the young man's voice.

The next morning, Beau hurried in the cold, taking his clothes off the aspen branches. The frigid air had removed most of the moisture. He donned one of the washed pairs of long johns. There was the familiar itch of the clean wool clothes. Soon the oil and sweat on his skin would eliminate the discomfort.

Reiner decided to stay in the area a few more days before heading for the shanty. "We will have a chance for another bath," Beau suggested.

His suggestion brought a snort from the leader. The dry mountain air did a good job on the wolf skins.

They caught two more beavers from the pond. Any howls of wolves were now only in the distance. There were large, lazy flakes falling when the men struck their camp.

The trappers went around the end of the pond, fording the small stream that flowed into the Green River. The leader was looking out over the valley. A hiss from Beau caught his attention. The young man was pointing toward the steaming spring. It was surrounded by several large, wooly beasts. Buffalo.

Reiner swung down from the horse, excited. "Damn it Levesque. This is a pond that just keeps on giving."

The spring was 800 paces away, twice the effective range of the Hawken carried by Reiner. Beau would not have felt confident shooting such a large beast unless he was something less than half that distance. There was open ground between them and the buffalo. To their right were the aspen that surrounded the pond.

Whispering, the leader told Beau, "Buffalo don't scare easy. I think we can walk alongside our horses and get in close enough for a shot. The wind is in our favor, and if they look this way, they'll just see the horses, which they have no fear of."

"Your Hawken has better accuracy and range than the 1803," the young man said. "You should take the shot as soon as possible."

"All we can carry is the meat and hide of one buff," Reiner said. "You can take the shot if you want."

"You know your rifle, best. You take the shot," Beau said.

As they slowly moved toward the spring, Reiner continued to talk softly. "I hunted these woolly beasts for two summers. Many a time I stood and shot a dozen animals and they would just continue grazing. Then next time, one shot and they were off. I had one charge me once. It killed the horse I was riding. Climbing on the hide wagon was the only thing that saved me. All in all, they are unpredictable."

The leader stopped about 300 paces from the spring. They were near a wash that ran to the left of the spring. "You hold the animals here," Reiner said. "I will crawl up the dry bed and try and get a bit closer. If they run before I shoot, you try for one, and aim at the lead buff."

Beau crouched next to the horses and watched Reiner's slow progress. So far, the buffalo had paid no attention to them. The meat from one of the beasts would feed the company for a month. There could be several uses for the hide, not to mention it could be sold.

The young man felt his heart start to beat more rapidly as he saw Reiner position himself to fire. There was a large bull standing a short distance from the others. Beau guessed that it was the animal he was aiming at.

At the sound of the Hawken, Beau's eyes were fixed on the bull. It didn't move. Could Reiner have missed? He was beginning to wonder if he should take a shot when movement from the rest of the herd caught his attention. Lying on its side was a buffalo. The others were moving around it, as though to protect the downed animal.

Beau saw Reiner finish reloading his Hawken, then, ducking low, he hurried back along the wash.

The bull that the young man had been watching advanced a few steps toward the movement. It snorted clouds of frozen breath and moved its head back and forth.

Watching the bull to make sure it didn't continue toward Reiner, the young man held the rifle at the ready. He breathed a sigh of relief when the leader arrived back at the horses.

Gasping to catch his breath, Reiner said, "The others are protecting the buff I killed. I seen 'em do that before. I noticed the bull watching me. Good thing it didn't come at me."

For an hour, the men watched the buffalo stand around the dead animal. Finally, Reiner said, "Take the mule and your horse into the trees. I am going to ride up there and try to chase them buggers off. Another hour and we'll have to use our hatchets to skin the buff."

Once Beau got into the aspen, he heard the leader take off. Shouting at the top of his lungs, Reiner charged the buffalo, his horse at a full gallop. Beau saw the protective animals lower their heads and watch the oncoming charge. As he got closer, the buffalo began to mill. They were either going to charge or run. The young man prayed that they would run.

Suddenly the herd broke, running down the valley, their tails in the air. "All right!" Beau shouted as he ran, leading the animals toward the spring. Reiner was already on his knees making the first slits for skinning the buffalo.

Looking up, he smiled. "I was only a couple seconds from wheeling the horse around and putting distance between me and the buff, when they give up and run."

The animal Reiner had shot was as large as the one Beau had been watching. The massive size impressed the young man. As they worked at removing the hide, he couldn't imagine doing this to a dozen or more animals each day. They worked, trying to keep the dirt off the meat while removing the hide. Then Reiner slit the stomach open. Removing the heart and liver, he placed them on the hide. He then reached inside, cut the base of the tongue and withdrew it from the animal.

"Some good eating meat there," he said. Agreeing, Beau worked at removing the hind quarters. It was early afternoon when they finished butchering the buffalo. The meat was tied in the hide and then lifted onto Reiner's horse. The young man smiled, thinking, He will be walking the rest of the way.

They dragged the remaining carcass a short distance away from the spring, before cleaning up in the warm water. Reiner started a fire and the two men sat roasting strips of liver. Their mid-day meal was enjoyed with a pot of coffee.

"Beats the hell out of wolf meat," the leader said. With juice dripping down his beard, Beau nodded in agreement.

Good travel and fair weather brought the men to the valley mouth five days later. Reiner led the way to a cluster of balsam trees. Evidence of previous camping let Beau know that this was probably a regular stop. A crude lean-to was nestled in the evergreens, and a snow-covered fire pit surrounded by logs for sitting was situated in front. While Beau pulled the packs off the animals, the leader cleared snow from the pit and front of the lean-to.

After he got the fire going, Reiner crawled into the lean-to and brought out a folded piece of paper. Getting comfortable on one of the logs, he opened it.

> We was here on the full moon. Not many beavers. Saw some grizz sign. No luck gitting it. See you at the shanty.
> Kinney

"That would have been a week ago," Reiner said. "A grizzly hide would make up for lots of beaver."

"You always leave notes in the lean-to?" Beau asked.

"Been doing it the last few years," he replied. "Helps let the teams know where each other are."

The young man sat at the fire putting their meal together, feeling a sense of excitement inside. Here in the middle of the wilderness, they had just gotten mail. The emptiness of the mountains felt just a bit less lonely.

The next morning, Beau emerged from the lean-to, anxious to get started. He was looking forward to seeing Eli and comparing their experiences of the past month. Reiner sat near the fire with a chew of tobacco, smiling at his young companion.

"You seem mighty fidgety this morning," he said.

"I must admit, I am in a hurry to be heading for the shanty," Beau replied.

"Well, don't get your hopes up too much," Reiner told him. "We put it up in a hurry some years back, and it is kinda small. By the time the snow melts, you'll be damn glad to be leaving it."

"Don't matter," the young man replied. "Eli and the others will be there. For me, it will be like coming home."

An hour later the two men were leading their animals into the valley. Snow was falling and made seeing any distance difficult. Beau got the sense that the valley was getting wider as the morning went on. Before they had left the shanty, Reiner had left a note. He didn't tell Beau what he'd wrote or who it was for.

The men's beards were coated with the fine flakes as it blew in their faces. The snow was knee-deep with a light crust. They chose to walk side by side, leading the animals. Reiner entertained Beau with past hunting stories. The leader had some cold buffalo meat to eat mid-day as they continued to walk.

The snow ended shortly after they had eaten. The sandstone walls of the valley rose skyward on both sides. Weather and wind had sculpted the walls, leaving stone chimneys and pinnacles to be marveled at. Gnarled trees and brush grew in the rubble of collapsed sandstone rocks along the base of the walls.

Then the valley opened into a wide basin that continued to drop in elevation as far as the eye could see. "A fair amount of game likes to winter in this area," Reiner said. "The basin must drop a mile to the back, where it comes up against the North Beaver."

"Any beaver in this basin?" Beau asked.

"Was full of beaver in the streams, but they've been trapped out long ago," Reiner said, regretfully.

All of a sudden, something that wasn't right caught Beau's attention. It was most of a mile away, but seemed to have appeared from nowhere. It was dark against the bright snow. If it was an animal, it had to be facing in their direction. Turning to Reiner, he told him, "We might have some more meat ahead."

The two men held up and Beau turned to point at the animal, but it had disappeared. Blinking several times, the young man wondered if his eyes had been playing tricks on him. "It's gone," he said.

"Could have been a deer, or even a shadow," Reiner suggested. "We are a couple hours from the shanty. If we see some tracks, you could come this way hunting tomorrow."

"I'll be ready to rest tomorrow and we got plenty of buffalo for a while," Beau told him. "Like you said, it was probably a shadow."

The two men continued down the basin, Beau watching for the tracks. Suddenly, he caught movement to his left. Turning, he swung his rifle, then broke into a broad smile. "Eli! You come to guide us in?"

"We're short fresh meat and I was hoping to bring down a deer," the slender black said as he walked over, his bow in his left hand, a quiver of arrows on his back.

Reiner slapped the buffalo hide on the horse. "We got plenty of meat for the time being. How was the shanty?"

"We had to do some work on the roof," Eli told him. "A couple poles had broken. The fix should keep the snow out for the rest of the winter."

The sun was low in the west when they reached the shanty. It was a low building with log walls and poles on the roof that overhung the back, offering storage. To the left was a mud and stick fireplace for heating and cooking. In the back was a lean-to for the animals and a rather large pole corral. Most days a couple of men would drive the stock out into the basin and let them forge for grass under the snow.

Beau entered the shanty, ducking under the low doorway. Three narrow, double high bunks lined two walls. In the middle of the room was a handmade table with two stools and a couple of split log benches. Next to the fireplace was a sideboard that held the cooking supplies. The floor was packed dirt. A lean-to that ran the length of the outside wall opposite the fireplace held their pelts and traps.

The overflow was stacked in the shanty, using up most of the spare space. It was apparent that one either sat at the table or laid in a bunk. There was a stack of wood next to the front door and another, smaller stack inside, near the fireplace. Candles or the fireplace were used for light. A small shelf held some books, a deck of cards, flint, striking steel, and writing material.

The dim shanty had a strong smell of the occupants and wood smoke. Beau smiled as he looked things over. It would be a fine winter home. His cabin on Crowley Ridge seemed long ago and far away. Here he was part of a team . . . a family.

The tight quarters were kept warm by the fireplace. A pot of water was kept heating at all times. Coffee was down to the last bag of beans. The men decided that a pot would be brewed once a week. Tea would be the morning drink until it was exhausted. They had another month's supply of beans and the same of cold flour. With the buffalo and wolf meat, they had enough to take them to the end of January. With the sedentary life, they ate only two meals a day.

While trapping the south part of the Green River, Kinney had traded some tobacco for two bags of pemmican. When the men made their first meal of the pemmican, they found it to be half pounded leaves and sticks. While they cussed plenty at the poor trade, they all knew that toward the end of the winter, it would all be eaten, sticks and all.

Eli had found two old saddles in the shanty. They had been there since the days of good trapping, when Reiner and Kinney had to use the riding horses to help pack out their catch. Both had been chewed on by hungry rodents and what was left of the straps was brittle.

The prior owners had no use for them, so Beau and Eli set to repairing the saddles. They could use the blankets from their sawbuck saddles with the repaired saddles to ride their ponies on their hunts. Reiner's only warning was, "Don't ride the meat off your stock. You'll be carrying your packs on your backs come spring."

Days were spent herding the stock, cutting wood, or hunting. A couple of trap lines were set for marten, fisher, raccoon, and other small animals. In the evenings the men read, played cards, repaired clothing and gear, or told yarns. The cooking was shared, although those with the knack were more often encouraged to make the meals. On calm nights, the men slept in the narrow bunks. When a storm blew, they would drag in their blankets near the fireplace and crowd together on the packed dirt.

Beau and Eli talked a lot about the grizzly sign that had been seen. The young black believed that he had found the den dug into soft, sandy soil at the base of a towering pine. The dirt and tracks had been fresh, but it would have been early for the bear to have gone into hibernation.

"Do you think you could find the den again?" Beau asked.

"It was a way up the slope on the north side. The pine could be seen from our last camp," Eli said. "Maybe a week's ride from here."

"At the rendezvous, we were told that they den up after the storms come," Beau recalled.

Agreeing, Eli said, "The storm just before we headed here would have driven it into the den."

The two young men talked for hours about the grizzly and how much the skin would be worth. While herding the stock one afternoon, they made their decision. The saddles were repaired and the weather was holding. Tonight, they would propose going after the bear to Reiner.

After a meal of boiled buffalo, the men settled in for the evening. Wes and Kinney were playing cards, while Reiner was whittling. Beau and Eli sat on the floor next to the leader. "Eli and I would like to go after the grizzly."

Reiner stopped his whittling and slowly closed his clasp knife. Setting it into his possible bag, he looked at the two men. "What grizz would that be?"

Eli told him about the den near their last camp. With the look of doubt on his face, Reiner said, "Grizz are hard to kill. Many a man's life has been cut short by coming face to face with the big silver tips."

Beau chimed in, "We got us a plan. The bear should be sleeping now. We locate the den and crawl into the opening and kill the thing before it even knows we're there."

"You ever poked at a sleeping bear before?" Reiner asked. "I've heard stories of the damn things coming out of a den with blood in their eye in the dead of winter. It's like they're waiting for you before you reach the den."

No amount of discouragement deterred the young men. They had a plan and felt it was fool proof. Finally, Reiner said, "I want you two to think on it for a day or two. If you haven't changed your minds, I'll send you off with a week's rations."

"It will take us a week to reach the den," Beau objected.

"Why hell, you'll be eating bear meat after that," the leader said, chiding the young trappers.

Little did the two young men realize that Reiner didn't ever expect to see them again after going after the grizzly. It didn't make sense to waste their scarce rations. Reiner hoped that the men would change their minds.

CHAPTER ELEVEN

Once they'd been bitten by the thought of bagging a grizzly, there was no changing the young men's minds. They packed extra clothing with their blankets. Ground cloths protected the outside of the blanket rolls. The round-bellied ponies were in reasonable shape for the trip. They used the experience gained working for Peter to get their rifles and revolver into top working order. Sitting in front of the fireplace, Beau melted lead and poured it into their molds for extra bullets.

The air was cold and the sun was shining the morning they left. Their three fellow trappers stood outside the shanty and wished them well. Reiner handed Beau a small leather bag containing a handful of coffee beans. "Save it until you get the bear, and then brew a pot to drink to your success."

There was worry in the leader's face. He felt responsible for each man on his team. One man had already been lost, and should something happen to Beau or Eli, he would have to live with that. With smiles of confidence on their faces, the young men waved and turned their horses up the valley, starting their quest to get the silver tip.

Their saddles didn't have stirrups and even if they had, the calf-high moccasins would have been too wide to fit. The ponies stepped out briskly, looking forward to travel. They used simple hackamores to control the horses.

They carried their rifles across the front of their saddles. The broad belt on the outside of their buckskins held a knife and hatchet. Their powder horns were in their possible bags with other items needed for living in the wild. Eli carried his bow and quiver of arrows tied to his blanket roll. Both men carried a water bag under their buckskin coats to prevent freezing.

The sun was low in the winter sky behind them, eliminating the glare from the snow. Every hour the men would slide off their ponies and lead them, giving the horses a breather and help keep themselves warm. They planned to ride to the lean-to the first day, then head down the Green River valley to find the bear den.

While leading the horses, Eli suddenly asked, "I wonder if it has been Christmas yet?"

"I hadn't thought about, it," Beau said. "Could be coming up, I suppose."

Eli began to sing a Christmas hymn. Smiling, Beau joined in. By the time the two men reached the lean-to they were both feeling the Christmas spirit. The snow-covered campsite looked much the same as it had the last time Beau had been there. After pulling the saddles off the ponies, they found a place to tie them for the night that would provide some grass and branches to chew.

Eli got a fire going and was melting snow in a small pot. He had two pieces of frozen meat that would be their meal once thawed and roasted. Forcing sticks into the meat, he set them over the fire. It had been 10 hours since they had eaten the cold flour porridge.

"I was hoping we'd see a rabbit or grouse today," the young black said.

"I agree, some fresh meat would be good," his friend said. Thinking back, Beau added, "I hunted a lot of bear back on the ridge. If we do find the den, not only will the meat help out, but the fat will be good. I used to make more money from the fat than the meat."

For the first time, Eli sounded concerned. "When we find the den, you won't take any chances, Beau."

"From what I've heard, this grizzly is much more dangerous than the black bear I hunted in the past, and they were bad enough. We won't take any chances."

It was fully dark when the meal was done. After checking on the horses, the men crawled into the lean-to. Using their saddles for pillows, they settled in under the blankets. Beau laid his rifle under the edge of his blanket and the revolver under the saddle. They didn't have to worry too much about danger in the dead of winter, but it paid to be careful.

The next morning, before leaving the lean-to, Beau wrote a short note: *Gone hunting grizzly.* He stuck it in the crack in the log with the other note. He hoped to add, *Got the grizzly,* on his return to the shanty. Feeling cold and stiff, the two men led the horses until their limbs warmed up.

Three days later, Eli got two rabbits with his bow. The extra meat was a welcome addition to the lean mountain men's diet. They took time to scrape the skins. The fur would be helpful to line their moccasins if needed. The men talked little that night, knowing that they were getting close to their quest.

Arriving at the campsite near the den, the men tied their ponies in the aspen. Eli pointed to the tall pine about a half-mile away. "It dug its den under that tree."

It was late afternoon when they arrived, so the decision was to stay clear of the den until morning. Should the bear be wounded and require tracking, they would have all day to do so.

"You realize that the bear may not have used the den," Beau said that night while chewing on jerky.

"There was a good amount of dirt dug out of the hole," Eli said. "If it had hit boulders or hardpan, the bear wouldn't have worked on the den as long."

Both men sat with their own thoughts. Who would go in and take the shot? That question had not been answered. If the den was empty, they had little food to get back to the shanty. And then again, what if the bear was in the den? Beau thought about the amount of lead the much smaller black bear could take without being killed.

Neither hunter slept well that night. It was mostly the excitement of killing a silver tip and bringing the prize back to the shanty. The howling of wolves in the distance and the hoot of an owl nearby were the only sounds they heard as they lay awake.

The wind had picked up, driving a light snow as the two men finally crawled out of their blankets. The sky was overcast, threatening more snow. "We best make a plan in case this becomes a blizzard," Beau suggested.

"Once we kill the bear, we could use its den," Eli said, chuckling at his reply.

"In that case, we should put off killing it and let the bear help keep us warm," Beau replied.

His face becoming more serious, Eli said, "The Flathead tell the story of a brave that was cold and looking for shelter. He met a bear that was hungry. The bear invited him into his warm den. Later, the bear came out. No longer was he hungry, nor was the brave cold."

"In that case, should we become cold, we won't look to the bear for warmth," Beau said. Suddenly, they both burst out laughing, releasing some of the tension.

They found a cut in the rocks just above the grove of aspen. It would give them some protection should the wind and snow get worse. They tied the horses near the rocks, making sure it was a loose tie just in case. The two men then readied their rifles.

Arriving at the tall pine, they found the base of it covered with a deep drift. "I sure wish we had a shovel right now," Eli said.

Not far away they found a tree that had been killed by a lightning strike. Large slabs of bark were loose. Tearing two good size pieces off, the two men returned to the drift. "We'll dig until we hit the opening," Beau whispered. "Then you move back with your rifle at the ready in case he comes out."

The two of them worked on the drift, removing blocks of packed snow. The progress with their crude tools was slow. After 30 minutes they hit some of the sandy soil that the bear had dug out. The two men rested for a moment. While the wind continued, the sun was now shining. The warmth felt good.

"We only have a couple more feet of snow, before we break through," Beau said, keeping his voice low. "You move back with your Hawken. I'll finish the digging."

Eli moved back several feet from the den. Nodding, Beau turned to continue digging. As he raised the slab of bark to cut into the snow, the drift in front of him exploded! The impact of the flying chunks of snow and the huge mass going by knocked him onto his back while a terrific roar erupted.

Fighting for breath and struggling to get away, Beau rolled, his hands over his face. There was a shot and the horrible sounds made by the silver tip. Everything seemed to be right on top of him. He couldn't open his eyes and he could taste blood in his mouth. Try as he might, he still couldn't breathe!

Beau was aware of someone, or something, pulling at him. Pain shot through his chest. He tried to cry out but ccould not make a sound. Everything went black . . . he was floating up and up. To where he didn't know, but he no longer felt pain or fear.

Eli stuck the butt of his rifle into the snow and hurried toward his friend. The bear had gone out of sight, up the hill. He gasped when he saw Beau's blood-covered face. His features were slack and the friend was dead weight as he pulled him away from the den. Whether Beau was breathing or not, he didn't know.

It had all happened so fast. Eli saw the drift in front of Beau burst out, followed by the bear. It had run right over his friend. After rolling and sliding a couple of feet, Beau laid still. The bear had turned back toward his injured friend when Eli had fired. That was when the silver tip ran.

Knowing that it could come back at any moment, Eli searched in the snow for Beau's rifle, which had been knocked over. His hand closed on the barrel and he pulled the Model 1803 from the snow. Leaving the injured man unattended for the moment, he brought it over to his Hawken. Leaning the rifle against a tree, he loaded the Hawken, his hands shaking. Eli didn't know if it was the cold or fear that was causing it.

"You best be alive, Beau." he shouted, as the growling and crashing of the bear continued above him in the trees.

* * *

All of a sudden, he was awake. Beau's eyes stung as he blinked to clear them. He was lying in some trees. He tried to sit up, and the pain in his ribs made him cry out and he collapsed backward. Gritting his teeth against the agony in his chest, the injured man again fought to breathe. He felt gentle hands holding him down.

"Stay down, Beau," Eli whispered. "You're safe. Just relax and breathe."

He lay waiting for the pain to subside. Finally, Beau was able to ask, "The bear . . . where is the bear?"

"Gone for now," Eli assured him. "The silver tip ran right over you. With the bright sun, it was unable to see right away and I managed to get a shot into it when it came back toward you. It turned and headed up the hill, making an awful racket. Your rifle was buried in the snow. I grabbed you and dragged you to the trees and got the Colt out before I went after the rifles. For an hour, I could hear the bear up on the hills."

Licking his dry lips, Beau said, his voice little more than a rasp, "I should have given you my rifle to hold." He lay breathing for a moment and then added, "I didn't expect it to come out like that. I figured we would be shooting a sleeping bear."

Eli helped Beau sit up and use an aspen to lean against. He gave his friend a mug of hot water. The tasteless brew felt good going down his throat. Beau coughed and froze for a second to let the pain pass.

"When I got to you, your face was covered with blood. I thought the bear had killed you. Turned out it had broken your nose. You also have a cracked rib, Beau," Eli told him. "I'm going to wrap it for you. It's going to hurt, but if I don't wrap it, you won't be able to move."

He went to the pack and came back with strips from a cotton shirt. While removing his friends buckskin coat and shirt, he said, "Once I do this, I'm going after the bear."

"No." Beau hissed, his throat soothed by the hot water. "Hell with the bear, Eli. We got to let it go. It's wounded and will be too dangerous to go after."

"For all we know, it's lying dead up on the hill," Eli objected. "It wouldn't be right to leave it to rot."

"A wounded bear will lie in wait for you," Beau warned. "If it is wounded too bad to run, it will do everything it can to catch and kill whatever is a danger to it."

Speaking calmly, the young black replied, "That will make it easier to find. I have stalked plenty of game. Once, I killed a wild boar with a spear."

Beau winced as his friend tied the strips around his chest. For the moment he was unable to speak. He knew the dangers of killing a wild boar and respected Eli's bravery, but one well-placed hit on a boar will kill it. The grizzly might take several shots, and still kill a man after the fatal one.

Realizing that he had been unconscious for some time, Beau figured it would be dark soon.

"Give me the night to rest, and then we'll both go after the bear. The sky has cleared and we shouldn't get snow tonight, so it will be easy to follow the animal," Beau suggested.

Eli feared that the silver tip would come back in the night. He wanted to make sure that the tracks led well away from their camp. He didn't tell this to his friend, and he doubted that Beau would be in any better shape to help track the animal tomorrow.

Before he had a chance to say anything else, Beau said, "Bring the ponies in. They will warn us if the big bugger comes back."

Neither man slept well. Eli lay with his Hawken at the ready and listened for any sound of the bear's return. Once, he heard the snapping of some twigs, but the horses didn't seem concerned by the noise. Beau awoke from the ache in his ribs every time he moved. While the wolves howled in the distance, the owl had moved on, no doubt due to the commotion of the bear.

It was still dark and Beau was sitting up when Eli threw off his blanket. "The ribs feeling better?" he asked.

Shaking his head, Beau replied, "Makes no difference. Lying or sitting up, they hurt the same. Only difference is now I can breathe through the pain."

They made breakfast from the last of their cold flour. Again, they drank hot water with the meal. "If we find the bear, we'll roast the beans and have some coffee," Eli said.

While Eli cleaned up after the meal, Beau took care of the ponies. He found that the pain was tolerable as long as he didn't make any sudden moves. It would get his attention if he coughed. The men took time making sure that their rifles had not been affected by the snow. They would have felt better if the rifles could have been shot and reloaded. They had no desire to do anything that would alert the bear.

Once again, they tied the horses, leaving the knots loose, just in case. Eli led the way up the hill. It wasn't until they had gone several paces up the hill before they sighted the first blood trail. It appeared that the bear had stopped and let out a growl, which forced blood to spray from the wound.

The two men spread out several paces. If they did come in contact with the animal, it wouldn't be able to attack them both, leaving the other to get off a shot. Beau's Colt was back in his waistband. While it wouldn't be very effective against a bear, it offered some comfort.

The tracks showed clearly that the bear had continued to run a short distance before stopping and looking for its attacker. Splintered trees and smashed brush marked the trail. The wounded animal was raging mad.

They found the area where the bear had ripped and torn up everything within reach. The blood trail had all but disappeared, which wasn't a good sign. The animal had thrown up once, and the evidence of blood was an indication that the bear may have been gut-shot. If that was the case, it would live for days, even weeks, before succumbing to the wound.

The tracks continued across a ridge about 1,000 feet above the camp. Then Beau felt a cold feeling inside. The bear was circling back. His first thought was that the animal was working its way back to wait at its backtrail, but they had come up and had not seen the bear. It must be heading toward the camp.

Fearing to call out, Beau raised his hand to get Eli's attention. He leaned against a lodgepole pine and waited for his friend. His ribs were throbbing and he felt weak. "What do you want?" Eli asked, whispering.

"I think the bear is headed back toward the camp. It may have been watching us this morning or may be after the horses," Beau said.

"We should go wide and hurry down the hill," Eli suggested. "We might get there before it gets the animals."

"I got to rest a minute," Beau replied. "I'm having trouble getting my wind."

"You're breathing too shallow due to the pain," Eli pointed out. "You wait here and I'll go down wide. You come when you can."

"The bear made this turn last night. It is already down the hill. More than likely it's just waiting for a chance at us," Beau said. "Then again, it might be headed back for its den. Give me a couple more minutes and we'll both go down. Let's keep to the tracks."

The curly-haired man stood, trying to remember everything he had learned about bears he had hunted. This bear could have made the turn and be waiting just a short distance in front of them. Walking back down the hillside was more painful than walking up. The jar of each step was felt in his ribs. Beau was also struggling not to slip on the snow-covered rocks.

Sure enough, the bear was headed toward its backtrail. Ahead of them, the tracks disappeared behind a thicket of balsam. The evergreen branches were weighted down to the ground by the snow. Beau motioned to Eli that he was going high around the balsam and that his young friend should go low.

The balsam thicket was about 30 feet long and as wide. Slowly, the two men walked around the balsam. Beau wished that the knee-deep snow made less noise as it crunched beneath his boots. A rock wall skirted the uphill side of the trees. Beau moved carefully, the rock brushing one side and the evergreens brushing the other. The snow became waist-deep between the two.

All of a sudden, he smelled the bear. Beau's heart began to pound. If it came at him, he would be trapped between the trees and rocks, mired down in the snow. Then came a snort! Unable to stop himself, he shouted, "It's in the trees!"

Then the snow gave way below him, and he felt himself sliding under the balsam branches. Desperately, he tried to bring his rifle around. He heard Eli shoot. Landing in an opening under the trees, the bear was 15 feet away. As he saw the bear standing, looking toward Eli, an arrow hit it in the neck. Beau lined up his rifle, hoping that the snow hadn't disabled it. He squeezed the trigger and the report of the rifle was deafening beneath the trees.

The bear wheeled around, then another arrow hit it in the shoulder. Beau jerked up his buckskin coat to get at the Colt. Pulling it free, he emptied the revolver into the behemoth. The bear roared, turned to run, and then collapsed at the edge of the thicket. Beau sat, unable to move as his legs were tangled in branches and his ribs were throbbing. He saw Eli moving slowly toward the grizzly. Poking it with the end of his bow, he said, "It's dead, Beau. We killed it."

With the help of his friend, Beau made his way over to the bear. "I'll go down and bring up a horse. You wait here," Eli said, taking charge.

Beau sat next to the grizzly. Pain racked his ribs from the fall under the branches. He thought about the number of shots it had taken to kill the animal. He knew that one well-placed bullet could do the job, but the silver tip lying in front of him hadn't stood still long enough to allow time for taking careful aim.

It took the men two hours to drag the bear down the hill. The thick brush and tree cover continually snagged the animal. Beau wished that he could have been more help, but he mostly stayed out of the way and followed the progress down. It was mid-afternoon when they made the camp. The temperatures were plunging. With his rib feeling a bit better, Beau pitched in skinning the bear, his Green River knife quickly removing the hide from the flesh. The head and paws were left attached to the hide.

As they worked, Beau said, "You were damn fast putting arrows in this bugger."

"I saw you come sliding in and figured I best keep its attention away from you," Eli replied.

"That was mighty thoughtful of you," the curly-haired young man replied.

As they skinned and butchered the grizzly, the two men looked for a kill shot. None of the rifle balls had hit a vital organ. The four shots from the Colt were nicely grouped, but had hardly penetrated the hide on the bear's chest. The arrow in the bear's neck had come close to the artery, but hadn't punctured it.

"I figure we put so much lead in the grizzly that it got too heavy to move," Eli kidded.

Laughing at his friend's joke, Beau replied. "We got lucky, Eli. We had put enough holes in it that the bear finally bled out."

"Yes, a lot of button holes in this hide," the young black said.

It was a sobering thought for both of the men, how much firepower it had taken to bring the silver tip down. Using the ponies and two lengths of rope, they raised the skinned carcass off the ground into a sturdy pine. In their urgency to get the bear skinned before it began to freeze, they hadn't started a fire. While Eli retrieved the heart and liver from the entrails, Beau started a cook fire. He then joined his friend to remove all the fat from the guts before they froze.

Beau also took one of the kidneys and the bladder, heading for the fire. The other kidney had taken a bullet. Eli was smiling when Beau joined him. He was heating a pot of water and roasting the coffee beans. "Our celebration drink," he said.

The men made their meal out of a good portion of the liver and the kidney. It was topped off with steaming cups of coffee. Beau reflected on the hunt. "Other than some banged-up ribs, I'd say we were very successful."

"We will definitely never forget the hunt," Eli said.

They sat around the fire well into the night, reliving the kill, quickly forgetting the danger they had faced and how easily it could have resulted in their deaths. The fire reflected off the large bear carcass. It resembled a huge, headless man hanging in the tree.

It took eight days to get back to the shanty. The bear had been loaded onto the two ponies' and the men walked single file, leading them. The celebration grounds were used for making four more pots of coffee before they became too weak to use. They spent a day and a half hunkered down while a storm blew through. Beau added to his note in the lean-to. *We got the bear.*

As the shanty came into sight, the two men walked tall and proud. Walt was bringing in an armload of wood. Dropping it outside the door, he shouted to the others. Reiner and Kinney joined Walt in front of the shanty and gave the two hunters a hero's welcome. Not only would the bear meat help for the rest of the winter, but the skin would make the winter more profitable.

CHAPTER TWELVE

The lack of change in the routine during the dead of winter made fighting boredom the men's toughest job. They read and reread the few books they had. They competed at throwing knives against the inside wall, next to the door. The deck of cards had become so stained that they could be easily read from both sides. Highlights of the day were tending to the stock and cutting firewood, or checking the trap lines.

Eli had removed the claws from the big cat's paws and made a necklace out of some of them. The rest would be used for trade. Kinney showed Beau and Eli how to make moccasins using some of the elk hide. Candles were made from the bear fat. Tempers tended to become shorter as the winter dragged on, and some days the men would sit by themselves in the cramped shanty without talking.

When the first hints of spring arrived, the door was left wide open, welcoming the sound of dripping eaves and the warmer air. With the melting of the snow came the leaks in the shanty roof. Soon, packs were stacked high in the remaining dry spots. The men had to make do with the leaks in the rest of the shanty. They moved their cooking to a fire pit outside. The spirits of the mountain men quickly rose, as they looked forward to leaving the shanty and getting back to trapping.

They were down to eating the last of the cold flour and the pemmican. Coffee was just a memory, the tea was gone and the tobacco had run out shortly after getting to the shanty. Beau's boots had come apart so many times that he had given up sewing them back together. He and Eli spent most days hunting and had managed to add some rabbit to the daily fare.

Having some powder to spare, the men competed in friendly target practice. Eli would challenge Beau's Colt against his bow. At the end of the shooting, the blocks of wood were split to retrieve as much lead as possible.

Bare patches in the snow-covered valley were showing when Reiner announced that they would be moving out. The news was welcomed by the men. The leader wanted to work two valleys to the south and east of them which had had decent beaver some years back. After that they'd be moving down the Green River, where there was a small trading post that just might have some coffee and tobacco.

The horses and mules were gaunt and covered with shaggy winter hair. The men kept them picketed on the short, brown grass exposed by the melting snow. It did not offer the nutrition that would soon be provided by new growth, but it would do for now. To survive the winter, all of the edible branches around the shanty had been chewed as high as the animals could reach.

The shanty was readied for the next season before the men left. Reiner jotted a note and left it on the wall near the fireplace. Beau read it before leaving the shanty. It simply stated that Reiner and crew would be back to winter next year. The five men had six horses and two mules. The packs were divided evenly between the mules and five horses. Reiner put a saddle onto his horse.

Beau and Eli walked together, leading their packed ponies. Both men had thick, long beards and bushy hair that needed cutting. Their stained buckskin coats were tied to the packs. The morning was crisp, but the long, cold winter had conditioned the men to endure the chill. Their wool shirts and long john tops were enough.

There was plenty of chatter between the men as they walked, most of it having to do with what they'd get once they got to the trading post. Walt believed that the old man who ran the place had a couple of women for comfort. Kinney snorted, "All I want it a chew of tobacky and a mug of strong coffee."

Riding out in front, Reiner called back, "For me, it's a bottle of rye to warm up my innards after this damn long winter. If you want a good drink, there's a Mexican village near Ham's Fork. They have tequila that will help you forget the winter. Haven't been there in a couple years. Maybe I'll make it there before the rendezvous."

"I've had that tequila," Kinney replied. "It don't suit my taste. The trading post will keep me satisfied just fine until rendezvous."

All of the men knew that they had several weeks before they would get to the trading post, and it might even have gone out of business. But talking about it gave them some degree of satisfaction.

This year the rendezvous was on the Green River, where Horse Creek joined it. It was less than a two week walk from the shanty. Reiner's plan was to trap the Beaver Creek and its many tributaries, slowly working in that direction. Once finished, they would be only a few days from the rendezvous site. It was now late March and the gathering would not be until July.

The trappers were traveling farther into the basin toward the North Beaver Creek. There they would split up and work in two teams again, searching for beaver activity. As they went toward the trapping grounds, the men were surrounded by snow-covered peaks and ridges. Beyond the end of the basin there were multiple ridges facing the men. Hours of travel would be spent crossing in knee-deep snow, to descend into the next grass covered valley.

There was a campfire near the Beaver Creek as they neared it. Reiner and his men had been traveling in sight of the fire for several hours. Whoever was camping at the creek had been watching their progress. Suddenly, Reiner called out, "It's Wes and Hoss."

The leader trotted ahead of the rest toward the camp. Wes stood up and was waving wildly as Reiner approached. Dog tired from the long day's walk, the rest of the men quickened their pace. "I bet they got coffee," Walt said.

"Probably tobacky also," Kinney replied.

The long faces of their friends indicated that Reiner had already told them about Uno. Men working the mountains became brothers, and the loss of one was taken hard. Beau and Eli began to pull the packs off the animals. Hoss came over to help them. "Sorry to hear about Uno," he said.

"Eli here shot the cat out of a tree. Damn near fell on top of me," Beau told him.

"I had no choice," Eli said. "Beau here had stood under it to get a better look up in the tree."

"You got any coffee or tobacco?" Beau asked.

"We been out most of the winter," Wes replied. "We was damn near down to eating our boots when a scrawny elk came by. We ate about every part of the animal except the hair."

That night the men ate a meal that was meager in substance, but was supplemented with stories of their winter adventures. Meanwhile, the rushing waters of the Beaver, swollen with the spring thaw, raged in the background.

The men spent four days at the camp. Each was spent resting the animals while the men hunted. One evening a herd of mule deer came out from the trees to forage on the new grass poking up. They were less than a quarter-mile away. Having no way to sneak closer, the men lay prone on their stomachs with the support hand beneath the rifle. Each man chose a different target.

Wes whispered, "Now."

The rifles thundered, the reports echoing off the distant hills. For a moment, the mule deer stood as though nothing had happened and then, in unison, they leaped into action, bounding back into the trees. On the grass lay three deer kicking their last.

The men leaped up, leaving their rifles, and ran toward the downed animals. All were claiming their shot was a hit. The truth was that once the animals had moved, and with the smoke from the black powder, no one could be sure if the deer on the ground were theirs.

Beau had his Colt out in case a second shot was needed. Eli had his bow and the others carried their knives. While the trappers were checking out the three deer, Eli followed the tracks of the departing mule deer.

"One of them is leaving a blood trail," he called to the men. "I'm going to see how far it got."

At a trot, the young black followed the trail. He disappeared into the trees. There was less than a half-hour of daylight left, and unless it fell after a short run, there wouldn't be enough time to find it.

The trappers carried the three mule deer back to the camp, looking forward to fresh venison for their supper. Beau and Hoss had dug some cattail roots from a cove on the creek and they would be baked to add to the meal. Just after dark Eli returned, carrying the fourth deer across his shoulders. The rest of the men cheered his success.

The next day the mule deer hides were scraped and stretched to dry. They would probably bring in a dollar or less, but the season had been poor and every saleable fur would be kept. Wes and Hoss left the camp the next day and headed north. That would leave the south and east to Reiner and his men.

The mule deer would keep everyone eating for the next couple of weeks. By that time, they should have beaver to eat. The leader assigned Beau and Eli to go with him, while Kinney would trap with Walt. There were several small streams that trappers rarely worked because the yield would be few beavers and the time spent too much. Considering the conditions that they had found in the fall, the leader recommended that these streams be explored.

One of the things they had to be careful of was that they were packing their winter's catch and could be the target of thieves looking for easy pickings. Some of the tribes considered the beavers caught by the mountain men to be stolen from their lands. Soon their winter camps would break up and bands of Crow, Flathead, Blackfeet, and others would be wandering the upper meadows in search of meat and furs. Some of the free trappers who'd had a poor season would invite somebody into camp with a smile and leave them bleeding and without their stock or furs.

While the catch of Reiner's trappers was nothing to boast about, it would make them even with the American Fur Company. The catches, other than beaver, would help buy supplies for the coming year. These would be sold and split evenly between the five men. Nothing had been said about the extra horse that had been owned by Uno.

The grass had greened up quickly and the trees were budding at the lower elevations. The breeze brought the scent of renewal and there were splashes of color from crocus near the forest edge. The stock had been hobbled and allowed to graze day and night if they wanted to. Beau knew that the matted hair on the ponies masked their true condition, but he was sure that they had started putting on some meat. He and Eli planned to ride the horses when searching the streams.

The trappers left the camp, wishing Kinney and Walt, who were heading south, good luck. Reiner headed east, riding his horse with the two young men following. Their gear and furs were distributed between the mule and the ponies. After splashing across the swollen Beaver Creek, they headed toward a snow-covered ridge. By noon they were trudging through a foot of the white stuff. While taking a breather, Beau pulled his water bag from under his shirt.

After taking sips, he looked around the snow-covered high meadow they had stopped in. It would be several weeks before the snow would disappear and bring spring to this elevation. In the distance, he could see mountain peaks that might have snow year-round. What Beau saw around him was breathtaking. He vowed that he would return to these high meadows come summer.

By that evening they had reached the first valley that Reiner wanted to trap. The tree-covered hillsides were still shrouded with snow, while only patches remained on the valley floor. Several streams and creeks ran through the area. They set up camp under some willows next to a babbling brook. The site had been used by others over the years. A log had been dragged next to a fire pit that was lined with rocks. The remnants of past fires had been scattered by time.

While roasting venison over their fire, Beau said, "In the morning, I'll work my way up the valley, looking for sign."

"Good idea," Reiner said. "Pack enough grub for a couple days. If you hit some good sign, work it. Eli and I will check out the lower valley."

The valley was two miles wide where the camp was set up. It remained that way as far as they could see. The lower valley was several miles wide. The leader told Beau that if they needed to move down the valley they would camp on the west side, so he could find them. By this time, the young men knew that Reiner never left a camp without leaving a note in a sheltered spot next to the site.

After the meal, Beau put on a pot of water to heat, dropping in a gob of bear grease. Once it was boiling, he dunked his traps, coating them to prevent rusting. It would also remove some of the man smell. Placing the traps into a canvas bag, he then went through the supplies, selecting what he would need. If he found good beaver sign, a few days could stretch into a few weeks. Some extra salt, grease, and castor should cover the contingency.

The next morning, Eli offered Beau the fly tarp. Shaking his head, he said, "I will be traveling light, Eli. You'll need it when you set up camp down below."

With his packing done, the two young men stood for a moment. This was the first time that one of them was going off all alone. "I will be back in just a few days," Beau assured his friend. "Save some of the beaver below for me."

Taking the lead rope of the pony, he started away, looking at a valley that was filled with new discoveries. Before going over a small rise, Beau looked back. Eli was waving. With a quick wave in return, he strode away quickly, deciding that he didn't much like goodbyes.

* * *

Beau found himself keeping to the snow patches as he walked. The bare patches tended to be soggy from the melted snow trapped by the frozen dirt below. Water trickled out from under the snow on the hillside, creating rivulets flowing into the streams. After a few hours of walking, he picketed the pony on a patch of brown grass.

Up on the hillside, he could see a rock outcrop that was a couple of hundred feet high. That would give him a wide view of the valley. Taking some rope from the pack, he patted the horse on its shoulder and said, "I'm going into the trees and climbing to the rock yonder. You eat your fill and I'll be back soon."

Climbing up the snow-covered hill, he slipped and slid on the heavy, granulated snow. He had to kick toe holes as he worked his way up. Grabbing saplings and brush to help pull himself up, he finally reached the outcrop. A sheer cliff ran out from each side of the rock structure. It would take over an hour to work his way around the cliff.

Stuffing his leather choppers inside his shirt, Beau started climbing the side of the rock. Forcing his fingers into the cracks, he pulled himself up, searching for toeholds for his feet. The hillside he had just climbed now looked like a sheer drop to the bottom as he hung on the side of the outcrop. He finally reached a narrow ledge near the top of the rock and was able to gain a foothold and push himself over the top edge. Lying on the rock, he gasped for breath.

His nails were torn and his hands were scraped raw. He pressed them against the cool surface of the rock. Rolling to a sitting position, he looked toward the valley. The view was absolutely beautiful. Mountains rose up around the valley, and farther in the distance other higher peaks could be seen in the haze. On the valley floor he counted four ponds, each more than a mile apart. All were near stands of trees. That gave him hope that there would be beaver. For a moment, he thought that he saw some smoke. Straining his eyes for another glimpse, he could not find it again. Below him, the horse stood grazing.

Leaning back, he wanted to rest a few more minutes before heading down. His hand felt something on the rock. During some past time, someone had chipped crude symbols on the granite surface. Each one had a line leading away from it, possibly showing a direction. The same rock he now sat on had been used as a lookout in bygone years.

Looking over the other side of the rock, he was surprised, "Well, I'll be." Below him were indentions cut into the rock. They were foot holes for climbing to the top. Moving slowly, Beau climbed down from the outcrop. Shortly he was back on the snow-covered hillside. Bumping from tree to tree, he worked his way down to the bottom.

The closest pond was toward the middle of the valley. He took the lead rope. "Let's go, horse."

The two of them headed across the spongy surface of the valley floor. The sun had warmed the air and soon he was stripped to his long john top. He seldom wore the buckskin coat during the day. The pants were needed to protect his trousers as he pushed through brambles and low brush.

It was time to make camp as he neared the first pond. The beaver activity he had hoped for was there. The dam had flooded a section of the trees. Several had been dropped into the water by the busy beavers. He was only able to see one lodge in the tangled mess. Tying the pony to a high spot away from the pond, he took out traps and stakes.

It was dusk when Beau returned to the camp. He collected wood for his fire and placed a pot of water next to the flames. Into the water he dropped a handful of beans and a little rice. He sat against an aspen tree thinking, *Tomorrow I should be eating fresh beaver.*

As he sat in the dark, Beau felt loneliness for the first time. The only comfort was the sounds of his pony grazing. Back on Crowley Ridge he had lived and hunted alone, but he'd always known that there were folks only a couple hours walk away. Here in the valley, the closest people he knew of were Reiner and Eli, and they were over a day's walk away. Then he thought about the smoke again. It could be trappers, or . . . He shook his head, muttering, "You're thinking too much."

The next morning, he made a meal out of the leftover mixture from the night before. Using a wooden spoon carved during the long winter, he scraped it right up from the pot. Anxious to check his traps, Beau left the dirty dishes for later. He fetched the pony and headed out, hopeful of success. Out of the four traps he had set, he caught two beavers. Their winter coats were both plew.

After resetting the traps, he headed back to the camp with his catch. He was humming a song that his father used to sing to him. The west wind was cold, promising a chance of a few snowflakes, but he was happy. If the other ponds provided the same success, the trip up the valley would be well worth the time. The climb to the rock outcrop had saved him hours of zigzagging across the valley searching for the ponds.

The next week was busy. He pulled and set traps from pond to pond. He passed several breached dams used by beaver in other years. One of the ponds was without sign or beaver. No doubt it had been trapped out last fall, or predators had gotten to the beavers during the winter. Quite satisfied with his success so far, Beau sat under a cottonwood and roasted some beaver for his supper. In the morning, he planned to pull the traps from this pond and head for the final one he'd sighted from the rock.

After two days of chilling air and snow flurries, the warmer wind had returned, making the evenings comfortable. Beau awoke at daylight and huddled near the fire in his long johns. His clothes were draped over some low brush, drying. In the high elevations, low humidity dried things quickly and after warming the clothes near the fire, he planned to put them on.

The fire felt good, but he sorely missed having coffee to drink. He had taken to having hot water in place of coffee with his meal. Cold water could quench the thirst, but the hot liquid running down his throat was comforting. When he had run out of tobacco, he had chewed on twigs in its place. Somehow it had seemed to help.

He bent down to add some wood. The small sapling behind him splintered, followed by the sound of a rifle shot! Beau dove for the ground, lying flat next to his fire. Clothed only in his long johns, he had no guns or the possible bag. Craning his head around, he looked desperately at his gear on the other side of the fire. "You damn dummy. Never be without a gun within reach," he muttered, scolding himself.

The pony was raising a commotion, having been scared by the shot. Unable to stay put, Beau rolled over the ground toward his rifle. Another shot from the attackers sprayed sparks from the fire as a ball hit a hunk of wood as he rolled by. Grabbing the rifle, leaning against an aspen, he lay prone with it in front of him. Beau groped for the possible bag. While the rifle was loaded with powder and a ball, the pan was empty. He heard arrows rattle in the tree branches and then saw one stick into the ground only a few feet from him.

He feared that that the arrows were meant to pin him down, allowing someone to crawl in and get him. The possible bag contained the Colt and the extra cylinder. He took them out along with the powder horn. Beau primed the pan, and with the Colt lying next to him, he searched for any movement. He heard a sound beyond some brambles. They were coming!

Then he saw something dark appeared in a small opening. Lining his sights on it, Beau fired the rifle. His view was obscured by the pan smoke blowing in front of his eyes. The sound of a grunt and the crash of brush confirmed that he had struck something solid. Then came the shrill cries of attacking Indians.

Clutching the Colt, Beau rose to one knee, using an aspen tree for cover. Three Crow braves were dodging through the trees and tag alders, coming at him. Suddenly cold inside, Beau put the front site on the nearest brave and fired. The shot spun the attacking Crow. He then fired at a second, missing as the brave disappeared into the undergrowth along with the third Crow.

Then it was quiet, not even a bird singing. The feeling inside was replaced by panic, as he watched for the braves to reappear. Beau realized that he had two shots left in the revolver. Crouching, he moved back, beyond the pony, away from the attackers. If they were after his horse, Beau would let them have it, if it meant saving his life. Hiding in a thicket, he reloaded the rifle, straining his ears for any sound. He wanted to break down the Colt Paterson and put in the loaded cylinder, but that would leave him with only a single shot with the rifle until he made the change. For now, having three shots made more sense.

For the next hour, he crouched in the thicket, his legs cramping from inactivity. The pony was beyond his sight, cropping grass. Beau hoped it would make some noise if anyone came to take it. The shrill cries haunted him. He expected to hear them again at any second.

Then Beau noticed that the birds were flitting from branch to branch around him and all seemed peaceful. Moving back to the camp, Beau tried to keep the tag alders and trees between him and the direction of the attack. He gathered up his clothing and dressed. He didn't bother to make any breakfast, but kicked dirt over the fire instead.

Returning to the thicket, Beau spent several hours watching his camp and listening to the sounds around him. It was late afternoon and his stomach ached with hunger. He couldn't remain in hiding any longer. With the Colt, knife, and hatchet in the broad belt around his waist, he took the rifle and went south, out of the aspen grove he was camping in. He could see the pond in the distance and several other groves of aspen, and cottonwood across the valley. There was no sign of the Crow. Circling around, he saw a cluster of boulders just to the north.

Walking to them, Beau found where the Crow had left their horses. Climbing onto the largest boulder, he could see into his camp. This had to be where the shots had come from. Beau determined that there had been four horses. He could see by the tracks that the Crow had come and gone from up the valley. Then he spotted blood on the grass.

Following the blood trail, Beau moved back into the grove of trees where he had his camp. Stopping several times to listen, he slowly went ahead. He found lots of blood from the Crow he had first shot. The wound had continued to bleed and there was a trail showing where he had crawled away. He wondered if it had been a killing shot with the rifle. There was less blood near the second brave he had hit. Beau went back into his camp. Were the Crow gone for good, he wondered?

Vowing to never be separated from his guns again, he went to check on his pony. After watering it, he picketed the horse on fresh grass. Beau went to his pack and dug out some jerky for his meal that night. After drinking some water, he took his blankets and went back to the thicket to sleep. Beau lay for hours listening, before finally dozing, sleeping fitfully for the rest of the night.

Waking at first light, Beau chose to leave his trousers in camp and wear stained buckskin britches to go check and set the traps. He was standing in knee-deep water and securing the stake when movement up the valley caught his eye. About a mile away was an animal near some trees, maybe an elk or . . . a horse! Could the Crow be coming back? Fear clutched his insides.

His hand shaking, Beau applied castor to the bait stick, left the water and got the pony. Hanging from the bucksaw saddle were two dripping beavers from the morning's catch. Whispering, he said, "We got to get back and move the camp, horse. They might be coming for a second round."

Returning to the camp, he hurriedly put the gear and beaver pelts onto the pony next to his new catch. Leading the horse from the grove, he moved as quietly as possible. Beau stopped at the edge of the aspens, searching for any movement across the valley floor. Satisfied that it was safe, he crossed the open ground toward the tree-covered hillside. He found a place with some crisscrossed windfalls. The hill was steep at his back, and the trees formed a buttress in front of him.

Adding a few large branches to improve what nature had made, he then cleared an area to give himself free movement along the windfalls. Satisfied with the results, he tied the pony nearby with sparse grass to feed on. "If I'm still here tomorrow, I'll find you some better grazing," he promised the horse.

Beau liked the defenses he had found. It felt safe enough that he decided to light a small fire and roast some of the beaver meat. He hadn't eaten since the day before and then it had only been some jerky. The two fresh pelts were stretched on sapling hoops and leaned against a windfall. Beau cut strips of meat from the beaver to roast. He put a pot next to the coals to heat water for drinking with the meal.

That night Beau felt safe behind the windfalls surrounding him. It might have been a false feeling of security, but it helped him rest. He no longer slept soundly. He was always listening for a signal from the horse, or an unexplained noise. Man has always had fear of bad things coming out of the dark. It would take time before the night sounds could be determined as good or bad. Waking before daylight, he sat behind the windfalls, ready in case of another morning attack. Everything remained quiet.

Once again, he carried all the weapons at the ready as he led the pony toward the pond. Using the grove for cover, he stood within the aspen, looking for anything that was out of place. The pond was only 20 paces away. The sound of chickadees and mourning doves let him know that nothing was lurking nearby. Out on the valley floor there were some mule deer feeding.

Within Beau's body there was a tightness that he couldn't shake. The peaceful valley that he had been working in was now a place where a careless move could cost him his life. Leaving the pony inside the trees, he walked out toward the pond. Even though he had weapons hanging at the ready, Beau felt naked to the dangers that could be lurking.

Two days later, he decided that it was time to move from this pond. Wading into the water, he checked the traps and then pulled them. Emerging from the chilling water, he tossed the trap onto the bank before moving to the next. One of the traps had a beaver. This he carried as he walked to the pony. He was physically shaking by the time he reached the horse tied to an aspen. The wet moccasins and buckskin britches had little to do with it. It was the constant fear of the Crow appearing from nowhere and attacking him. Dropping the beaver, he leaned against the pony.

"I don't know if I am cut out to be a mountain man, horse," he said. "When I come out here, I knew there would be dangers to face, but I didn't realize what it would be like. There is no way to prepare for what you can't see."

Sitting close by the pony, Beau skinned and stretched the pelt. It was another quality plew. With the chore done and some of the meat saved, he took the lead rope of the horse. In the distance, he could see the traps lying near the pond. There was a splash on the pond. Beau crouched, bringing up his rifle. The screech of an eagle brought his attention to the sky.

"I should be trapping this pond for another day or two," he said to the horse.

Suddenly, he was angry with himself. His father had taught him to never back down. If one doesn't face their fears, they will spend their life running and hiding. Beau knew what he had to do. It was time to stop hiding from shadows. The Crow had attacked him. By now they might be far from here. He thought about the tracks leading away from the boulders. He had to know where they led.

Caching his traps and pelts in the windfall fortress, he saddled the pony and tied his blanket roll onto the back. He had cleaned the rifle and revolver and loaded the extra cylinder. His Green River knife was razor sharp. Climbing onto the pony, he rode toward the boulders. As he went, he watched and listened to his surroundings. The valley appeared peaceful.

Trusting his senses and knowing that the pony would alert him to things he might not see, Beau was quickly feeling more confident. He no longer felt helpless. The sign was still clear on the ground. Had it rained or snowed, much of it would have been lost. The tracks of the Crow ponies were plain to see. From the vantage point of his horse, Beau could see much farther ahead than if he'd been on foot.

The tracks continued up the valley. It was evident that one of the ponies was being led. An hour later, he found the spot where they had been camping on the edge of some cottonwoods. The few trees had no undergrowth, giving him a good view of the area. Swinging down from his horse, Beau walked around the camp. It appeared that they had been there for some time. The remnants of a mule deer had been tossed beyond the spot where they'd had their fire. He squatted next to the dead coals. Using the Green River knife, he poked in the ashes. He found a partially burned book.

It was an unlikely item for the Crow braves to be carrying. Looking more closely around the camp, he found empty tins that had once contained molasses and cornmeal. There were two smashed bottles that had held whiskey. Beau figured that the Crow he was following were young braves on a raiding trip after being cooped up all winter. Somewhere they had come onto some trappers or hunters and had taken the items from them.

Emerging from the cottonwoods, Beau looked down the valley. In the distance, he could see the rock outcrop. He could also see a gnarled pine that was near the pond he had been working. No doubt the braves had seen him setting traps and had chosen him as another target.

Then he remembered the smoke that he'd seen from the top of the rock. It could have been their cook fire. It was doubtful that they could have seen him on top of the outcrop, due to the distance from this point. As he prepared to leave, he saw his pony dozing in the sunshine and heard birds out in the valley. Smiling, he thought, *I'll never be alone with all this around me.*

He continued to trail the Crow. They now had six horses. The two extra horses must have been kept at the camp. The tracks showed that three of the six horses were being led. Beau had no doubt that one of the four braves was wounded badly, or tied across a horse being led. It could be either of the two braves he had got lead into. Beau felt no remorse, he'd been defending himself.

For another two hours, he tracked the Crow. The hoof prints were deep in the spongy surface, showing that all the horses carried a load. He became more confident that they were headed out of the valley. They were probably going back to their main camp to sing of their successes around the fire. The tracks of the ponies were filled with water and the sides were caving in. They were days old.

Confident that there was no immediate danger, Beau decided to turn back. Whether he had killed one of the braves and angered the Crow enough to send someone to exact revenge was impossible to know. He would depend on his wits and his horse to warn him should it happen.

Near a small stream, Beau stopped to rest and water the pony. He was emptying his water bag and refilling it when he caught the smell of burnt wood. While it was common to smell wood smoke in the wilds, this had the smell of something bigger, like a burnt building. The smoldering caused by goods in a building had a different odor than clean-burning wood.

The breeze was coming from Beau's right. The sun was bright, and the Crow were headed out of the valley. He felt in no hurry to get back to his camp with all this beauty around him. Two eagles were circling on the afternoon updrafts and white puffy clouds were floating across the valley. Climbing back onto the pony, he urged it in the direction of the wood smell.

Beau was admiring the fine stand of lodge pole pine on the hillside when he caught sight of the charred remains of a cabin. The smell of fire grew stronger as he rode closer. The pony began to prance, unsure that it wanted to go near the burnt building.

"You're a smart one, horse," he said. "I'll take a quick look and we'll get out of here."

Sliding off the horse, he muttered, "I hope the owner got out." Beau led the pony to the charred ruins. Not much was left of the cabin. One would expect that the fire had been caused by a faulty fireplace. Many a cabin had found its demise that way. As he got closer, and by the smell, Beau could tell that the fire had been recent. What remained left little doubt that it had been the work of the young braves he had fought. Scattered in front of the cabin were bags and containers that had been ripped open or smashed. It also explained the items he had found at their camp. Reflecting for a second, Beau wondered how the owner had still had any whiskey come spring.

Smiling at the thought, his expression then changed to concern. He caught the smell of something rotting. It wasn't coming from the cabin. The pony shook its head and snorted. Patting it on the shoulder he said, "You been smelling that for a while, I bet."

There was a crude lean-to and pole corral 30 paces from the cabin. That is where Beau found the cabin's occupant. The trapper had been hit in the side with two arrows. The Crow had scalped and mutilated the body. Birds had also pecked at the flesh. There was an empty whiskey bottle lying near the body. The young man felt nauseous as he looked at what was left of the man. Closing his eyes, he prayed that death had come quickly to the poor soul.

"I couldn't help you when you were attacked, mister, but I will give you a proper burial," Beau promised. He found a shovel near the lean-to and dug a hole, breaking through two feet of frozen dirt beneath the thawed surface. The cold nights had prevented flies from finding the body. The young man was thankful for that. He had found a moth-eaten blanket in the lean-to which had been used to cover or rub down the horse that had once been here.

Laying the blanket out next to the body, he rolled the man onto it, the arrows snapping from the weight of the trapper. Before wrapping the blanket around the body, the young man searched for anything that would identify the deceased. The trapper was clad in long johns and leather britches. They had been sliced to ribbons by the braves. Finding nothing, Beau wrapped the body and dragged him over to the grave.

The smell of the rotting body was almost overwhelming. After filling the grave, the stench remained strong from Beau's contact with the man. He piled as many rocks as were available onto the grave, then knelt and prayed for the man and for his own safety. The fate of this man could have so easily been his had the ball struck him instead of the wood on the fire.

Beau went to a small stream and scrubbed his hands and arms. It did little good, for the smell was upon him. It was beginning to get dark. The young man felt sure that the departed trapper's ghost would mean him no harm, for he had done the right thing burying him. He decided to camp in some evergreens near the stream. Had the conditions of the lean-to been better, he would have slept there, but the floor was churned to a mixture of mud and manure.

When he went to get the pony, it wanted nothing to do with him. It backed up, pulling on the hackamore tied to a sapling. After a bit of coaxing to make the horse accept him, Beau led the horse to the corral. "You can spend the night in here, horse. I will be near the stream trying to air out."

Roasting beaver meat over his small fire, Beau thought about what he had found here. Many a man had disappeared into the wilderness, never to be heard from again. He was sure that once he got back to the rendezvous, someone would know of the trapper in this valley. Rolling out his blankets, he crawled under them, keeping the Colt and rifle close. Sleep came quickly to the exhausted man.

All of a sudden, Beau's eyes were wide open. Something wasn't right. Something had awakened him. He could hear the pony in the corral. It was restless. Beyond the stream there was a sound. Something or someone was moving around. Then there was the sound of metal on metal. It wasn't a wild animal.

Not daring to get anyone's attention by moving suddenly, Beau slowly closed his hand around the Colt. In the dark, at close range, it would be much more effective. Clouds had moved in during the night, blanking out the stars and the crescent moon. Again, the sound of metal on metal. He now was sure that it was a rider. Someone was sitting on a horse a short distance from him. Friend or foe, how could he know?

He almost jumped out of his skin when his pony whinnied and whatever was out there snorted back. Lying still and wishing that he hadn't made his camp away from the lean-to, Beau stared across the stream into blackness. Again, his horse whinnied. It was followed by a nicker from across the stream.

There was a horse across the stream and the pony was not being hostile toward it.

Taking great care, Beau climbed out of his blankets, moving to the side and keeping low. Just then the clouds moved away from the sliver of moon, and in the faint light Beau saw the horse standing on just the other side of the stream. It was saddled, and what he had heard was the bridle and bit. Sticking the Colt into his waistband, he waded the stream and caught the reins that were dragging beside the animal.

Beau led the horse to the corral and tied it to one of the poles. Returning to his banked fire, he added some kindling and encouraged the coals back to life. Adding more wood to the flames, he lit up the area. He removed his soaked socks and wrung the water out of them. Then he pulled on his moccasins and went to bring the horse closer. In the fire light he could see an arrow sticking out of the back of the saddle. It had gone through the rider's blanket roll and stuck into the cantle.

This had to be the trapper's horse. Why didn't the Crow go after it once they had shot the trapper? Then he thought of the whiskey bottle he had found near the body. It could have been that the trapper was carrying the bottle, and when he'd fallen the braves had had a few snorts, causing them to forget about the horse at the time. Later, he surmised, they had found more in the cabin and the horse might have gone too far by the time they'd sobered up. He was sure that the other two horses and packs that the braves had been leading had come from there. It really didn't matter why. At least the Crow hadn't gotten this horse.

Beau removed the saddle, saddlebags, and bridle from the animal before putting it into the corral with his pony. Placing the saddle next to the fire, he sat by it, his legs folded. It made little sense to do any more before morning. It was partly cloudy, hiding most of the stars, so he had no idea what time it was. He decided to stay near the fire and wait for the sun to come up. Three hours later, when the eastern sky began to lighten, Beau sat near the cold fire with his blanket around his shoulders, dozing.

Stiff from sleeping sitting up, Beau got up, went to the back of the lean-to and relieved himself. He then dropped two poles off the corral to get the pony and horse. Glancing into the lean-to, he saw three places to keep horses. He was sure that the Crow had the trapper's stock. Leading the two animals to some good grass, he picketed them. The trapper's horse was a long-legged, reddish sorrel with a slightly lighter mane and tail. The animal's rump had been creased by an arrow during the attack on its owner.

Beau walked around the area, looking about as he collected wood before heading back to start his morning fire. It looked like the trapper had been returning from hunting or checking traps when the Crow had surprised him with a shower of arrows. Severely wounded, he had fallen from the startled sorrel. The rest was too gruesome to think about.

Beau ate the last of his beaver meat as he stared at the gear from the horse. His feelings were mixed. In front of him were the items lost by the trapper who was killed. On the other hand, they were a gain for himself. It wasn't right, but Beau knew that it wasn't his making. Wiping his hands on his britches, he took the saddle first. He broke the arrow to get the bedroll off. Prying the remainder out of the cantle, he tossed it into his fire.

The bed roll was wrapped in a ground cover. Inside the blankets he found a rain slicker and cooking utensils. The saddle was in fair condition, but had no identifying markings on it. Beau then pulled over the saddlebags. For a moment, he looked at them. *Gus* was carved into one of the flaps.

"Well, Gus," he said, "let's look what you had here."

The first thing Beau's eyes fell on was a twist of tobacco, with only a chew or two taken from it. The saddle blanket was spread out next to him. As he emptied the bags, Beau set the items on the blanket. There was some jerky, a fry pan, a leather packet, a bar of lead, a ball mold, a pouring ladle, a small bag of coffee beans, some cold flour, a couple of tools for working on a rifle in the field, fishing hooks, a sewing awl, waxed string, pigging strings, some glass beads, ribbon, and small things for trading.

Beau picked up the leather packet. It held various coins, an old letter, and a receipt for a Hawken .53 caliber rifle. A chill ran through the young man as he remembered the attack. The braves had probably been using the trapper's rifle. Carefully, Beau unfolded the brittle old letter. It had smooth, flowing handwriting.

The date on it was July 10, 1812. It was written to Gustave Woodland, Private, U.S Army. It was a letter telling the young private that his woman was marrying another man. The end of the letter was too faded to read the young woman's name. Gus had gone to fight the British while the love of his life had found another. It was remarkable that he had carried it all of his life.

Beau walked over to the grave and removed a large rock. He put the letter on the dirt and replaced the stone. "Gus, this here letter was important to you and should be here with you for all time."

Walking back to the fire, the young man thought about the few women he had known. He remembered a hazel-eyed brunette from his past. At the time they were too young, but he remembered the hours he would wait by the road for her to walk by. Even now he felt a flutter when he thought of her.

There was no reason to spend any more time at the trapper's. Beau did check inside the ruins of the cabin. He found some steel traps, but no sign of any furs. There was a Dutch oven that he took to the stream and cleaned. It was a luxury that was too heavy for a trapper's life, but now, with the extra horse, he might as well carry it. Beau smiled since he had nothing to cook in it for now, but once he got to the trading post he could make cornbread or biscuits.

That afternoon, Beau rode away from the charred cabin on the tall sorrel. The low-cut moccasins fit in the stirrups. The saddle had a scabbard which he put the rifle into. Ten days later he rode into Reiner's camp. Eli was working on supper and the leader was scraping a beaver pelt.

The two men stopped what they were doing and watched him approach. He saw Reiner's hand go to his Hawken. Beau stood in the stirrups and called to them, "It's me, Beau!"

The two men ran toward him, "What the hell are you riding there?" the leader asked.

Eli was smiling from ear-to-ear. "I got some cattail root and beaver stew going."

Swinging down from the sorrel, Beau walked back to camp with his friends. They were all busy talking and no one was listening. That night, over a chew of tobacco and hot coffee, Beau told him about the attack and finding the cabin and horse. Though he had wanted to, he hadn't touched the items in the saddlebags until he got back. They were things that should be shared.

Reiner remembered a trapper named Gus. The old man left the rendezvous each year with one horse carrying supplies and the other carrying whiskey. He would drink one bottle each week to keep track of the date. A sad look came across the leader's face. "He was a good man."

CHAPTER THIRTEEN

At the beginning of June, Reiner said that it was time to cache their furs and trapping gear. The trading post that they had hoped to visit had been found lying in ruins. The trappers' desires would have to wait until they got to the rendezvous. Beau had been disappointed when the leader had told him that everything gained on the trapping venture was to be shared by the group. Gear and animals brought by each man continued to be his property. Anything caught or found belonged to the group. The benefit that Beau got was being able to ride a fine horse until then.

Once they got to the rendezvous, Reiner would make inquiries to find out if Gus had had any family back east. Many trappers had wives or children they'd left behind. The goods would be sold for money to be put into a letter letting them know what had happened to the departed. If none were found, the money from the goods would be split by the group.

Their cache was a two-day ride from the Green River rendezvous site. It was dug into a sandy hillside and lined with poles cut from pine. It was then covered with additional poles and a layer of dirt, sod and brush which made it almost impossible to be seen by passerby. Most trappers cached their furs rather than carry them around for a month while waiting for the rendezvous.

The leader had no doubt what he was going to do. Reiner had talked about a trip south to the Ham's Fork area several times since leaving the winter cabin. There was a Mexican village that had a cantina he'd come across after the rendezvous of 1834. They served fine tequila, good food and had some pleasant women to look at. He would have liked to have trapped the area, but it was Mexican territory and the army didn't favor gringos.

With the last of the brush tossed onto the cache, Reiner wiped his hands on his britches. "I'll see you all at the rendezvous. I got a bottle of tequila waiting for me."

"I've never tasted anything called tequila," Beau said.

"Well, I can't explain it," Reiner told him, "but I passed many a pleasant evening with a snoot full. Come to think of it, the owner has daughters that would be about your age. You might like coming with me and meeting them. Hell, if you behaved yourself, he probably won't even shoot you."

"Should we check out what tequila tastes like, Eli?" the young man asked his friend.

Beau knew that his friend was anxious to get to Green River and look up one of the Flathead women he had met the year before. Knowing that the tribe wouldn't be at the Green River for a few more weeks, Eli grinned at him. "It sounds good to me."

Kinney and Walt planned to meet up with Hoss and Wes and go after some buffalo hides. After settling on a place to meet before the rendezvous, Reiner and his two companions headed on the five-day trip to the cantina. The trip south wound through canyons with majestic peaks on both sides. The money that had been in Gus' gear had been put aside, and would become part of the funds once everything was sold. Both Eli and Beau had enough money to enjoy their time at the cantina.

They entered a willow and sagebrush-covered valley. Beau rode tall on the sorrel. He was intent on spending every penny he'd made this season to buy the horse. It was the best horse he had ever ridden, with a smooth gait and staying power. He figured that he would sell the pony for a few dollars to help with the purchase.

A cluster of adobe and stone buildings came into view. A dusty street wound through the village. Most of the homes had small gardens in the front, surrounded by fences made from woven willow branches. They could hear the ring of iron being shaped on an anvil from a building in the back. In the center was a large structure with a low, wide porch. All of the buildings had long overhangs and stone foundations to keep the rain from softening the mud and straw bricks.

The hills around the valley had ample pines to provide logs for construction. No doubt the Mexicans who had built this little village were more knowledgeable using adobe. Another advantage would be that the adobe remained cool in the summer and warmer in the winter.

A sign on the front of the large building read: Cantina Garcia. Someone inside was singing and strumming a guitar. The double plank doors were wide open, revealing the shaded interior of the building. The men swung down from their horses, tying them to a well-chewed rail. Walking into the cantina, they saw a low ceiling supported by hand-hewed square logs. A long bar ran along the back wall, with a scattering of tables on each side of the room. The singer was a white-haired Mexican dressed in homespun clothes.

Two posts held up the beams spanning the room and two lanterns were mounted on each. The back wall of the cantina had a painted mural of a Spanish woman, daringly dressed and lying on a red cushioned chaise longue. On each side of the painting were shelves containing bottles of tequila.

Behind the bar was a slim Mexican dressed in a crisp, white shirt with bloused sleeves and a short apron which protected his dark pants. His silver, wavy hair was combed back and he had a thin, trimmed moustache and bushy eyebrows. The man's face was creased from years in the sun and the wide smile.

"I am Emilio Garcia," he said, introducing himself. "Welcome to Cantina Garcia."

Reiner walked up to the bar. "Tequila, Señor Garcia. Tequila."

The man's eyes widened, "Señor Wells! Welcome back." Turning quickly, the owner took a bottle and glass from the back bar and placed it in front of Reiner. "This is for you, on me."

"Thank you, my friend," Reiner said. "Could you get me a couple more glasses for my friends?"

Placing the glasses onto the bar, Emilio replied, "Your friends are my friends."

Reiner filled the three glasses and held his up for a toast. "To the good year, men."

Beau and Eli picked up their glasses and tossed the drinks down. Both of the young men gasped for breath, trying not to show the tequila's effect on their throats.

Reiner filled the glasses again. "Kind of tough to swallow, ain't it?" He then called to Emilio, "Could we get some lime to cut the bite?"

Smiling, the owner came with a clay bowl of sliced lemons and limes. "Just came in from Mexico. Let me know when you're hungry. Alisa has some frijoles ready."

"You should let that sweet wife of yours come out of the kitchen and have a drink with us," Reiner kidded.

"You, my friend, I would have to watch all the time," the owner replied. "Now, your friends look like honorable men. In need of a haircut maybe, but honorable."

They all laughed at the bantering between the two men. The trappers moved to a table, taking the bottle and bowl with them. Beau found that the lime did help cut the bite of the tequila. His stomach was burning with hunger and he hoped that Reiner would order the food soon. A young man came in who looked a lot like Emilio. The owner said something to him in Spanish, and he hurried out.

Emilio came over to the table with another bottle of tequila. Feeling light-headed and hungry, Beau was about to order some food when the owner said, "I have asked my son to order some frijoles for you and then bring your horses to the stable."

"We appreciate that, Emilio," Reiner said. "Felipe has grown into a handsome young man. He has the look of a matador, like you."

"Fighting the bulls is very exciting, but no way for a family man to live," the owner replied.

"It could be worse," the leader said. "He could become a mountain man."

Emilio pretended to be concerned. "Don't even kid about something like that."

The conversation was interrupted by the sound of his wife, Alisa, bringing the food. She carried a large, steaming bowl, which was placed on the center of the table. Smaller clay-fired bowls were placed in front of the men. A young girl followed her in with a ladle, spoons, and a plate stacked with warm tortillas. Beau's and Eli's attention went immediately to the young Mexican girl.

"Could this be Ana or Evita?" Reiner asked Emilio.

Before he could answer, the girl replied sweetly, "I am the youngest, Catalina."

The ladies hurried away to the kitchen. Emilio looked after them. "Yes, she is my youngest daughter. She is gifted and I do worry."

Beau and Eli were busy scooping the savory beans into their bowls. Taking a tortilla, Beau folded it and dunked it into the broth. Taking a bite, he hesitated a moment. "They're kinda spicy, Eli," he warned.

The frijoles had been seasoned with side meat and chilis. The men ate the meal without talking. They'd had very little for breakfast and it was now late afternoon. The young men were thankful when Catalina returned with a pitcher of cool buttermilk and cups. Beau was wiping the last of the juice from the bottom of his bowl when Emilio came over to the table with a pot of coffee.

"I will get you clean cups," he offered. All three of the trappers shook their heads and held the buttermilk-coated cups for him to fill.

The owner joined them for coffee. Reiner pushed back his chair a little, satisfaction from the meal and coffee clear on his face. "I imagine the older girls are off and married," he said.

"The middle one, Evita, is married to a fine man that runs the store in our village. Ana wants more than this village offers. She talks of traveling to a city, maybe San Francisco," the owner replied.

"We should be around here for a couple weeks, Emilio. Maybe we'll do a little hunting," Reiner told him.

"Alisa can always use fresh meat in the kitchen," the owner said. "The casa across the way is available and you can stay there."

Soon it was dark and the cantina was filled with local men playing cards and drinking tequila. A second man joined the one who was singing. A heavy-set Mexican named Jesús took over behind the bar. He had a wide face and a gold tooth that could be seen when he smiled. Felipe helped out keeping the shelves stocked and the glasses clean. Three women in colorful dresses, worn off the shoulder, mingled with the men at the tables.

"Let's go check out our quarters," Reiner suggested, tossing down one last shot of tequila. Beau was feeling the effects of the drink. Both his mouth and stomach were burning from the food and tequila. Eli had quit drinking when the food had come. He had kept mentioning Catalina.

The house that Emilio told them about was small, with a low door and one window on the side. The foundation was stone and the walls adobe. The floor inside was carefully fitted split stone. A perforated tin lantern with a candle hung outside the door, offering some light. Reiner carried it into the building and set it onto the table. Their gear from the horses lay on the floor near the fireplace. The room had a small table with four stools, a bunk, a small sideboard with pots and cooking utensils, and a basin. Next to it was a wooden bucket filled with water.

"All the comforts of home," Reiner said as he rolled out his bedroll on the only bunk.

The fireplace was swept clean of ash and had kindling and wood ready for the morning fire. A stack of split wood was stacked alongside. The remaining floor was just large enough for Beau and Eli to roll out their blankets. Eli kicked off his moccasins and crawled right into bed.

Feeling restless, Beau dipped a cup into the bucket and went over to pick up the lantern. A small mirror on the wall behind the table reflected his bushy beard and unruly hair. "Damn, you do need a haircut and shave."

He stepped outside and hung the lamp next to the door before sitting on a low bench in front of the house with the cup of water. The evening was warm, with a soft breeze that brought the scent of flowers. The sound of singing drifted across from the cantina. This was the closest he had been to civilization since leaving Fort William. The Colt in his waistband was cutting into his full stomach. Pulling it out, he put it onto the bench beside him.

"Are you getting ready to shoot someone, señor?" a female voice demanded.

Startled, Beau quickly stood up, spilling the water on himself. Bushing it off, he said, "Excuse me miss, I was just . . . ah, I was . . ."

"I can see, you were just taking a bath," she kidded. "From what I can see, it had been some time."

Recovering some, he looked toward the girl in the shadows and replied, "It was probably a mistake to take the lantern out with me. I can assure you I look much better in the dark."

"I would agree," she said. "You have a pleasant voice, but even in the dark the lack of bathing would be telling."

Before he could answer, she continued, "You are in my casa."

"We were told it was empty," Beau replied, surprised at her assertion.

"When my brother told me to move to my sister's for a while, it did become empty."

"You must be Ana," the young man told her.

The mysterious girl was quiet for a moment, then said, "You know my name."

"I do," Beau replied. "My friends and I would be happy to move out and sleep outside of town. We didn't mean to force you out of your home."

"It is okay to stay. My sister had a baby that I can help with. Tomorrow I will bring two mats for you and the other to sleep on. The stone floor can be cold." Without waiting for an answer, she turned and disappeared behind the building.

"My name is Beau," he called after her.

The smell of flowers lingered for a bit before being whisked away by the breeze. She must have been watching him for a while before speaking. Smiling, Beau went back into the casa and crawled into his blankets. After a bit he thought, *Not only cold, but also hard.*

The sound of roosters crowing woke Beau. He lay listening to the morning sounds. Birds were singing and someone was pumping water, the handle creaking with each thrust. Someone else was chopping wood. Sometime in the night he had crawled out from under his blankets and was now on top of them. It was more comfortable than the stone floor.

Getting up, he struck a flint and got the fire going. Next to the coffee pot was a tin of ground coffee. He filled the pot with water and put it next to the flames. He then headed to the outhouse. Leaning against the wall next to the bench were two woven straw mats. His thoughts went back to the girl in the shadows. Today, he vowed, he would get a bath and a haircut. With luck he could find someone to launder his clothes.

When he got back to the house, the others were up. Eli was adding coffee to the steaming pot. "We got a couple of mats outside that we can sleep on," Beau informed him.

"Good," Eli replied. "Not much give or warmth to the stones."

Sitting at the table, drinking coffee, Beau asked Reiner, "Aren't we supposed to be paying for some of this stuff?"

The leader swirled the coffee in his mug. "Emilio is an old friend and opened his home and cantina to us. It would hurt his pride if we offered money. The trick is to find other ways to re-pay him."

"Such as hunting?" Eli asked.

"That is one way," Reiner replied. "Gifts is another."

"Well, Eli and I will do some hunting today," Beau said.

They made a meal out of some cornmeal mush, then Beau and Eli went to the stable to get their horses. The stable was a long building with a wide door on each end. It would hold a dozen horses. A sign above the street side door said: Emilio's Stable. They found Felipe busy cleaning out the stalls.

"You work very hard for your father," Beau told the lad.

"For myself," Felipe said. "Someday I will own all this."

He was right. All that a man built would eventually go to the eldest son. It would become his responsibility to take care of unmarried sisters and, if need be, jobs for married sisters' husbands.

"I met your sister Ana last night," Beau said.

"She likes the night air," Felipe replied. "Be careful, senor," he cautioned. "She carries a sharp knife."

"And a sharp tongue," he said.

"Yes," the young Mexican said, laughing.

"Is there a place that I can get a bath, haircut and my clothes cleaned?" Beau asked.

"Just outside of town there is a stream. A man named Pepe has a place near it that can take care of you."

Their horses were impressive. Both had had some of the rough winter coat left, but now were cleanly curried, their coats shining. Eli and Beau saddled the animals and rode out of the village, stopping by Pepe's. They both left their dirty clothing to be washed and said they would be back for a bath and barbering later in the day.

The valley was thick with willows and sage brush. They passed a small farm that had hacked out enough area to plant some vegetables and graze a couple of cows. The man working in the field waved at them as they rode by.

"This is a friendly area," Eli said.

"This is Mexican territory. They welcome visitors but may not be as nice if we decided to move in and start our own business," Beau replied.

"They won't have to worry about me, unless that young Catalina keeps smiling my way," Eli said, chuckling.

Beau held his hand up and pointed to a small opening. There were three mule deer grazing on the lush, green grass. The two men got down off the horses and walked a few steps closer to the deer. Taking careful aim with the rifles, Eli whispered, "Now."

The rifles belched fire and two of the deer spun around and fell into the grass. As the third ran into the willows, the two young men ran to the opening. Both of the mule deer were dead. While Eli retrieved the horses, Beau started gutting the animals.

It was late afternoon when they rode up to the cantina. Carrying the deer over their shoulders, they brought them to the kitchen door. Alisa was thrilled to see the fresh meat. They had also saved all the organ meat for her. Feeling good about supplying some food for the table, they rode toward the bathhouse. Beau caught a glimpse of a young Mexican girl working in a small garden. She had been watching them and looked down quickly when he noticed her.

For the next hour, the two young men watched their shoulder-length hair and shaggy beards disappear. Eli chose to keep a short beard, while Beau went for a clean shave. As Beau got into his bath, his bare face felt strange after having the beard all winter. Soaking in the warm water, Beau thought of the pile of hair around the barber chair.

"I bet we could have gotten a couple dollars for those pelts lying on the floor," he told Eli.

They scrubbed themselves all over with the homemade brown soap. Climbing out of the bath water, they shivered while drying with the rough towels. Two piles of clean clothes lay on a bench near the metal tubs. The ones they had worn in were now being washed.

The wool pants and shirts were a little worse for wear, but smelled fresh and were a marked improvement on how they'd looked when they'd ridden into town. Beau decided to visit the store run by Emilio's son-in-law. He hoped to buy a pair of boots.

Reiner was almost speechless when Eli and Beau walked into the adobe house. "Who the . . . What . . . My God! Was you boys scalped?"

"We decided to become civilized again," Beau responded.

"Emilio's daughters wouldn't have something to do with it, would they?" the leader inquired.

Beau's freshly shaved cheeks blushed. "Every so often it is important for a man to remember what he looks like."

"Well, you both smell mighty pretty." Then Reiner busted out laughing.

Eli kept busy at his packs, seeming to avoid all the kidding. His thoughts had drifted to the rendezvous and a particular Flathead woman. Beau changed the subject and told Reiner that they had gotten two mule deer and dropped them off at the cantina.

"Emilio told me he'd come into some fresh venison and we're invited to supper with his family this evening," the leader informed them.

Beau looked down at the tattered moccasins on his feet. "I got to go and do some quick shopping." Without waiting for an answer, he hurried out and headed for the Mercantil Garcia.

He had only $12 left to last him until the sale of the furs. There was a fancy pair of calf-high riding boots adorned with silver for $9. After much debating, Beau left with low-heel work boots for $3. He would have liked to show Ana how he looked dressed up, but a fancy pair of boots and worn clothing would prove nothing.

For another dollar, he got two pairs of wool socks. Pulling the new socks on, he pushed his feet into the new boots. While they had a few tight spots, the fit was good. Beau walked back to the small house. As he went he looked at the fine new boots. They just made the rest of the clothes he was wearing look more dilapidated. Stopping in front of the adobe, he kicked and rubbed dirt onto the boots. Then he kicked against the bench to remove the loose dust. While it helped, he wished that he had been through a couple of rain storms with them.

In the back of the cantina there was a courtyard with low walls around it. Six tables with benches were arranged for eating. A mariachi group was playing and singing. They had dark clothing with bright trim and broad sombreros. There was a clear area for dancing. Pitchers of a citrus-flavored drink were on the tables.

The three men arrived and went into the cantina. Emilio ushered them to the back and had them sit at a small table in a shaded part of the courtyard. "You wait here until the others come. I will have Felipe bring you out some tequila."

Beau looked at Reiner. The leader had combed and brushed his hair and beard, slicking it back with something. He was also wearing a shirt and trousers that they had never seen before. He even had a nice-looking pair of boots on. All they had ever seen him in were his long johns or old woolens under his buckskins.

"Where did you have those hidden?" Eli asked.

"I always figured if I died up in them mountains, I wanted something along to be buried proper in," Reiner told him.

"Well I didn't know you had them along," Beau said. "When we were alone, and if you up and died, I wouldn't have dug you back up when I was selling your things and discovered your outfit."

The sound of laughter caught their attention. A group of families and friends of Emilio came into the courtyard. The three trappers were introduced around. Most of the newcomers only spoke Spanish. Reiner chatted away with the group while Beau and Eli caught a word here and there.

Soon the ladies came in with large trays of venison and vegetables. They were placed on the table and the men sat down. The ladies returned again with more food and placed it on the tables they were sitting at. Emilio stood up and made a short speech and a prayer. Then everyone dug in. Beau kept glancing toward the tables with the ladies and tried to pick out Ana. He had met Catalina and the mother, but not the others.

The venison was tender, and there was some type of dish made with cornmeal and the organ meat. The vegetables had a sweet glaze on them. Beau and Eli talked a bit as they ate, and wished that Felipe had been seated closer to them. Several times someone said something to them and they struggled to know if they should nod or shake their heads.

Once the meal was done, cakes were brought out. They were covered with wild berries from the hillsides. Beau had eaten little cake in his life and found the dessert wonderful. Then the dishes were quickly cleared away. The men broke into smaller groups to drink tequila and smoke short, thin cigars. Felipe came over with some for Beau and Eli.

The mariachi band began to play again and the crowd moved back so Emilio and his wife, along with other couples, could dance. The traditional dances they did fascinated Beau. After a couple of dances, they left the floor with a loud hand of applause. Beau had picked out three different young women that he hoped were Ana. Finally, he turned to Felipe, "Would you point out your sister Ana?"

The young Mexican looked around and replied, "She is not here. Ana must have gone back in the kitchen with our mother."

The band continued entertaining and when a slow love song was played, couples would go out and dance. Beau had turned down several offers to have his glass filled, wanting to keep his mind clear when he met Ana. He had experienced her wit and wanted to be ready.

The meal was over and people began to leave. Emilio and Reiner continued to drink tequila and smoke the short cigars. Beau and Eli sat listening to the conversation, now being spoken in English. Not wanting to look like an improper guest, the young men kept waiting for Reiner to finish. All of the women had gone back into the kitchen. Felipe was in the cantina helping.

Finally, the leader was ready to leave. "You have provided a wonderful evening, my friend."

"Your men here provided the best part of the meal for us, and we were pleased to share," the owner replied.

One more shot was poured as the men stood up, and Emilio toasted to good health. Reiner led the way toward the small casa. Beau stopped when he heard a voice behind him.

"You are leaving so soon?" the sweet voice of the mystery woman inquired.

Beau turned. The footsteps of Reiner and Eli faded behind him. "I was hoping to see you tonight, but thought you had already gone."

Into the light stepped a vision of beauty. Ana was wearing a colorful fiesta dress pulled off her slim shoulders. While her full skirt came to her ankles, it left no doubt of her stunning figure. She smiled and came closer to Beau. He could smell the scent of flowers.

Looking up at him she said, "I did not recognize you tonight. I expected a bushy hombre in buckskins. It was Felipe that told me you were here."

"I took your advice and went to the barber," he replied.

"It is a shame to hide your handsome face behind all those whiskers," Ana said.

Her comment made him blush. Beau had never considered himself handsome. Good enough looking, but handsome? She was standing too close and he felt awkward. She was staring at him, waiting for him to say something.

"Would you . . . Would you like to walk?" Beau asked.

"I would like that," she said, getting even closer as she moved by him.

Giving a quick laugh, Ana replied, "You need not worry. I do not bite."

With nothing else coming to mind, he followed her and blurted out, "Your brother warned me that you carry a knife."

Stopping quickly, she cocked her head at him. "He told you that?"

The move being unexpected, Beau continued walking and brushed past her. She felt soft and smelled great. "I apologize, I did not mean to bump you. Yes, he told me that."

She smiled. "It is a stiletto from my abuelo." Seeing the confusion on his face, Ana added, "How you say, my grand . . . grandfather."

Struggling to think of something else to say, Beau asked, "Where do you hide it?"

"I should not tell you, but . . . If I reach under my hair, you best keep away," she said, her smile letting him know that she was kidding.

The night breeze was taking away the warmth of the day. The village was filled with music from the mariachi band still playing in the cantina. Ana swirled her dress back and forth with her hand as she walked.

"I am going to leave my father's village and live in a city," she told him with conviction.

"Why would you leave?" Beau asked. "This is a beautiful place, and your family is here."

"Have you been to a city?" Ana asked.

"Some," he told her. "My father traveled for work and we visited some in the east. Then on the way west, I saw St. Louis."

"You must tell me what they were like!" she said, excitement in her voice.

"I was young and my father would be working. I remember it was very busy. Lots of people. I was mostly scared," he admitted.

"I want to go to San Francisco," she said. "I will shop for dresses and go dancing and to parties."

"I don't believe you could find a party nicer than the one your father gave tonight," the young man replied.

They kept walking and she told him of her dreams. Beau's new boots were hurting his feet, but there was no way he wanted to stop their walk. The village was small and they went by the cantina several times. Once, Beau heard Reiner calling for another bottle of tequila.

Suddenly, Ana shivered. "It has gotten cold and I must go home. Will you walk me there?"

221

Beau did as asked as she walked closer to him. Despite his hurting feet, he now wished that they were miles from her home. "I didn't mean to keep you out so late," he said. "I can't say I even noticed the cold."

"I like to walk just before sunset each day. I would be pleased if you would join me," Ana told him.

"Maybe we could walk to one of the higher meadows sometime and watch the sun set," Beau suggested.

"I would like that," she said. "I could make us something to eat while we wait for the sun to go down."

They had arrived at her sisters. A low lamp was burning and they could hear a baby crying. Moving quickly, she gave him a kiss on the cheek and hurried into the house.

After a short hesitation, Beau turned and walked toward the cantina. The touch of her lips remained on his cheek. He hadn't been kissed since his mother died. This was different. Feelings were surging through his body. The closeness of her when they walked made him want to take her into his arms and never let go.

Stopping short of the cantina, he changed his mind and went to the small casa. He sat, taking the weight off his aching feet. The mats were on the floor and Eli was lying with his blankets covering him. He sat up while Beau was removing the boots.

"Four times you walked past the house," Eli said. "The girl was talking every time. I never heard you speak once."

"I was enjoying listening to her," Beau replied. "I didn't want to say something that would scare her away."

"When Emilio finds out you are spending time with his daughter, he might take the rest of your hair off, gringo," Eli said, laughing, before laying back down.

Beau sat on a stool, thinking and smiling for some time before he got under his blankets and tried to sleep.

They awoke the next morning to find that Reiner had not come home. Beau was humming while putting the coffee on. Eli shook his head. "I hope this isn't what I can expect from now on. All your happiness makes me feel envious."

"Does Reiner being gone make you feel that way?" Beau asked. "He probably spent the night with one of the pretty ladies at the cantina."

"More than likely he slept on the floor of the cantina," Eli replied. "He was really enjoying the party last night."

They were just finishing the meal when the leader came into the small casa. His good morning was more of a grunt as he headed straight for the bunk and collapsed, his feet still hanging on the floor. Grinning at each other, Beau and Eli went outside.

"I don't think Reiner wanted any breakfast," Eli said. The two of them broke out laughing and headed for the stable. Much of the venison they'd brought back had been eaten at the fiesta. They wanted to ride back toward the clearing and see if more mule deer had come in.

For the next week, the young men went out hunting each morning and Beau waited in front of the small casa for Ana to come by. Twice he visited the bathhouse for a shave and another bath. He endured the endless kidding from Eli and, on occasion, Reiner.

On this day, he went to Ana's sister's house to meet her. They were going to the high meadow. Ana came out with a basket containing their meal. Taking it from her, the two walked past the cantina, hand in hand. The path to the meadow was steep and winding. Several times, she let him help her as they worked their way to the meadow.

Ana put a blanket under a spreading oak tree. The yellows, reds, and blues of wild flowers were scattered across the little meadow. They had a grand view of the western snow-capped mountains. They sat close while eating the food Ana had packed. Beau chewed and swallowed, but could not have said what he had eaten. The closeness of the girl and the smell of her perfume was all that he was aware of.

The meal was finished and she let him put his arm around her as they watched the western sky turn red and orange. As the sun disappeared, Beau was enjoying her soft hair against his cheek. Slowly the colors in the west faded. As darkness settled around them, he whispered, "Should we start back down the trail?"

"Not yet," she whispered as she pressed closer and looked up at him. Beau kissed her, his body tingling. They sat making small talk, sharing each other's warmth.

After leaving Ana at her sister's, and a final goodnight kiss, Beau returned to the small casa. He sat on the bench in the cool night air. What he had felt this night was not something he wanted to share with anyone else. The lights, laughing, and music coming from the cantina didn't begin to break into his thoughts.

"Does Eli have someone in the house?" Reiner asked, startling Beau. "Why are you sitting out here in the cold?"

Begrudging the mood being broken, Beau mumbled something and went into the small casa with Reiner.

Beau felt anxious when he awoke the next morning. He wanted to see Ana, but worried about it. He was a little edgy during breakfast and Eli asked him if he was having woman troubles.

Abruptly he said, "No!" Seeing the startled look on his friend's face, he said in a gentler voice, "Actually, things might be going too good."

Reiner left right after the meal to meet with Emilio. Beau and Eli saddled their horses and rode away to hunt farther down the valley. Beau craned his neck as they went past her sister's place, hoping to catch a glimpse of Ana.

As they wound through the willows, Beau was intent watching for deer or other game. They stopped near a small stream to rest and water the horses. Several large trout were hovering in the rapids, waiting for food to wash toward them.

Digging into his saddlebag, Beau brought out some hooks and line. In the next two hours the two of them had a fine stringer of large fish. Eli touched his friend's shoulder. He pointed at the mule deer that had come to drink downstream. Picking up the bow that was lying beside him, Eli stayed low and, using some brush for cover, he snuck closer to the deer. He stopped 30 paces away and notched an arrow. Drawing the bow back, he let the arrow fly. It struck the deer just behind the shoulder. The deer leaped away from the stream and bounded a couple of jumps before collapsing.

The two young men rode away from the stream, looking forward to showing off the day's success at the cantina. They pulled up at the sound of horses coming rapidly toward them. Within seconds they were surrounded by Mexican soldiers. They were staring down the barrels of a dozen rifles.

The Mexican who was in charge was shouting at them in Spanish. While they didn't understand a word he was saying, it was obvious that they best drop their rifles and knives. Beau's Colt Paterson was in the saddlebags. He hoped that the soldiers wouldn't search them.

One of the soldiers dismounted and tied their hands behind them. Beau tried to tell them they were guests of Emilio Garcia, but nothing he said seemed to dissuade their intent to take the two hunters prisoners. Two other soldiers took the fish and deer. With their weapons collected, the soldiers fell into columns and led their horses. Beau watched as one of the soldiers stuck his Green River knife into his bedroll.

In a low voice, Eli asked his friend, "Are we at war with Mexico?"

"Not that I know of, but I figure these soldiers think so." Beau winced as a quirt hit him across his back. The soldier behind him was shouting at the two prisoners, leaving no doubt that they were to keep quiet.

Beau sat on the horse, remembering stories of James Fannin and all of his men being executed after surrendering to the Mexicans at Coleto Creek few years back. The "no quarter" used by the army meant take no prisoners. If captured, one would face the firing squad. Suddenly, he realized that they were heading toward Emilio's village. By saying his name, Beau wondered if he had brought danger to their friend.

Dread went through him as he envisioned Ana being forced to witness him and Eli being shot. He thought about the Colt. If he could get his hands free, he could get to the revolver and try to shoot their way free. It would be better to die fighting than helpless at the hands of the Mexicans.

He began to work at the bonds on his wrists. Again, the quirt cut across his back. Gritting his teeth against the pain, he was determined not to let them hear him cry out. Eli rode wide-eyed next to him. He wanted to tell his friend not to worry, but felt no confidence in that.

The column rode into the village and stopped in front of the cantina. Ana and her mother stood near the courtyard. Beau saw fear on her face. The man in charge of the soldiers dismounted and walked into the cantina. Loud voices could be heard inside.

Suddenly, Emilio emerged with Reiner beside him. He was shouting angrily in Spanish at the soldiers. The man in charge of the soldiers stood by them, his face angry but saying nothing. Quickly the bonds were removed from Beau and Eli. He saw that their rifles and Eli's knife were placed near the cantina.

Reiner walked up to them. "Are you both okay?" he asked.

"One of the soldiers has my knife," Beau answered. "Other than that, we are okay."

The leader went over to Emilio and spoke softly. Once again, the cantina owner shouted angrily in Spanish. Soon Beau's knife was sitting with the rifles.

The fish and mule deer were dropped into the dusty street and the soldiers rode away, their displeasure plain on their faces. Beau and Eli remained on their horses until the soldiers were out of sight. They then dismounted.

"What the hell just happened?" Eli asked.

"I don't know, but I've never felt so close to death," Beau admitted.

Before he could say anymore, Ana was there, throwing her arms around him. She was crying. Beau blinked rapidly, fighting back his own emotion. It hurt him to see her cry. "I'm okay," he said quietly.

Evidently, Emilio wasn't ready to settle down. He barked some additional orders in Spanish and Ana pulled herself away from him and helped her mother carry the fish and deer into the kitchen. Reiner waved the young men to follow him into the cantina. Felipe took the horses to the stable.

There was a bottle of tequila sitting on the table with glasses. They sat down and Reiner filled them. Raising his glass, he said, "We survived a close call today."

Swallowing the sharp-tasting liquid, Beau asked, "What did Emilio tell the soldiers?"

"I didn't catch it all," Reiner said, "but he called you two hunters for hire and that he had paid you to provide meat for the cantina. He demanded to know why the soldier had interfered. Truth was it was mostly bluster and he outshouted the Mexican lieutenant."

"I was sure we would be shot by sundown," Beau said.

"I didn't know what to think," Eli said. "Every time you said anything, the brute behind you would give you a swat with his quirt."

"Well, it was a close one for sure," Reiner said. "We are in territory claimed by the Mexicans and they don't much care for gringos. It's just bad luck that they come by this way while we were here. We'll have to leave first thing in the morning. Odds are the cocky lieutenant will rethink things and come back hunting us."

A jolt ran through Beau. He hadn't thought about ever leaving here, at least not in the near future. He wanted to protest and tell the leader that he couldn't leave Ana. He let the words die within him because he knew that if they were to stay it would only being trouble to Emilio and his family.

Emilio came to the table. "Alisa is making you a meal of some of the fish." He placed another bottle of tequila on the table.

Beau wanted to get up and run into the kitchen and find Ana. He was feeling desperate. To do so would be to insult their host and now benefactor. The fish was sweet and tender. The fillets were served with black beans, tortillas, and wild greens. Beau kept glancing toward the door leading to the kitchen, hoping to catch a glimpse of Ana.

With the meal finished, Reiner said, "We best pack up our things. I want to move out before daylight."

"I am going to give the sorrel to Emilio," Beau said. "It will be payment for all he had given us."

"You know that you only have a share in that horse," the leader reminded him.

"Okay, I am going to give him my share then," the young man said.

Eli interrupted, "He can have my share also."

229

"Well, you two are mighty generous with other people's shares," Reiner said. A moment later he added, "What the hell. He can have mine too. If the others want their share they can come and take it."

Beau suddenly felt a little less pain of the thought of leaving. The horse would remind her of him and he fully intended on coming back here. When he presented the horse to Emilio, the owner was overwhelmed. Beau made sure that he knew it was from all of them. He still had his pony to ride and planned to keep the saddle and saddlebags.

That night he went to the sister's house to meet Ana. The two of them walked around to the back of the home and sat in the small courtyard. "We are leaving in the morning," Beau told her.

"My father told me this," she said. "He is worried that the soldiers will come back and he won't be able to stop them from taking you."

Ana stared at the ground as she spoke. Beau wanted to take her in his arms and hold her. He wanted to tell her that she would never lose him, but it would be a lie. With any conflict between Mexico and the U.S. things could get worse. If found, he could be taken and shot or thrown into prison. While he didn't fear for himself, he did for Ana.

He took her hand. She looked up at him. "You must go and stay away. The soldiers told my father that they would be building a post in the area."

Only last night they had held each other, free of worries, their whole future in front of them. He wanted to tell her that she could come with him, but to where? She would not be happy with him living in the mountains. She wanted to see cities. Beau loved the mountains and hadn't thought of being anywhere else.

She looked at him, and he pulled her close. For the next three hours they sat in the courtyard talking softly, avoiding the subject of the coming morning. Eli came to the gate. He cleared his throat to get the attention of the couple holding each other.

"Beau, Reiner wants us to pack everything and have it in front and ready to leave. He also wants the horses ready in case the army comes back."

"I'll meet you at the stable in a couple minutes," he told his friend.

Their lips met in a long kiss. "If I can, I will come back. I can't say when that will be."

Ana did not promise to wait. She was young and it would be a shame if she wasted her young life waiting for a man who might or might not return. She pulled away and stood up. "I have never met someone like you before. What I feel inside now would not be good for us. You must go now."

Tears were running down her face as she turned and hurried back into her sister's house. Beau knew by delaying that he might put the others in danger. Quickly, he strode to the stable and got the horses with Eli. The sorrel was left in its stall. "You were a good horse," he told it before leaving.

They got back to the small casa and found all their gear out front. Emilio was standing there with a mule. He handed the lead rope to Beau. "The mula is not young. Ana wanted you to have it."

"Pack up men," Reiner ordered. "We ride tonight."

Numb with the realization that he had seen Ana for the last time, Beau put the sawbuck saddle onto the mule and his packs. Emilio had provided them with coffee, tobacco and a few other supplies

231

they were short of. The sound of bottles clinking told Beau that at least one of the packs on Reiner's mule had tequila.

Beau's newly gained mule carried Eli's packs also. All of the heavy things had been left in the cache. Digging into his saddlebags, he found a pencil stub and paper. He wrote a short note to Ana telling her goodbye and that he . . . loved her. Quickly, he went back into the casa and placed it on the table.

While he had hoped that she would be there as they left, only Emilio was there to say goodbye. Reiner leaned down and shook his friend's hand. "I'll see you next season. Maybe the army will have gone back south to warmer places."

They rode north, leading the mules. The men traveled without talking and kept to cover. An hour after they left, Reiner spotted the fires of the Mexican soldiers. The camp was given a wide berth. The three men continued to ride until just before daylight. Reiner then pulled up near a stream to make camp. The men would sleep a few hours and then continue.

CHAPTER FOURTEEN

The Reiner group arrived at the confluence of Green River and Horse Creek. There were several trappers waiting for the arrival of the American Fur Company. They were also expecting the Hudson Bay Company. It was the end of June 1839 and some men who had traveled ahead of the American Fur Company caravan said that they were about a week behind them. The Hudson Bay Company would be coming from Fort Hall.

There had been some confusion as to where the rendezvous would be this year. Some even thought it would not happen. A note had been left at the Popo Agie location letting trappers know of the new location. The change had been made to try to confuse the Hudson Bay people.

Some of the tribes had arrived and were setting up their teepees. Trappers and Indians had camps set up all along the Green River. The gathering remained quiet for the time being. The whiskey was still a week away. All complained about the poor beaver harvest and had hopes that the price had improved over last year.

Reiner selected a site next to a cottonwood tree. The Green River was close by and there was good grazing for their stock. The nearest source of fire wood was a quarter-mile away and Reiner sent Beau and Eli to haul enough in to last several days. Fly tarps were put together to make tents and rocks were collected from the river to make a fire pit.

Beau was using the mule given to him by Ana and Emilio. He carried the Colt in his waistband, leaving the heavy rifle back at the camp. Eli had his bow slung across his back with a quiver of arrows. There was a good-sized windfall at the edge of the trees. Taking their axes, the two men began to chop it into useable lengths. Two pieces of the trunk were kept for seats next to the fire. These would be dragged behind the mule and horse back to camp.

The others in the group began to sort the catch, readying it for selling. Most of the beaver pelts would be given to the American Fur Company in payment for their past winter supplies. The grizzly and mountain lion would be money for the trappers, along with other various furs and hides they had. Some would be traded with the tribes in exchange for new buckskins and moccasins.

Three days after arriving Eli came back to camp, excited to share news with Beau. "Peter and Joshua are here. They said that the other caravan is only a day behind them. He also has work for us if we want."

"Once Reiner has finished the trade, we will be free to do what we want," Beau said. "I think we should work."

Each day more trappers and Indians arrived at the river. When the caravan was sighted, a cheer rose from up and down the river. Reiner stood at the edge of their camp. "Looks like a smaller caravan. Only four carts and the rest on pack animals," he observed. "They best have brought the damn whiskey."

Kinney agreed that it looked smaller. "Looks like we'll be looking to the train from Fort Hall."

The two young men had gone to visit with Peter. They were helping him get set up when the American Fur Company came in. Peter had been aware that it was a smaller caravan this year. Joshua had coffee and some cornbread for a mid-day break. The four of them sat around the fire as the caravan went by.

"I thought I should warn you," Peter said. "There was a poster at the fort on both of you. They had one on you, Beau, for assault and stealing slaves. Another was for a runaway slave named Elijah."

"Well, it is all lies," Beau said.

"I was given my freedom by Massa Weber," Eli explained. "Only I didn't get the papers before he died."

"Well, we are a long way from Arkansas and the troubles you might have had," Peter said. "I figured you should be warned. Men from back east travel with the caravans. Some may have saw the posters."

Then the gunsmith smiled. "Looking at the two of you after a winter in the mountains, I doubt anyone would recognize you."

It was July 5th and the trading companies were quickly setting up for business. Independent vendors such as Peter were scattered around the Green River area. Beau and Eli arrived back at Reiner's camp. The leader was gone to meet with the American Fur Company representative. Kinney had a bottle of tequila open in front of him.

"Get your mugs," he said. "The boss wanted us to have a drink to the rendezvous."

The next few days were a frenzy. The fur prices were lower than last year, leaving less money for merriment or supplies and the trappers were short-tempered. The haggling got noisy and threats of selling to the Hudson folks could be heard. One would think that the smaller supply of available beaver pelts would drive the price up, but the demand back east and in Europe had weakened and no amount of threats budged the price. The best a trapper could hope for was whiskey to drown his sorrows and enough left over for essential supplies.

While some trappers, such as Osborne Russell weren't at the rendezvous and might not have been aware of its location, those who did attend were ready to celebrate their winter's work. Beau and Eli were kept busy by Peter. They had each earned $53 for their share. Reiner had invited them to join him for another winter. Neither had committed. Earning only about $5 a month, plus some supplies that they didn't catch or shoot, would take some thinking on.

Eli was spending all his free time with the Flathead. He had confided that he might marry one of their women. He had given her father the claw necklace so far. Beau returned the kidding that had been directed at him when he'd been with Ana.

They were staying busy working for Peter. Again, he promised them $10 and their meals. There had also been some bonus items last year. Beau noticed that the gunsmith had brought fewer items this year. He had the anvil and forge, plus some muskets from his cache. After his warning about the posters, he did not bring it up again.

A trapper named Chess Handlin stopped by to have his Hawken worked on. He had a short beard and a round top hat with a drooping brim. He carried a knife in his belt. Chess stuck around and visited with Beau while he converted the flintlock to percussion. The man rode a buckskin and left it with reins dragging near the cart. In the past, he had trapped for the companies, but for the past year he'd been a free trapper and had come out ahead, despite the low prices. He had plans of going north into the Yellowstone this year.

Beau liked the man and asked him who he trapped with. Chess said that he had been trapping with a man named Doo, but gold fever had gotten to the man and he was going to try that for a while. After test firing the Hawken, Chess smiled. "No smoke in my face, and no misfires to worry about. I should have done this sooner."

The trapper climbed onto the buckskin and waved before riding back to his camp. Beau glanced at the blanket that Joshua was selling from. There was a percussion Hawken that someone had traded. The rifle had had a broken frizzen spring when they'd gotten it. He thought about his Model 1803. Maybe a swap plus a couple dollars, but that would leave him with less money for supplies.

With the day's work finished, Eli headed for the Flathead camp and Beau decided to look up Reiner's crew and have a few drinks. The area around the company tents was crowded. A couple of fiddle players were entertaining some hard-drinking mountain men, hoping to be tossed a few coins for their efforts. He had stopped to listen when he heard Reiner. "Levesque, join us for a drink!"

Turning, he waved, and then froze. Behind him was another voice. "Levesque?"

He turned and the first thing he saw was the gray gelding. Sitting on top of it was, . . . Angus! Very much alive. The scowling face glared at him as the man pushed through the crowd on the gray.

"I been looking for you," he snarled. "You and that runaway!"

The shock of seeing the brute alive was replaced with loathing. In front of him was something hateful from his past that could now destroy his future. Realizing that if he backed down now, he would be running for the rest of his life. He turned to face the man, his eyes cold and his body ready.

"Well, you have found me," Beau hissed. "Doing so may not be healthy for you."

"You little sons-of . . ." His arm was raised, the whip in his hand.

Beau pulled the Colt Paterson from his waistband and lined it up on the hateful man's chest. "You come at me with the whip and I swear I'll kill you right here," the young man said, his voice cold.

Shocked at being challenged, Angus pulled up the gray. "I got paper on you!" the brute shouted.

"You or your paper ain't worth spit out here," Beau replied.

Reiner and his trappers came up and backed the young man. "What's this all about?" Reiner asked.

"Angus here thinks he can push around everyone unable to fight back," the young man replied.

"I thought I'd killed him once and will not hesitate to finish the job right now."

Not liking the odds, the brute wheeled his horse, knocking some onlookers over and rode away from the company tents. A hail of rocks and insults flew after him from angry trappers. Trembling inside with anger, Beau joined Reiner and the trappers for a drink.

After Beau had downed a couple drinks, the leader asked, "You thought you had already killed him?"

"Back in Arkansas he tried to whip me and ended up with my knife in him." Beau replied. "I thought he was dead. I guess I should have made sure."

"Was Eli the runaway?" Reiner asked.

"He was talking about Eli."

Laughing, the leader said, "He best keep clear of Eli. He got him a Flathead woman and they'll scalp him and make a necklace out of his teeth."

At they drank, he felt the tension go out of his body. Beau realized that he was with "his people" and Angus was on the outside. Trappers and mountain men didn't much care about what had happened back east. They judged a man by what he did here in the west. The young man had not backed down, but rather had stood up to the brute.

The next morning, Beau told Eli about Angus being at the rendezvous. The young black man picked up the bow as he listened to his friend. "If I see him, I will kill him," Eli said flatly.

"All we have to do is watch our backs," Beau said. "The man is a bully and a coward. I doubt there is a man out here who would back his claims against us."

They let Peter know about Angus. He had already heard about the confrontation and how Beau had backed the man down. The young man had to admit that a Colt against a whip did give him the advantage. The gunsmith went to his pack and came back with a flintlock U.S. Model 1826 Navy pistol. Handing it to Eli, he said, "The .54 caliber ball will make short work of Angus should you need it."

For the next several days, Beau only caught a couple of glimpses of Angus on the gray. Peter had learned that he had tried to plead his case at the American Fur Company and had found little interest in his claims. Word of what Angus had done had gotten around quickly along the Green River and the man had found himself unwelcome at most fires.

The mid-July sun was blazing in the blue sky above the Green River. The rendezvous would be over in another week. Peter and Joshua were doing some blacksmithing for one of the trappers, repairing traps. All of the other work was caught up. The boss let the young men off early.

Beau had heard that a German was selling a decent beer on Horse Creek. He saddled the pony and called out to his friend, "Your woman won't be looking for you this early. Come with me and we'll try out the German's brew."

Climbing onto his pony, Eli smiled. "The day is hot. I wouldn't mind something for the thirst."

They found the brewmaster's tent in a grove of willows. Several trappers lounged under the trees, enjoying a mug of the stout brew that had been cooled in the waters of the creek. Beau waved to Chess, who was in a dice game on a blanket. After purchasing some foamy mugs of the beer, the two young men went over to watch the game.

Chess collected his coins and joined them with a fresh brew. "My guess is those dice are as loaded as some of the players. We all been donating money to the German's brother."

The beer was satisfying in the afternoon heat. Most of the trappers might drink one or two at mid-day, but come evening it was whiskey they wanted. The shade of the willows felt good and there was a breeze from the west.

"I heard that the American Fur Company won't be contracting any trappers this year," Chess said to Beau. "I'm looking for someone to join me this winter."

"I haven't talked with Reiner about the coming year," Beau told him. Looking at his friend, he continued. "I figure Eli and I can free trap ourselves if we don't go with Reiner."

Looking at Eli, Chess said, "You're both welcome, even split."

The young black bought the next round of beers. Three trappers were throwing hatchets at the end of a log propped up on a boulder. "I'll bet you both the next beer that the tall fellow hits closest to center," Chess said.

For the next hour, the three men talked and wagered on the various contests going on under the willows. Finally, Chess drained his last brew and said, "Whiskey and women are waiting on the Green River. I best head that way."

He took a few steps and turned back. "I just remembered. That fellow that was giving you trouble.

I heard he is camping downriver with two men that are suspected of stealing pelts. The word is they may also be responsible for some trappers that came up missing."

"I'm surprised that the other trappers haven't taken care of them," Beau said.

"No real proof," Chess said. "They best tread lightly, though. Some angry men don't need much proof."

Beau and Eli watch the man ride away on the buckskin. "It is good to have another trapper we can partner with, Eli."

"I best go now," the young black said. "The beer was good. I'll see you in the morning."

The next day an old trapper everyone called Grits came hurrying to the camp. He had left an older Kentucky Long Rifle for cleaning and sighting in. With the rifle in hand, he said, "I gotta git to the shootin match. Could win me some whoosky."

It was near closing time, so Beau decided to try his luck with his flintlock. There were almost two dozen men standing with their rifles, waiting their turn to shoot. The target was out 100 paces and the shooter was lying prone.

Beau shook his head. "I'll wait for the closer target. I tend to miss to the left at this distance. If the target is as big as a buffalo, I can hit it."

"Do ya settle yarself afore ya shoot?" Grits asked.

"Settle myself?" the young man asked.

The old man leaned over, his stained beard and yellow teeth close to Beau's ear. "Most don't know this. Ya git the target in the sights. Close yar eyes. Open yar hand and then grip the rifle agin. Open yar eyes and see if yar still on the target. If it ain't, then move yar legs so's its thar. Do it agin and if yar on the target, pull the triggar."

Beau watched the old man ready himself for the shot. He moved his feet a couple times before squeezing the trigger. The clay jug shattered when his ball hit it. Standing up, he smiled and nodded at the young man. When his turn came up, Beau decided to tried the method. Every time he did so, the sights were off the target. Finally, he sighted and fired, missing to the left.

It took four rounds of elimination before Grits took home the whiskey. Walking past Beau, he said, "Ya keep practicin'. The whoosky will be yar's."

Toting his rifle, Beau went to the company tents and found Reiner and the others. He bought a bottle to share. The leader told him that no one knew of any family back east for the trapper Gus Woodland. Also, Uno had no family. He handed Beau some coins which was his share of both. There was no talk of the sorrel.

Reiner asked, "Have you seen the brute called Angus lately?"

"Nope," Beau replied. "Me and Eli are being watchful of him."

"Will you two be trapping with me this winter?" Reiner asked.

"We do have another offer, but haven't decided yet," the young man replied.

"You both carried your weight last season. I want you to know you're both welcome. If the company don't take on any one, we will be free trapping," the leader said.

Thanking Reiner for the offer, Beau headed back to camp. He was adding wood to the cook fire for Joshua when Eli came over and sat on one of the logs. "I figured you would be gone to see your woman by now," Beau said.

Looking a bit uncomfortable, Eli replied, "I can't see her until tomorrow."

"Well, you'll have to put up with my snoring tonight."

"I can't go because . . . I am getting married tomorrow." Eli said. "I guess it is custom that you can't see your bride the night before."

Beau dropped the rest of the wood and exclaimed. "Married!"

Smiling at his friend's surprise, Eli said, "Yes, Beau. I am getting married tomorrow."

Concern crossed Beau's face. "Reiner might not let us take your wife with us when we go trapping."

"Many men do. But, there is one more thing I have to tell you." The young black hesitated for a bit before continuing. "I will be wintering with the Flathead."

A jolt of regret went through Beau. "You will be with the Flathead?" He turned away and ran his hand over his whiskered chin, realization settling in. Then he turned back to his friend. "Of course, you will want to be with her family. I will miss having you to back me up next time I go after a grizzly."

* * *

In the dim light of a crescent moon Beau walked back toward Peter's camp. He had just come from the Flathead wedding ceremony for Eli and his new wife. He'd been the last to leave. The exchange of presents and promises had happened hours ago. His friend had been dressed in traditional Flathead clothes and looked every bit a warrior.

His boot caught on something, and suddenly his feet were pulled out from under him. Landing on his stomach, it knocked the wind out of him. He fought for his breath and rolled to get free. There was a *crack*, and pain burned across his chest and side. He raised his arms to protect himself and something wrapped around his arms. He gripped the braided whip with his left hand and jerked it for all he was worth.

The man wielding the whip was pulled forward, stumbling to his knees. Beau managed to get to his feet. He gasped for air. The enormous frame of Angus came up in front of him. The young man grabbed for the Colt. It had fallen from his waistband! The brute leaped at him, arms spread. Beau ducked under the grasp and stuck out his foot to trip the man. Again, Angus fell, but his mass also tripped the young man.

Beau's hand touched a large rock next to him. Gripping it, he got to his feet in time to see the brute coming at him with a knife. Spinning to avoid the blade, he felt the burning from the sharp edge as it cut him. Angus turned to come at him again. Beau swung the rock attempting to stop his rush. It struck Angus across the head. The big man went down like he had been pole axed. Feeling the blood run down his side, Beau dropped the rock and headed for the camp. After a few steps, he wished that he had continued to brain the man, but there was no way he was going back.

Joshua had returned earlier and was having coffee when the young man reached camp. Beau collapsed near the fire. "Angus come at me. He cut my side."

Joshua dropped his cup and checked Beau's side. "He got you pretty good. It ain't deep, but its long. Lots of blood, but it won't kill you."

He helped Beau get his shirt off. "Looks like he got you in a couple other places."

"That was with the whip," the young man replied.

Hearing the two near the fire, Peter came out. He looked at the wounds. "You say Angus did this." Anger was plain on his face. "Tomorrow we'll deal with him."

"It's my fight," Beau insisted. "I don't want him hurting people I consider friends."

"It's not your choice. He has hurt one of ours, we hurt him," Peter said as he put the bandage on the young man's side.

The next morning, Beau's body ached. The lashes across his torso and arms, along with the slash on his side, left him moving carefully. He took Peter to the site of the attack. They found his Colt lying in the dew-covered grass. There was no sign of Angus. When they returned to the camp, they found that Reiner and Kinney had come for coffee. The men had brought a bottle of tequila for Eli and some *foofooraw*, or doodads, for his wife.

Peter told them what had happened to Beau. A half-hour later the four men rode out of the camp to find Angus. They would not stop short of hanging the man. They came across Chess, who was heading out to hunt. He asked Peter where they were going. "Beau here was attacked in the dark by the brute named Angus. Reiner and Kinney have come with us to witness the hanging."

"Well, hell! I ain't been to a good hanging for a while. I'll go along as another witness."

The group rode to the last known place where Angus was staying. It was evident that the camp had been hastily abandoned. The tracks showed three ridden horses had left and one that had been led. The men discussed whether it would be worth chasing them and decided it was good to be rid of the men. Peter would let the people from the companies know of the attack and request that they alert them if Angus returned.

Eli was at the camp talking with Joshua when they returned. The young black offered to have some of his new family go after Angus. They could be back with their scalps in short order. Beau convinced Eli that the likes of Angus were not worth the chase. He was probably heading back to Fort William, hoping that he could make a case with the army.

The rendezvous was winding down. Some of the trappers were leaving and the Flathead had plans to strike camp. Eli was looking forward to leaving with his wife, Saka'am, and starting a family. Peter had given Eli some blankets, along with two knives and hatchets and his pay. Beau cautioned him again about Angus. The man might still come looking for them.

Eli smiled and said, "If he does, I will have the first scalp for my lance."

Beau watched him ride away with mixed feelings. He was happy for Eli. The life of a trapper offered little for his black friend. The Flathead and his wife offered him a future and happiness. Beau had also made a decision. He had told Reiner that he wouldn't be joining the group this year. He planned to go to the Yellowstone with Chess.

Next spring, after trapping was done, he would go back and visit Ana. Word was that the U.S. and Mexico had not resolved their differences and at some time in the future it could develop into a war. But the risk was worth it to see the young Mexican woman.

Peter and Joshua started getting ready to head back to the fort. While Peter had made out okay this rendezvous, he told Beau that he would not be back next year. He took Beau to his cache that contained a few muskets, the forge, the anvil and a few tools. "If you don't see me here next year, you are welcome to any of this. Use what you want. Leave the rest."

The cache had been dug into a sandy bank and lined on the inside with logs. Though a little larger than the one Reiner had, the design was much the same except for a thick plank door which allowed entry. It reminded Beau of root cellars back on Crowley Ridge. The door swung out. Once Peter closed it, he put a large boulder against the door and piled sage brush over it. There was a rock pinnacle just beyond the cache to mark its location.

Along with his pay, Peter gave him some clothing and a pair of boots. After he had climbed onto the cart, he handed Beau a bag with some powder, lead and a worn holster to carry the Colt. The American Fur Company was pulling their tents down while Peter and Joshua rode away. Like last year, there was talk about whether they would be back next year. The Hudson Bay Company had again undercut the prices of supplies in trade for pelts.

Beau had a new set of buckskins, high and low moccasins, and a good supply of coffee and tobacco. He also had salt, side meat, jerky, beans, cold flour and other items needed for the coming season. Loading the supplies onto his mule, he saddled the pony and headed toward Chess' camp. He found him stirring a pot of beans. "I figure we'll leave in a few days," he told Beau.

"Reiner and his crew left this morning," the young man said. "No one got contracts with the fur company. They'll be free trappers this year."

"It's hard to believe. In two weeks, there won't be a trapper or Indian along this stretch of the Green," Chess said. "A few good rains will wash away most of the marks left by the rendezvous."

He then said, "Set your packs down. By the time you're done with the animals, the beans will be done."

Once the meal was finished, Chess was off to meet with a Crow woman he had been spending time with. Beau wondered if any of them were riding Gus' horses. They might even have the dead trapper's rifle. It was hard to believe that conflicts that happened in the mountains were mostly forgotten once everyone got to rendezvous.

The Hudson Bay Company had left for Fort Hall. The American Fur Company had men readying the pack train for the trip back to Fort William. The main tent was down, but they still had a makeshift bar selling whiskey. Each day the empty bottles had been collected and washed in the river. They were then refilled from kegs of high proof alcohol. The liquor was cut with water to prevent killing the trappers from alcohol poisoning.

The crowd had shrunk to a few dozen trappers, but they did their best to keep the party going. More than one trapper would be forced to go back east with the company, due to having no money or supplies for the coming winter. They would try and join the army as scouts, or go out onto the plains to hunt buffalo.

Beau bought a bottle and rode the pony toward a bluff just to the south. Gaining the top, he found a spot under a gnarled, wind-buffeted tree and looked across the basin. The remaining camps were scattered along the river. There were a few teepees marking the camps of the remaining tribes. It was remarkable how everyone showed up each year to trade and celebrate. With prices and demand for beaver dropping, he wondered how much longer it would last. *It will be a sad day when it is gone*, he thought.

CHAPTER FIFTEEN

Excitement filled Beau as he and Chess rode away from the Green River. He would again be in the mountains he loved. It was toward the end of July and the plan was to hunt and jerk meat for the coming winter. The beaver would be busy storing branches at the bottom of their ponds for easy access under the ice. Chess had found a couple good streams the year before that had been overlooked by trappers, and they had good possibilities of beaver.

Chess was out front, riding the buckskin and leading a brown packhorse. He had his round-topped hat pushed back on his head. Following him, the wind blew the bareheaded Beau's curly brown hair. His flat-brimmed hat was tied to his bedroll. Chess had told him that they would start out trapping along the Snake River.

The area where they camped the first night was familiar to Beau. While trapping with Reiner he had seen the same mountain peaks in the distance. The wind was carrying the smell of rain. They were camping in the open near a small stream.

"Should we set up the fly tarps?" Beau asked.

Chess was chewing jerky while drinking their evening coffee. "We might get some rain, but I figure it's coming down in the mountains and will be all over by the time the clouds reach us."

"Well," Beau said, "no sense in setting up more than we need."

He put his packs close together and rolled out his blankets near the fire. Using his saddle for a pillow, he put the Colt underneath. His rifle was under the edge of his blankets. He laid an extra ground cloth over his blankets to keep the dew off.

The sound of thunder woke Beau with a start. The wind was tearing at his blankets, and ash and sparks were blowing out of the cook fire. He grabbed at the ground tarp just before the wind had a chance to rip it away and send it flying. Sparks and ash were landing on his blankets. There was a flash of lightning, giving the river basin an eerie light, showing swirling dust being blown by the wind. It went through the camp with sandblasting force, hitting his exposed face.

Turning away from the wind, Beau covered his head, trying to get the dust out of his eyes. Then came the rain and hail. Pulling the blankets tighter for protection, the young man was pummeled by the downpour and biting pieces of ice.

"Rain in the mountains!" he shouted at Chess, the words being ripped from his lips and lost in the storm.

For an hour, the storm raged. Beau could feel the flood waters from the stream running under his blankets while the rain soaked him from above. He had a grip on the extra ground tarp, but had no opportunity to pull it over him. As quickly as it had come, the rain stopped, the wind driving the storm to the east. The heavy clouds remaining made it ink black outside.

Then he heard Chess. "You still with me?"

"What happened to rain in the mountains?" Beau asked, mocking his partner.

"Well, hell, Beau," Chess said. "I imagine there was rain in the mountains. I figured it would be done before it got here."

Beau could hear Chess shaking his blankets and trying to arrange things enough to get back to sleep. "You're lucky you had that ground tarp to cover you," he told the young man.

"I sure am lucky," Beau snorted. "That was the first thing the wind blew off. Then there was the river running under me."

The young man could hear Chess laughing as the two of them tried to arrange their bedding enough to get back to sleep. Beau was curled in the fetal position with the extra ground tarp wrapped around him when the sun came up. He was thoroughly soaked and covered with dirt. He sat up shivering in the cool morning.

Chess' blankets were empty and Beau saw him with the animals. A single tree stood a quarter-mile away, so the young man pulled his boots on over his wet socks. The firewood they had collected last night was half-buried in mud from the rushing groundwater. Grabbing his hatchet, Beau headed for the tree to fetch some dry wood. It was almost an hour before they had coffee ready. The small stream they'd slept near had overrun its banks and soaked everything.

"I suggest we pack stuff just like it is and head for the trees that we'll find at the base of the mountain, yonder," Chess recommended.

The men quickly loaded the animals and rode in search of trees. After two hours of riding in damp, dirt filled clothes, they reached a stand of aspen. Both the rifle and Colt were useless after the soaking. Looking around, Beau could only see one benefit from the storm. The late summer grass seemed to be greener. They would have good grazing for the stock.

Both men stripped down to their long johns. Shaking as much dirt out of the clothing as possible, they hung them on branches. Then they shook and hung their blankets. They unpacked their extra clothing and buckskins to hang up. Chess started a fire while Beau began to go through the supplies. It reminded him of the trip from Fort William with Peter and Joshua. Almost half of their dry goods were damaged by water. He spread the white beans and coffee beans out on a ground tarp to dry. The tobacco twists he hung on branches. The cornmeal was wet and the cold flour was hopeless.

Beau set the cornmeal by the fire to be cooked. The cold flour he looked at with regret. The salt was wet, but would dry in a hard block. Chess went by wringing out another pair of socks. "This was our misfortune for this trip. Glad we got it over with."

"I surely won't be asking you to predict rain again," Beau promised.

The day was spent drying and dusting out. Beau kept a pan of thin, crisp corncakes going. They would store for a few days, providing for their meals. The jerky they had was dried over the smoky campfire. Once the clothing and blankets were dry, they were shaken to try to get additional dirt out of them. Beau worked on the rifles and revolver to get them back into working order.

The next morning, what was left was packed and the men continued. It was late morning when Chess held up his hand to alert Beau. Beyond a swale in front of them was a small herd of elk. They were mostly female with a few young males. Chess swung off the buckskin. Getting off his pony, Beau joined him.

"We got jerky on the hoof, right out there," Chess said. "We can lead the horses to the marsh area and then crawl within range of the elk."

"We best stay close to our horses," Beau said. "That way they won't be able to pick us out from our animals."

"I agree," Chess replied. Putting their horses between them and the elk, they walked down the depression, working diagonally toward the willows near the swampy area.

Tying the animals in the trees, the two hunters crouched as they worked their way closer to the game. Finally, they had to crawl on their stomachs through the short grass and sage toward a low ledge of rock, where they could hide before rising to take aim. The men lay beneath it, catching their breath. The elk might have wandered from the area, since they'd left the far side of the swale. Hoping that wasn't the case, Chess removed his hat. They were ready.

Coming up slowly, they saw the elk just over 150 paces away, well within range of their rifles. Excitement building in them, the two men took aim. On Chess' command, they fired. The shots echoed off the ridges on both sides. The startled elk began to race across the valley. One fell, rolling to a stop. Then a second one stopped. It stood with its head hanging for a couple of seconds before sinking to its knees and falling over.

"Yes!" Beau exclaimed, as Chess slapped him on the back. Two shots, two elk. Before venturing out, the two men loaded their rifles. Once finished, they climbed over the rock ledge and trotted toward the elk. Between the two animals, there were probably 1,000 pounds lying on the valley floor. Each elk would provide about 250 pounds of meat. Once dried, it would be just over 100 pounds from each.

The thrill of the hunt was soon replaced by the vast job in front of them, deboning and drying the meat. Beau gutted the elk while Chess went after the horses and mule. They used the horses to drag them to the willows. Hoisting the elk into the trees, Chess began to skin the first animal. Beau collected wood for their fire and started cutting poles to make racks for drying the meat.

They were glad that the threat of rain had gone. In the higher elevations, the meat would sun dry in as little as six hours. Beau built a rack about four by eight feet and weaved willow branches on the long sides. They planned to build a smoky fire and let the west wind carry it through the meat. It would not only add some flavor, but would also help keep the flies off.

Beau then cut a log six feet long and split it. Using the hatchet, he smoothed one half as best he could and set it off the ground on two blocks. This they would use for cutting the strips of meat. He sunk two fork sticks next to the log, to cradle the poles used to hang the meat before placing them on the rack.

Chess began to cut chunks of meat and laid them on the hide near the cutting log. "You built us quite the processing system here," he complimented the young man.

"We got a whole lot of meat to dry," Beau said. "It could take a week."

Soon the rack was loaded with fresh meat. There was a fire on the west end, allowing the smoke to flow through. On some green sticks Beau had strips of liver roasting for their meal.

Both of the men were covered with blood and fat as they continued the cutting. There was a creek running from the swamp next to them. The two men used it to rinsed their hands before dining on the liver.

They were thankful that the nights were cool, to help preserve the meat. After the second day, they started rubbing salt onto the meat to stop spoilage. At the end of the third day, with little sleep at night, the drying was done and they used one of the scraped hides to make bags to carry the jerky. Each bag was 100 pounds.

Leaving the area for nature to clean up, the two men were happy to get away from the now rotting smell of the elk bones and discarded flesh. On the last day, buzzards had been walking around their camp, looking for opportunities to steal a scrap here and there. Within another day, wolves or coyotes would be after whatever remained.

* * *

The men and horses were slowly moving west. It was the first week of August. "We have to go to Fort Hall," Chess said.

"I thought we were headed for the Yellowstone," Beau replied.

"The beaver will wait, and the pelts will only get better," Chess explained. "We lost much needed supplies in the flood. We now have more jerky than we need and can trade some for supplies at the fort."

"How far do you figure the fort is?" the young man asked.

"Five, maybe six days. We should be back by the end of August and have out traps in the water. The fort is on the Snake River. We can follow the basin right up into the Yellowstone."

During one of the nights the two men were camping at nearly 10,000 feet above sea level. The sky was clear and the air cold. Beau sat with a blanket wrapped around him, looked up at the stars and swore that if he looked hard enough, he would be able to see heaven. The brightness of the larger stars and the millions of the distant ones in the milky way gave him the feeling that he was being pulled into them.

Chess found him the next morning, curled up in the blanket next to the dead cook fire. "Did you spend the night keeping watch? There's not too many enemies up this high."

Chilled with just the blanket on him, Beau shivered. "I figured by morning I'd be sleeping in the stars."

"Let's get some breakfast," Chess said. "By noon we'll be at the fort."

Fort Hall was situated on a grassy bluff near the Snake River. The white stone and log wall surrounded the fort. The Hudson Bay Company had purchased it in 1837 after successfully competing in the fur trade against the prior owner, Nathaniel Wyeth. They controlled the Snake River and beyond to the Columbia River valley. Chess had cautioned Beau not to mention that they would be trapping along the Snake.

The main gate stood open as the men rode into the fort. Several log buildings lined the inside of the walls. Chess stopped in front of the trading post. A second building connected by a curtained doorway had a bar and several tables. It could also provide a traveler with a meal. Three loafers were sitting in front of the building. Chess and Beau tied their animals to the metal rings fastened to posts in front of the buildings.

The two men walked into the trading post. Chess told Beau, "We'll talk to this gent a moment before we go have a drink."

A grizzled looking fellow ran the post. He was thickly built and covered in hair. His moustache was yellow from pipe smoke and he was missing his teeth on the right side. He took a long look at the two men.

"Is there something I can help you with?" he asked.

"We would like to talk about doing some trading," Chess said. "We got . . ."

He was cut off by a voice behind him. "Zeke, these boys were at the rendezvous and traded with the Americans."

The men looked back. It was one of the loafers from the front. Not denying it, Chess said, "Your right, we did trade our furs at the rendezvous."

"Well, then," Zeke sneered, "you best head for St. Louis to finish your trading."

"It ain't furs we got," Chess argued. "We got jerky made fresh from elk. I figure we got 100 pounds."

Zeke looked for a bit at the man standing behind them. Then he said, "Bring it in here and let me taste it."

Beau went out to the animals. He took the bag that they'd made from the second elk. Hefting it onto his shoulder, he carried it inside and placed it on the counter. The trading post owner reached inside and sniffed a piece. He then tore a hunk off with his good, left side teeth. Slowly, he chewed with little expression on his beard-covered face.

Rolling the bag, he dug toward the bottom and brought out another piece. He handed it to the man who had followed them in. "It's good jerky," the man said.

Chess figured that they had near $20 worth of jerky in the bag. It was time to start dickering. "What we need is some cornmeal, cold flour, salt, some tobacco, coffee, and tea." Looking at Beau, he asked, "Did I miss anything?"

Zeke interrupted him, "What in hell do you think you got here? Gold?"

Beau wandered outside and looked around the fort. Inside the two men went back and forth on the value of the trade. Zeke could use the jerky and wanted to give as little as possible for it. There was a British flag flying over the fort. He took a seat on the bench in front of the trading post.

"Where'd you shoot the elk?" the man who had come into the store asked.

Beau figured that was a leading question and what he really wanted to know is if the elk were shot on British territory. "We got then near the south pass," he lied.

The man snorted, "You didn't trade it at the rendezvous?"

"Chess here kind of takes a liking to this fort and wanted to bring it here," Beau replied. "We plan to trade furs here next spring." He figured that with nothing to lose, he might as well lie all the way.

For an hour, the dickering went on. Finally, Chess emerged with most of what he was after. They would have to do with the coffee they now had. Zeke followed him out, carrying the cornmeal. He eyed the second bag of jerky.

"You looking to trade that also?" the owner asked.

"We'll be brewing that instead of coffee this winter," Chess replied.

The fort had an unfriendly feel about it. Beau knew that the U.S. was at odds with the Mexicans but he had figured that the British would be easier to get along with. The men from the Hudson Bay Company who'd gone to the rendezvous seemed happy to see the trappers.

Chess wanted to have a couple of drinks before leaving. Beau tied the animals in front of the open door and kept one eye on them while they downed shots of whiskey.

After picking up some bottles to go, the two men mounted their horses and led the pack animals out of the gate. The haze was off the mountains, which stood rugged, rising from the grassy plain.

* * *

The ride up the Snake River was beautiful. While Chess seemed to ride without noticing, Beau's head swiveled back and forth, trying to take in everything. It was the end of August when they came onto sign of beaver activity. It was two miles off the Snake River, on a small stream. There was a cut into the foothills where the stream originated. The cut was filled with aspen.

The pond had a dam that was a hundred paces long. Chess smiled and pointed. "From here I can see a half-dozen lodges."

Both men knew that some were probably abandoned, but they had found an overlooked stream and would have a good start for their first wetting of the traps. They set up their camp away from the pond. By the time that they had their supper ready it was dark. In the distance they heard a tree fall. It was a beaver at work.

Both men awoke, looking forward to the day. The traps had been boiled and oiled with fat from the elk. They had their stakes cut and peeled. All was ready. Leading the mule, Beau crossed the stream and went to some canals he had seen on the far side of the pond.

The air was comfortable so, as before, he removed his trousers and socks. Putting the low-cut moccasins on, he waded into the water. The muck on the bottom oozed into the footwear. Clearing debris from the canal, he placed the set trap. He then drove the stake into the bottom, securing the trap. Tying the leather string to the stake, he untangled it and tied it to a low bush on the bank. He then put the bait stick over the trap and applied the castor.

Slogging out of the water, he walked over to the mule, muck squishing in his moccasins. Beau continued on to the next canal and set another trap.

Continuing along the edge, he ended up with four traps set. He headed back for their camp. Walking into camp without trousers brought the expected laugh from Chess.

Beau sat near the stream and rinsed the mud from his moccasins and from his feet. The legs of his long johns were almost dry. Putting on his trousers and socks, he then pulled on the low boots and headed back to the fire.

Chess' buckskin britches were drying over an aspen branch. "I may look funny without my pants, but come cooler weather, I won't be waiting for them to dry."

It was a weak argument and did little good to stop the kidding from Chess. The two men spent the day making hoops in anticipation of beaver pelts to stretch tomorrow. The pond turned out to be a good start for the season. They ended up with six beavers before they moved on. Days were spent following streams to find beaver. The Snake River had been worked hard in the past years. The two men traveled miles along streams in hopes of finding a pond.

On one deeper, fast-flowing stream, they found some bank dens. The beavers had built the den on the bank of the stream and could depend on the water remaining open for access to food on the shore throughout the winter. Setting the traps were more of a challenge. Most of the places where the beavers exited the water was flowing too fast for a trap.

Chess dug into the bank above the den with hopes that a beaver would choose that exit or be drawn to the castor. Four additional dens were found over a three mile section of the stream. The men spent a week trapping the stream, catching only two beavers. Finally, they gave up and went to find another place.

Beau was digging through his pack when he came across the worn holster. He used some fat and rubbed it into the leather. Then he took the Colt Paterson out of his possible bag and tried it in the holster. It fit well, except for the flap the went over the revolver. He decided to flip it back and make a belt loop out of it. Using leather string, he poked holes with the tip of his knife and sewed the flap into place.

His trousers and buckskin britches were held up by a leather strap that was tied. While the waistband would support the Colt, the belt alone would not. The broader belt worn outside his buckskin coat would work well. He could wear it over the top of his shirt and trousers. Beau liked the feel of the Colt at his side. He put a loop on the holster to prevent the Colt from falling out.

Pulling the revolver, he noticed that he didn't have to worry about it catching his shirt. Beau was standing near the cook fire drawing the Colt when Chess came back from relieving himself. He stopped and watched his partner.

"You're going to shoot your toe off if you keep playing with that revolver," Chess warned.

"I just want to make sure how the holster works." Beau liked the feeling of the Colt on his hip.

After a week of searching, they finally found an active pond surrounded by maple trees. It was early September, but there was already color showing. Sharp slaps of tails were heard as they rode near the water's edge.

The maples continued up a steep hillside and the two men decided to make their camp at its base. In the next couple of weeks, the ground would be covered with the red and orange leaves. It was one of the favorite times of year for Beau. It had always signaled the time to hunt. Living in the mountains, they shot game year-round, whenever the opportunity presented itself, but fall still had special meaning.

Chess got the fire going and put a pot of beans to boil. Beau decided to go and set a couple of traps in the ebbing light. He rode the pony back to the pond. Tying it to a maple, he got his traps and stakes ready. He hung the possible bag on the saddle horn while he pulled off his boots and trousers. Slinging the possible bag over his shoulder, he decided to leave the Colt and powder horn.

With a trap and stake in hand, he waded into the water. A short distance up the bank he could see a spot where the beaver climbed out of the water. The bottom was sandy and firm, which made walking easy. Several rocks forced him to wade in hip-deep water. The cold nights had dropped the temperature of the water.

Pushing against the water, Beau stepped out and the bottom disappeared! In his haste to set the trap, he had not felt his way with the securing stake. Suddenly he was underwater, weighted down by the trap in his grip. He had stepped off a ridge, hidden by the pond. He released the trap and stake and fought to swim to the surface. Without his feet touching bottom, he had no idea which way was up. He paddled furiously, he lungs burning for air and his mouth full of water. The possible bag was dragging like an anchor.

His head finally broke the surface and Beau gasped for air, only to slide under again. He was choking and trying to cough. Again, he broke the surface. Stroking for all he was worth, he struggled to stay above the water. Violent coughs shook his body and he tried to get the water out of his lungs. He stared wide eyed for the safety of the shore. He was out almost 30 feet.

Fighting down the panic that was surging inside, he began to swim for shore. Between the coughing and the drag of the possible bag, his progress was slow. His frantic kicks were causing cramps in the back of his legs. He feared putting his legs down to feel for the bottom, knowing that he would never be able to kick his way up again. After what seemed like an eternity, his hand finally grasped a low bush at the shore. For several minutes he stood, trying to work the cramps out of his legs. Finally, he began to climb onto the shore, his clothes and the bag weighing heavily on him.

Beau collapsed onto the grassy bank and lay there coughing, his lungs aching. He managed to pull the possible bag's strap over his head and sit up. His legs continued to spasm from the cramps. He looked at his feet. The moccasins were gone. Out on the pond he saw them floating. Nearby was the stake for securing the trap. A soft breeze was blowing them away from shore, toward the dam.

Staring at the pond, Beau realized that the trap was lost. There was no way that he was going into the deeper water to find it. He opened the flap on his possible bag. It was nearly full of water. He drained what he could without dumping the contents. He continued to cough, his body attempting to clear the lungs. Standing up, he felt drained of strength. Dragging the bag, he made his way to the pony. The act of climbing into the saddle seemed like too much of an effort. He hung the bag on the saddle horn and then walked beside the horse, heading for the camp.

It was dark when he arrived and Chess was scooping beans onto his plate. "Maybe we'll have a beaver in your traps in the morning. We could use the fresh meat."

When the fire light fell on Beau, Chess looked at his partner, shocked by what he saw. Dropping the plate, he rushed to help him. "What in the hell happened to you?"

After another coughing fit, Beau said, "I damn near drowned myself."

Once he had settled him near the fire, Chess poured a cup of coffee and handed it to Beau.

The hot brew was difficult to swallow, yet made his throat feel better. "I was setting the first trap when I hit a drop off. Me, the trap and everything went under water," Beau explained.

"Damn the trap, Beau," Chess said. "We can get more. Burying you in the morning couldn't be undone."

Kicking the spilt beans into the fire, Chess refilled the plate and handed it to Beau. He then filled another for himself. The coffee was helping the young man to recover. He continued to try clearing his throat as he ate. He began to shiver in the cold night air. Moving closer to the fire, he soaked in the warmth. Chess laid a dry shirt onto the ground and dumped the contents of the possible bag. He separated the items to help them dry. The bag was propped open in front of the fire.

Slowly, Beau told Chess about the experience as best he could. He was sure that he wasn't in the water very long, but it had felt like it. Chess promised to go and look for the moccasins and the trap left on the bank first thing in the morning. He also pulled the saddle off the pony for his partner. He set it and the Colt near his blankets.

Stripping down, Beau put on dry clothes. Chess dug out a bottle of whiskey and poured a good measure into the coffee mug. The young man drank sips of the liquor. It helped to warm his insides. He then got under his blankets and was soon sleeping.

It was full daylight when Beau awoke. Chess was back with the trap that had been left on the bank. "I fear your moccasins went to the bottom before they floated across the pond. I poked around where you went in and the water after the drop off was damn deep. We best be careful in this pond. The stream they dammed was a deep one."

The near drowning experience took more out of Beau than he had expected. He had chills and fever, along with a deep cough. He stayed around camp doing what he could and resting. The pond was trapped out by the time he regained his strength. Chess kidded him regularly about milking his fall in the water. Deep down he was worried about Beau. There weren't any doctors in the mountains and if a man got ill, it was only the ability of his own body to fight the affliction that would save him.

They rode out of the maples, looking for the next pond. While the young man had a catch in his throat that he continued to try and clear, he was feeling ready to work. The leaves were changing, bringing brilliant colors to the hillsides. The next hard rain would strip most of them from the trees. They had started waking to frost. Beau was wearing his buckskins over his wool shirt and trousers. He would continue wearing the low-heel boots until snow came.

It was early October and the trappers were heading for streams on the east side of the Snake River. The mule was carrying a spring buck that Beau had shot earlier in the day. They were riding over a rise when there was the smell of smoke. In the valley below they saw it filtering through evergreens.

Chess led the way down the slope, toward the smoke. He doubted that the camp was trappers. With the coolness of the day, he would have expected a bigger fire. He also pointed out that there was a stream a quarter-mile across the valley. Trappers would have camped closer to the water.

They rounded the grove of spruce, their rifles ready across their saddles. The trees had an opening that held the camp. Stopping just in sight of the teepees, they heard dogs barking and saw the Indians. Three of the braves leaped onto their ponies and rode out to meet them, stopping within range of their bows.

Chess knew some sign and indicated that they had come in peace. He pointed at the spring buck and made a gesture of joining them to eat. The braves moved to the side, allowing the trappers to approach the camp. Beau was not comfortable having armed braves behind him. He had memories of finding Gus, who had been attacked from the back.

Riding ahead, Chess spoke softly, "They're Flathead and they are coming from hunting for meat. They are headed for their winter camp."

As they got closer, Beau saw the women and children farther in the camp. The men stopped at the fire near the front and dismounted from their animals. One of the braves rode into the camp and spoke to the others. Two women came and retrieved the buck from the mule. A short distance from the fire they began skinning the animal. There were several dogs watching them, looking forward to whatever was left.

"You see those dogs?" Chess said, pointing. "The spring buck will give one of them another day or so to live."

The young man knew that the Indians were practical. The dogs would be used to help carry packs, alert them of intruders, or provide them with a meal. "Do you think they know of Eli or his wife?" Beau asked.

"It is unlikely," Chess replied. "My guess is these Flathead have been traveling the mountain valleys all summer and are now headed to join up with others, which may include Eli."

The trappers tied their horses and mule to evergreen branches and sat near the fire. An older Flathead joined them. His face was creased and his hair white. He spoke some English and began to asked them about where they had been. He told them that their hunt for meat had been good, but beaver pelts for trade had been poor.

They were interested in the rendezvous and hoped to be at the next one. Beau told him about Eli and the wedding. The old man repeated this to the other braves and they seemed to lower their guard just a little. The women finished cutting up the spring buck and added much of the meat to a large pot of water steaming on the fire. The trappers would have been happier roasting the venison over the fire, but would not complain of how their hosts cooked the meat.

This was the first-time Beau had visited an Indian encampment. He watched the activity going on around him. The women were busy with the duties of getting food ready and bringing in wood. The braves sat around the fire, listening to their elder visit with the trappers. Children stood outside the circle, curious about the strangers. The camp had a harmony he liked. Life would be good for Eli if all the Flathead lived like this.

While they ate the meat, fishing pieces from their clay-fired bowls. Chess told the elder about the close call Beau had had in the pond. The trapper used a bit of humor telling the story, and when the elder translated to the braves it got a laugh out of them. They pointed at his feet, enjoying the story.

The elder looked at Beau and said, "They say losing your moccasins is why you have to wear the clumsy things on your feet." Beau looked down at the worn boots on his feet and smiled at the old man agreeing as he picked another piece from his bowl. The meat was a little chewy and had the flavor of the sage that the spring buck had been eating. There was little other seasoning in the pot.

After the meal was finished, Chess presented the elder with a twist of tobacco. A pipe was brought out and smoked. It was slowly passed around to all the men at the fire. The trappers thanked the elder for their hospitality and told him that they would make camp near the river. The old man insisted that they sleep in one of the teepees. Thanking them, the trappers took care of their animals. The packs were placed just outside the teepee.

There was a small fire inside the teepee, the smoke rising through an opening at the top. Two poles on the outside were used for adjusting the opening. Skins lined the floor for sitting or sleeping. There was a strong smell of smoke, evergreens, and the occupants in the teepee. One of the women pointed to the spot where Chess and Beau would sleep.

The young man worried about their packs outside, but Chess seemed comfortable with the arrangements. Beau had his Colt on his hip and carried his rifle into the teepee. He wasn't sure if they had been expected to leave them with the packs or not, but there was no way he was going to allow any distance between the rifle and himself.

Beau discovered that the skin he rolled his blanket on had a lining of spruce boughs under it. Sleeping in the teepee offered little privacy. Four other Flathead joined them inside. The young man laid awake for some time, listening to the night noises of the Flathead camp. The bed of boughs was comfortable and finally he slept.

The next morning the camp was busy. The Flathead were moving. Beau ducked through the opening of the teepee. A quick glance told him that the packs were still there. Then he stopped. Sitting on top of one of the packs was a new pair of moccasins. Looking up, he noticed several Flathead were grinning at him. Smiling back, he removed the boots and slipped on the moccasins. It seemed to please their hosts.

He was stuffing the boots into the packs when Chess came out of the teepee, followed closely by a young Flathead woman. She hurried to the fire and filled two bowls from the cookpot. Handing one to Chess, she gave him a sweet smile. She handed the second one to Beau and then went to help the other women.

Digging into his possible bag, Beau brought out a spoon. The two trappers sat near the packs and tasted the food. It was some kind of crushed grain, ground with wild berries. It had been boiled to the consistency of mush. It had a pleasant taste, slightly sweet from the berries.

Between spoonful's, Beau asked, "Did you sleep well, Chess?"

"Yes, I did," he replied. "I surely did."

"I am surprised you slept at all," the young man kidded.

Swallowing the mouthful of mush, Chess said, "Nice moccasins you got there."

By the time that the two men had the packs on their animals, all of the teepees had been taken down. Some of the poles were used as travois and put on horses or dogs to carry the Flatheads food and gear.

The elder came over to the two trappers. "It is good to share with our brothers in the mountains."

Chess handed a knife to the old man. "May this knife provide food for your families, and protect you from those that would bring harm."

Beau was impressed by the amount of ceremony and respect that was given with a chance meeting in the mountains. At another time with different circumstances, the meeting could have been one of conflict. He was sure that this meeting would create a lasting peace and friendship for them with the Flathead.

With the braves in the lead on horseback, the Flathead departed on the way to their winter camp. Chess and Beau sat and watched until they were out of sight. The two men then continued toward the stream and on to the Yellowstone.

CHAPTER SIXTEEN

There was snow on the ground when the two trappers reached the Yellowstone. Trapping in the Snake River region had been okay. Chess told Beau of days past when the beaver were plentiful and a man could work the whole season without venturing further. Now with many of the beaver depleted, the trappers spent much of their time looking for the next pond.

The Yellowstone offered grass-covered meadows, plenty of streams, meat for the winter, and another thing which left Beau in awe: Geysers! He sat on the pony with his mouth open as he saw steaming water shoot out of the ground while the temperature around them was below freezing.

It was not the first time that the young man had seen warm springs, but to see it bursting forth into the sky was new to him. They ate their mid-day meal near a huge geyser that shot twice over 100 feet into the air while they watched. One lasted almost five minutes.

The men continued riding north, passing several smaller geysers. Chess told him that the ground was white near the geysers, summer and winter. They also saw green and yellow steaming pools. Again, like so many places he had been to in the mountains, Beau wanted to come back here and camp for a summer.

They passed a herd of buffalo grazing, sweeping the snow away with their massive heads. Chess pointed to a young bull. "We can use some fresh meet."

Beau swung off the horse and removed the feather that he used to prevent moisture from getting in the touch hole. He then primed the pan. Beau had learned about tuning his flintlock from Peter during the first rendezvous. Since then he had been more confident of the rifle firing every time.

Pulling back the hammer, he lined the sites on the bull. He squeezed the trigger, smoke and fire belching from the rifle. The young buffalo's head came up quickly before it rolled onto its side. The other buffalo were undisturbed by the sound of the flintlock as they slowly moved away, grazing. Beau reloaded the rifle before they rode up to skin the animal.

On the second day in Yellowstone they found beaver dens on a fast-flowing stream. They spent more time in the frigid water setting the traps than it would have taken on a pond. Beau was wearing the buckskins to give him some protection from the icy water. It was getting close to November and soon all the ponds and streams would be frozen over.

"We'll be riding north to Gardner's Hole for the winter," Chess told Beau.

Back in the '30s a trapper had given the river headwater area his name. Off and on since then, trappers would winter there. Chess had used one of the abandoned cabins for several winters. The area backed up to the foothills of mountains to the west. They offered some protection from winter storms.

The men had scraped the young buffalo's hide. Although it was green, it could be used during the cold of winter. The trapping continued in streams that were kept open by runoff from the geysers. They were setting traps on land as well as in the water and had managed to catch several otters and some mink. Chess and Beau had also shot two wolves that were chasing a young elk. Wolf skins could also be used during the frigid days of winter.

The temperate weather allowed the men to continue trapping until early December. When they finally arrived at the cabin at Gardner's Hole, the wind was howling and snow swirled around the building. It was situated in a sparsely wooded area near a river, which was frozen over except for areas of rapids. Chess mentioned that he had caught trout in the rapids during past winters.

The cabin had one window that was shuttered. A plank door hung on leather hinges. It swung in and was partly open when they arrived. The dirt floor was covered with snow, with some drifts a foot high. The roof and fireplace appeared sound. The south side had a lean-to for the horses and mule. The wind was keeping most of the ground blown clear, exposing brown prairie grass. The Yellowstone River ran a few miles east of the cabin.

Beau's feet were numb when he climbed down from the pony. The thick hair and eyes of the animals were crusted with snow. They had plenty of daylight left to take care of unpacking and getting the cabin habitable, but with the blowing snow the task seemed insurmountable. Chess fought the door for a bit and finally got it open enough to haul their packs and gear in. They chose a spot with the least amount of snow to place them for now.

Beau brought the animals around the cabin and put them in the lean-to. They would not get much protection from the swirling snow with the south side being open. He would have liked to hobble them on the grass so they could graze, but they would have moved with the wind and could be a mile away by morning.

There was a pile of wood to one side of the lean-to. Beau picked up an armload and carried it into the cabin. Chess was using a plank that kept the door shut to scrape and push the snow out. "I found wood!" Beau shouted over the wind.

"I guess we have the last squatter to thank for that. I wish the bugger had closed the door," Chess growled.

The fire helped to add some light to the dim interior of the cabin. Beau brought in a couple more armloads and stacked it near the fireplace. Several of the logs had gaps where the chinking had fallen out, letting wind and snow filter in. Beau pitched in removing the snow from the cabin floor. Finally giving up, realizing that the amount blowing in the open door was making their attempts futile, Chess pushed the door closed and leaned the short plank against it to secure it.

Once the chimney warmed up, the fireplace drew well and stopped filling the cabin with smoke. The window's shutter hinges had stretched and they rattled in the storm. The cabin was furnished with a crude table and two three-legged stools. There were two shelves made from hand-hewed planks. A couple of rusty tins sat on one. Dead evergreen boughs were the only evidence of where prior occupants had slept.

Beau was surprised at how quickly the small cabin warmed up with the fire going. The men were soon stripped down to their long john tops. Dirt from the floor clung to their calf-high moccasins as the remaining snow melted. Chess dug the coffee pot from the packs and filled it with snow. Setting it near the flames, he went back to dig for coffee beans. Beau pulled the old boughs into a pile and put them next to the fireplace for kindling. The floor in that area was covered with old needles and was fairly dry.

Sitting at the table, the young man looked around the cabin. "It kinda reminds me of my place on Crowley Ridge," he said. "Of course, there I had sound walls, a bunk, and even a sideboard for putting meals together."

Confused, Chess asked, "How could this remind you of your old cabin? This has none of that."

"Yes, but it *is* small."

* * *

After a few days, the two men had the cabin quite comfortable. The storm had blown out and they had brought in fresh evergreen boughs to soften their beds. Most of the cracks had been chinked with strips of green hide. The routine of taking care of the animals had been set up. Chess even caught some fish in the river. One morning Beau had spotted some deer feeding on a distant hillside. Plans were made to build a blind to lay for the animals. Both men did some distance shooting at targets to pass the time. Beau also did some practicing with the Colt. The practice did pay off. Chess brought down one of the deer that ventured in the cabin's direction. Beau managed to shoot a couple of rabbits with the revolver.

The snow in the hills was nearly two feet deep and made hunting difficult. One day, Chess came back with some slender saplings. He demonstrated how to make snowshoes out of them and strips of deer hide. They had set up a trap line in the foothills. Beau found that the snowshoes worked well for walking the line.

They had a worn deck of cards and played some. Neither had any books or other reading material. The back wall of the cabin was scarred from where they competed throwing their knives. Winter was hardly half over when Beau roasted the last of their coffee beans. Tobacco was also just a memory.

It was the end of February and the day was cold and clear. Beau had a frozen marten in his game bag and was making the turn back toward the cabin when he heard a scraping sound. It was a porcupine's quills rattling against balsam branches as it climbed looking for tender bark.

Beau drew the Colt Paterson and fired without holding it out and aiming. The ball struck the tree just beside the porcupine. "You're getting better," he said with satisfaction. He then took careful aim at the animal, which was now moving more quickly up the tree, and fired.

The porcupine stopped climbing, holding on to the tree. Then, as though in slow motion, it fell, tumbling through the balsam branches. Beau tied it onto a stick and carried the animal, taking care not to let the quills poke him. It had been a couple of weeks since he and Chess had eaten fresh meat and the porcupine would be a nice change.

The beginning of March brought a late blizzard. Chess had been out hunting when the snow had started. By the time he arrived back at the cabin the wind was tearing at his clothes. Beau was bringing in the stock when Chess appeared out of the storm. Shouting back and forth to be heard, they led the animals in the lean-to, secured the lead ropes and then began carrying wood into the cabin.

The shutters and roof boards rattled from the impact of the wind. "We sure don't need more snow," Chess complained.

"We'll be boiling our boots for supper if the weather doesn't break soon," the young man replied.

It was three nights before they awoke to silence outdoors. Inside, the cabin was covered with a thin layer of snow. There was a rope secured to the outside wall near the door and it had been used as a lifeline for checking on the stock, getting wood, and relieving themselves during the blizzard. Each day of the storm the first chore of the day was brushing snow off the table and the packs of supplies. The wood supply was all but depleted, and had the snow continued for another couple of days they would have had to burn the furniture.

While Beau took the horses and mule to the river and chopped a hole so they could drink, Chess went to cut wood. Beau led the horses to help bring the felled trees to the cabin. There was lots to do near the cabin cutting the wood, so they let the animals graze at will. Chess caught sight of a wolf looking over their stock and sent a shot in its direction. The startled wolf ran into the foothills.

The trappers had finished soup made from bits of meat and raccoon bones and a little cold flour. Unsure of how long the freezing temperatures would last, they gleaned all the food value out of animals caught in the trap line. Beau picked up the pot and headed for the door to toss the bare bones out. When he pulled the door open, less frigid air promising the coming of spring filled the cabin. "If this keeps up, we'll be trapping in a couple of weeks," he called.

Spring came in fits and starts. A few warm days would give promise, only to be followed by cold and snow. The only saving grace was that the days were getting longer and the grip of winter would soon be defeated. The horses and mule were gaunt from the long winter. They would need time to gain their strength before carrying the men and packs around the rivers and streams.

Two weeks of warm weather broke the ice on the river. Melting snow from the foothills raised the water, causing large slabs of ice to tumble and crash as it was washed downstream. The sun against the hillside helped the life-giving grasses to sprout earlier than the prairie. The animals spent their days grazing and gaining strength. The same grass brought in the hungry mule deer. Beau had been practicing closing his eyes and re-gripping the rifle and had gotten the procedure down. He tested it out on one of the distant deer and scored a hit.

Two weeks of cold spring rain took care of most of the remaining snow. The cabin roof allowed ample water in during the storm. Thunder and lightning crashed as the heavy clouds rolled across the foothills and prairie. Spring flowers were up in the woodlands and the swiftly running rivers and streams were quickly carving new routes through the lowlands.

It was April before good weather returned. The two men were making ready to leave the cabin. They would be heading back into the Yellowstone. The mountains in the distance were still snow-covered. Beau was roasting mule deer on a fire in front of the cabin. After the long winter cooped up in the cabin, the two men spent as much time as possible outside.

Three trappers came in from the north. They stopped short of the cabin and hailed Beau. Looking up, he waved them in. "We ain't got much, but you're welcome to share what we do have."

"That's mighty neighborly of you," a heavyset trapper said. The other two were much younger. Probably the man's sons.

"We got some coffee to add to the meal," the man added. "You wouldn't have some chew by any chance?"

Chess came around the cabin. He had been out of sight with his rifle ready. "Our tobacco run out months ago, but the coffee sure is welcome."

While trappers were cut of the same cloth, when they met in the mountains certain precautions were taken. It was sort of like two wild animals coming together. Once the smell and character had been looked over, they could let some of their guard down. Beau's Colt remained on his hip and Chess set the rifle within easy reach while the three visitors climbed off their horses and joined them around the fire.

The coffee smelled like heaven as the beans were roasted. Once crushed they were added to a hot pot of water. "How's your year been?" Chess asked.

"Fair," the big man said. "We was north near to Canada and found a couple good streams. Most had been trapped out."

"Don't much make a difference," Chess said. "They don't pay much of beaver anymore."

"Were going to work our way to Fort Hall and trade," the visiting trapper said. "Don't believe there'll be a rendezvous this year."

"I'm hoping as long as there are mountain men, there will be the rendezvous," Beau said, taking the venison off the fire.

The table had been brought out next to the fire and the young man used it to cut the venison haunch into pieces. The trappers stuck their knives into the hot, juicy meat and began tearing at it, the drippings running down their beards. The coffee was saved until after the meat was eaten. Chess and Beau did not want to hurry drinking the dark brew. While they sipped the coffee, the heavyset trapper said, "We run across a couple of dead Cheyenne a day ago."

"Are tribes that-a-way fighting?" Chess asked.

"They was scalped, but it weren't Indians," the man said. "Looked like it was whites. Probably will be selling the scalps at the forts. They'll be worth three beaver each."

Beau looked at Chess. "Other Cheyenne will be looking for revenge."

"More than likely," Chess replied. "We'll have to watch our topknots."

With the meal finished, the large man hefted himself up and said, "Thanky for the grub. You cook good deer." The two younger trappers followed him to their horses. "I'd recommend you leave the area soon."

Chess and Beau watch the three trappers ride away, leading their pack animals. Speaking in a low voice, Beau said, "I wonder if the younger ones speak?"

"I wonder if they got a couple of scalps in their packs," Chess replied.

There was no law against killing Indians, so if they had done it or not did not matter. What might was the rest of the tribe coming after them. Both Chess and Beau knew that their tracks led right to the cabin and if the Cheyenne came they wouldn't be asking if they had seen anyone else before they attacked.

After retrieving their packs and gear from the cabin, Beau went and brought the animals in from grazing. Chess made sure that the slab door was firmly closed before joining the young man. They saddled the horses and loaded the pack animals. Then they led them to the river before mounting. For the next mile, they rode in the rushing water. If the Cheyenne came, they wanted to make sure that it was the three trappers who were followed.

The two trappers rode southeast before cutting back west. In the distance, there were white bluffs. "Looks like some of the snow or ice hasn't melted yet," Beau said.

"That's not snow nor ice," Chess told him. "Wait till we get there and you won't believe your eyes." As the white bluffs got closer, Beau was still sure that it was ice. The air around them was comfortable, but he could swear that he saw icicles.

Then he saw steam blowing off toward the back. "What the . . ." the bewildered young man said. "It looks like ice, but it ain't, is it?"

"The white stuff comes from the hot water flowing out of the spring," Chess explained. "It started building up long before we saw it and will continue long after."

Then Beau noticed the streaks of brown and orange, even some red. "It sure is a wonder," he said.

"When we get back toward the other geysers, you'll see the ground covered by the same white stuff. Looks like snow all year round," Chess told him.

The two men camped within sight of the hot spring. They kept their fire small, attempting to avoid attracting any attention. The three men who had come to the cabin would travel further west to go to Fort Hall. That would lead any pursuing Cheyenne well away from Chess and Beau.

Chess wanted to work to the east. The streams between them and Fort Hall had been trapped by the British and was protected by the Hudson Bay people. The Yellowstone had been trapped hard in years past, so there was little chance of finding any beaver. Chess scratched out a map of the rivers he knew, pointing out the ones he hoped would provide pelts.

Before leaving the Yellowstone, Chess showed Beau some of the other sites he had come across in the past. There was a towering waterfall running through a gorge. The fishing was good and they caught enough to dry for future meals. The trappers passed up herds of elk grazing in meadows along the rivers. It would be too much meat and take too long to dry it. Prong horn and mule deer were another story. The two men could put away a small deer in two to three days.

It was two weeks after they'd left the cabin before they found an active pond. The furs they got were still plew. For the next two months the trappers searched, trapped, and moved on. The once new buckskins and moccasins were now stained and full of holes and tears. The larger holes were stitched closed, smaller ones ignored.

They spent the night with some Flathead who were headed to the Yellowstone to hunt elk. Chess told them of the herds they had seen. The braves had met Eli at the winter camp. They called him a skilled hunter and brave warrior. Beau and Chess traded beads and fish hooks for new moccasins. The rest of their footwear had patches on patches. Beau was in good spirits as they left the Flathead. He was thankful that Eli was doing well, and he had his feet covered.

It was the middle of June when the two men decided to split up. Chess wanted to check another place further east and Beau wanted to head for the Mexican village and see Ana. For half a day, the two men dickered as they split up the winter's catch. It was done more for fun than a serious affair. The next morning, they each rode their own way with promises that if the rendezvous happened at the Green River they would share a few drinks.

CHAPTER SEVENTEEN

Beau stopped at Peter's cache and stowed his furs and extra gear. He let the plank door slam shut and rolled the boulder into place before tossing sage brush over it. His stuff would be well-hidden until he returned to go to the rendezvous. The village was about five days south. If he spent a week there he would be back to the rendezvous before it ended.

He smiled as he started south. He knew that he looked like a wild man with his long hair and beard. His clothing was shabby and his weathered, worn hat drooped on his head. He planned to get a bath and shave before looking her up. There was not much he could do about his clothes. The wool shirts and trousers were threadbare and faded. He had patched them the best he could, but he hoped that she would overlook his attire. After all, he had nice-looking moccasins. He laughed at the thought.

"When I leave you at the stable, horse," Beau said, "they'll give you grain and a good brushing. You too, mule."

As he rode, he sang songs that he remembered from his childhood. The sun was bright and he was going to see Ana. For two days, he rode from dawn to dusk. The long hours were showing on his animals, so he gave them a half day's rest to graze. He spent the time cleaning his rifle and revolver, trying to improve his wardrobe, and thinking about Ana.

The area where he was traveling was familiar right down to passing the spot where the army had been camped when he, Eli and Reiner had left the village. Beau was fully aware that he was riding into hostile territory because of the friction between the U.S. and Mexico. As he got closer to his destination he stayed off the trail and weaved through the willows. It would take a little longer, but would give him time to check out the village and the area around it.

The sounds from the village came through the trees before he could see it. There was music coming from the cantina. Someone was chopping wood. There was the ring of a hammer shaping iron. Beau came up behind the cantina. He swung off the horse and loosened the cinch. "You'll be enjoying grain before you know it," he said, patting the pony on its shoulder. He started to lead the animals around front when he changed his mind.

He decided to go in through the kitchen and surprise Alisa. Grinning from ear-to-ear, he went inside. Emilio's wife was so surprised to see the bushy headed, bearded man that she dropped the bowl she was carrying and fought to stifle a scream.

"It's me, Beau," the young man said quickly. "I was with Reiner."

The look of shock turned to a look of fear. "You must not be here," she hissed. "They will arrest you, too."

Confused, he asked, "Arrest me too? Who else has been arrested?"

"They have Señor Reiner," she said. "Get your horse and ride away."

"Where is Emilio?" Beau asked, keeping his voice low. "I want to talk to him."

Her eyes were filled with tears. "No. You must go now," Alisa begged.

Suddenly, Emilio came into the room. "What fell . . ." He stopped short when he saw Beau. He motioned the young man to follow him. They stepped out back of the cantina. He saw Beau's horse and mule. "It is not safe here," he said. "There are soldiers in the cantina."

Beau started to object when Emilio said, "Go to the high meadow. Do not make a fire, and stay in the trees. I will come later and explain."

With that, the owner went back into the kitchen and said something to his wife. Beau got his animals and led them into the trees behind the cantina. Using them for cover, he worked his way to the path. The mule and pony climbed the steep path without much trouble. Reaching the meadow, Beau went to the trees where he and Ana had watched the sunset. Memories of the night washed over him, making his heart beat a little faster.

He picketed the pony and mule on a part of the meadow that couldn't be seen from the village. He then settled down under a maple and took out a piece of jerky. He chewed on the dry meat and sipped from the water bag while trying to piece together what had been said in the kitchen. Reiner was in trouble, and if he was seen he would also be taken. He wondered if the army had taken the town over, or had they come back knowing that trappers stopped there in the spring?

Twice he moved the animals as the afternoon passed. Waiting was difficult and Beau was filled with anxiety as he fought the urge to go down and find out more. Just before the sun set, he caught sight of movement toward the path. He moved deeper into the trees, waiting. He tested the Colt in his holster. He looked around a tree and froze. It was Ana! He wanted to run out to meet her, but what if she had been followed?

Then he heard her whisper, "Beau. It's me, Ana. Come out."

"I'm in here," he said, keeping his voice low.

Beau stepped out from behind the tree, and she saw him. Suddenly, she was in his arms, holding him tight. He held her close, feeling her body shake. "I wanted to get a haircut and shave before I saw you," he said lamely.

The young man knew that she was crying and had no idea how to comfort her. Finally, she pulled back and looked up at him. Tears stained her cheeks. "My father sent me to tell you to go back north. If the soldiers see you they will arrest you and take you to Mexico City to be tried and shot as a spy."

"Your mother said they had Reiner," Beau said. "Have they taken him south already?"

"He is being held in their camp," she told him. "They wait for more Americans to come before they leave. They had learned that trappers come each year."

"I must free him, Ana," Beau told her. "What can you tell me about where he is being held?"

Her eye grew large. "You must not!" she insisted. "You will be killed. Go now. Go back north. I will wait for you."

"I can't leave Reiner," he said. "I will be careful."

"There are many of them," she warned him. "Go back now. If you want, I will go with you right now. Please!"

"Your being with me is all I dreamt about this winter," Beau confessed. "If I left Reiner, even having you with me couldn't wash away the regret I would have to live with. I would be no good to you."

Ana sank to the ground, her head hanging. "I am going to lose you," she whispered.

"No, you won't," he said, trying to assure her.

Realizing that she did not believe his promise, he added, "If they do catch me, your name will be the last word on my lips. That is all I can promise you."

Slowly, she began to speak. Her voice was resigned as she told him about the camp. It was south of the village, with maybe 20 soldiers. Her father had let her take food to Reiner and tequila for the soldiers. She had been treated rudely by the soldiers, but they had not hurt her. Reiner was tied to a pole in the center of the camp. They had beaten him after capture. He had to lay on the ground to eat or drink out of a bowl, like an animal. Twice a day he was taken to relieve himself, always with four soldiers.

Sitting next to her, she felt cold in his arms. Beau realized that once she had told him, Ana had already began mourning for him. Regardless of the lack of emotion from her, he sat holding her and thinking. The camp was close to the village. The only chance to free him would be during the middle of the night while most of the soldiers were sleeping, or when he was taken to relieve himself.

Once free, their escape would be a race to the north, with the hope of losing the pursuers in the many hills and valleys. Beau figured that he would ride the mule and let Reiner have the pony with the saddle. He would leave his packs here for Ana. There was little of value in them. Everything they would need could be put into the saddlebags.

"Ana," Beau said, "I will need you to put the horse and mule behind the stable. Bring them tonight and leave them. Give them some water and grain twice a day until I take them. I will watch and wait for the chance to free Reiner. Once I have him, we will run for the stable and take the animals. Your father can say they were stolen if the army asks."

She spoke, barely audible. "Okay."

They sat silently for a while. Then Beau told her, "After I have gone, be ready. There will be a night that I come back for you. There will be no chance to say goodbye to your family. You and I will disappear."

Sitting a bit longer, he continued, "We will go away until the time comes that it is safe for us to return, and then I will bring you back."

Forcing himself to release her, Beau went to the animals and took what would be needed and put them into the saddlebags. Then he added some things to the possible bag. Once done, he led the horse and mule to Ana. She took the lead ropes. "Follow me," she told him.

Crossing the meadow, Ana led the animals down another trail that swung wide around the village.

Beau walked beside her, carrying his rifle. "We forgot to watch the sunset," she said.

"When this is over, we will go to a place with a perfect sunset and live there all our days," he promised.

He almost missed her low reply. "Only if you get a haircut and shave."

He smiled and put his arm around her. She leaned back against him as they walked.

Short of the stable, she stopped. She pointed the direction to the army camp. Starting to turn away, Beau stopped her. She looked up at him and Beau kissed her. For a few seconds, he held her close before heading toward the camp. He could smell her sweet perfume on his beard. Despite the benefit of the face hair catching the smell, he enjoyed feeling his skin against hers much more without the thick beard between them.

He was wearing his buckskins and moccasins. The drooping hat covered his unruly hair. Beau moved silently through the trees. The clink of metal ahead stopped him. He was still a distance away, but it had come from the camp. Crouching, he continued. Then he saw the light of their fire. A two-acre area had been cleared of willows and they had set up tents for officers and enlisted men.

As he got closer, he could see Reiner tied to a post in the center of the compound. Two soldiers stood watch near the prisoner. Reiner lay on the ground, his hands behind his back around the pole. There were eight soldiers sitting around the fire, drinking tea or coffee. A flash went through Beau. One of the soldiers was Felipe. Ana's brother had been pressed into service.

One of the thoughts that Beau had come up with, as a last resort, was blasting his way in, killing everyone that moved and grabbing Reiner as the soldiers ran for their rifles. Or, doing the same when they took Reiner to relieve himself. The problem was, Felipe could be one of the guards. Throughout the night, Beau watched the camp. There was little movement except when the guards changed watching Reiner.

Lying in hiding, Beau dozed on and off until daylight. He then watched as they pulled the trapper to his feet and untied him. To prevent him from running, two additional soldiers came and surrounded the prisoner. Reiner was taken into the bush to relieve himself. The trapper's beard was matted with food and dirt. The group stopped about ten paces from Beau. He lay almost holding his breath, fearing to even look at them in case they felt his eyes on them.

Beau found it difficult to watch as Reiner was pushed and shoved while returning to the pole. Once, a bowl of some kind of gruel was placed near him. Beau noticed that it was far enough away that he was forced to stretch while lying on the ground to reach the food. There was a slight movement of the pole as he struggled.

The young man estimated that there were between 15 and 20 soldiers in camp. He guessed that there were only a couple in the cantina. He saw the scrappy lieutenant who had taken them prisoner last year. He strutted around the compound, snapping orders at the soldiers. As he walked by Reiner he poked him with the toe of his boot and laughed. Beau decided that if he was not able to do anything else, he would put a bullet into that man.

Beau moved away from the camp and dug some jerky out of his possible bag. He took the extra cylinder, which had five chambers loaded, and put it into the Colt. He put a small piece of wood between the hammer and the cap to prevent firing if it was bumped. He had decided that he would make his play when they took Reiner to the bush tonight. He just hoped that Felipe wasn't one of the guards.

Crawling back to his cover, he settled in for the afternoon. He noticed the soldiers looking at something toward the village. It was Ana. She was leading his mule packed with bags. The lieutenant stopped her, angrily challenging her. She said something to him and he smiled. He went to the packs and rifled through them. He then shouted at a couple of soldiers and they came and removed the packs. The sound of bottles clinking told Beau that at least one of the packs was tequila. They were placed near the officers' tent.

Ana went over to Reiner with a small bucket of water. Using the dipper, she gave him a drink. The trapper stared at her while taking the water. Evidently, she was taking too long, because the lieutenant ordered a soldier to remove her from the camp. The soldier pulled her up, tearing her dress. Suddenly, Ana's knife appeared, flashing in the sun as she took a swipe at the soldier. Her attempt narrowly missed the man.

Felipe stepped in, grabbing the knife-wielding arm. He took it from her and shouted something which seemed to please the lieutenant. Shoving her toward the mule, he took Ana to the edge of the camp and sent her away.

Beau lay hidden from view, mad clear through. He had just witnessed a good friend and the woman he loved being treated poorly. The only thing he could think of in his rage was to take no prisoners. He had now grouped Felipe with the other soldiers. He knew that he would have to gain control of his emotions. To run blindly into battle would leave him dead and save no one.

It was time for the soldiers to have their meal and the packs were opened. One bag was filled with various types of food normally reserved for fiestas. The other had bottles of tequila and limes. The lieutenant and another officer took their time selecting from the food. They then took two bottles of tequila each. They had barely gotten into their tent when the rest of the soldiers ran for the bags to grab their share.

Seeing the confusion, Beau almost made his move to get Reiner. At the last moment he settled back down, his heart pounding. The amount of time it would take him to get to the trapper and then cut the bonds would be too long. They would then have to make it back to the woods without being shot. Beau wasn't even sure if Reiner could run.

Crouching in his cover, the young man decided to let the tequila take effect. The heavy foods would also slow the men down. Suddenly, he realized that this was the edge Ana's family was trying to give him. The soldiers ate and drank. It was near dark and they hadn't taken Reiner to the bush. They had swapped the guards so all could get their share.

Beau heard Reiner complaining. One of the guards shoved him with their foot. The trapper continued to talk, no doubt asking to be taken out so he could relieve himself. Beau checked his Colt and rifle. His Green River knife was razor sharp and in his belt. He could feel the tension growing in his muscles.

He then saw Felipe and another soldier come to assist in taking the prisoner to the bush. It was obvious that they had had plenty of tequila. The other soldiers sat in groups, drinking and gambling. Some had even gone to their tents to sleep. A light was burning in the lieutenant's tent. Shadows on the tent walls looked like he was at a table reading.

While he watched, Beau made sure that there was nothing that would make noise as he moved closer to the guards. His plan was to strike the nearest soldier with the barrel of his rifle and if possible strike a second. He would then shoot whoever appeared to be the most danger. Then to the Colt for the rest who were standing. Then he prayed that he and Reiner could make their break, and that the trapper would be able to run.

Beau's heart sank when he saw that Felipe was the furthest of the guards and would surely be the one that he would have to shoot. He could try and wound him, but the reality was that he would be aiming for dead center. Beau removed the piece of wood from under the hammer of the Colt. Carefully, he slid it back into the holster. Gripping the rifle, he waited.

Reiner was weak and unsteady on his feet as they moved across the compound. He almost tripped at the edge of the woods and one of the guards grabbed him, holding him up. He uttered something that Beau was sure was a curse. Once in the bush, Reiner started fumbling with his pants. *Now*, the young man thought.

In a swift move, he struck the unsuspecting guard closest to him. He turned toward the second in time to see Reiner knock him out with a roundhouse punch. Beau turned to the remaining guards, the rifle cocked. Felipe had already knocked out the third guard. "Run!" he hissed.

Without wasting a second, the trappers plunged into the brush and ran for all they were worth. There was a shot from behind them and Felipe shouted in Spanish, "Two men have grabbed the prisoner!" Then Felipe shouted for the other soldiers.

Beau handed the rifle to Reiner in case they were separated. Behind them there were more shots. The young man feared that he would become disoriented in the dark woods and run wide of the stable. He needn't have worried. Reiner took the lead and soon they could see the horses. There were four animals. Reiner's horse, the mule, the pony and . . . the sorrel.

They saw nobody when they reached the stable. Deep inside, Beau was hoping that Ana would be waiting with them. The men checked the cinch straps on the horses before swinging into the saddles. They rode hard away from the village, Reiner leading his mule, Beau on the smoothly running sorrel, leading his pony. In the distance shots could still be heard. The soldiers were shooting at shadows.

* * *

The two men rode north throughout the night. The knowledge that they would be shot if captured kept them alert. When the sun came up they were miles from the village and Reiner had taken them off the trail to the east. The horses were lathered and needed rest. Dismounting, the trappers led the mounts to cool them. They stopped in a thick grove of willows with a stream. They allowed the animals a little water to begin with and would give them more later. Beau pulled the saddles off the horses. The animals stood picketed on a grass-covered patch with their heads hanging.

"I couldn't be prouder of how the horses ran through the night," Beau said.

"I see Emilio swapped back the mule for the sorrel," Reiner said as he sat heavily at the base of a willow.

Handing the water bag to his friend, Beau replied, "Could be he loaned it. Whatever it was, I am glad to have the horse."

"We can start off on the mule and pony when we leave here," Reiner said.

Beau open the saddlebags to get them something to eat. It would be too dangerous to make a fire, so jerky and water would have to do. To his surprise he found cheese, some ham, and biscuits, along with his jerky. "Thank you, Ana," he whispered. There was also a bottle of tequila.

Reiner had been treated roughly by the soldiers, but the beatings had only bruised and split the skin a bit. There were no broken ribs or other bones. After the food and dirt was washed from Reiner's beard, Beau used the tequila to clean the cuts, much to the objection of the elder trapper. "Don't be wasting the damn stuff on the outside. What I need it for is on the inside."

"There will be enough left for the inside," Beau replied. "If some of these cuts go sour, there won't be enough tequila to fix you."

They needed to get some sleep before continuing north. It would be safest to travel at night. Beau was awakened mid-afternoon by the sound of running horses. He went and got their animals, bringing them closer to camp. They had been grazing, which would help keep up their strength. He let them drink their fill and then saddled the mule and pony before tying them to a nearby willow.

Beau sat watching his sleeping friend and thought about their situation. The soldiers were ahead of them, looking for tracks. Beau was pleased that they hadn't discovered theirs as of yet. The soldiers had been on the more traveled trail to the west of them.

That evening they went slower, watching for any sign of the soldiers. As they rode, Reiner told him about Ana's visit. "She's a gutsy woman. Ana told me and Felipe that you were hiding in the trees. She told me about the horses. When Felipe acted the way he did, it was to make sure that the lieutenant didn't suspect him of being part of any plan. You heard him shouting as we ran. He was telling them that there were two men helping with the escape. I figure it was to explain the soldier near him that he hit. He probably shot hoping they would believe he was trying to stop, or kill us."

Riding in silence, Beau thought about the risk that Emilio's family was taking. Rather than be angry at what he had seen, he should have realized that they were doing things to help. He shuddered to think of how close he had come to shooting Felipe.

Beau knew that the steep ridges on each side of the valley narrowed a few miles ahead. If the soldiers were laying for them north of the village, that would be the logical place. Reiner knew of another route, but that would take them south for a day and then it would be a difficult climb to the next valley. "We'll have to lead the horses and keep to the east wall," Reiner said. "Keep that Colt ready for action."

Just short of the narrows, Beau climbed to a high point and searched the valley for any sign of the soldiers. He had sat for some time when he caught the glow of a soldier's face as he lit a cigar from a tin lantern. As quickly as he saw it, the glow disappeared as the lantern was put behind some rocks. What he had seen was enough. They now knew where the soldiers were.

Climbing down, he told Reiner, "They are holed up in the rocks on the left side."

"Could you tell how many?" Reiner asked.

"It was too dark," Beau replied. "By the sound when they rode past, and the pass being narrow, I wouldn't figure more than six. Others would be watching the village or searching south."

Passing clouds covered the moon, preventing the narrows from being bathed in its pale light. With little natural cover available, they would easily be spotted by the army in the moon light. They led their animals up the right side, trying to use what little tree and brush cover it offered. Tension ran up and down Beau's back as he anticipated being discovered at any time.

The soldiers' horses started snorting as they passed. Beau prayed that their animals wouldn't answer. There were some rocks and brush that they could use in case of a firefight, but he had no desire to kill anyone. He heard the soldiers calling softly back and forth as they discussed the restless animals. The sandy ground in front of the east wall muffled the sound of the horses' hooves. The trappers put their animals between themselves and the soldiers. If the army decided to fire at shadows, the horses would be hit first.

They continued to walk a mile beyond the soldiers before mounting up. They kept their animals at a walk. "We got lucky," Reiner whispered. "One of the Mexicans saw a coyote just before dark. They figured that it was back bothering their horses."

Well past midnight the clouds opened and the moon lit their way. They stopped at a shimmering pond to switch the saddles to Reiner's horse and the sorrel. Kneeling at the edge, the riders washed the dust off their faces. After watering the animals, the trappers continued through the rest of the night, riding at a lope for a while and then slowing the animals to a trot. By morning they were sure that they were out of Mexican territory. There was still a danger of pursuit. Which country claimed the area made little difference if the army wanted them bad enough.

Short of the rendezvous, the two men split up. Reiner headed for his cache while Beau rode to Peter's. The two men promised to spend time together and split a bottle. Beau rode the sorrel using the rock pinnacle as a guide. With his horses tied nearby, Beau leaned the rifle in the scrubby brush next to the door. He cleared the sage away and, rolled the rock clear. Then he pulled the heavy door open and entered the cache. It smelled strongly of the beaver pelts and other furs. Removing the possible bag and his wool shirt, he grabbed the sawbuck and blanket. Taking his time, he carried the packs and gear out of the cache.

Beau placed the sawbuck pack saddle onto the pony. He loaded the packs, keeping them balanced to each side of the sawbuck. Beau was excited knowing that soon he would be seeing Eli again. The young man had much to tell him about the Yellowstone. He went back into the cache to get his possible bag and shirt. There was a slam, and then darkness.

Turning quickly, he hit his head on the plank door. Beau fell back, holding his bruised forehead. He heard the rock fall against it on the outside. "What the hell's going on!" he shouted.

"I'm sealing your tomb, Levesque, just like Jesus was," he heard Angus say. "You'll be meeting him soon enough."

Through the thick plank door, he heard the ugly laugh of the man outside. There were scraping sounds as the monster beyond the door piled sage brush against it. Beau drew the Colt and fired into the door, hoping that he could penetrate it and hit Angus. The door was too thick for the .28 caliber ball to go through.

He heard the man outside shout, "Save the last shot for yourself. That way you won't have to die of thirst."

Instinctively he touched his chest. The water bag was hanging on the sorrel's saddle horn. Beau realized that whether he died of thirst or starved made little difference. There was the fading laughter as Angus rode away. Beau now realized how sick the man was. He'd had ample time to shoot him for a quick kill while loading the pony, but had chosen to wait in hiding until he could lock him in the cache.

Groping around in the inky darkness, Beau put his hand on the anvil, then the hammers and muskets. He continued until he found an axe. Feeling around the door, he located the cross boards used to hold the planks together. Crouching, he stepped back in the low cache. Beau swung the axe, striking a glancing blow off the door. He had nothing with which to judge up or down. He sank to his knees and felt for the cross piece. Closing his eyes, he pictured the target in his mind.

He began to swing, sweat running down his back as he made little progress. He had to continually fight panic. Resting a moment, his hand touched his possible bag. "I have flint and tinder!" he shouted.

Feeling around, he found loose bark on the inner logs. He shredded it and placed it on the tinder from his bag. Holding his flint, he struck it with his knife. The shower of sparks was blinding. He had missed the tinder. After several tries he had a smoky fire going. Most importantly he could see. Beau realized that the smoke would rapidly become a problem. Wasting no time, he gripped the axe and began to work on the door. Within minutes he was prying the planks open and pushing the brush away. He gasped for fresh air, coughing the smoke out of his lungs.

Crawling out, he squinted against the bright sunshine. Almost quarter-mile away he saw Angus riding the gray and leading his horses. Beau looked for the rifle where he had left if in the brush. A flood of relief washed over him, it was still there. Angus had missed it.

The Model 1803 had an effective range of 200 yards, but the ball could carry twice that. Beau took the powder horn from his possible bag. Placing some powder into the pan, he laid prone. The words of the old trapper came to mind. Close your eyes and regrip. The wind was coming from his back, blowing toward Angus, which would help.

Beau repeated closing his eyes and regripping several times until it repeated. He was thankful that he and Chess had practiced distance shooting and that Angus was big. He aimed for the center of the huge man with an elevation a little above his head. Beau hoped to but the ball into him somewhere between the shoulders and his waist. Taking his time, he squeezed the trigger. Fire belched out of the rifle, sending the ball across the valley floor. The young man watched his target, fearing that he had missed. Then Angus slumped forward on the gray. He slid sideways off the horse. The brute was gripping his rifle as he disappeared into the prairie grass.

Reloading the rifle, Beau knew that Angus was a dangerous man. Wounded, he would be even more dangerous. When the man couldn't run, he would do whatever he could to injure those coming after him. Angus also had a Hawken, which had an effective range of 400 yards. From his first step, Beau would be in the rifle's effective range.

With his rifle ready, Beau crouched, running diagonally across the valley, trying to make himself more difficult to hit. Keeping to a wide zig zag pattern, he kept closing in on the man. The horses had stopped just beyond the spot where Beau had seen Angus fall. It was unlikely that he was still there. Angus would have moved to better cover.

There was a shot! Beau threw himself to the ground. He lay breathing heavily, looking for any sign of the man. The young man feared to rise up. He had been lucky that the first shot had missed him. Angus would have the Hawken loaded by now and be waiting for Beau. He fully knew that by the time that he had heard the shot, the ball had already gone by. It would have made no sound and have landed well behind him.

He was still an eighth of a mile away. Beau crawled forward on his elbows, pushing with his toes, watching for any movement in front of him. The young man's skin crawled, knowing that the enemy could lie in wait until Beau could see the cruel smile. Then the crack of the Hawken would end Beau's life.

Slowly, Beau snaked along the ground, the sweat from his brow making his eyes sting. He blinked trying to clear them. His hands were wet, making gripping the rifle more difficult. He stopped, knowing that he would be unable to react fast enough when Angus rose up to finish him. He lay listening for any sound, praying to hear anything that would give him any idea of where the brute was waiting.

Almost shaking with fear, Beau slowly looked above the grass. He envisioned himself with a dark hole in his forehead. He saw nothing in any direction. For all he knew, the man could be lying in a dip, knowing that he could not be seen. Stretching his head a little higher, he saw something. It was Angus' shirt showing just above the grass. Readying the rifle, Beau rose just a bit more. The big man did not move. Slowly, the young man got to his knees. Angus lay still upon the grass. Could he have died after firing the single shot at Beau?

Beau walked forward, holding the rifle at the ready. His jaw dropped. The side of Angus' head was blown away. Walking closer, Beau saw that there was blood low on the man's back. Standing near him, Beau realized that Angus had killed himself. Beau's shot had hit him near the spine, just above his hips. The young man guessed that the severe pain and realization that he would be paralyzed had been too much. He had chosen to take his own life.

Seeing the brute lying on the prairie grass sent a wave of anger through Beau. Angus had locked him in the cache and had left him to suffer a slow death. Now, when he'd had to face up to what he'd done, he had taken the coward's way out. Pacing back and forth near the man, Beau kicked him several times. "You sons-of-a-bitch!" he shouted. "You drove me and Eli out of Arkansas with your meanness!"

The young man dropped his rifle and sat heavily near the brute. His body shook with the emotions surging through him. "You spent your life bullying and hurting others. Now you're lying here dead. For what" he demanded.

Beau was fully aware that he had been the cause of Angus's death. His shot had broken the man's back and had forced Angus to shoot himself. Suddenly, all of the frustration, anger, and hate drained from the young man. He looked down at the lifeless body and thought back.

Beau had been living in a small cabin on Crowley Ridge, without freedom to leave until the contract would have been completed. Elijah had been a slave without any hope of freedom. The truth was that Angus had forced both of them to leave Arkansas and build new lives. They had chosen to go west. West, which offered freedom and the beauty of the mountains. He and Eli had been happier here than they could ever have been back east.

Looking at Angus, he said, "The debt is paid in full. Despite all your cruelty, you did give us a new start."

Returning to the cache with the horses, Beau retrieved a worn shovel from his earlier tomb. He dug the grave deep for Angus. It was deep enough to make sure that none of the meanness could ever surface again. Before filling the grave, he tossed the whip in. Once finished, he looked at the horses. He now had the pony, a sorrel, and the gray gelding. He had a newer Hawken rifle that used caps. The gray's saddle and saddlebags were filled with things that would be useful. He had no doubt that Angus' future was in hell. He and his whip could give the devil trouble.

Before leaving, Beau did repair the cache door. There was a good chance that Peter would never be back, but just in case he came for things he stored, the young man didn't want to let the weather in. For the first time, for as long as he could remember, Beau felt at peace. His past would stay to the east. What could come west was buried with Angus. It was time to go to the rendezvous.

CHAPTER EIGHTEEN

The rendezvous was in full swing when Beau rode in. There were mountain men and Indians camping all along the Green River. The young man's first order of business was to sell his catch to the American Fur Company. Their tents had more supplies than the prior year, but Beau found out that the amount of fur traded had been down. Many of the trappers had not expected another rendezvous and had gone to Fort Crockett or Fort Hall to trade. Prices for fur were lower than the previous year due to lack of demand. While there were those who would celebrate until they were broke, many of the trappers would be facing a tough future after selling their furs, receiving little money to purchase supplies.

After two hours of haggling with the company, and purchasing some coffee and tobacco, Beau left with just over $70 for his winter's work. He would have made more money back east working as a logger and he would have had his meals supplied. The young man was undaunted by the low prices. He considered the beauty and freedom of the mountain life to be part of the pay. He walked out and planned to find a spot to set up camp. Someone shouting his name stopped him.

"Join us for a drink, Levesque!" Reiner called.

A broad grin breaking out on his face, Beau led his horses to the group. Kinney, Hoss and Wes were sharing a bottle with Reiner. "I hardly got enough for my furs to pay for a good drunk," Beau replied. "I would be happy to share yours."

"I see you got yourself another horse since we parted," Reiner said.

"I come by it after the owner had no more need," the young man said.

Digging a tin cup out of his gear, Beau poured a good measure before handing it back. Taking a drink, he enjoyed the bite of the liquor going down his throat before saying, "If the price of fur goes down anymore, I'll have to pay the company to take them."

Reiner looked at the gray gelding, but asked no more about it. "Most figure this will be the last rendezvous. Word is they brung more supplies than last year. It don't make sense, since there are fewer beaver caught each year."

"You best watch your horses," Kinney advised. "Stealing horse flesh has become the only way for some trappers to pay for supplies."

Beau bought the next bottle and the men continued to talk about the future, or lack of it for the trappers. Hoss and Wes were going back east. Rumor was that guides were needed for folks coming west. Most of the mountain men knew the best routes through the mountains and they could make money with this knowledge. Reiner hoped to put a crew together and try trapping another year. He still believed that there were mountain valleys full of beaver that hadn't been found. He could then haul the catch east and get better prices.

Beau hadn't thought much past going back to the Mexican village and spiriting Ana away. Once that was accomplished, he would worry about what came next. The only thing he knew was that going east was not an option. With the bottle gone and a nice glow on, Beau bid the men a good day and went to claim his piece of prairie grass to camp on. Tonight he planned to get a good night's sleep, then look up Eli and Chess.

The clouds were threatening rain, so Beau put up his fly tarp and stored his gear under it. A small stream ran near the camp, winding its way toward the Green River. Nearby were aspen and oak trees. He gathered a store of wood and covered it with the ground cloth from the gray's blanket roll. Beau thought about what he had gained by the death of Angus. Not only had the man been well outfitted, he'd had almost $200 in a money belt. The young man guessed that it was money taken when Angus had left the Weber plantation. Beau knew of no family that survived Horst, except for Elijah. He planned to give it to his friend before the rendezvous was over.

It was getting dark by the time Beau finished taking care of the horses. He ate a cold meal and then rolled his blankets out under the tarp. He wished Peter had come to the rendezvous. He had enjoyed working for the gunsmith. He had also liked listening to Joshua's stories. Beau lay using his saddle for a pillow. He had the Colt under it for quick availability. Both the Hawken and flintlock were under the edge of his blanket. He finally fell asleep to the sound of those with money enjoying the whiskey sold by the company.

The young man was suddenly wide awake. He didn't dare to move. Someone, or something, was nearby. Slowly, he moved his hand toward the Colt. "Do you think you'll get that gun out before I get the fire going?" It was Eli.

Kicking his blankets off, Beau rolled out of the fly tarp. "How did you know I was here?"

"Reiner rode by my teepee this morning and told me about the adventure with the Mexicans," Eli said. "Finding you was easy. Your snoring led me to your camp."

Over coffee and frying pan biscuits, Beau told his friend about killing Angus. "I saw the gray with your horses and wondered how you came by it," Eli said. Both men agreed that the world would be a better place without the likes of the brute.

After they had eaten, Beau dug out Angus' money belt. "I figure this money came from your father's plantation." Handing it to Eli, he continued, "You're the only relative I know of, and figured it should be yours."

Elijah opened it and fingered the money. "Half of this is yours."

"No," Beau replied. "I got plenty with Angus' horse and gear. The money is yours."

His friend would not have it. Eli said, "I would have never gotten away from Arkansas without your help."

Finally, Beau accepted half of the money, but only after Eli agreed to take the Model 1803 and some of Angus' gear.

Satisfied, Eli said, "You must come to my camp. Saka'am wants to see you."

Fearful of leaving his horses unattended, Beau rode the sorrel and led the other two as he followed Eli to the Flathead camp. It looked much like the one he and Chess had come across near the Snake River. The teepees were neatly arranged to the back with the communal fire in the front. The Green River meandered next to them and some of the children were playing in the shallows.

While Eli went to get his wife, Beau tied the horses to some low bushes. He became aware of the occupants looking at him. Some waved, recognizing him from Eli's wedding. Debating whether he should sit down next to the fire, he was grateful when Eli and his wife came out of their teepee. Both approached him smiling broadly.

"We have something to show you," Eli said. With that Saka'em turned, revealing the cradleboard on her back with a . . . baby.

"You . . . You have a child," Beau said in wonder. "You just got married."

"That was over 10 months ago," Eli said, looking every bit a proud father.

"Is it a boy or girl?" Beau asked.

"The baby is a girl," Saka'am replied. "It is okay. The future will bring us many sons."

"You speak English," the surprised young man said.

"Eli teach me," she said, "and I teach him mine."

Eli was thrilled to have the rifle. He had given Saka'em's father his Hawken as part of the gifts of marriage. Beau stayed and ate with them. He even had a chance to hold the month-old baby. Eli and Beau talked of their adventures during the past winter. The months apart had changed Beau little. He wore stained buckskins britches and a faded wool shirt. His unruly hair poked out from under the drooping brim of his hat, and his beard was long and thick.

Eli wore his hair off the ears and had it swept up on the sides and braided down the back. His buckskin britches fit well on his wiry frame. His shirt, which was more of a vest, was decorated down the front with quills from a porcupine. He had lost much of this youthful look. The gentle manners learned as a house servant were gone, replaced by a self-assured attitude. The softness only appeared when he spoke with his wife or held his daughter.

Beau left the camp realizing how much more his friend had grown than he had. The life he now led was little different than that on Crowley Ridge. His only responsibility was for himself. He killed or gathered what he ate, and slept on the ground with nothing more than a tarp to protect him. Smiling, he realized, *Not even as good as the cabin I had on the ridge.*

He was passing a broken-down teepee when he recognized his trapping companion. "Hey, Chess," he called out. The trapper was sitting with a tall, serious-looking man. A brown dog lay at his feet and growled when Beau approached them.

"Don't worry," the tall man said. "Most of the time he don't bite."

Chess stood up. "This here is Tom Franklin. He's a buffalo hunter and mountain man."

"Mr. Franklin. My name's Beau Levesque. It's a pleasure to meet you."

Tied near the teepee was a bay and mule that Beau figured belonged to Chess' new friend. "I heard about horses being stolen by those that didn't make enough on their beaver. You best watch your stock, Mr. Franklin."

Smiling, Tom said, "You got a mighty polite friend here, Chess." Then, to Beau, he said, "I see you keep your horses close. And you can call me Tom."

The young man joined them for coffee. He told Chess about Eli being a father. "I liked Eli," Chess said. "I am mighty glad for him. I hear you were out saving trappers caught by the Mexican Army."

"You talked to Reiner," Beau replied. "It was a challenge getting him free. Ana and her family made it possible."

"Who is Ana?" Tom asked.

"She is a Mexican woman Beau here took a fancy to after the last rendezvous," Chess explained. "I heard about her all last winter." Then he turned to Beau. "Tom here has a young Arapahoe woman he's got his eye on. An old geezer bought her from her pa and plans to make a profit on the resale."

The tall man didn't appear to want to talk about the Arapahoe woman and the conversation changed over to the price of beaver pelts and the lack of good trapping areas. After an hour of visiting, Chess suggested that they go buy a bottle. Tom declined, but offered to watch Beau's stock if he wanted to go.

The two men spent the rest of the afternoon sharing a bottle and watching those who'd had too much to drink acting up. Reiner caught up with them and brought another bottle. It was not long after when Chess excused himself and went to look up a woman he had met. The sun was about to slide down behind the mountains when Beau left the party. He stopped by the old teepee and got his horses. Tom offered him some supper, but the young man was feeling pretty light-headed and figured he'd best head back for his camp and sleep it off.

The next morning, he awoke to a pounding headache. He sat up in his blankets, holding his head. "Did you have a good night?" a familiar voice asked.

He looked up at Eli and groaned, "I think I had too much fun."

"I mixed up a pan of biscuits and got some coffee on," the friend told him.

"Coffee first, then maybe biscuits." Beau crawled out from under the fly tarp and went to relieve himself. Steadying himself against a tree, he fought down the urge to vomit. "Never again," he moaned.

While Beau drank coffee, Eli suggested, "We should go hunting. If we get a deer, venison steaks will straighten you out."

His friend was in such a good mood, and Beau felt so awful. He figured that he would feel just as bad sitting in camp as hunting. "After a little more coffee, we will do that."

By mid-day Beau's head had cleared and his stomach was settled. He was riding the gray and carrying the Hawken across the front of the saddle. Beside him, riding a pony, Eli cradled the Model 1803 in the crook of his arm. They were several miles from the rendezvous, riding across a grass and sage brush-covered valley. Movement on the far side caught their attention. There were pronghorn grazing.

Stopping the horses, Beau pointed to the right. "We can move into the pine and work our way close enough for a shot."

The sun was bright, with a breeze in their faces. Eli squinted as he looked at the game. "If we work our way to the ridge, just into the trees, we may be able to knock a couple down."

He tapped his pony with his heels and led the way toward the pines. Beau pulled his hat down to shade his eyes. His throat was dry and he wished that he had drank some water while they had stopped. The gray walked smoothly as it followed the pony. Once in the trees Eli swung off his horse. Following suit, Beau led his horse alongside his friend's.

The lodgepole pines were thick, causing them to weave back and forth, looking for a way through. "These are good for our teepees," Eli said. "They grow tall and thin."

After traversing the tree-covered side hill, they came to the ridge. Leaving their horses behind, they climbed the rocks, gaining the top. Removing his hat, Beau slowly looked over the edge. To his dismay, the pronghorns were in full flight away from them. They were downwind from the animals, so it must have been some slight movement they had seen, causing them to run.

Sitting on top of the ridge, Beau drank from his water bag. Eli watched the pronghorns run over a rise and disappear. "We need to follow them to see if they stopped on the other side."

Drinking water and chewing on a piece of jerky, Beau agreed. "They are mighty jumpy. We have to go slow once we reach the rise. They've probably been chased before by hungry trappers."

Returning to their horses the two men mounted and rode through the trees toward the valley. The trees thinned as they approached the edge. They had their horses at a trot when they broke out of the pines. Riding around the boulders below the ridge, they came face to face with two burly trappers. Beau removed the loop off his Colt.

"I think we spooked the pronghorns," the man riding a chestnut said.

"We had hoped to take down a couple," Beau replied. "I figure we'll find them over the rise."

The four men sat with their rifles across their saddles. Beau and Eli waited for the two men to ride on. The men seemed to be waiting for them to move. They were both looking at the gray that the young man was riding. The man on the chestnut moved his horse, bringing his rifle to bear.

"You may want to move that rifle," Beau said, his voice cold.

"I don't think so," the man said, his voice cruel.

The other man riding a bay asked, "Did you kill the man that had the gelding?"

Before Beau could answer, the man on the chestnut said, "We hear your black is a runaway. He's worth good money back east."

Beau and Eli were looking down the bore of the man's rifle. Beau spoke in measured words. "He's not anybody's black."

The other man began to turn his horse to bring his rifle around. Without a warning, Beau let his rifle drop to the ground and drew his Colt. The men were watching the Hawken hit the ground when Beau fired the revolver. He didn't take aim, he just fired two quick shots at the largest part of the big man in front of him. Swinging the Colt Paterson at the other man, he saw him clutching a knife protruding from his chest. Eli had thrown it.

The man Beau had shot fell backwards off the chestnut. The one clutching Eli's knife turned the bay and tried to ride off. Beau fired the revolver. His shot went wide as the trapper slid off the saddle, and rolled onto the ground. Eli had his rifle to his shoulder and brought it down without firing.

"They're the men that were with Angus," Beau said.

"If we track them back, we'll probably find their camp, where Angus was supposed to meet them," Eli replied.

Forgetting the pronghorns, the two friends loaded the two bodies across the horses and followed the tracks to their camp. There were several packs lying about and a troop tent with their blankets. A quick search of the packs revealed personal items from other trappers. It was difficult to say how many victims they had left behind. Any furs or animals had been sold at one of the forts, or traded with various tribes.

They brought the two bodies back to the rendezvous and then returned to the camp with pack horses and the closest thing they could find to an official. All the packs with personal items from missing trappers was taken back to the rendezvous, including one of the rifles with a missing trapper's name carved in it. The rest of it was left with Beau and Eli. The official called it a reward for bringing in the murderers.

The two friends discarded the worn or broken items and what was left was put onto the remaining pack horse. "These are for you, Eli," Beau told him. "I took Angus' stuff, so this should be yours."

"You're damn fast with the Colt," Eli said.

"I never even saw you throw the knife, yet there it was in the man's chest," Beau replied.

"I figured at the very least one of us was going to die," Eli admitted.

"We were lucky," Beau said. "Or maybe they were just too confident."

Either way the two men knew that the standoff could have just as easily gone against them. They left the troop tent standing with the discarded items inside. Just maybe someone from the rendezvous with even less would find it.

* * *

The rendezvous lasted another week before the company started packing up. The number of fur purchases was the least of any year. Many attributed it to trappers going to the forts. The excess supplies brought from Missouri would be sold at Fort William to help cover the losses of the rendezvous. Beau learned about Tom Franklin's horse being stolen and the dog killed. He also heard that the old geezer had been killed and his investment taken. Tom had gone south after the Arapahoe woman. Beau hoped that he didn't run into any Mexican soldiers.

The deaths of Angus and the two trappers had left both him and Eli better off. Beau had expected to feel some remorse for killing two men. It did not come. They had been cruel and cold-blooded killers. Angus alone had made it impossible for him to go back east. The man had made sure that he was known for attempted murder and stealing slaves.

The only freedom for Elijah was in the mountains, or Canada. Without papers from his father, he could show no proof of being freed. It made little difference to Eli. He had chosen to become part of the Flathead tribe. If changes came from the east that made his freedom uncertain, he had told Beau that he and Saka'am would move north to Canada.

The two friends sat together in the Flathead camp sharing a meal prepared by Eli's wife. They realized that the golden era of the mountain man was over. Even Meeks had been heard to say that it was time to go west to Oregon and become farmers. Those who remained in the mountains would do so just for the love of high places and life far from the shackles of the orderly world to the east. Each year more and more emigrants had been coming west. They would follow the trails improved by trappers and be guided and protected by the men who had spent much of their lives on the trails.

"You are going after Ana," Eli said.

"Yes, I have to," Beau replied. "I love her and believe she loves me. I have little to offer her except for three horses, two guns, and some gear. I left my traps in Peter's cache and doubt I'll ever go back for them."

"If the Mexican army gets its hands on you, they will stand you up against a wall and shoot you," Eli warned.

"Then I best not let them catch me," the young man replied and smiled with less confidence than he felt. "I know my way around the valley near the village and am sure I can get to Ana and safely leave with her."

Saka'am came and sat near the two men, holding the baby. The child was in a cradle fitted with a board that pressed against the front of the skull. This would flatten the shape, a tradition of the tribe. While it made no sense to Beau, he did not question her about it.

"Will you be leaving early tomorrow?" Eli asked.

"I have to meet a man with a camp near the Green River before I go," Beau replied.

"What does he sell?"

"Shaves and haircuts," the young man told his friend.

Both men broke out laughing, causing Saka'am to wonder what was so funny. The two men stood up, facing each other for a moment. Then Beau held out his hand and they shook before parting. The young man had much more that he wanted to say to Eli, but was unable to find words that could describe how he felt.

CHAPTER NINETEEN

Beau rode south, his face stinging from the shave, the cool morning air hitting his neck. The barber had come west with the clergy who had accompanied the caravan, bringing supplies to the rendezvous. The man planned to continue on to Oregon with the clergy in the next few days. He felt that cutting the hair of mountain men was doing God's work. He converted the men from the wild look to a more civilized look.

God's work had cost Beau a dollar. The young man had to admit that the barber had done a great job. He'd left a full moustache and sideburns to the bottom of his ears. With the protective whiskers gone, Beau's face would soon be burned red by the sun and wind.

The pack horse held enough supplies to last him two months. With more than one person eating, they would be depleted in just over a month. He worried as he rode that she would not be willing to join him in the mountain life. Her saying that she would leave with him without question the last time gave him hope. Yet it might have just been to avoid the guilt from luring him back, should he be killed.

Beau had found many beautiful valleys and meadows that would make a wonderful place to build a cabin and raise a family. He would choose one that wasn't too far from a fort or town. Towns would be coming soon with people moving west. They would need places to work and purchase goods. Beau even thought about the anvil and forge in Peter's cache. He could retrieve them and do some blacksmithing, or even be a gunsmith. He was sure that he could work something out with Peter to get parts and supplies he would need.

He had left the rendezvous being told that there would not be another. Beau thought about last year when there had been doubt. Yet this year there had been another. The young man couldn't ignore the fact that there were fewer beaver and even less demand for the pelts.

Beau remembered Chess talking about buffalo hunting. Hoss and Wes had also hunted the wooly beasts. There was demand for the hides, and buffalo were plentiful on the plains. Yet living on the open plains around rotting buffalo carcasses covered with flies was not a life he would take a wife into.

Wife, he thought. Beau knew that he was getting ahead of himself. Suddenly, he caught sight of riders to the west. Five braves were riding hard to intercept him. He had been riding the sorrel and had Angus' saddle on the gray. Tossing the pony's lead rope over its back, the young man leaped from the sorrel and quickly switched to the gray gelding. With the sorrel's reins in his gloved hand, he kicked the gray's flanks, bringing it to a gallop.

The pony was carrying his supplies, but with the cries of the braves who were bearing down on him getting closer, it would be better to lose his packs than his life. The gray was a powerful, and fresh, horse. It began to put distance between him and the attacking braves. The unburdened sorrel ran alongside, easily keeping up the pace. Beau's Hawken was in a scabbard on the sorrel. If the braves managed to get close, he would let the sorrel go and use his Colt Paterson.

The wind blew Beau's hat off and it slapped on his back, held by the leather tie under his chin. The cries faded behind him and he glanced back. The braves had stopped, giving up the chase. The gray was running well and the young man wasn't ready to slow the horse down. After putting more distance between him and the braves, Beau felt the gray faltering. He slowed it to a trot, and then let the horse walk, cooling it off. Beau glanced at the sorrel. It shook its head, snorting. To his relief the pony was just a few lengths back.

Beau pulled up the gray and swung down. The pony came up and stopped short of the sorrel. All three horses were lathered and breathing hard. The pony had accomplished a supreme effort to keep up with the other horses while carrying the packs. The lead rope still lay on the packs, which prevented it from being stepped on. The young man was thankful that the pony refused to be left behind.

For the next mile, Beau led the three horses while keeping an eye on his back trail. He figured that the braves had seen the three horses and decided to go after one or two by scattering them. They hadn't figured on the saddled gray, nor the pony, continuing to run. Many horses carrying packs would have gone a short distance and then slowed, or come to a stop.

Still concerned about his pursuers, Beau mounted the sorrel and brought the horses to a trot, continuing south. He caught sight of some high ground ahead. A stream ran alongside before turning across the valley. The young man let the animals drink and then rode in the water for a way. Once beyond the ridge, he turned and rode behind it. He then led the three horses toward the top, using a narrow animal trail. He picketed the horses in a depression just below the top. Pulling the gear off the animals, he used handfuls of grass to rub them down.

He took extra time with the pony. "You did a good job keeping up, horse. Without the groceries you were carrying, I would have been put in a hurt." He patted the animal's shoulder. As he left, he glanced toward the gray. "You too, horse. You too."

Then Beau went to the top and laid near the edge, watching his backtrail. He chewed on jerky and drank from the water bag as he searched for any movement. Some pronghorns were feeding on the valley floor. Beau figured the braves had probably come from the rendezvous and had chased him more for sport than his scalp. Foregoing a hot meal, he rolled out his blankets near the horses. They continued grazing as the young man drifted off to sleep.

The next morning, Beau led the horses back to the stream. He filled his water bag while they drank. The valley beyond was empty. There were splashes of color from paintbrush and other wild flowers. The walls of the ridge were layered with red and gray rock. To the west he saw thunderheads building. July and

August were generally dry months and a little rain would be welcome.

Feeling good about what he had seen, Beau built a small fire and fried up some side meat to go with his coffee. He was about three days from the Mexican village and the army, but here on the rise he was safe. While getting the horses ready to go, Beau noticed that the sawbuck saddle had rubbed a couple spots on the pony. He put the extra saddle on it, and the packs on the gray. He rode out on the sorrel, leading the other two.

Rain swept over the valley that afternoon. Beau had a slicker in the bedroll, but figured that by the time he got it out the storm would have blown through. The summer rain felt good, taking away the heat of the day. Water dripped off the drooping brim of his hat, soaking into his wool shirt. Once the clouds blew over, the west wind dried him. The fresh, rain-washed air helped maintain his positive mood. He thought about the evening in the high meadow, watching the sunset.

As he got closer to the narrows where he and Reiner had eluded the army, Beau's thoughts went from Ana to the dangers he might be facing. Having made a couple of trips into the willow-covered valley, he was sure that he could avoid the soldiers. He would have to go to the small adobe under the cover of darkness. His stomach was tight, as much from concern of being seen by the army as the worry that Ana would not leave her family.

Beau was riding the gray when he arrived at the narrowing of the valley. He rubbed his hand over the whiskers on his chin. He wished that he had a razor to use so he could show up clean-shaven. His Green

River knife was sharp enough to scrape them off, but he feared that it would tear up his face. It was mid-afternoon with the sun blazing down from above. It was doubtful that the army would be in the area. They could possibly have a man watching who would ride back with information of anyone coming through.

He guided the horses into the trees. The packs were back on the pony and he swapped from the gray to the sorrel. Should he be chased by the army, Beau wanted a fresh horse under him. He felt a flutter of excitement as he thought of how close he was to Ana. His face became creased with concern. He knew that this was not the time to have his mind elsewhere. He rode out of the narrows without seeing any sign of soldiers.

He stayed to the left of the well-traveled trail, keeping more to the route he and Reiner had used fleeing the village. He pushed through the low-hanging branches of the willows as he looked for a clear route. The close cover protected him as well as preventing him from spotting danger ahead. Finally, Beau dismounted and led the horses. Traveling through the thick trees prevented the young man from knowing how far he had gone. The village was just over a day's ride from the narrows.

The plan that Beau had come up with was taking the path that Ana had shown him to the high meadow. He would hide there with the horses until dark. Then, on foot, he would go down to the village and locate Ana. Cloud cover moved in, hiding the sun and threatening rain. It made the air feel cooler on Beau's sweat-covered face. He finally stopped for the night, fearful that he would get turned around in the thick willows. As he pulled the gear from the animals, he checked the pony's back. The places rubbed by the sawbuck saddle looked good. He noticed that the horses were stripping leaves and bark off the tree limbs. He tied them to brush that would allow them to eat their fill.

That night he had no fire and was not near water. His horses had drank shortly before stopping, so they would be good until morning. After some jerky and a drink from the water bag, he took a chew from his tobacco twist. He was too wound up to sleep. What happened tomorrow could set the course for the rest of his life. He thought about the meadows and valleys he liked the best. He hoped that he was able to describe them well enough for Ana to be able to visualize the beauty and want to go to them.

Sometime during the night, he finally fell asleep, curled under a willow tree. The early morning chill awoke him. He got a horse blanket and wrapped it around his shoulders as he sat against the tree. The warmth of the blanket felt good, and he dozed on and off for another hour. Beau debated whether he should chance a fire and make coffee. His jaw had hung slack while dozing and his mouth was dry. The coffee sounded good.

The sound of the iron rim of a wheel striking stone brought him fully alert. A short distance from him a wagon, or buggy, was passing by. Evidently he had meandered closer to the main trail while pushing through the trees. He was tempted to go out and see if it was a local villager. He might be able to gain information on the army. Caution prevailed. The traveler could be a friend of the army and alert them to his presence.

Rinsing his mouth out from the water bag, he then took a long drink. He decided to get the horses ready to travel and then go to the trail. There might be another route within the trees, but he hadn't been able to find it. Beau led the horses to the main trail and looked for any travelers. The marks of the wheels that he had heard were plain on the narrow road. Riding the sorrel, he continued south, taking his time. He did not want to catch up to the wagon head of him.

Beau arrived at the trail to the high meadow an hour before sunset. The cloud cover had cleared, promising a stunning sunset. He turned his horse up the little-used trail and felt less tension, knowing that he was no longer on the open trail that was more traveled. Twice during the day he had pulled off to avoid travelers he spotted in the distance.

He swung off the sorrel, deciding to lead the horses to the meadow. He had eaten little during the day and his stomach ached with hunger. His lips were cracked and skin peeled on his face from the sunburn. He smiled, feeling the sting on his lips. He was fortunate that it would be dark when he met Ana. She would not be able to see his wind and sun-damaged face.

"But I want to see hers," he whispered.

Beau stopped before walking into the meadow. He looked at the grass and flower-covered opening. Although they had been brief, he had fond memories of being here. The shadows were getting long as he stepped out. He could see the oak where the two of them had watched the sunset. Staying close to the edge of the trees, he led his horses. It was only an hour or two before he would see Ana again. He stopped short of the oak and tied the horses. He loosened the cinches of the saddles and started to pull the packs off the pony.

"You're going to miss the sunset," a voice behind him said.

Startled, Beau jumped ahead, putting the pony between himself and the voice. He had the revolver in his hand. Bringing his head above the back of the pony he looked into the eyes of . . . Ana.

"I did not mean to scare you," she said, surprised at his reaction.

His eyes were wide and his mouth open, as Beau came back around the pony, rushing to take her into his arms. Ana threw her arms around him, holding him close. He opened his eyes and saw his Colt, still in his hand, in front of his face. Beau didn't even remember drawing it.

He tried to move his arm to put the Colt back into his holster, but Ana just held him tighter. "I was afraid you and Reiner would be caught," she said.

She looked up at him and then over her shoulder at the Colt. "Oh, Beau. Not the gun again. By now, you should know I will not hurt you."

"I thought . . . Ah, I heard . . . I . . . I didn't know . . ." She put her finger on his lips.

"I know," she assured him as she let him put the Colt back into his holster. "It is time to watch the sun go down."

She led him to the blanket that she had spread under the oak. "I try and come here every evening. I would think of you and pray you were safe."

"I came here to wait for dark to avoid being seen by the army," he explained.

"They have left," she said. "There is trouble to the south and they were called away."

The two sat together, watching the sun go down, providing the fiery red sky that they had hoped for. As the darkness engulfed them, Beau whispered, "So it is safe to go to the village?"

"Yes," she said. "First, tell me what happened. We heard shots and horses running and then you and Reiner were gone."

With his stomach growling with hunger, Beau replied, "We couldn't have done it without the help of you and your brother."

She placed her hand on his cheek. "You shaved for me."

Taking her hand, he pulled her close. Together in the darkness, Beau told her about running from the army with Reiner, the rendezvous, and about Eli being a father. In the future, Beau planned to tell her about Angus, about him and Eli running from Arkansas, and when the time was right he might even tell her about having killed two men.

She told him that her father had paid money to get Felipe out of the army. Then Ana told him bad news. Her parents and her family were closing their businesses and leaving the village. They planned to settle in Nogales, where her father's brother lived. Fear of conflicts between Mexico and the U.S. in the future was the reason.

Beau knew that without the cantina, stable, and mercantile the villagers would soon leave and the adobe and log buildings would fall into ruins. Nogales was deep in Mexican territory and it would be too dangerous for him to go there. With this news, the young man avoided talking to Ana about their future. He feared that her decision was that she was going with the family. Quite possibly she would not have a say and have to go to Nogales. It was late and Ana began to gather up the blankets.

"Leave your horses," she said. "I will send Felipe to bring them to the stable in the morning. He will take your packs to the cantina. There is a room in the back of the cantina that you can stay in."

The village streets were quiet as the couple walked down from the meadow. Light from the open door of the cantina spilled out onto the dirt. Beau had his saddlebags over his shoulder and the Hawken rifle in his hand. Ana led him to the back of the building. There was a low doorway to the room.

Ana handed him a lantern hanging near the kitchen door. Giving him a quick kiss, she said, "I will make you a big Mexican breakfast in the morning."

Then she was gone, leaving him alone. He pushed the door open, ducking as he stepped into the room. It was small, with a cot on one side and a sideboard and chair on the other. Beau had no doubt that Reiner had spent more than one night in this room, and probably not alone.

For a moment, he thought of going into the cantina for a drink and to see if he could get something to eat. He worried that he might have to explain why he and Ana had come down from the meadow so late. Digging into his saddlebag, he took out a piece of jerky and sat on the cot, chewing it.

It was full daylight when Beau stepped out of the low doorway. He squinted at the bright sunshine. He walked around to the front of the cantina. The village was quiet. In the next hour, the streets would be busy with people heading for the shops that had just opened. Large plank doors were closed in the front of the cantina. The windows were shuttered. Beau went around to the kitchen door. He saw Ana who was hurrying to put her apron on.

Felipe was leaning against the door jamb, eating a burrito. Ana spoke rapidly in Spanish to him. He smiled and waved at Beau. Stuffing the rest of his meal into his mouth, the brother headed for the meadow. Alisa was busy rolling out tortillas and putting them into a hot cast iron pan. Ana picked up a couple of hot tortillas and handed them to Beau.

"This will keep you until I finish your meal." She then went to the pantry and started collecting the things she would need.

Alisa pointed to the table in the corner of the kitchen. "You can sit there. I will bring you some coffee."

Beau could never remember anything that tasted as good as the corn tortillas and coffee. It might be the fact that he was almost starving, having eaten little the day before. It would be a long time before he would forget them. He heard Emilio in the cantina opening the shutters and front door. A breeze blew through the kitchen, taking some of the heat from the stove to outside. It also brought the smell of the food through the streets, drawing in hungry customers.

Ana set a clay-fired mug in front of him. It was filled with a lemon-flavored drink. Beau tried to sip the beverage, but it was too good and he gulped it down. He was quickly feeling much better, the edge taken off his hunger. Emilio came from the cantina and sat across from Beau. Alisa placed a mug of coffee in front of him and a small pitcher of milk. The young man watched as Emilio put sugar and milk into the strong coffee.

After tasting it, he seemed satisfied and said, "It is good to see you are well."

"Thank you," Beau replied. "I am pleased to let you know Reiner is also well."

"The young black, Eli. Have you seen him?" the owner inquired.

"My friend Eli is married," Beau said proudly. "He has a baby girl."

"He is married," Emilio said. "That is good. It is proper."

The young man began to feel uncomfortable. It seemed that the owner had something unsaid on his mind. Ana placed a platter of meat, vegetables, peppers, and tortillas in front of the two men. Alisa followed her with two plates and more coffee. The men filled a tortilla with the contents on the tray and began to eat. As hungry as Beau had been, he now had lost his appetite. He continued to eat, only to avoid having to talk.

The young man wished that Reiner was here to add some humor to the meal. The owner wiped his mouth with the back of his hand. He then pushed back his chair and took out some small, slim cigars. He offered one to Beau and the young man took it.

Alisa came over with a burning stick and lit the cigars. She went back to the stove and tossed it into the fire. Ana stood next to her and they were speaking too low to hear. Emilio stood up.

"It is warm in here," he said. "Come, it is cooler in the courtyard."

Beau thanked Ana and Alisa for the good meal, and followed the father outside. The young man wasn't sure what was expected from him. One thing that Beau did know was that he had to tell Emilio he wanted to marry Ana and then ask the father's permission. What if Emilio asked him how he was going to support his daughter? Maybe he would demand he join them in Nogales. Beau hoped to stay in the mountains.

The owner cleared his throat. "Ana was late for work this morning."

It took a few seconds before Beau realized that he had spoken. Unsure of what explanation Ana's father would consider acceptable, Beau went with the truth. "It was my fault, Señor Garcia," Beau said, choosing his words carefully. "I arrived at the meadow near sunset. She was there and I kept her talking late. She must have had trouble getting up."

To prevent Emilio from thinking too hard on his excuse, Beau continued. "I am glad we have this time, Señor Garcia. I have known your daughter for two years now and have come to love her. I would like to ask your permission to marry Ana, if she will have me."

The owner's face was without expression as he stared at the young man. Beau was sure that this wasn't going to end well. He should have tried to spirited her away in the night and avoided what was to come.

"Ana is a good girl," Emilio replied. "She speaks of you all the time. I have warned her about marrying a gringo. Where would the two of you live? How would you provide for her? War between your country and mine is coming. It cannot be avoided. We may never see her or our grandchildren if you take her away. If war comes, you and Felipe may be fighting against each other and may be forced to kill . . ."

The owner's voice faded. Beau sat, a sinking feeling going through him. The questions had been asked, and he had no answers that would satisfy her father.

Emilio looked at the clouds above and squinted as though looking for guidance, then shook his head. "No matter what, my daughter is lost. Her dream has always been to go to San Francisco. If you take her into the mountains, she will be lost to me. If she chases her dream, again, she is lost to me." Tears filled the old man's eyes. "I have asked her to come to Nogales, but it will be her decision."

Beau was hopeful. Though it was against her father's wishes, Emilio had given her his permission to say yes. He saw Felipe leading the horses toward the stable. Beau needed space to think. Thanking Ana's father, he went to help with the horses.

"You have another horse," Felipe said. "You must have had a good year trapping."

"I have had some good fortune," Beau said, not wanting to explain how he had actually gotten the gray.

He thought of what he would say to Ana. Beau helped the young Mexican give the horses a good rubdown. "When will your family be heading south?" he asked.

"My father has purchased wagons and mules for the trip. They will be here in two, maybe three weeks," Felipe replied.

With the chores completed, Beau rubbed his chin. He needed a shave. Tonight, he would ask Ana to join him in the meadow and then ask her to marry him. Finished in the stable, he headed for Pepe's. He sat in the hot bath and let the water calm his nerves. Beau had money and thought about getting new clothing, but feared it would make him look too much like a dandy. He would meet her with a fresh shave and clean clothes. If necessary, Beau would leave the mountains and live in San Francisco.

Walking back into the village, Beau saw Felipe sweeping the front of the cantina. Emilio came out to tell him something when he noticed Beau. "Come in my friend and have a drink with me."

Forcing a smile, the young man replied, "I would like that."

Sitting at a table near the door, Emilio poured tequila into two glasses. "I will miss my friend Reiner when we go to Nogales," he said. Raising his glass, he added, "To good friends."

Beau touched his glass to the owners. He thought of Eli. "To good friends."

"I understand your brother lives in Nogales," Beau said, making conversation.

"He has a ranch there," Emilio replied. "I will build another cantina, maybe a hotel."

The tequila warmed Beau's stomach and helped calm him. He held the glass out for a refill. Taking a sip, he set it down. As though Emilio had read his thoughts, he said, "Ana will be through work in a little while."

Then the owner called to Felipe, "Have your mother bring us something to eat."

Suddenly, Beau realized that he was really hungry. A plate of meat and fresh vegetables was brought out. Ana placed some bowls of chili sauces and tortillas onto the table and smiled at Beau. "I see you have been back to see Pepe," she said before returning to the kitchen.

With their meal finished, he sat smoking slim cigars with Emilio when Ana walked around the building, heading for her casa. Excusing himself, Beau hurried out to catch her.

"Ana," he called. "Can I talk to you?"

Stopping, she said, "Give me an hour to remove the smells of the kitchen and then come by."

Beau waited until she went into the adobe before returning to the cantina. Emilio was behind the bar. He looked up at the young man. "Come. We will drink to our futures."

The young man tasted the amber liquid. It was an excellent brandy. "This is very good," Beau replied. "We will always be friends."

"Yes, we will," Emilio agreed. "When you see Reiner let him know I think of him often."

Feeling restless while waiting, Beau thanked Emilio for the drinks and food. He walked around the cantina to the small room where he had spent the night. He took out the leather packet that he had gotten from Gus' gear. Beau had put his extra money into the packet. It contained $132, a small fortune for the young man. He was sure that it would be enough for him and Ana to make a start in San Francisco. He would miss the life of a mountain man, but love required sacrifice, and he was prepared to do so.

His walking money Beau kept in the pouch hanging around his neck was almost gone. He debated adding some from the packet to his pouch. Changing his mind, Beau placed the leather packet back into the saddlebag. Sitting on the cot, he went over what he would say to Ana. He remembered the night she had asked him to take her and leave rather than go and rescue Reiner. He felt that this was a much better way to take her away from her family. Her father had not given his blessings on the marriage, but he had not forbidden it.

Beau left the dim room, stepping into the bright sun. He figured Ana should be ready by now. If she wasn't, he would wait on the bench in front of the adobe. Walking around the cantina, Beau felt a mixture of excitement and fear. All would be right when he heard her say, "yes."

He walked up to the door, passing chickens scratching in the dirt. He hesitated a moment, thinking over what he was going to say before knocking lightly on the door. After a few seconds, he knocked again, a little louder. There was no answer. He wondered if she'd gone back to the cantina to look for him?

Again, he knocked and the door opened slightly. He caught the smell of her perfume. Pushing the door open slowly, he called softly, "Ana. Ana, it is me Beau."

Hearing nothing, he pushed the door open and stepped inside the room. It was empty. He turned to go check in the cantina when he caught sight of a letter on the small table. Stepping over, he saw "Dearest Beau" at the top. He began to read.

> Dearest Beau,
> I am writing this letter because I could not bear to see the disappointment on your face. My father told me that you planned to ask me to marry you. He made it clear that the choice would be mine to make. The pain I saw in his eyes was difficult to see. It had been there only once before, after the death of his father.

I know he wants me to go with the family to Nogales and I will. It is important that you know he is not making me go, but for him I must. I fear going with you would leave a lasting scar on my father and haunt me for the rest of my days.

If I were to ask you to join me in Nogales, you would be in constant danger of being arrested. I have seen the glow on your face when you talk of life in the mountains. This too, I would be taking from you.

Do not come looking for me. I will always cherish the time we have spent together and must apologize for letting it go so far. Take care of yourself and think of me when you are in the high country. I will never forget our time together.

Love, Ana

Hardly able to breathe, Beau stood looking at the letter. He had never received a letter before. But this letter telling him of her love clearly told him that it was not his to keep. He held it close and caught the scent of wild flowers. With the letter in his hand, Beau stepped out of the adobe. His only thought was that he had to find Ana. She could not have meant what was written on the paper.

His first thought was that her sister would know where she'd gone. Feeling numb inside, he walked toward the house. He was about to knock when he heard crying inside and someone speaking softly. He caught the words, "You are doing the right thing."

Beau's throat tightened. He could not remember the last time he had broken down and cried, but if he didn't step away from the door, it would happen right here. His eyes blurry with tears, he went back to the small room. Leaning on the door jamb, he fought to control himself.

"Thank you, my friend."

The sound of someone behind him startled Beau. He turned, blinking rapidly and looked into the sad eyes of Emilio. The old Mexican looked tired. Unable to speak, Beau nodded and went into the small room to get his gear. When he stepped out Emilio was gone. Fighting the urge to run back to the sister's house and beg Ana to stay with him, Beau walked woodenly to the stable.

Felipe was working on some harnesses. "Your horses are ready," he said. "I will help you put on the saddles."

Clearing his throat, Beau was finally able to speak. "I am leaving the gray and its saddle. Give it to your father as a thank you."

Staring at the stable floor, Felipe said, "I wish things were different. I envy you going to the mountains."

After saddling the sorrel, Beau lifted the packs onto the pony. They were heavy and there was the sound of bottles. He looked at the young Mexican. "My father wanted you to have tequila when you see Reiner next."

Not only were there bottles of the liquor, but there were also the supplies he would need in the mountains. "Thank your father for me," Beau replied.

After swinging into the saddle, the young man told Felipe. "If anyone wants to get ahold of me, send the letter to Fort Hall. I will be doing most of my trading there."

As he rode out of the stable, Beau ducked under the doorway. As he left the small village, he looked neither right nor left.

* * *

For several weeks, the young man wandered the Wind River range. When he found a place he liked, he would spend several days as he sorted out what had happened. During a couple of nights he had tried to focus better by drinking a good portion from a bottle of tequila. It had done nothing to help clear his head, but had only left it aching the next morning.

He thought about his father a lot and slowly came to realize that, like Ana, if his father was still alive, it was doubtful he would have gone off and left him. It helped him to understand what had happened with Ana. Several times, he took the letter out of the leather packet and re-read it. It helped make him feel a connection to Ana. One day a broad grin came across his face. He now understood why Gus had kept the letter.

The young man was riding toward Square Top mountain. He was wearing new buckskins that he had acquired in trade with some Crow that he spent a couple days with. In the distance, there was smoke from a camp. Riding with the Hawken rifle across the front of his saddle, he slowly worked his way toward the camp. The sound of his horses crossing the Wind River alerted the camp's occupant. Immediately he recognized the man. It was Reiner. "Hello the camp!" Beau called. "Anyone thirsty for some tequila?"

Feeling like he was home again, Beau joined Reiner and they broke open a bottle of tequila and passed it back and forth. "Emilio sends his best along with the tequila," Beau said.

"I will miss the old Mexican," Reiner replied. "You say he and the family are headed for Nogales."

"He will ride in in style on the gray," Beau said.

"That he will," Reiner said. "By the way, I went to Fort William and noticed the posters on you and Eli are gone. I guess nobody else will be looking for you two."

Taking a drink, Beau replied, "That is good to know. I figured on doing business with Fort Hall anyway."

"The rest of my trappers have taken up buffalo hunting. There are herds a mile wide in some areas," Reiner informed the young man.

"Give them time and the hunters will make them go the way of the beaver," Beau said.

"I made some inquiries at the fort," Reiner said. "Word is Newell and Meek are cutting the trail from Fort Hall to Oregon. It will open the way for lots of emigrants looking for good and cheap farming land. They will need men that know the mountains to guide the wagons through. One trip pays more than a winter of trapping. I don't plan to hunt buffalo, so we should team up guiding them through. We pick them up at Fort William and leave them in Oregon."

"That would keep us going in case we can't find any grizz," the young man said.

"So you didn't learn anything the last time you tangled with a grizz?" Reiner asked taking a drink and handing the tequila to his friend.

"I guess I didn't, although I like the sound of Levesque and Reiner mountain guides," Beau said taking a swig from the bottle.

"It's a deal then. Reiner and Levesque mountain guides," the young man's partner replied.

NOTES AND COMMENTS

Thank you for reading this book.